RIVER IN THE MOUNTAINS

RIVER'S END SERIES, BOOK THIRTEEN

LEANNE DAVIS

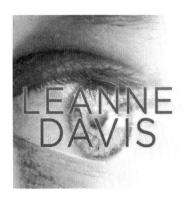

River in the Mountains

Print ISBN: 978-1-941522-79-0

The River's End Series, Book Thirteen

Edited by Teri at The Editing Fairy

Copyediting: Joan Nichols JRT Editing

Cover Designer: Steven Novak

In memory of the real Monty.

PROLOGUE

*V*IOLET RYDELL WHOOPED LOUDLY as she pressed her knees into the flanks of her horse, urging the mare to the right with her leather rein. So well were her horses trained that it only took a flick of her fingertip for her horse to respond. Right, left, stop, go. Easy-peasy. Almost like toddler-talk to her extraordinarily intelligent horses. Naturally, she was the one who taught them everything they knew and so much more. Her Uncle Jack often crowed she very well could have possessed a special knack for training horses, something even he didn't have. And Jack was the best horse person she'd ever known.

The crowd was right with her and the energy in the arena, reflected in the throngs of captivated faces, was impossible to ignore. She relished the unlimited fun, joy, shock, positivity and in all honesty, utter amazement, she received as she and the crew performed the routine tonight. As the lead attraction, she never ceased to have the time of her life doing it.

"And now, ladies and gentleman, Violet and Princess will show you how well they can dance…" The announcer's deep voice burst through the sound system, echoing throughout the huge building and amping up the already elevated crowd. Amidst all the cheering and clapping, Violet turned Princess toward the bleachers and stopped her dead. On cue, Princess then lifted a front leg and straightened it out forward, shifting her weight downwards as if she were bowing.

The large arena was fully enclosed and most of the central floor was a semi-circle of sand where the horses were always featured as the main attraction. On the long side of the semi-circle were bleachers for spectators to watch the presentation. A high, half-wall of boards separated the bleachers from the horse arena, protecting the viewers. The opposite side of the arena was dedicated to horse stalls and conference rooms, while the second floor housed the Rydell Family Bar and Grill. The restaurant had glass walls that overlooked the arena, allowing the diners to watch the goings-on in the main arena without subjecting them to the smell of it.

Tonight, Violet was performing one of three shows that week. Guests from the Rydell River Resort, which was located on the same grounds as the arena, often enjoyed the dinner and entertainment. Plenty of locals and passing tourists through the area attended also. Most Friday and Saturday nights, the shows, like tonight's for instance, were sold out. The income supported the general maintenance and upkeep while also providing a nice profit.

Tonight, Violet wore a sequined hat, blouse, jeans and chaps: her performance outfit. Her signature boots, always flashy and fantastic, were pink with fringe and a tassel that swung to and fro.

The things she trained the horses to do, and their eagerness to do it were testament to her talents. The experienced professionals of high caliber brought a truly spectacular performance to the valley. Violet started Princess down the center line of the arena. She lapped up the howling yells of excitement from the audience. Soon, the three other riders and horses came out of the shoot to join her as the music started blaring.

The audience roared at the rousing, exciting opening sequence as it proceeded at full speed. First, they rode one way before two broke off and started running the opposite direction, neatly passing each other on each end of the arena's semi-circle. The music pulsed a beat, magnifying the energy level, and the riders' bright outfits, all complemented each other and the magnificent steeds they rode. Even the horses displayed their own finery as they pranced and cantered.

The crowd never failed to collectively hold their breaths as the horses cantered in opposite directions before breaking into a full gallop. For merely two laps, the riders pushed the horses and themselves into a dangerous exhibition of speed, control and coordination. The music rose to a crescendo and the anxious moments always managed to make Violet's heart soar with crazy, fast, happy beats, as if she were doing the final steps of an Irish jig. The rush of adrenaline was a natural high, unlike any other. Nothing even came close to it. She was flying and gliding over the earth, the air blowing in her face, yet still connected to the ground. She considered it the most beautiful experience she could ever imagine.

While galloping on the inner loop, she passed her fiancé, Preston Green. His horse followed the gentle curve as hers did but nothing remained long in her view before becoming a blur of colors, sights and sounds. They exchanged a brief smile before her gaze returned to the performance and she focused only on it again. She did love doing it all but it required unflawed timing and concentration and Violet never compromised her safety.

She met Preston during the two years when she attended

the community college, earning a degree in general accounting. Her career choice surprised many since her entire work history revolved around horses: riding, training, caring for and performing with them. She wasn't shy in sharing her passion with others either. She had been giving private riding lessons for years and intended to continue them her entire life. She made good money at it. The accounting degree was necessary to help her set up a life-long dream: her own small business. Someday, she intended to make a business out of training horses and giving private riding lessons, but she didn't stop there. She also harbored a vision of designing a program that she could sell to people who couldn't come to the arena. She hoped to offer them a step-by-step method that featured the best practices she knew. Someday… It was just one of her long-term goals. She hoped to create a course that would appeal to all levels, from beginning basics to what she was doing right that second.

Spinning the horse in frantic circles.

Preston earned the same degree as Violet but had no idea what to do with it. They met in class, started dating and he visited her often at her home. She introduced him to her passion and he fairly quickly succumbed to the horse-bug. A total newbie, Violet supplied the one-on-one instruction, and he quite competently managed to become a part of the show. He lived at the ranch with some of the other workers. For now.

They shared their plans. Dreams. Ambitions. Goals. Huge ones. They often escaped to the top of the arena, accessing the roof and looking out at the endless views of Rydell land, river and the mountains beyond. They liked to talk and make love as they discussed their future. Marriage was naturally a big part of it. They wanted to create a partnership with each other, and a business involving horses that they could do while married. The best union she could imagine combined her personal goals with her professional ones.

Preston rode Wallace, a new and feisty recruit to their stables and equine show. There were two other riders spinning on their own horses at the moment. All four horses and riders were in perfect sync and precise placement.

Like clockwork, they practiced and drilled by the hour to create a performance as involved as this one. The first event at every show starred the animals, creatures that were not naturally prone to doing tricks on cue for a show.

Anxious excitement and loud cheers. The crowd seemed more raucous tonight than usual. A large bachelor party was previously hosted at the restaurant and obviously, the attendees followed it up with the horse show. Smiling under the lights of the arena, Violet simply guided Princess through her routine with more focus... and smiles. People got uncomfortable watching a performer scowl and frown as if they were concentrating too hard. Which they were. But like every performance, it required a bit of acting.

As a rule, Violet tried to reflect her ease and confidence with a smile. Hers was a routine she'd perfected and honed for years before performing it in front of an audience and now she did it several times a week. It was never safely predictable because horses aren't machines, yet her confidence in her horse's obedience and abilities assured Violet another wonderful outcome.

The music changed into a Country/Western twang. Smiles, cheers, and intense excitement filled the air. She caught the eye of Asher Reed. At twenty-six years old, he was one of the workers on the ranch that she'd recruited to help her perform a few years ago. He quickly became her second in command. Asher was a foster child who stayed with the ranch foreman, AJ, and his wife, Kate, but they'd adopted him at age thirteen. He winked at Violet with just as much confidence in their skills and training as she. Asher also agreed that every time they got to perform was so damn fun.

They changed the formation and began doing a figure eight. The horses took turns crossing the center of the arena with precise speed and flawless timing.

The crowd was clapping to the music. Violet's heart swelled and the adrenaline rushed through her veins. With breathtaking accuracy, she spun fully around before crossing straight over the center of the arena and then retracing the curves into almost stopping the horse as they followed the curve to come back around. The figure eights required less speed, but they still managed a pretty rigorous pace. Designed only for extremely advanced riders, the faint of heart need not apply. Passing each other in blurred sequences, the crowd cheered and roared as always to indicate how much they loved it. As they did now.

Then… Crack. Boom.

What the fuck?

Gunshot? No? What? But it was. The loud shot echoed in the arena before shrill screams and yelling followed. Violet pulled sharply back on her reins, squeezing her mount with her knees while trying to stay on as Princess shied and bolted out of formation… Then Asher and Calvin's mounts followed suit. Preston was headed straight for the wall if his horse failed to stop and turn. She saw Wallace, his gelding, instantly trying to bolt forward.

No.

Galloping directly at the wall, he careened in a hard left a split second before smashing right into it at full speed. His movements were so unplanned and they happened in the span of a nanosecond.

"Preston!" Violet screamed his name. He was catapulted forward when the horse stopped without warning, but as Wallace turned, Preston's body was launched directly into the board wall that ran the length of the arena. He hit his head before his entire body slammed into the restraining wall.

It was so unreal.

Slow motion. And seemingly endless. Violet was still screaming. She heard other sounds, like the gasps of the crowd and thumping of the horse hooves, her own mare included. She was already galloping towards Preston.

His limp body flopped onto the ground.

Like one of the flowers the audience often threw at the end of the show, Preston flopped on the ground, a spent offering. That's how Preston was lying. He hit the ground and flopped onto his back.

He was so still.

Completely lifeless.

The crowd continued to scream as they shuffled about with panicked confusion. The horses nickered and neighed in protest, but moments later, their experienced riders brought them under control.

Including Violet. She dismounted from her horse, dropping to her knees beside Preston's motionless body.

He was mute. Wallace ran to the far side of the arena.

Then there was almost a shared gasp as the growing silence from the spectators became deafening.

Violet's mouth dropped open. Her gaze was confused and unsure. She touched his chest and shoulder, but tears blurred her vision. She couldn't see him clearly. Nor could she make any sense of it. But Preston's chest wasn't rising and falling. Why not? Kneeling beside him while weeping hysterically, she couldn't figure it out. She didn't understand…

"Preston? Preston!" She began screaming into his face. Someone yelled louder. At her.

"Violet, don't move him!"

Jack? Uncle Jack was running very fast. For a man of

sixty-eight years, he sprinted like an Olympian towards them.

Violet emerged from her trance when Jack's drawn, tight, fearful face registered in her brain. Jack was frantic and her uncle never looked like that. But he did now. He dropped down beside her and started doing something. What? Violet didn't know. She just slunk out of the way, crying uselessly. Oh, yes, duh! Jack was gently touching Preston to check for wounds. Or maybe for broken bones?

Yes. Yes, that was it. Violet instantly started to soothe herself. That's the worst of it. They had to go to the hospital and have Preston checked out for a concussion. Yes, that's obviously what would happen next.

"Jack? Jack? What happened?"

"I think one of the fucking stag party-goers shot off his gun to celebrate."

That's it? Someone shot their gun in the air? Someone deliberately startled the horses which caused all of this? Preston lying motionless in the arena?

"Wallace threw him. Hard. He... he hit the sideboards... with his head... we need to check it... at the hospital..." She blinked to clear her gaze but it remained fuzzy and strange.

She heard screaming and calls all around her. She didn't know from whom or where they came. Movements as more people were coming forward. "We need an ambulance... now!" She yelled at Jack, her tears streaming.

He nodded. "Ian's calling." He was her other uncle. Sure. Yes. They could fix this, handle it and take care of it. There was no one better in an emergency than Ian and Jack.

But Jack was sitting back on his heels... and his hands were not on Preston anymore. His shoulders slumped forward.

Preston seemed too still. In dire need of medical assistance. So much need. Panic started to lodge in Violet's throat. Maybe it was more serious. Maybe he needed surgery or... or physical therapy or something like that? Whatever! Anything he needed was attainable... She'd be right there beside him, so eager to help save him. She would never leave him. Yes. They could face anything... anything at all... but first, he had to wake up...

"He's... help him! Jack! Jack, please... You have to hurry!" she sobbed incoherently.

But Jack wasn't hurrying anymore. He reached forward and leaned over Preston before sitting back on his boots. He didn't try to hurry. He moved with thoughtful precision and grace, making purposeful movements. Why the fuck did he stop hurrying? Why wasn't he doing something more? Like rushing to call an ambulance? Or the police? Or someone? Shouldn't they be asking people to help haul Preston off the dirt floor and get him the medical assistance he required?

"We have to hurry!" she sobbed and Jack jumped to his feet, turning to catch her. He took her against this chest and held her tightly.

"Violet, no!"

He deliberately turned her body away from Preston. *Away.* What the fuck was wrong with him? She needed to hold Preston.

"No... No, honey. Just... stay here with me." He almost yelled at her, clamping his arms around her body with steely strength, despite his age. She was no match for Jack's strenth but she pushed on him as hard as she could, panicking.

"Fuck! Let me go! Let me go! I need to help him!"

Jack had tears in his eyes as he gazed down at her with a tender expression and replied, "You can't anymore. You can't help him. I can't help him either. Violet... I'm so sorry, honey... he's... I'm afraid it's too late."

Too late? What did that mean? She snapped her head back and screamed up at him. "Let me go! Let me go! *Let me go!*"

More sobs escaped her. She refused to hear what he was saying. Pushing hard, she finally managed to loosen her uncle's hold and she spun as she collapsed besides Preston. She stopped crying. Screaming. Moving. She sniffed and wiped off her snot as she blinked to clear her eyes. Preston's neck didn't look right. She gasped and started shaking her head.

"Preston? Preston? I'm right here. I'm here. Honey..." She tried to rest her head on his chest and wrapped her arms around his torso as far as she could reach. Then she leaned quietly on top of him. Her ear was pressed on his chest, which was so... silent. Her gasp nearly choked her as she tried to hear his heart. His heart... The heart she loved, adored and *needed*... why wasn't it beating?

Starting in her fingertips, she felt a tingling. Then numbing. Her breath was heavy in her chest. Her sobs unrelenting. Was she making all that noise? Her chest jerked with each sharp sob as her hot tears fell onto his shirt. No. No. "Preston? Preston? What happened? How? What?" He was just there with her. Smiling at her. Then... how could he be gone? It couldn't happen that fast. It couldn't just end in a split second. How could it be over?

She glanced up but her tears distorted everything she saw. "Jack! Jack! Please... please help him..."

Jack had his own stream of tears falling as he knelt beside her. "I can't, honey. I just can't. I'm so sorry..."

"He's... dead?"

The words were so unforgiving and they came out in a pitiful croak.

Jack's gaze held her as his own tears reflected his concern and pain. "Yes. He's dead."

Nothing registered in Violet's mind. Not Jack's words. Nor their meaning. Nor where she knelt and lay on Preston's chest. There was nothing. No breath. No heartbeat. But...

how? How could he have died? Why did it happen so fast? Right before her own eyes? While she was watching him? Performing the act she taught him to do? She'd encouraged him from the beginning to learn the skills so he could join the show with her. She told him to come here. She taught him to shine in his role.

And now she could only cradle his empty shell of a body? Her tears became huge, gasping sobs. She was crying out to the universe… what the hell was that din? Her? That inconsolable grief? It was a wounded, vicious, beaten wail… what was it? She sobbed and cried, becoming incoherent. Nothing mattered. She wished she could die and be with him.

She begged and pleaded… "No! No! Please, you can't leave me. Come back now. Please… Preston? Please?"

More sounds came from her lips. None of it held any meaning to her. She had no idea what she said or failed to say. She didn't understand what any of it meant.

Then, two arms enveloped her and lifted her up. She felt a massive chest. She'd recognize her dad's leathery smell anywhere. He must have just heard. "Violet… it's Dad, honey. I'm here. I'm here, baby girl… come on, baby, come with me. He's…"

"Don't say it!" she screamed in reply as she struggled in his arms. "Don't you dare say it! Don't you…even, just don't…" His huge body held her up and his arms were under hers. Her legs collapsed like rubber, simply out of her control. She whimpered pathetically and sounded so sad against this chest, "Let me go!"

He kissed the top of her head and said softly, "Never."

The one person she never wanted to lose was gone. Right before her eyes.

~

Later, she would learn that a man named Coop Trellin got so drunk at the bachelor party that he accidentally shot off his gun. It wasn't for fun and crazy excitement, but just an accident. The errant bullet hit the metal stairs and ricocheted, without striking anyone. But the loud surprise disturbed the horses, which responded by seeking flight. Preston's horse inadvertently throwing him straight into the rail caused his neck to be snapped immediately. He died before he even knew what happened.

Right in front of Violet.

The whole family tried to support her. Rose, her oldest sister, came home with her husband, Mateo. They lived in Rhode Island, where Mateo attended medical school and Rose tutored dyslexic children. Iris and her husband, Quinn, also arrived, along with Daisy, the sister who was just a year younger than her. She was back from college. Everyone came home. Everyone was very sorry. Unspeakably sorry.

But there was nothing anyone could say that could help her.

No one could do anything to help her.

Nothing could change the reality.

She stared with unresolved bitterness out the window. Tears randomly rolled down her cheeks. She slept very little and ate even less. Ignoring all the family advice, she rarely responded or commented on their attempts at providing consolation. From the funeral to the settlement of the case, Violet barely reacted. She was numb. Gone. Dead as Preston. She sometimes wished she were killed that day.

One day, Jack came over and asked her, "What do you think about selling Wallace? I think we can all agree that no one will ride him again. It's too traumatic. Such a sad reminder…"

Wallace? Wallace darted forward before he turned so sharply he jack-knifed, throwing Preston off and murdering him. It was the first thing to evoke some feeling and passion inside Violet, and it consumed her. Rage. Red and angry, rage filled her brain. Her tone was lethal as she replied simply, "Sell him? I think you should render him into glue. Make sure I never see him again or I'll do the job for you."

She turned and spun on her heel, slamming her bedroom door. She didn't come out again for any reason except to eat and go to the bathroom. That went on for weeks.

Maybe even months.

She never found out if the horse was reduced to glue. She simply fantasized that he was.

Meanwhile, she tried to ignore the idea that Preston was no more than ashes now. It became such a fitting symbol of the rest of her life.

CHAPTER 1

"I'LL BE FINE. WE'VE been through everything. Double-checked what I packed. Triple-checked our plans and how we're going to communicate. It'll be okay. Really."

Gage Sullivan glanced down at his mini-me and sighed. She was fine. He wasn't. "It's a long time."

"It is, but it's not forever. In the blink of an eye, I'll be back." Yes, his daughter was comforting *him* about their coming separation. She was already booked in back-to-back summer camps, one for horseback-riding and the other for track. The camps were in Georgia. Freaking across the whole country. Her grandparents, who so nicely provided these experiences for her, lived there. Sure, he was grateful. But God damn! How he hated the rigid scheduling and time away from him. Each lasted a week, and then she was off to her grandparents.

Every damn summer. Every August, he lost Andy to her grandparents.

He hated it. No, he detested it. Worst of all, he knew it was good for her to go and be with them. Her mother died when she was very young. Her maternal grandparents were Andy's only connection to her deceased mother. They both doted on Andy, and cherished their time with her. Gage tried to remind himself of that, even though it did nothing to alleviate how much he'd miss his daughter.

Damn! The separation. It was a long way for Andy to travel all alone, but she'd already done it for three years now. Every Christmas, her grandparents stayed with them; and in return, Andy spent four weeks in August at their house. In Georgia. There were plenty of weekly phone calls and lots of text messages as well as care packages sent to her. They tried to remain as involved as they could despite the distance of twenty-seven hundred miles.

"I know. I just… I won't be fine." He sighed as he shook his head. "But that isn't your problem and I refuse to burden you with my issues."

She easily wrapped her thin arms around him. He hugged her tight, patting the silky straight hair she pulled into a ponytail. An old soul since she was born, it seemed, Andy would probably be fine while Gage would continue to miss her. Andy adored her father as much as he did her.

Single right after she was born, Gage learned how to be a dad on the fly, although Andy always seemed to know exactly how to be the best daughter. At least, that was his take on it. Her mom, Dierdre, and he were no love match. More like just an oops! At merely twenty years old, a casual relationship with a woman he barely knew but was simply having fun with, popped up pregnant.

They never married. Nor did they panic or fight. They became congenial friends and decided to remain so in order to have the baby together. Her parents were disappointed but supportive as they helped them find lawyers to hammer out a fair child support agreement that included Gage's visitation. It worked for the first six months of Andy's life, until Dierdre died in a car accident. Grieving for the mother of his child, out of his unconditional love for his child, Gage knew she lost a major factor in her life. He was already madly in love with his infant daughter, and developed a new respect for Dierdre's parents who were consumed by their loss and grief. When they requested more time with their granddaughter, Gage wanted to be generous although he despised any separation from her. He agreed to it only for Andy's wellbeing.

Everything in his life revolved around Andy's wellbeing.

And damn if she didn't reflect a genuine happiness. Always a straight A student, she ran cross country and track and now, she was just entering eighth grade. She was funny, sweet, kind, intelligent, worldly, yet innocent, hopeful, and pragmatic. Gage did a stellar job in raising her. Well, to be fair, maybe she was simply born that way. Someone with innate charisma, caring, intelligence, maturity, and good decision-making without any previous guidance. She was, in a word, amazing. It seemed that everyone who met Andy adored her. Her genuine attitude was an asset that most people longed for and responded to.

"You're going to do all that hiking we talked about. Right?"

Andy hated to hike. And camping. That was her only flaw as far as Gage was concerned. "Yeah," he sighed in a petulant tone which made Andy giggle.

He loved her spontaneous giggle especially when she was fully laughing at him. "Dad... I can't stand walking for a whole day just to sleep on the ground. To work so hard to do the things I could do here in this house. So you go and do your outdoor activities. It'll be good for you."

"How could you be my daughter when it comes to survival skills?" He liked to tease her about that. Her mother's side was pure suburbanite. He was from the country and always preferred it. Born and raised in Winthrop, Washington, Gage joined the United States Forest Service, working as a recreation technician after college. He took mostly outdoor assignments in the past, but was promoted three years ago. Now he managed the entire program for his area and could no longer pursue the outdoor assignments. His official capacity was ensuring public safety whether it be in accessing the hiking trails, campgrounds, rivers, or lakes, while also working as a liaison in providing information about the diverse recreational opportunities in the forested areas.

While evaluating the viability of the Hunter's Creek Trail after a large section of it succumbed to a landslide, Gage managed to finagle a rare opportunity. He asked to rebuild the trail himself although it wasn't in the scope of his usual maintenance work. It required a complicated repair and Gage wanted to be the one to do it. Since Andy was gone for half the summer, he had the time and the freedom to get back out in the wilderness and fix it.

It would also fill the hours of a summer that would have otherwise been nearly intolerable to him.

There were no motorized vehicles or any gas-powered equipment allowed in the section of trail he was addressing, so the trail and work crews had to hike in with it or use horses to carry their supplies. Trees were still felled with two-man hand saws. The backbreaking work could take the crews days just to clear a few yards of trail from the blowdowns.

Gage had to set up camp, hauling in his own gear for survival. He scheduled three days to find a camp and get it all set up. Three weeks were allotted for the trail maintenance and another five days to break down camp and haul everything back out. He would also receive temporary help from some of the college students they hired for the summer hours, in the form of them hiking in all the materials and tools he'd need to do the repairs.

Gage was eager for the break from his usual computer files and the paper-pushing job he managed at his desk nowadays. He often complained he was managing people more than the forest.

The biggest drawback was that he could only contact Andy once a week. He had to hike out to the trailhead to get cell phone service. He didn't like that part at all. He preferred to talk to her daily. "I'm worried you won't be able to call me if you need me for anything."

"I have Uncle Rory's number. He said he'd hike his butt in there day or night if I needed you, right?" Sigh. Yes. The emergency arrangements were already in place. His younger sister and her husband, Rory, would check in on Andy daily. Along with his own parents. Andy would have more supervision than if he were at home. But since Andy wasn't with him, Gage didn't like it. He enjoyed the daily reports of what Andy did and the sense of control it gave him. It wasn't easy for him to give up any part of it.

Andy was the planner in the family. She could make any dad the star of the year simply by being herself. She was that great a kid.

"Yeah." Glumly, his hangdog look hit home as he hugged her again.

"Dad?" She released him from a hug and looked up at him. He still had plenty of height on her although she was on the tall side, like her mother.

"Yeah?" He sounded like a petulant teenager again, unhappy at what his parent was about to say, not the other way around.

"You're going to have fun. Right? Get away? Do your outdoor thing. We'll come back together in the fall and say what a fun August we both had, right?" He sighed as he hugged her tightly for a moment. What would he do with her? Now she was chiding him!

"Don't forget, we still had July. Practically an entire summer."

"We spend all our time together. Maybe it'll do us good to have a break."

Then she had the nerve to give him a cheeky smile. And yes, they did spend all their time together since school got out in mid-June. He even took her to Disneyland at the end of June for one week. Just the two of them. It was exquisite. Fun. Amazing. Another perfect example of how lucky they were to have each other and a celebration of the relationship they shared. Andy never appeared to suffer from any hardship in her life, despite having only a single parent.

Gage had a large family, which neutralized the feeling that it was "just" the two of them. His parents lived down the road and were involved with Andy from the time he announced the startling, but disappointing (at the time) news that he was about to become a dad with a woman he didn't love. He did care about Dierdre, however. It was bitter news, but only at first. His parents scolded him for being so careless about something totally preventable. But well, there was no undoing what was already done. They came around as soon as Andy was born. Who wouldn't have? She was Andy and there was no more perfect being ever born in this world.

Gage's little sisters were the surrogate mothers Andy might have missed. The entire family jumped in to pick up any slack in Gage's fatherhood experience.

"Andy… you know I love you…" He all but suffocated her as he pushed her into him again.

"Duh, Dad. I doubt I could have missed that." Then she patted his back. "I love you too, Dad." She released him and turned with the signature ease and confidence that was so Andy and started towards the line. She was headed through security and into the bowels of the airport towards her flight. Damn. His heart hurt. He had to blink hard to fight back the sting of tears.

She was leaving. Going out of state. He hated it. From the beginning to the end. He almost ordered her to come back to him. But when she turned with a huge grin and a wave and a wink, knowing he'd be staring after her with longing, regret and doubts, she let him know she would be just fine. Great. Good. Ready. Old enough. Independence also seemed to be congenital in her.

Not Gage. Not anymore. Not when it came to Andy. She gave him another wave and a little head bob, as if she were saying, *go, Dad*.

He put his hand up and smiled. He had to let her go. Despite every instinct that told him not to. That cord that tied him to the most important person in the world was tugging hard at his heart. He simply wanted to tug her back. And keep her beside him.

But that wasn't what was best for her. Which was why he allowed her to go.

Gage insisted on doing what was best for her. Even if it hurt him. Or it meant letting her go.

But only for the month of August.

He waited until she passed through security and with one last wave and an air kiss, she was gone.

Gone.

She was no longer there. He was all alone.

Text message: *Dad, I'm fine. I'm going to get a pop and watch the planes come in. Go home. I swear I'll text as soon as I get there.*

Yeah, she could read his mind too. He told her he loved her and to call him if she needed anything and he got a winking face and a heart emoji back from her. The emphatic message from her was in capitals: GO HOME, DAD.

Easy for her to say. Emojis. What stupid ways to communicate. Who decided those were a good way to convey his depression?

He departed the airport, slogging to his SUV and dumping his sad, empty heart and ass inside it. Sighing, he glared at Sea-Tac International Airport, and the blue sky and brilliance of the sun shining over the mostly concrete world. Far off, the horizon of mountains and city-scape could not lift the sad, heavy feelings in his chest.

Now he had to focus on the long-assed drive home. Taking Highway 2 through Wenatchee and up the Columbia River, he finally exited where the Rydell River joined the Columbia River. Up the valley beyond River's End and just outside of Winthrop, he and Andy lived in a single-story rambler on a one-acre lot. The neighborhood was paved with a half dozen lots of one acre and custom-built houses. Each featured neatly manicured lawns. The flat land offered a full three-hundred-and-sixty-degree view of the mountains surrounding them. Downriver was a view of the lower, rounded mountain closer to River's End. The north was much sharper, with jagged crests that comprised the North Cascades and toward the east, the tree-studded Sawtooth Mountains. That was where Gage intended to spend the whole month of August.

But first, he had to enter the quiet house. Sad. Alone. So alone. He dropped his phone and keys on the entry table and shook his head. Why should he bother to make dinner?

Thankfully, his phone rang, sparing him the decision. He grabbed it, his heart lurching. *Was it Andy?* No. The person on the other end was his mother.

"She get off okay?"

"Yeah… she was fine."

"And let me guess… You're not fine?" His mother's tone was tongue-in-cheek but he failed to appreciate her dry humor.

"Well... did you expect anything else?"

She gave a soft laugh. "No. That's what makes you such a good father, Gage. Have I told you how proud your father and I are of you for that? Few men would have accepted single fatherhood as readily as you did, never mind actually loving it."

"Any man worth his salt would. It's all because of Andy. How could she *not* become the greatest part of any father's life?"

His sister, Greta, called next. After heating up a frozen dinner, his younger sister, Savannah, called too. Both called to check up on him. But the best call came from Andy. Hearing she was safe and sound with Nana and Papa, who were thrilled to have her, elated Gage. They took Andy to her favorite local restaurant where she ate pan-fried chicken, field peas and collard greens. She raved about the meal. He couldn't relate to it at all. It didn't sound appetizing to him in the least.

But Andy was okay. He sighed as he flopped onto the recliner and finally allowed his heart to relax. *She was okay.* Yes, he was lonely and he missed her. The quiet house was disturbing without her, but most of his anxiety was thinking about Andy on an airplane. Being alone, without him, if anything happened while she was in the air and he was help-lessly on the ground—

No. Nope. His brain never finished the thought. He was physically lighter upon hearing her voice. She was so happy and girlish and obviously enjoying Nana and Papa.

"Okay, Dad, I'm exhausted. Can we talk tomorrow? Before you go in?"

"Yes, Princess Ann. Tomorrow it is."

"Dad..." She groaned at his pet nickname, one he wasn't supposed to call her anymore.

Tomorrow, he'd embark on his own adventure. He hung

up after a few more *love yous* and walked into the garage. His truck was parked in one of the three garage bays, and the other two were filled with all his camping and outdoor gear. Kayaks occupied the far wall, and the life jackets, oars and other paraphernalia were scattered about. The snowmobile and snow skiing stuff were also stored there.

Gage started preparing his stuff during the last month. Everything was all laid out. He took his list and covered it one last time, fully satisfied he had everything he needed. He meticulously loaded it all into his truck, glad that the hard work and late hours would force him to sleep, and maybe he could manage to ignore the deafening silence of the house without Andy's presence to console him.

FINALLY, Gage was ready to go. Loading his backpack onto his back. The pack contained his tent, sleeping bag, cooking gear and an assortment of freeze-dried, pre-packaged meals, he was well-prepared to hike the eight miles where he could make a semi-permanent camp. Calling Andy one last time to check in, he smiled when he heard how excited she was on her way to the horse camp. Nana was taking her to get cinnamon rolls at her favorite bakery. He bit his tongue and didn't say that it wasn't exactly the ideal sustenance to handle a full day of physical activity, but… Her voice sounded invigorated. Eager. Optimistic. So he ignored his nagging *dad* thoughts.

He also had to remind himself she was no longer four years old and he was no longer her entire world and universe. It was healthy and normal for her to get more anxious and eager to hang out with teens her own age who shared her passion, than spending her time by missing him. He was grateful she was so independent and could go out in the world without needing him at her side twenty-four/seven. It's how he raised her, right? Yes. But damn. It didn't make letting go of her any easier. No one warned him how hard parenting would be. No matter how much he prepared for it, he never learned any trick to make the next phase any easier than the last.

It wouldn't be long before she'd be dating. Gage shuddered at the thought. So far, she practically scorned the middle school dating scene. Sure, she had plenty of friends who fluttered between multiple boyfriends or girlfriends. Her friends seemed innocent enough to Gage although he heard enough scuttle from other parents to know there were plenty of others who weren't and the thought of that turned his stomach. Some twelve-year-olds were sending gross pictures to each other. Or worse... He couldn't think about it for long without getting physically nauseous. It was so wrong. All wrong. Little kids were doing that shit?

Luckily, with Andy? Not so much.

They survived the start of puberty. Something he dreaded silently for years... When she started seventh grade, she got her first period. They handled it together. A trip to the grocery store after a discussion with her aunts to find out what to buy, and Gage also bought a book about child psychology. Andy had a health class. Despite it being a little awkward, they worked it through. Now, Andy wrote down whatever she needed on their grocery list, including the brands of the products, and Gage was more than familiar at picking them out as well as taking advantage of any sales.

He lifted the straps of his fifty-plus-pound backpack onto his back and snapped all the comfort straps across his chest and waist. That distributed the weight better and eased the strain on his back and neck.

Wearing his most comfortable hiking boots, and lightweight nylon hiking pants, he did not need too many clothes.

He began the eight-mile journey after locking his vehicle. He noticed a truck and horse trailer parked at the trailhead. He checked the trail log. Yep, one person was listed with two horses. The mountains seemed empty otherwise. It was only Tuesday. Normally, there were a handful of people up there most of the time.

Hunter's Creek Trail read the sign. Gage stepped onto the trail, disappearing into the pine trees. Dirt puffed up with every step. The spicy smells of sage and pine filled his nose and lifted his heart. Yep, this was the only comfort he could find to fill the emptiness of Andy's departure: the great outdoors. Damn, he loved it. The house made him feel lonelier, more isolated and eventually, depressed. In the woods, he could share the miles with nothing but birds, deer, bear, raccoons and who knew what else could be out there? It was pure heaven. Joy. Fun. Inspiring. He rarely felt lonely in the woods.

It was the perfect morning for a hike. The trail was fairly free of brush in the valley of pine trees. One end of the trail dropped precipitously towards Hunter's Creek and roared in the canyon below. It was a very rugged, steep canyon in spots. A wall of mountain filled up the opposite side of the creek. A gloriously long, craggy, vertical line of rocks followed him for a few miles. Then it was covered in green pines and firs before plunging dramatically towards the rushing water. As the trail bisected his side of the mountain, he looked for the sign to indicate he reached the Sawtooth Wilderness Area. No motorized vehicles were allowed here. It was pristine, raw land. Gage loved knowing that. There were so few places in the world like it nowadays.

The trail became less distinct as the brush crept over it. Some of the bushes came up to his chest and blocked his view as he slowly snaked his way through the harsh, root-laden trail. Some places, however, were clear meadows, surrounded by remote mountains and mostly blue sky filled his view. Perfect vistas for waterfalls were everywhere. He observed huge pools and small, cascading waterfalls. The rotting logs in the forest provided shelter for all kinds of animals, and boulders as big as a car forced the creek to go around them. Everything he saw overwhelmed his senses. He could feel it lifting his spirits. Sometimes the trail became a meandering, easy walk through the flat forest, under a canopy of gorgeous trees in their natural setting. He also had to climb steep, rocky, winding trails that made his thighs burn and his breath short.

Crossing Hunter's Creek required a walk over an old log, now carved as a pedestrian bridge. It was fat and weathered, like a natural landmark. Someone carved a wide trench into it that provided passage and *voila!* A bridge was established in the middle of nowhere.

Gage stopped to drink and eat some nuts and dried fruit he brought. It always seemed to taste better out here in the middle of nowhere. He liked feeling earthy and healthy, although he wasn't particularly that way in the course of his real life.

Rested and refreshed, he moved on. Halfway there. He traversed an old slide area that was a bit intimidating. It was all made of sand. The trail was barely wide enough for two human feet, let alone horses, but their hoof prints were proof that horses had been there. Several hundred feet below, down an old landslide, the rushing, icy creek crashed over the rocks. Above him, an aspen grove was growing straight out of the landslide area. Being an ancient slide, it wasn't dangerous anymore, and the thick-trunked trees were evidence of that. But still, it was steep and it felt eerie to cross it. It also seemed very long although it was no more than a quarter mile.

Finally, he found gentler terrain and managed to regain his equilibrium.

He knew exactly when he hit the last two miles of his trip for the day. The timber changed from Douglas pine and lowland brush to alpine firs, that were denser and skinnier. The wild blueberry bushes comprised most of the brush now. It was getting into higher elevations and steeper mountains. Finally, he spotted the trail to the campsite he planned to use. Weaving a few hundred feet through the forest of trees, it opened up at Hunter's Creek. A deep pool of water glittered under the afternoon sunlight. The color was a cobalt blue as it rushed crystal clear over the subtle colors of pebbles below. It looked artificial, but so inviting. The cleared tent site was flat enough. Gage sighed with pleasure as he finally set his pack down.

Pulling out his water bottle, he downed the remains of it before refilling it from the creek. Then he stood up and stretched as he prepared to make camp for the night. Using a pair of clippers that he tied to the outside of his pack, he started clipping the invasive bushes that littered the tent site. Then he quickly erected his lightweight, small tent, placing the blue tarp over it, and tying it off securely in case of wind or rain. One never knew when the higher elevation would bring in stormy weather, even in summertime. The blazing sunshine forbade a speck of rain although the clouds persisted until well into September, but a random storm could bring flooding at any given time. He was ready for anything up here.

Filling his sleeping pad with air by blowing it up with his mouth and tightening the valve, he topped it with his eider down sleeping bag. The next supplies consisted of a single burner and fuel to heat the water for his dinner. A small pot and mess kit were all he needed. He tossed his personal items into the tent. Building a small fire, he set his small camp stool beside the rock-lined circle, Gage felt more than satisfied. He poured the heated water into the foil-lined bag of his freeze-dried beef stroganoff.

He enjoyed the cozy warmth as the little fire crackled and snapped. He warmed himself and stared up at the stars peeking brightly over the tops of the trees and the impossibly high mountains. Oh, yes... this was the only comfort to ease the ache of Andy's departure.

He smiled as he began thinking of her out there. She hated walking. Carrying the heavy gear. The dark. Of course, she'd frown at all of this.

Tomorrow, he planned to walk up and find the trail that was washed out. Then he could start to figure out how to fix it. Physically exhausted from the day, Gage fell asleep as contented as a baby.

CHAPTER 2

*M*ORNING FOUND GAGE TENDING to the camp. Nothing was easy or fast. But eventually, he lifted his light daypack and headed across the creek, going up the trail towards the meadows. It was a good two miles, he believed, and darn near straight up. Steep, rocky and densely forested.

He quickly found the washed-out trail. A freak flash flood was his first guess, judging from the large rocks that obscured the path. A wooden side wall next to the trail had also been destroyed. Gage walked up and down to assess all the supplies he needed. It required a lot of debris-clearing first. Then rebuilding the wall and creating another trail. Wood and hand tools. Directly above the destroyed trail was fresh horse poop. He glanced at the high brush all around. Damn. Someone actually circled the hillside on horseback and walked all around the spot. It was very steep and no place Gage would dare to *ride* an animal, much less, *drag* an animal through. He shuddered at the very thought of it. How could anyone attempt something like that?

He ate his lunch before heading out towards the meadow.

Rarely venturing to the end of the trail this way, since it was the lesser used side of the mountain, he continued to climb towards the meadow. It was steeper and narrower than the other direction. Two ranges of mountains ran into Hunter's Creek: one north and one south. This was the southern range. Hiking until the trees opened up to the first clearing, Gage reached his destination. It was not a flat meadow like the ones you see in Disney movies, more like an opening in the great expanse of trees. Grasses clung to the steep hillside that ended in a rocky outcrop, which was most likely due to the snow drifts that tended to form there and kept the forest from taking over. He doubted horses could find enough food to graze on in this spot. Plus it was too steep. He could not imagine anybody bringing horses here. Why would anyone bother to detour around the washout just to end up on the south side? Why not simply choose the lush meadows of the wide open trail on the north side? There weren't any decent camping sites on the south side either. None were flat, let alone, open enough for horses to stand, and none were near the water.

Walking a mile further, Gage saw no signs of a camp. Huh. Maybe the horse poop was from another trip and not the same person who logged in at the trailhead. That made the most sense. Someone on a day ride perhaps?

It had to be a long day ride, close to twenty miles round trip. Then Gage spotted fresh horse poop on the trail again. Huh.

He walked up the first steep rise and meadow just to take in the view. It offered a panorama above the tree lines. Wow, all the trees. Like a dark green carpet that hid the creek and other scenes of beauty in its corners and depths. The creek rushed on loudly but remained hidden. The gray mountains towered across from him, scraping the sky, giving him a sense of eternity.

31

But wait…

Yeah. It was smoke. A wispy stream was barely visible in the clear day. It was coming from beneath the dense trees. A camp? In there? Having patrolled this area for years, Gage never remembered seeing a camp up this far, and in the forest that ran along the creek? No way. It was too densely populated with evergreens. Not to mention being too steep and rumpled with no flat land to speak of. How could anyone try to camp there? Especially with horses?

Estimating where he should turn off the main trail to reach the slender wisp of smoke, the treetops revealed nothing. Suddenly energized, he started down the trail and half jogged, carefully making his way to the main trail before it dipped back into the forest. Relieved to be out of the sun in the cool depths of trees, Gage kept his eyes on the right side of the trail, which led towards the creek. He was looking for another trail, a side path he'd obviously missed.

He spotted it easily now that he was actually looking for it. He also saw why he'd missed it the first time. The spur trail started right where the main trail began to ascend. Someone walking on it would have no doubt been looking up the trail they were on, and not toward the left side of it. Besides that, it appeared to be no more than a path created by deer and other wildlife that often ran through the woods. Most of those paths soon petered off into nothing but forest and forced you to turn around.

But this one had horse hooves on it. He started going down it and noticed something on the right. Metal? Leaning down, he pulled up what was once a tea kettle. It was very old. Cast aluminum maybe. Now it was dented and rendered unusable. Huh. He left it there.

He continued down the hill, which turned right before dropping down again, then right again… He saw the creek and looked across it up a small incline… Something white caught his eye. A tent. Smoke. A campfire.

Horses.

Two horses were huddled in the trees further down from the campfire.

Holy crap, he wasn't wrong.

He walked to the bottom of the trail, which ended at the creek. A large, flat rock stood in the center, and several more footholds were scattered around. Gage stepped on a flat one. The rocks were a strange turquoise color that glowed green under the clear water. They looked so pretty. He jumped over to the far side and ran up the dirt and rocks until he reached the clearing. It was small, barely enough for a canvas wall tent, which stood on his right. A tarp overhead served as the entryway to the tent. The tarp was supported by a framework of buried logs that were tied together, making a square. The firepit was surrounded by rocks and still burning, although now it was mostly a bed of hot coals. An area had been cleared of dirt and roots, with a primitive fence made of random logs and tied off with rope to create a makeshift corral. Two horses were staring at him, their ears pricked forward with curiosity and interest.

"Hello?" he called out. He was worried he might scare the person whose camp he entered. No doubt. There was no one nearby for at least ten miles, so he doubted anyone expected him to pop by for a neighborly visit. No answer.

He walked further into the camp. A tent flap was pinned back and two cots were inside, one covered with bedding. There was also a black stove with a stovepipe that popped straight out of the top like a little chimney.

He saw a small, portable cooking stove with a green propane bottle attached to it. There were a few large, plastic totes that were probably used as boxes to pack on the horses. He saw a couple of camp chairs and a lantern hanging from the structure. It was more than comfortable, far more comfortable than his camp. He walked around, glancing at the construction of the corral. It was used for more than just this visit, of that he was sure. It wasn't legal to do that in the designated Wilderness areas, like this was. No permanent structures were allowed. Not even the ones that were made of logs from right there. The special designation, with some exemptions, prohibited motirized and mechanized vehicles or machines, timber harvest, new grazing or mining activites and any other kinds of development. Obviously, this enclosure was a form of human development, rudimentary as it was.

Just a few steps past the fire was a small, trickling stream. It was only several inches deep and a foot or two wide. It carved a slim pathway over the terrain with a soft *swoosh.*

Comfortable quarters. Fresh drinking water closeby. A bigger stream for other water needs. Flat ground to sleep on and the tent site dug out so the cots would be level. Huh. What the heck? Could it be some kind of hunter's camp maybe? Why would anyone else be out here? It wasn't very well-suited for horseback riding as far as he knew. No one else ventured up this way, and the land was too rugged to use. Outdoorsy people may have used it for day hikes, mostly from where he was staying to further down below where the north and south ends diverted.

He crossed the trickling stream and ducked his head under the branches of aspen firs. A junk pile lay there. But it was all old stuff. Maybe from the forties, fifties and sixties, judging by the brand names and obsolete items. Old stoves, two broken Coleman lanterns, some metal coffee cans and Rainier beer cans that still had the original triangle pop-top tabs from the sixties. Whatever this was, and whoever was using it seemed to have claimed the space for several decades. It was no accident they were there. Gage didn't think of the pile as being so much trash as a time capsule of history.

"Who the fuck are you?"

Gage was squatting beside the small pile of metal scraps, having moved a few just to gawk at them. Turning slowly, he simultaneously rose to his feet, catching a glimpse of a woman moving behind the tent. A second later, she appeared at the side of it.

She carried two round stumps of wood. She dumped the large, heavy stumps at her feet, beside the campfire where some other rounds already were. An axe was propped against one of the log posts.

He blinked in disbelief. Had he been transported to an old western?

The woman… (or was she a girl?) was maybe in her twenties. No visible lines around her eyes indicated her youth. She wore a cowboy hat that she'd pulled low over her forehead, jeans, a shirt that she'd tucked in and a wide belt. He noticed a pistol slung on her left hip. She hadn't drawn it yet, but only rested her hand on the grip. Clearing his throat, he raised his hands to let her see he came there peacefully. Had he ever done such a thing before? No. Nope. No way. But crap. Was that a Glock sitting in her holster? He squinted. Yes. That could do some serious damage to any black bear in the area, never mind what it could do to him.

She was slim, but stout with wide shoulders and muscular arms. Her brown hair was pulled back in a low ponytail.

"I'm sorry. I was hiking and happened upon your camp. I called out when I arrived but there was no answer. I didn't mean to scare you."

She snorted. "No reason I'd be scared. But…"

Maybe Gage should have been? That was the distinct message he received from her tilted head, raised eyebrows and unsmiling mouth.

Keeping eye contact with her was difficult and he had to break it to make sure he didn't step into the tiny stream. Once he was across it, he stayed on the far side of the camp- fire to give her plenty of space and not crowd her.

"Not many people could find this campsite."

"No. I was sure I would startle whoever might be here. I saw the fire from up above when I was taking in the view. Thought I'd best check it out…"

It was obvious by her pursed lips that she preferred he hadn't checked it out. "My name is Gage Sullivan. I work for the US Forest Service. I have a campsite below because I'll be fixing the trail that was washed out a mile back or so. You obviously are the horseback rider who went around it. Kudos to you. That was an impossible spot to get past easily."

"Can you prove all of that?"

Her face relaxed barely a centimeter. He shook his head, and continued to speak. "I'm sorry. I didn't bring my wallet with me. It's in my tent down where the two creeks meet. You know where that is?"

"I know it."

"I didn't think I'd run into anyone this far out…"

"Me neither." She didn't let go of the butt of her gun. He never had a woman confront him with her hand on a visibly holstered gun. He felt like he was back in the Wild West. She did not flinch or move.

"Right." He licked his lips and stuck his hand in his pocket, trying to appear less threatening. She didn't say anything but her eyebrows rose towards the brim of her hat. He tried again. "So… this is quite a camp you've got."

She gave him a small, flippant smile. "Yeah. It sure is."

Huh. Nothing. No ease. No conversation. She didn't seem at all scared of him even if she appeared suspicious. But there was no reason for her to doubt him. And there was no way to determine how long she'd been up there.

"Uh… permanent camps are not allowed in any of the national wilderness areas."

"Right. Good thing it's not." She all but yawned and smirked. She was silently telling him, hell no, this was a frequently used camp. She couldn't have constructed the corral, or created a damn gate with two logs across it, and all the framework for the tarp just this year. Her lips remained in a small, mocking scowl. Grabbing the axe beside her, she uncovered it and leaned down to set one of the wooden rounds flat. She placed another round on top of the first. Raising the axe above her head, she brought her arm down with a sharp crack and split the wood nearly halfway through. She repeated it until the round broke in half.

Impressive. Not that Gage couldn't split a stump of wood. Sure. But she was swift and on point; displaying the ease and skills of a pianist on a keyboard. Gage was in pretty good shape, but she had complete control of her muscles and dealt with her work methodically and without any complaints.

"Are you going to enforce that law?" she inquired, leaning down to toss the wood aside and pull another one up.

"Uh… you mean the camp? Not at this moment. Besides, you did it all, right? On this one trip? Long as you take it all down again and leave it how you found it. You know the rules; leave no trace or trash. Right?"

"Absolutely. That's why I handsaw all my firewood."

"That's your story then? You did all this on this one trip?"

She paused and gave him a little smile. "That's my story."

"Well… then who am I to doubt it?"

She nodded. Grinning. She set the freshly cut wood in a little triangle over the fire, leaning down to blow on the hot coals until the flames started to lick at the wood. She dropped a handful of tiny little branches to serve as kindling to make the flames higher.

He stayed back but assumed her stoking the fire was her

permission to take a few steps closer. "Do you mind?" he asked, putting his hands out closer to the heat.

"Fine." She stood up, nearing the fire before resting a boot on one of the rocks. Then she stared at the flames.

She wasn't much for words.

"Your horses are beautiful." He waved at the two matching horses. Both were white with speckles of gray and black. Were they Appaloosas? One had more black than the other.

"Yeah."

He was obviously disturbing her and she wanted nothing more to do with him. She seemed to disdain company in general. Hence, the reason she was here, obviously. But Gage found her intriguing.

"So you're obviously not seeking any visitors or companionship. I'll let you go. I was just surprised to find anyone up this far. There aren't many comfortable campsites to use."

"Exactly zero campsites as far as I know. Except this one."

Wow, she actually said something. "Yeah. How did you discover this? It's not easily located, that's for sure."

Her mouth twisted but her gaze was riveted on the fire. She finally glanced back at him. "My family used it hunting and horse-riding base. We've been coming here for as long as I can remember."

"Ahh… a family refuge."

"Yeah. I guess."

She left Gage feeling visibly uncomfortable. He wasn't used to such a sensation. Nor striving so hard for an innocuous conversation and interest of the person he saw before him. Especially since they were out in the middle of nowhere. Together and both surprised. But she wasn't reacting the way he expected someone to under these circumstances.

He cleared his throat and finally simply took a step back. "Well, then... I'll let you get back to your..."

What? Campfire? Handsawing? Camping? Solitude? He almost snorted as he pictured the lack of schedule-keeping up there. Stuff had to be done. Sure. Survival stuff. It was important, but there was no timeclock to punch or meetings to attend or any real demands on either of them. Their timelines and schedules were exclusively their own to decide. More reasons to see the beauty of this wonderful place. Maybe she was afraid of him. She was in the middle of nowhere, quite obviously alone and miles from any help if the scene turned ugly. He could see that his presence might cause her more stress than she was used to.

"Okay."

That was it. The end of the conversation. This cowgirl wanted nothing to do with him and pressing further conversation would just make him appear pushy. Or scary. Or creepy. There was no reason to be like that. "It was nice meeting you... I'm sorry, but I didn't catch your name."

She smirked. "I'm not telling you my name. There's no reason you need to know anything about me."

"So if I see you again, what shall I call you? Woman? Mountain girl? Horseback rider? What exactly do you prefer I call you?"

She pressed her lips together. "Okay. Fine. Call me Vee."

"Vee? Like the letter?"

"Like the letter. That'll suffice, right?"

She acted oddly paranoid. He glanced around again and she seemed prepared for more than just a few days. "You don't live out here on a permanent basis, right?" He was kidding. But honestly? Not totally.

She didn't seem totally maladjusted. "Nah."

"But you must have intended to stay for awhile."

"What makes you say that? And why do you need to know?"

"I don't. Sorry. I'm just in the habit of making casual conversation."

"Well, I'm not."

Ouch. Damn. She turned her back on him and ducked back into her tent, closing the door. Okay. All right, he got that hint. Backing away from the fire and taking one final glance, Gage started back down the trail and left the strange woman in her campsite all alone.

She seemed to prefer it that way.

GAGE SULLIVAN. With the US Forest Service. That was who he said he was. Not anyone Violet had expected to find so high in the mountains. He'd materialized from out of nowhere; that was a fact. She'd been having a normal day until his shocking appearance. Running low on firewood, she'd climbed upstream to saw more of the old snag she was currently using for dry firewood. It was hard work to saw single-handedly through the old log. It took a good twenty minutes per round to saw through the ancient, dense, dry timber. She'd left four more rounds up there and would have to carry them back to camp.

Returning to her campsite, she'd sensed something was different. The energy had changed at her quiet spot on the earth. She'd stopped dead. Sunlight had surrounded her. Peaks of the stunning mountains towered like castles in the sky above her. But something unexpected and new was invading her camp. She'd scanned the view through the bushes and trees. Was a bear poking around it? Or a cougar? A deer maybe? She'd highly doubted any animal was there. Fearless and curious, she'd wondered if it were a bear? It was no match for the gun on her hip so she had no apprehension, but she also knew how rare it would be to even have to shoot a bear. No. Nah. There were only a few times when a black bear refused to go away.

But she'd seen movement. Across the creek. What the hell? What was it?

A man.

She instantly glanced around for her faithful English Springer Spanial, Monty. She didn't see him. He was nine years old, and his hearing and eye sight were terrible. He'd have to smell the man to realize he was there. He often trotted way off into the woods while she worked. She didn't see him anywhere.

Oh well, not like Monty was a guard dog. He'd hide behind her or go beg to be petted, at the site of a stranger. Which was part of why she felt so protective of him and loved him so much.

But a man.

That had caused a jolt of fear to ripple through her. A man was crouched beside the old heap of metal detritus left from the late forties, fifties, sixties and seventies by random campers or hunting parties of her family and friends, since they were the only ones who'd used this campsite. Back then, people simply left the gear behind. That was before the whole area was designated as permanent wilderness for the national parks and recreation, binding it to all the rules and regulations that accompanied its status. Sometime in the sixties, these areas were preserved to remain as natural as possible. The mantra *leave no trace* arose about that time with the clear intention of conservation.

The only issue was that her family had been setting up camp here for longer than the law existed. Jack said they could be "grandfathered in" and allowed them to keep using the private, hidden camp. The corral was built long before the change in land status. Granted, they periodically repaired and reinforced the structure, but it was allowed to stay nonetheless.

Back in the day, they'd bury the used tin cans and coffee canisters in a holes scattered around the area, to dispose of them. Of course, garbage burying was something her family hadn't done in probably five decades. But it had been different times. Their garbage didn't include plastic back then, and metal and glass were usually buried for disposal. Honestly, it tickled Violet when she discovered a relic from fifty or more years ago. She imagined it being in the hand of a distant Rydell relative of hers. Randomly, their ancient refuse seemed to percolate up through the layers of dirt and rock after heavy rains and pop right out of the ground. The other day, she'd stepped on an old coffee tin while fixing one of the poles of the corral. She didn't recognize the brand name but assumed it must have been the most popular brand in the sixties. Like a settle reminder that they were here once too.

The man had risen from his knees to his feet. No. Damn. How could a man invade her space?

But he had.

Who the hell was he? Way out here? It wasn't any figure she'd recognized. She'd instantly known when her dad, uncles and cousins were around. But this guy? No way. Something had shot down her spine. Was it fear? No. She'd shaken it off. She'd refused to allow fear to determine her next move. Her initial reaction had been to turn around and hide in the surrounding trees and brush. There were endless miles of unused, raw, isolated land. The simple beauty of the creeks, streams, and rocks remained hidden under the canopy of coniferous trees. But hiding wasn't the best response. It might work for now, unless the guy decided to come back. Maybe he'd intended to steal from her. Or rile up her horses. He must have stumbled onto the place. To her knowledge, no one except members of the Rydell family could even find it. His arrival had not been by accident.

Who was this guy? Why would he show up when she was there? Great. Damn. Crap. Tightening her grip on the wood rounds she held, she'd prepared to drop them in an instant and grab her gun if necessary. She'd sucked in a deep breath to fortify her resolve. First, she would not be scared off. She'd fully intended to appear so unconcerned about her safety and downright tough that he would not question her resolve to defend herself to the death. Unnerved, if she were totally honest, she'd braced herself to deal with him. Her anti-social side was more than strong. It was the entire reason she'd chosen to come out here for the rest of the summer. She'd wanted to avoid any and all people, at least as much as possible. Being unprepared for anybody's presence, she'd cringed at the idea she would have to interact. Socializing didn't come so easy to her anymore.

She'd walked around the tent and he'd jerked up in surprise to see her when she'd simultaneously demanded, "Who the fuck are you?"

She'd said it as abrasively as she could to put him off. She'd had to establish her dominance. She'd had all the control. Caught off guard, Gage had sized her up initially, until his eyes noticed the gun at her side. Yeah, he'd seen it. And since he worked for the US Forest Service, he would instantly know the type of gun it was. Big enough to stop a bear and him. Never mind the hollow-point ammo she'd loaded in it.

Gage Sullivan, conservationist and trail builder. Yeah, a lot of good he was to let her find another way in when her tow horse was loaded with camp gear. The high side of the washed-out trail could not be safely traversed. In fact, it turned out to be one of the more death-defying rides she'd ever encountered, let alone, traversed.

It was extremely steep and all covered by old logs. They had to go high up to skirt the stumps of trees they couldn't get around. Gage had plenty of work before the trail could be deemed passable again, and that was more than evident. Alone? Right. It appeared to be too much for anyone to repair singlehandedly. But his story was plausible. How else to explain his presence in these mountains? He obviously knew the trail well enough to detect her presence without actually observing her.

She didn't fear or worry that he could be a crazy stalker who intended to sneak up later and cause her harm. But she couldn't fully discount it either. She had no desire to converse with him or make small talk. She chose to be alone on the mountain. She was actually very much alone for several miles of mountain range, so she hoped Gage would realize that she had little or no desire for chit-chat. The last thing she'd do was try to make him feel welcome. Judging by his hesitant departure, he didn't feel welcome there and wasn't used to such hostility.

Gage Sullivan was a gorgeous man. Violet doubted he ever felt unsure, especially with women. That just didn't happen to men like him. He probably was surprised to find a woman who did not eye him with unmasked adoration. No smile from her in greeting, or any kind of flirtation.

He seemed a little mature, definitely older than her, but she wondered how much older. He wasn't ridiculously older or she might have been compelled to show more respect due to their age difference. Perhaps he was in his early thirties. He had wide shoulders, and he carried himself with ease and fluidity. People who were younger or inexperienced just didn't carry themselves like that.

He seemed to know his way around the woods too. Not

so much horses, she guessed, but hiking and camping out here and braving the elements. He seemed fully at ease and confident and sure-footed. He was no day hiker or sightseer that stumbled onto her camp. God, she wished he hadn't though. She loved the sense of being invisible to the world as long as she wanted, and that's how she felt up here. She controlled who saw her and when. She had her own kingdom up here and she held all the roles: queen, king, princess and everything in between.

But now Gage, the hiking trail-blazer, knew where she liked to hang. Great.

She waited until after he'd made his awkward departure out of her camp. Sure, he probably wanted to stay there and enjoy her toasty fire, if only to figure out what she was doing here and why she came up here? What more was she capable of? She seriously doubted he ever met a woman who was as adept with horses, camping, and living up in the mountains by themselves as she was. Naturally, that would puzzle someone like Gage. If he'd found a man instead of her, exactly like this, he'd probably never consider it odd. For a man to be alone and so amazing was not unusual.

Violet chose to do this and she was thriving and succeeding and enjoying it.

That she was.

It was her escape from the ranch for the summer. That was when the Rydells offered two sessions of horse camp for at-risk youth. It was arranged through a Seattle-area-based organization called Shield Shelter. It was a good cause that she and many of her family members enjoyed providing. All year long, they had to organize and plan for it, between gathering the necessary supplies and trying to make the entire program successful. The foster kids were transported on charter buses and housed in the Rydell River Resort. They had full access to the river for swimming, floating in inner tubes and river rafting. They were also led into the lower mountain trails for gentle hikes and nature walks. Many have never taken nature walks before and their idea of the wilderness was something they saw exclusively in books.

Some of them liked to go horseback riding. So many kids hadn't ever done it before. It took a crew of adult riders like Violet to coordinate so many newbies on horses. She gave them lessons and helped saddle up the throngs of horses before embarking on the proper instruction and supervision. Violet began helping when she was barely thirteen. She had already proven she was more comfortable on horseback than on her own two feet.

Now? She couldn't stand to give any more lessons. Now she couldn't and wouldn't set one foot in the main arena. That was where most of the instruction and preparation for the kids took place. Most of the camp activities were confined to the arena, including all their meals. They ate at the Rydell River Bar and Grill. Hell no. Violet refused to go there. Ever. Period. No matter the reason or the person asking her. If someone yelled for help from the arena, and she saw that their hair was on fire, she'd never go in there or look for a bucket of water. She'd call someone else. She couldn't help the kids any longer and being there only reminded her of that. She no longer did the things she used to love doing. She hid herself away because her failure to do the things she loved made her feel worse.

So she spent most of the summer here. This was the second summer she'd done so. Two years had passed since Preston was all but murdered in that stupid arena. The arena she wished she could blow up. Only when it was annihilated would she be happy.

Her big sister, Iris, was raped in one of the outbuildings, the mechanic shop of Rydell Rides. After her dad learned what happened to Iris, which turned out to be a random act of violence, he swore he'd find the perpetrator. The man claimed to know her father Shane, but they still hadn't caught him. Shane threatened to burn the building down, but wound up disassembling it. All of it. The perfectly decent shop was dismantled and a new one was built. So? It wasn't impossible. Entire buildings could be destroyed.

Razed. Obliterated.

That's all she wanted. To take that fucking arena off her family land.

But the arena was not just her dad's. It belonged to the entire Rydell family and no one would destroy it. They felt bad for her and sympathized... Blah. Blah. Blah. Endless excuses for keeping it. But all Violet saw was the injustice. She thought she was owed some justice. What Iris endured was certainly not the same as her. Iris was the victim of sexual violence, while Violet was traumatized... Honestly? She still was. That's the only reason she sought the absolute silence and emptiness of the land she lived on right now. She had little interest or tolerance for anyone else. Especially people her own age of twenty-four years. They were always happy and healthy; they didn't know that real life was a harsh betrayal that ripped out your lungs and heart until you couldn't breathe or function.

But you were expected to continue regardless.

She shook it off. Not now. It didn't matter. She had to cut more wood for the fire tonight and start boiling some water. The horses needed to be fed and watered, and there was always something else to do up there. The physical exertion was a blessing in that it ruled her thoughts and took her heart and brain out of the past, planting them directly into the present.

She picked up the axe, balanced the next round of wood for splitting and started hacking away. The effort made her shoulders, back and neck ache but it was so satisfying to leave her thoughts of the past and focus on now. She could forget what happened. Let it be. She'd like to forget Gage too. She assumed he was telling the truth. He probably was a US Forest ranger and doing what he claimed to be doing. She didn't think he was a serial killer or a rapist or robber who just happened upon her. Any kind of criminal on the run could hide up here. She paused with the axe in mid-air. Could be a very good place to hide… but no way. She shook her head. *Don't let your imagination run wild. Go with the most logical and likely excuse. He works for the US Forest Service so he was seeing the lay of the land before starting the trail repair.* It was a whole year overdue, and very necessary. So his excuse was plausible.

He also had nice eyes.

She swung the axe way too hard as that thought drifted in. No. She didn't care about or notice guys, men or boys anymore. None of them interested her.

But he did have interesting eyes… that was just a fact. They were green. Oddly enough, her eyes were also green. Not many people had green eyes. Maybe only two percent of the population. And Gage Sullivan's eyes were big… no huge… and way too widely set for a man. Not like he could help that. Bright green as the moss and lichen in the stream, and framed with long, thick, black eyelashes. They almost reached his eyebrows. Could they be fake? That's how huge they were. Could be, but who cared? She preferred to think of him as being shallow or vain. That was primarily because she didn't need or want her sexual interest stimulated. But noticing beauty for the sake of beauty? Sure. She could do that too.

Gage had a beard, something she usually found attractive, and brown hair that matched his brown beard. All of it worked: the hiking pants, the flannel shirt, the utility knife hooked to his waistband, like any good Boy Scout. Honestly?

They almost looked like they belonged together. Brunette hair with green/gold eye color.

Oh, damn. How happy her family would be to realize a forest ranger was camped out at the base of her mountain? They'd be giddy with joy.

Sure, they all worried about her. They'd all tried to talk her out of coming here. Alone. For so long. She'd listened at first. But now she no longer asked, needed or wanted their permission. She'd told them to quit mentioning it and expecting her to do what they wanted her to do. They didn't get a say anymore. She'd decided. And honestly? If she were Ben, her cousin, who was fifty now, and equally matched her equestrian skills and training abilities, the family would never have questioned or worried about his decision. Not so with her.

Well, screw that. She was woman enough to handle all of this.

And careful too. She was in no danger because she took precautions. She kept her gun with her at all times, and took all the safety courses as any man did who worked at the ranch. She always carried a gun when she ventured out to the back country like this. Especially when it came to her horses. She would do her best to spare all of them any tragedy.

She kept a knife strapped to her belt as well for any unforeseen mishaps or emergencies. The horses might need to be cut free in case of a fire or worse. She also carried her GPS locator. Always. Even in middle of the night when she got up to pee. One click of the button and a helicopter would be dispatched to her location to airlift her out of there. She relied on having the ultimate protection. So no, she wasn't afraid. She grew up learning about horse care and horse tack. She knew as much as Jack and Ian and Ben and AJ... all the horsemen of her childhood. She'd followed them around and later worked with them to hone the masterful horse skills she possessed. And the camping gear was just the same. Having spent most of her summers up here for shorter amounts of time, of course, she wasn't naïve or inexperienced.

The only thing that threw her was finding a stranger at her camp.

She finished chopping the wood and stacked it up in the tent under the tarp cover. She tidied up the camp, fed the horses and finally ate dinner. As twilight started to fade, a strange, otherworldly whiteness descended over the mountains. It towered above her like the walls of a giant church and scraped the sky. Trees were silhouetted in the night sky and the last fading daylight succumbed to the night sky and stars. It always felt so different up here. At home, she'd be so occupied with her phone, or staring at the TV, or working in the barn, that she simply missed what happened outside. Always. She yawned as she lit a fire in the stove before bed. Summer temperatures didn't require a fire every night but she liked the hominess of it. Though not quite winter-chilling, the night reduced the temperature considerably up here, and the fire kept the chill at bay. She flopped on her cot finally and sighed with relief. Her sigh provoked Monty, to let loose with a huge sigh. He'd been long asleep on their shared cot. She had to wiggle around to get her legs around his prone body. He just one-eyed her and didn't move. Rolling her eyes, she leaned forward with a laugh and kissed his fluffy head. He was her constant companion and one of the few beings that brought her joy.

The only thing she could be sure of each and every night was a level of exhaustion that nothing at home compared with... No matter how long or how hard she worked with the horses at the ranch, she never felt as tired as she did after a day spent up here. The physical weariness comforted her as she lay down and shut her eyes, shutting down her brain for the night. The bliss of that exhaustion let her forget so much. Like the reason she came here. That kept her up most nights when she was at home. And the awful feelings that accompanied it. She savored this period of peace after a day well spent, and that was the real reason that brought her up here.

Peace. Her brain's silence. Sleep.

The tragic images were gone. The terrible sounds that repeated over and over in her brain vanished. Her regrets stopped suffocating her. Her grief that lodged so heavily in her chest, smothering her, faded away.

That night, she placed her gun right next to her head.

CHAPTER 3

*V*IOLET TRIED TO AVOID thinking of Gage. She went through her morning chores and took the horses up to graze for two hours on the farthest pasture from camp. It was a good mile ride and straight up. Not so far in distance, but certainly a workout for the horses and her just to get there. There was nothing easy.

The horses were relatively content after being fed and watered, so she tied them back to their high line so they could not wander in their makeshift corral. She tied them up anytime she went hiking or planned to leave camp for more than a few minutes.

She wanted to hike down the trail a mile or so to check out Gage's story and see if he were really there.

Not too weird.

Sighing, she finally admitted to herself that the only reason she was getting her chores done and the horses settled was for that reason. Damn it. She didn't want to indulge her curiosity, but here she was.

She grabbed her daypack and a bottle of water before starting down the trail. The forest was denser with aspen firs than she realized. She found it pleasant when the sunlight filtered in, and the shadows danced around all the tree trunks, branches and detritus. The creek made a loud, constant presence, while the blue sky played peek-a-boo. Yeah, not a bad day for a walk. Any time she spent in nature made Violet feel good.

She stopped when she heard a noise. It was man-made. A pinging noise. What was it? Metal?

She trampled further, making several more turns. The unique clatter did not let up. She finally came to the washout and found Gage. There he was in full glory, swinging a large metal mallet. He hit the spike below him, and then did it again. Again and again. She watched him pound out a rhythm: lifting the mallet over his head and then bam! Down it came and the spike he hit sank another inch or so. It reminded her of her own axe-swinging.

However, that is where the comparison ended. His arm muscles bunched up and relaxed. His shoulders were tightly strung and then not. His gray t-shirt stuck to his chest. Sweaty? Yeah. A sweaty man literally pounding a spike in the middle of the mountain. She nearly rolled her eyes. As hard as she longed to get away from it, here she was.

Attraction.

There was no way she could deny it. The man was tall, wide, muscled and lean... all at once. He was hot. She remembered his brown hair and eyebrows and long eyelashes. Perfect face. Mature face. Not the face of a boy, but a fully mature man who was well-developed. He was wearing shorts that clung to his waist and thighs while hanging loose at the tops of his knees. There was nothing douchey about him. He was what she expected a person working on a trail to look like. But oh! Could he wear it better than anyone else could! A camera crew should have been called out to capture his movements, they were so refined. The perfect subject for any movie or advertisement of a mountain man. In the woods. Doing manly-man activities. Doing strong, sweaty things.

He was right in front of her. In the mountains. Alone. With only her to observe him.

She all but shook her head. Damn! Was she becoming the weird, reclusive woman of the woods? She got a little worried when her thoughts so easily wandered there.

If she were another woman, she might have taken her water bottle and dumped it over her face, head, and chest... Yeah... Good thing she wasn't because she didn't want to be like that.

She finally unglued her gaze from his physical prowess and glanced at what he was doing more closely. A pile of metal spikes lay not far from him. And some lumber and several more tools. Clippers. Shovel. Rake. More than one kind of rake, actually. Hammers in various sizes as well as different-sized mallets.

"No way could you hike all of that in since yesterday."

Gage jerked upright, swiveling his head and scanning the nearby area until he found her. She stepped closer, emerging from the bowels of the forest. She gave him a small half wave. He wiped the back of his hand over the sweat that beaded on his forehead. "No, I didn't. A crew of several lithe, young, strong, energetic college students carried it all up here and left it for me. They are summer trainees. All I had to do was eat my breakfast, drink my coffee and haul my old ass up the trail. Pretty easy."

She snorted and surprised herself when she stepped even closer. He seemed so truthful. Honest. Real. Why shouldn't he be?

"Yeah. Looks real easy. Why didn't you keep those young, energetic college students and get them to do the work?"

"They weren't being paid to stay up here and camp. Or to

make any repairs. They were simply the hauling crew and when they finished their work, they took their butts out."

"Really? So it really is just you?"

"I volunteered for the detail."

"Why?" Her head tilted and he set his mallet down, wiping his face again.

"I work at a desk most of the time. I occasionally hike to oversee some of the areas, but I rarely get to do any field work anymore. I miss it. I like the exercise and exertion, so I offered to take care of the repair this summer. My personal life allowed me the time away from home, so *voila*."

"You *asked* for this work detail?"

He leaned down and popped back up with a water bottle, which he drank from long and deeply. "Yeah. You came here on purpose too, right?" He mimicked her exact tone and incredulous wording.

She inclined her head and replied, *"Touché."*

He grabbed the edge of his t-shirt to wipe his face, revealing the white skin of his stomach and pecs. She saw black hairs and muscles with his quick flipping of his shirt before he dropped it back down. Fine. He was an attractive man with an appealing body. Of course, she looked. She would have looked at a hot picture of any man too. It was nice but it didn't mean anything. It certainly didn't mean she *wanted* him. No. Nope. No way. Didn't even arouse her sexual curiosity. She didn't think about or desire or want sex anymore. Never. But that didn't stop her appreciation of a good-looking person. Most of humanity were average. Average in their faces, hair, features and body composition. Some people were considered homely and ugly by her although she realized it wasn't their fault. A very rare few were stupid-pretty like this guy. And that too was not due to any fault of his.

So she could freely appreciate the pleasant creation nature made.

"Were you trying to find me?"

Startled by his question, she watched him set down the water bottle and step away from the lower part of the trail on which he was obviously braced. Wooden planks covered the trail and he was hammering the spikes in to keep them in place.

"What?" Her response was reflexive. Trying to find him? No. Never. She didn't seek out strange men. Not even out here!

"Well, you didn't exactly welcome me to your camp so I didn't think I'd see you ever again."

"Did you want to see me again?" she countered. Her hand was on her hip and she bit her lip after voicing such a thought. It sounded flirtatious. Like she was a full-blooded woman and… what? *Hoped* he wanted to see her again?

A small smile curved his lips. "Actually, I did. I hoped you'd realize I wasn't a homicidal maniac who came up here to harm you. I hoped you weren't scared of me or disturbed by my presence here. I can appreciate how startling it is, thinking you're all alone in the woods where no one will find you, and miles from anywhere when a strange man shows up. I entered your private camp while you were gone and that could be very unnerving."

He seemed so genuine. His facial expression was open, and the words sounded honest, like something she'd say if the roles were reversed. Could he just be a normal guy? Doing exactly what he said he came to do? Well, the proof pretty strongly supported his purpose. She looked at the lumber, the tools and the washed-out trail. She found him sweating over it. Straining his muscles and… damn it! She wasn't horny.

Son of a bitch.

Maybe she was.

Anyway, he seemed totally legit. And even validly concerned that he could have scared her. That was nice, wasn't it? Courteous? Had she avoided human interaction so long that she was becoming a little paranoid? Maybe. She had to watch out for that. She didn't want to become a crazy mountain hermit, afraid of other people. He was an ordinary man who came to rebuild a hiking trail just as he said. Two days ago, there was nothing but a washed-out trail. She'd walked it so she'd know.

"I wasn't afraid. I was just startled. True. And your story seemed legit. But yeah…"

He held up his hands as if he were under arrest. "No. I get it. I mean, there I was. I honestly didn't think I'd find anything, much less, *anyone* out here. I saw evidence of the horses. But the smoke in the valley was a complete shock. I thought you were a couple of guys…"

"Why? There are more women equestrians than men. Next time you see a horse trailer being towed down the road, check out the driver. Only one in three will turn out to be a dude driving. Horses are mostly the passion of women. Older women, actually. Anyway, it's odd, but it's the truth."

"You got me. I assumed it all wrong. I didn't think I would find a woman alone out here, much less scare her."

She started to speak, but he held up a hand and immediately corrected himself. "Startle her, I meant startle."

A small smile brightened her face. Yeah, he already caught a bit of her number. "Okay, you made me nervous. But seeing this… your story checks out."

He nodded. "It does." He flopped down on a large boulder near him. "Mind if I sit and take a break? It's not the kind of work I'm used to anymore." He gave her a weary smile. "Being over thirty sucks and my body is clearly reminding me I'm no longer twenty."

"Can't relate." She nearly frowned at the unexpected flirty statement that emerged from her lips. What the hell? Why was she flirting with him? Was there any particular reason? The reality of her mistake made her freeze. No. There was nothing about this man to inspire her to flirt.

He stretched one leg out. His legs were golden tan, unlike his white belly and chest. His shorts slid up an inch and she freaking noticed that too. "No. Youth is truly wasted on the young. You've heard that before? Well, let me tell you. That's the truth when you're over thirty."

She chuckled and her face released the frozen scowl before she finally stepped a smidgeon closer. "You can't be that old."

"You can't be that young," he countered with a smile. "I'm a resilient thirty-three years young... although, this expedition could very well kill me."

He wasn't too far off saying that. Things could happen in the raw wilderness, which could be dangerous or even kill you. You could trip and fall over the tools, or accidentally cut your leg or finger off with a handsaw or sharp clippers. Yes, hand tools, but a wrong miss or fall could easily make them a danger. One simple fall could manage to throw out your back or cause you to break a hip or a leg. The possibilities for danger were unlimited. And adding horses to the equation? Well, that created a whole new peril. Accidents like falling off the horse, or having the horse step on you could be serious out here. Ropes getting caught around a leg or a hand could result in any number of mishaps. Things happened so fast. No, it wasn't as safe as sitting in your living room and watching TV.

Oddly enough, Violet felt safer out here than at home.

"Well, you probably qualify for grandfather status... so I'll keep checking in and making sure you're still kicking if you like every once in awhile."

He laughed. "Appreciate your support and concern, Vee."

Vee. Some people called her Vie but never Vee. It disconnected her from her own self and made it a safe interaction since he could never be part of her real life. He never would be. So, she could indulge herself by being a little more social. It surprised her to discover how nice this felt. She'd been out there for weeks without another human talking to her. She talked a lot to her horses and often narrated her activities. And, of course, to Monty. He was her primary source of interaction both here and at home. She'd have curled up into a sad, scared ball out here without him. He kept her focused on the work at hand and helped stave off any loneliness. Her lifeline in so many ways. She'd left him at the camp this time. She was unwilling to risk him getting too friendly to Gage if she decided she didn't want to stay there.

"So you're not a creep or a homicidal maniac. Should I take comfort in that?"

"Well, seeing how no one could possibly know where you were, then yes, I hope so."

"That's true. It's pretty far off the beaten path."

He stared at her for a long moment. "What?" she asked when it seemed she should know the reason why he stared so incredulously at her.

"Off the beaten path?" He scoffed and shook his head. "You could say that. But then again, I guess that's why you're up there. You prefer the unused path, huh?"

She arched a brow at him. "What makes you say that?"

He smiled. "The hostile aura you give off. The gun. Your belt of weapons and tools. The fact that you're up there all alone."

"And not a guy."

He pressed his lips together. "I keep alluding to that, huh? But actually, it was more the vibe you give off. I really didn't think I'd ever see you again."

"Are you disappointed?" Was she drawing him out to say he wanted to see her again? That was something she most definitely didn't want. Not as a woman to a man. Not in a mutual attraction way. Maybe as the only human around for ten miles… but definitely not from physical attraction.

"Yeah. You seem more interesting than anyone I've met of late. But I can understand if you came up here for some quiet solitude without any interference. I can respect someone's privacy. Hell, I often come hiking by myself for exactly that reason."

"Well, thanks. I mean, not that I really care what you thought, but I'm grateful for not just assuming I'm some kind of antisocial freak who's afraid of people. I was just taking a break. Yeah, that's a good way to describe it."

He gave a single head nod. "I won't bother you again. But if you need anything, I'll be here for a few weeks."

She tugged on the GPS locator hooked to her belt loop. "I have this. It's always on me. So if *you* need anything, a click of one button will dispatch a helicopter to lift me or you out of here. If it becomes necessary."

His eyes gleamed. "You are definitely prepared."

"Yeah. I might have been a big surprise for you to find me out here alone. But I'm not stupid."

"Can you also send a text on that GPS?"

"Yes. They're pretty simple, so it takes forever to send and receive. But yeah. It allows me to contact my home and let them know I'm good."

"I'm sure they appreciate that."

"They do. They'd prefer I didn't venture out here alone. They believe that because I'm a girl, it's somehow more dangerous and risky than when my male cousin, who matches all of my horse and camping skills, does it. But whatever…" She shrugged it off, even though their old-fashioned concern visibly irritated her.

"I've seen lots of evidence of bear nearby. More than the last time I came up this way. Did you see any?"

"No, but it seems one took up residence at this end of the valley this year. But I haven't come across one yet. At least, not yet."

"That doesn't scare you?"

"No. Nah. An encounter with a bear scares me less than you did."

"Startled, you mean."

"Right. Yeah, I meant startled." She released a tiny smile of amusement. "Besides, Monty barks so loud that I can't imagine any bear bothering with us when there is so much land all around us. If we happen to come across one, I hope it's just a black bear. Not so sure I'd be willing to camp all alone if grizzlies were any threat."

"Monty?"

"He's my English Springer Spaniel. He was way up behind the camp when I saw you and he didn't hear or smell you obviously. I left him back there today. He's nine years old now and he sometimes needs a longer rest."

"Huh. We might *think* there aren't any grizzlies around here but I've heard a few reports over the years from people who'd swear they spotted them. We hired a few wildlife biologists in this area and up towards Colville who intended to prove it. Some reports of there being several roaming around came from the Cascades. And someone from Mazama posted a picture of what looked to be a grizzly sow and two cubs a couple of years ago."

"They have pictures?"

"Yeah."

"Could just be a cinnamon black bear. Lots of people mistake the brownish, auburn and blond colors they sometimes are for grizzlies." Lots of black bears sport beautiful auburn red and brown fur. Violet saw one. She'd seen more bears while riding closer to the ranch than way up here in the mountains. She believed there was enough space out here to keep them in hiding without investigating all the noise that she, her dog and her horses made. But knowing how to shoot a gun provided the most confidence. No way, she believed, could they harm her. And if they tried, she would overcome them. That made her sick to even contemplate. She saw no reason to kill such beautiful creatures.

Her family included hunters who liked to shoot duck and pheasant as well as large game like deer and elk. Yes, the occasional bear was a target, but Violet was never a fan. Guns were only an efficient means of protection for her, in the worst-case scenerio.

She couldn't really complain since she often ate the game that Jack and Ian gave to her parents and her.

"Grizzlies can also be all those colors. A young grizzly can be smaller than an adult male black bear. So a young grizzly can be mistaken for an adult black bear. Size and color aren't the most reliable indicators. You need a combination of characteristics. Grizzlies have longer front claws that are gently curved for digging, while black bear claws are shorter and sharper for climbing and tearing apart logs. Their profiles are also different. Grizzly faces are concave while black bears are flat. Different in the ears too; grizzlies have shorter, rounded ones and black bears have longer, pointy, more erect ones. And there is no mistaking a black bear for a grizzly once you see either one up close and personal. Have you ever seen one?"

"No. Not a grizzly, but several black bears. Monty, treed one once. We were on a day ride near Foggy Dew campground. The poor bear was simply rooting around in a field and Monty took off after him until he started running and climbed up a tree. Poor thing was terrified. I called Monty back and we got out of there. But with your work in the

Forest Service, I take it you've seen plenty of them? Grizzlies, I mean."

"Years ago, the Forest Service collaborated with the National Parks and went to Glacier National Park to better understand the visitor usage. I stayed there one summer. There were close to three hundred grizzlies in the area. I saw quite a few. Damn. They were so huge and they easily outweighed the average black bear. It's one of those things. Once you see a grizzly with your own eyes, you will never again mistake it for another bear. They're magnificent. It's really something to experience."

She snorted. "They're also far more dangerous and aggressive. I imagine most visitors don't realize that, knowing human nature... I doubt many took the proper precautions."

"You guessed it. Every summer, every park has to deal with the wildlife. Especially grizzlies. They look so big that you'd think they're slow and sluggish. Not as fast as a horse or as graceful at swimming as a fish. One time, while driving I noticed a guy taking his two-year-old daughter on his shoulders to the edge of a river, which was no deeper or wider than the Rydell River. They were staring at a grizzly bear feeding on some huckleberries on the other side of the river. The guy just stood there like freaking bear bait with his baby. I had to approach him cautiously and try to talk him back. He wouldn't believe me. Meanwhile, if necessary, I could have shot the bear with bear spray and gotten them to safety, but I hated to disturb the poor bear just because of the idiot's lack of understanding and common sense. He had no clue that the bear could have crossed the shallow river in a matter of seconds before he could even start to turn and head for his car. He thought the water was a barrier to the bear."

She snorted. "I would so suck at your job. No tact. Especially when it comes to ignorance. And I consider most animals much smarter than humans so…"

He laughed, flashing his teeth and damn! did he have a nice smile. Wide lips and warm eyes. Stupid gorgeous eyes. "Somehow, I can perfectly understand that coming from you."

It was the truth too. Another idiot spooked the horse that killed Preston. For so long, she blamed Wallace, but she really knew he just reacted as a horse naturally does when startled and the fight or flight reflex kicks in. They invariably react to being startled by running away before stopping to evaluate the threat. A stupid tourist killed her fiancé. A fucking idiot. Lacking common sense. Disrespecting the animals. Any animal commands an air of respect and careful-ness around them.

Silence fell between them for a moment, which was oddly nice. The sun warmed the rock he sat on and she was so close, it warmed her shoulders and back through her t-shirt. Blue sky, bright sunlight and the lovely rushing of the creek and forest all around them. It was so peaceful. Only the occa-sional bird twitter or call.

"Quiet, huh? Lets you think. Forget about all the stress of daily life."

"It does. A quiet that most people never get to feel or hear. It's…"

"Unearthly. I've always thought that. It's nature and the world at its raw wildest for me. I'm used to more noises, even animal noises, which are seriously lacking this high up. It's almost creepy if I really stop and listen to it… there's almost nothing. But damn. Only the most real thoughts and reality can flow into your brain. All the mistakes and stresses of life get magnified."

"Yeah. But then again… I kind of feel far away, as well."

"Yeah. That's it. It magnifies everything but also makes

things fade in importance. Feeling connected to something much more than just you. Look at that mountain that all but blocks out the sky. How small one thought or concern seems compared to the overall fabric that makes up the rest of the world? Your worries are not really that big at all. For me, this place reminds me of that. What really matters and where I stand in it all. Not as big or self-centered as my brain often pretends it is when I'm so busy and stressed over the mundane problems of life. I come out here and have to survive by using my wits and my day becomes so much simpler and the important things seem... obvious. I can't always find that at home."

She tilted her head, listening to him, surprised at the things he said. They were strangely reminiscent of her feelings. She never analyzed her thoughts and feelings into any defined terms. But yes, that was it. That was also why she was here.

He glanced her way and surprised her when a blush turned his cheeks pink. For real. It was kind of.... cute. Sweet. He glanced away. "Damn, I sound like—"

"One of the few people who has a damn clue about what they're saying," she interrupted. She instantly glanced away and stared at the slope of the mountain. The gray rock and jagged crests looked so harsh against the bold blue of the sky. Yes, the world is huge, and the sky and land and entire ecosystem in which she stood were gigantic. They were such small pieces in the puzzle. This place and ecosystem would thrive much better without their presence. Individuals were no more than tiny gnats compared to the overall world. How easily that was forgotten and never even noticed. So many people were too narcissistic and self-centered to get it. Or appreciate it. But this man did?

His blush started to fade as he slowly turned his gaze to her. She felt his eyes boring into her profile. She finally tilted her head until she could meet his eyes. His back was stiff and a small smile appeared on his mouth. "Yeah? You don't think I sounded like a chump?"

"No. I think you pretty well articulated the same reason why I'm here. That's always why I seek out nature."

He nodded. "Me too. So few get that…"

"So few…" There was an odd strain in their gazes and a radiant warmth began blossoming throughout her entire system. Her blood felt hotter than a few moments ago, and that was just from staring at each other. What? Did they understand each other? Articulate their preferences in ways she never did with anyone else?

He cleared his throat. "My family always asks why I'm going off alone to nowhere. It's hard work. Hard ground. But it's so much more than that. I long for the simplicity that makes me feel completely different when I come out here."

She nodded and her smile was small. "Yeah. I get that."

Silence fell again but this time, it was comfortable and tinged with something new for her. A new awareness? Of him? She observed his finger tapping his thigh. His head was turned towards the creek, and his unseeing gaze aimed at the woods. He shifted a hip, pulling his foot up to rest on the rock and bending his knee. Acutely aware and mesmerized by his small movements, it was disconcerting when she realized how much she noticed them. Holy shit. Her skin prickled with heat. And he was just a man. A stranger.

She cleared her throat and this time, her nerves felt new and strange in her. "So yeah… if you want to make the walk up a mile on the mountain, you're welcome to visit me. I don't have much to offer, but I always have coffee and water. So…"

His gaze flipped back to her. She dropped hers and stared at her dirty, brown cowboy boots. "Seriously? You don't mind if I visit you?"

"No. I really don't. Again… you haven't been an asshole so far. But if that changes, then the invite will quickly be retracted." Phew. She was glad she found a cheeky smile and flippant voice. It immediately released the odd understanding that was wedged between them a moment before.

"I'll try not to be. Honest. If I am, you can let me know and I'll stop. I swear. And after laying new trail I'd like nothing more than to hike a mile up the mountain for a cup of coffee…" He gave her a smirk and her damn heart accelerated when she saw it.

Damn. His half smile, boyish charm, and the "ahh shucks" attitude. Damn it to hell. "Oh, you'll know when I kick you out of my campsite by using the tip of my gun."

He rose to his feet. "Somehow, Vee, I imagine that's exactly what you'd do. But don't be surprised to see me again at some point."

"Well, at least you won't startle me next time. I'll let you get back to work."

She started walking.

"Hey, Vee?" She turned at him calling her name.

"Thanks for the invite. I appreciate it."

Annoyingly polite as well as charming and genuine, he was smart and even interesting. Despite being a bit sweaty from living in the woods, he smelled good. He didn't stink. There was something very appealing about him. Damn it.

She waved him off as she quickly faced forward and high-tailed her ass away from Mr. Charming, the hardworking, nature nut who seemed to get all this just like she did.

CHAPTER 4

*H*OLY SHIT! MOUNTAIN GIRL came to see him before inviting him to her camp? Inviting him. Gage was almost giddy as he picked up the mallet before readjusting the spike and starting the hard, backbreaking work again. He was driving the metal spikes into the parched, crusty, virgin forest ground. It sure didn't like being disturbed. Neither did Vee. But she let him disturb her long enough to check out his story? Did she find it believable? He hoped so. He was genuine. Or she wouldn't have stayed, chatted and invited him up to her camp.

And damn… she could be the most interesting person he ever met. Hands down. Period. No contest.

A real-life cowgirl, a mountain girl, a wilderness pioneer woman… or whatever she was, living as a recluse out in the middle of nowhere with all of her tools and capabilities… and she actually invited him to coffee! In the damn city, they could grab a coffee at a café… sure… out here? How about a mile hike up a steep mountain? And then another two-mile hike from there back to his camp? But he wanted to take her up on her offer. It was worth it. He knew she would be well worth it. He almost begged her not to leave. He was disappointed as he watched her disappear in the trees. She was so damn interesting to talk to. Vee. Strange name. Maybe she'd tell him why she was called that when he went to visit her.

Tonight? This evening? Or was that too soon?

Would he seem too eager? Too obvious?

She was kind of hot too. Her sharp, angular body was a testimonial to hard work. He imagined the calories literally dripped off her with all the work she had to do, not to mention hiking all around the mountain.

He was eager to see her again. The thought alone invigorated his work. The afternoon was spent shoring up the lower edge of the trail and the hours sped by as he thought about Vee. Gage tried to recall everything they'd said and the way she'd reacted, both in words and body language. Her body language seemed to be more of a key to understanding her than anything else. Her behavior intrigued him. She'd seemed unsure at first and suspicious, obviously. She was worried to even admit such a normal reaction. Especially to a stranger that came up without any warning. But she'd tried to be as tough as she could appear. He remembered a few moments when it seemed like she might have eyed him up a little more thoroughly. But when she'd glanced away and grimaced, he'd wondered if she'd found him particularly distasteful. Or could it be more than that? Maybe she'd actually liked what she saw and got dismayed at herself for noticing.

There were a few flirty statements, smiles, and eye-locks. Of those he was sure. But she'd shut them down again in head-spinning haste. Mountain girl seemed unsure of what to think about him. But he had no doubt she'd liked him.

She was incredibly prickly about it, but that seemed more directed at herself than at him. And damn if that didn't make her more amusing and fun and interesting. As interesting as her camping out there alone. And not giving him her real name. Vee. Right. That obviously wasn't her name. But that's all she gave him.

Who was she? Where did she come from? What did she do? Why was she up here? What drove her to come all the way out here all alone? And who trained her to be so prepared? She seemed fully primed to stay an extended length of time. Perhaps that was the most puzzling thing of all.

She provided a distraction Gage never dreamed he'd find in the mountains.

She was also cute as hell. Her hair was once again pulled back in a low ponytail. Chocolate brown and all one color. Her closely set eyes fit her narrow face. She reminded Gage of a pixie with a soft smile that sometimes slipped—accidentally and beyond her control—into a wide grin. Jeans and a t-shirt exposed her strong legs and arms. Angular shoulders. She was sturdy, thin, and fit. With medium-sized breasts. She filled out her shirt and was well-proportioned. So yeah. He'd noticed her.

Her gaze had met his before it darted away. She'd smiled and seemed a little flirty and fun until she wasn't. She was almost cold… then not. So intriguing, Gage had found it hard to look away. The desire to see her again totally compelled him. She made his day fly by as he'd anticipated… and he looked forward to the freaking hike uphill. Not just an uphill hike but to an elevation where the roots and rocks obscured the trails, making it easy to stumble and trip. Especially feeling as physically exhausted as he was. But the impulse to see her again demanded it.

He drank some water and ate a protein bar before stowing his tools and supplies at the worksite and starting his hike.

Going up the mountain took half an hour. Glancing at his

watch, he noted it was five-thirty. When he dropped down below her camp at the creek, he called up. "Hey, Vee? It's me."

A dog, obviously Monty, immediately started barking and popped his head over the top of the incline. His big, floppy ears swung around and he tried his best to intimidate Gage by barking incessantly.

"Monty… buddy… hey… guy… it's okay…" Gage called up, gently warming his voice to soothe the dog. Monty tilted his head. His barking stopped and he slunk back a few steps. Gage started across the creek and headed up the last bit of trail. Monty barked again as he ran back in a circle, slinking away and afraid. He was definitely no use as a watchdog. If Gage were there to harm Monty or the horses or Vee, well, good Lord, this dog couldn't provide any protection. He was all but peeing on himself.

Gage chuckled as he kneeled down, putting one hand out and talking softly. "Hey… guy… it's okay. It's okay." Monty stared at him, slinking forward a little, leaning his neck out and sniffing Gage's open hand which he kept palm up as a sign of trust. The dog nudged his hand finally, then jumped back. Gage smiled. He talked some more nonsense in a baby voice. The poor beast was so overwhelmed with anxiety at Gage's unexpected presence that he couldn't decide whether to be nice and trust Gage or run away in fear. Finally, he whimpered and licked Gage's hand… barely. Gage smiled. "That's it, buddy. See? I won't hurt you. We're friends. Come here…"

Monty finally came forward and Gage rubbed his ears and the top of his head. Only then did Monty roll over and expose his stomach in a submissive display of trust that could have broken anyone's heart. Gage smiled as he scratched the dog, rubbing him enthusiastically while reassuring him over and over again, and saying what a *good boy* he was.

"He has terrible eyesight. He can't recognize anyone until they're right up on him."

Gage flipped a glance over his shoulder to find Vee standing in the opposite direction of where she stood yesterday. She'd been down to the horse corral and was leaning against a tree. Had she been watching him for awhile? Listening to his monologue with the dog? Crap. Yeah. Seeing the small smile on her face, he knew at once she must have been.

"I had to talk to him. He was terrified of me."

"Hard to miss all the ruckus. It drew me here."

"Oh." Gage rose to his feet. Monty flipped over and this time, his stubby tail kept wagging as he wiggled all around Gage. Great. Now he was a chump for talking baby language to her dog. But damn. The little guy was so sad and cute with all his barking and timidity. How else should he greet a terrified dog?

She stepped over the makeshift fencing that reached her crotch as she straddled it, stepping down on each side before flinging her other leg over. Monty spotted her and got all excited again with his butt and body wiggling while he rubbed against her legs. She bent down with a pat to his head and side as she kept walking toward the covered part in front of her tent.

"Didn't think you'd make it tonight."

"Am I too soon? Thought the walk would loosen my muscles before they stoved up." Oh, sure. That was pure shit. He knew it. She had to know it too. His walk back to camp would do the job, except he had to walk three miles instead of one. Whatever.

She nodded towards the fire and quickly stoked the hot coals until a flame sprang up. She fed it some dry twigs and the fire greedily ate them like a child licking an ice cream except with snaps and crackles. She added some dry, rotten wood she took from the forest floor. Putting her hands in the flames for warmth, she turned to the Coleman stove beside her, which she lit before setting a coffee percolater on it. She already had it all set and ready to go. Had she expected him or maybe even hoped he'd show up? And just in case he did, she wanted to be ready? Or maybe she simply prepared it that way every morning. She might always keep it clean and filled with water and coffee grounds for the next time.

Gage preferred to believe she'd hoped he'd show up.

"Sit down."

Gage eyed the two blue, fold-up chairs before flopping down gratefully on one beside the fire. His body practically collapsed. He was ready to fall asleep in the chair, he was that tired. He hadn't worked so hard all stinking day for many years. Paddling his kayak, he had to use most of his upper muscles, and also when he worked in his yard, but that was nothing compared to this. He consciously stifled the urge to release loud groans of pleasure just to be sitting. Resting, at last. In a lawn chair. His camp only had a hard log beside the firepit to sit on, or a little stool. He relished the present moment and sank into the luxurious comfort. Lounging there in the camp chair felt even better than his over-stuffed recliner at home. His most prized piece of furniture most of the time. But after his hard day of working and hiking through the mountains, this seemed like the most exquisite and relaxing chair he had ever sat in.

"You look like I just handed you a fistful of money. Does the chair feel that good?"

He couldn't hide it. She stood, crossing her arms over her chest and stepping closer to the fire before staring into it.

"Yeah. Honestly? It feels that damn good. My sleeping bag would have to suffice for a chair at my camp. And six p.m. is a little early for bedtime, even as tired as I am."

73

She snickered. He liked the sound of it. She was not acting suspicious or afraid of him now.

"So… can I offer you some dinner? It's just freeze-dried chicken and rice. But it would fill you up with a hot meal."

"I can't take your supplies. I brought my own with me, probably even the same brand as you, but they're down at my camp."

"A good two miles away and at least an hour's walk. Now, would you like some of this? I have enough. I can bring in a lot more than you can with two horses to carry it."

"Okay. Yes. I'd really appreciate that."

She smiled and clicked the other side of her small stove until the propane burner lit. She began heating a small pan of water.

"So, Vee, how long have you actually been here?"

She walked back and set a foot on the rock beside the fire. "Hmm… well, I guess it's been three weeks."

Startled at the duration, Gage jerked upright. "How? How is that possible? How can you have carried that much in?"

"Well, let's not forget I can ride out and stop at the store anytime I need to. I'm not exactly stranded here."

"Oh. Yeah. I guess your horses can carry a lot of food since the camp is already here." He started looking around; there was no way in hell that she and one saddle horse and one pack horse could have brought even half the stuff he saw around the camp. Even with several trips. There were years of accumulation here. Totally something he should address in an official capacity… but he expected her to clear it out when she left, although he had no plans to check to make sure.

"How much longer do you plan to stay?"

She shrugged. "Not following any timeline."

"Huh. Must have a pretty understanding boss. Or are you in college on summer break?"

"Nope. No college. No boss either."

"Oh. Then you must be one of the lucky few who is independently wealthy?"

"Nope. Not that either."

He put his hands up. "Okay, I give up. How can you afford to do this? How do you get this long off from work?"

"I work for the school district."

"Teacher?"

"No. But I have my summers off."

"Ah. Okay. What school district?"

Her head shook. "No. Nope. I'm not telling you any identifying facts about myself."

"Okay. Why exactly can't you tell me any identifying facts —as you call them—about yourself?"

"Well… no reason. You'll never see me again outside of here. So no reason. I'm just a private person."

He glanced around. "Uh… yeah, no kidding, mountain girl. I think that was obvious from the get-go. So… no last name either?"

"Nope."

"And Vee? Is it a nickname?"

"Nope."

"But it's not your real name either?"

"No. Never."

He sighed. The coffee finally percolated and she glanced at it, letting it bubble. The smell of roasting coffee wafted towards Gage and he almost groaned with pleasure. It smelled so good out there on top of the world, lost in the woods. He always cherished the homey, heavenly coffee aroma.

"Huh. You already know mine. Doesn't seem fair."

She stared at the fire and the side of her mouth lifted. "You offered it. I didn't ask you for your name. And how do I know you're telling the truth? Anything goes up here. It's kind of what makes it fun."

He sighed as he moved over to slip his hand in his pocket before he brought it out with his wallet. He leaned towards her. "I figured it might come up. So there. Proof I'm not lying."

She stared at his wallet, then at him. "What?"

"My ID. Look."

"I—I don't need to. I already believed you."

"Please, I would feel better knowing you have no reason to be suspicious of me."

She stared into his eyes as she reached out to grab the wallet, but curiously, her other hand immediately rested on the butt of her gun. Damn... like a reflex, it was automatic. "That's smart."

"What?"

"I asked you to reach towards my hand. I could have grabbed you, pulled you down and out-manned you with my strength but you had your gun at the ready. You're well trained in self-defense. I like seeing that."

Her eyebrows rose. "You do?" She was slightly incredulous.

"I do. I wish more women took those kinds of precautions. It sucks that as a woman, you're relegated to doing that, but I can't stand hearing stories about women being overpowered and harmed. Or worse. Disappearing. Did a few Search-and-Rescues in my career when we enlisted anyone who was willing to help look... some ended well, but some didn't and not because of the exposure or the terrain, but from a jealous husband or angry boyfriend... so, yeah."

Vee tucked a lip under her teeth and nodded. She took the wallet and leaned back in her own space before she glanced into it. She read the license and said, "Gage Sullivan, age thirty-three as noted. You live in Winthrop? Local here, huh? For some reason, I didn't get that."

She leaned over to hand the wallet back to him. He nodded, taking it and putting it back in his shorts pocket. "Uh-huh. Sure. Family's been here for years. Born and raised."

"Are you very close to your family?"

"Yeah. I still live near my mom and dad. Like three miles away. I have a sister in Pattison and another one in Winthrop. I see them regularly and they also email, text and call... a lot. So much. Oh, my God, do I have meddling, gossiping sisters."

Her head tilted. "That's sweet, actually. Are you married?"

It seemed to just occur to her. "No. You?"

Her face tightened. A flush crawled up her neck and reached her cheeks. She suddenly turned to grab the bubbling coffee in the percolator. Finding two tin mugs, she poured the coffee in each before handing him one. Staring into the dark liquid, she swirled it and shook her head. "No. Never. Never plan to or want to."

"Oh, yeah? That seems boldly determined."

"It is. You doubt me? Everyone tells me I'll change my mind and blah, blah, blah... like I can't possibly want that later on. Staying unmarried. How scandalous."

He stared at her, tilting his head as he considered her comment before he replied, "Actually, I believe you. I've never met a woman like you, with different goals and life choices than most of the women I know or meet. There are a limited scope of people I know and associate with, so not a broad sampling of society when it comes to scientifically speaking—but anyway, you're like no one I've ever met. So yeah. I see that. I believe that."

She sipped the hot coffee and nodded, dropping her gaze down. "That's a nice change... you believe me. You aren't trying to talk me out of it or set me up with your cousin or best friend or neighbor…"

"For real?"

"Constantly. Are you single?"

"Yes."

"That doesn't ever happen to you?"

"Not much. Though, I'm more than willing to be set up, so sometimes yes, but it's not unwelcome."

She shuddered. "Why would you ever willingly set yourself up for such an excruciating, humiliating experience? People send their cast-offs to you. I can't stand the phoniness, pretending it's fine. The weird habits, jobs, personalities, oh, no! Never."

He let out a laugh. "Sounds like you've had some nasty experiences that you could make me laugh about."

Her frown dipped her mouth. "No. No funny experiences with dating for me." Her tone was harsher. He got the hint and backed off that line of questioning.

"Yeah… I have some whoppers. Want to hear one?"

Her gaze returned. Was that relief he glimpsed in her eyes? "Yes. Actually, I would."

"Okay… you should sit down because you'll laugh so hard at this."

Her raised eyebrows and skeptical expression suggested she didn't believe him. "I was set up with a woman I used to work with, a friend. We met at a restaurant, doing all the usual, boring stuff you do on a first date. I sat down and it started off good. We ordered drinks. We were chatting about her job and mine. It was a few years ago, and at that time, I was doing fundraising in Washington DC for the Forest Service. Telling this woman about it, I said I was bi-coastal right now."

"Okay, so far not funny."

"Nope. She stopped, hesitated and said that was acceptable to her. She had no judgments. I was confused by her answer. I mean, how controversial can it be to work on the east and west coasts? But okay… I thought perhaps she was picturing us dating in the future and just reassuring me she wouldn't mind if I traveled. I don't know, honestly. Then with no segue or transition, the next thing she literally said was, 'Well, I slept with a woman my junior year in college. She was a friend and she asked me to…' Then she went into graphic detail all about how the hook-up happened. After that, she asked me to describe my times with men.

"I was so startled, I could only gape at her, unable to even answer. Struggling for words, I said I have never been with a man and even if I had, I wouldn't share that experience with her… and definitely not on a first date."

Vee's gaze sharpened and she leaned towards him, assuring him he finally had her undivided interest. She tilted her head. "Well… no judgment there. Lots of people experiment. You can tell me." Vee's snarky laugh and comment made him glare at her. "Seriously, what were the woman's issues? Why was she so awkward with social cues?"

"After a few more sex stories from her, I finally asked why she was telling me all this stuff. She said it was so I would feel more comfortable knowing it was okay with her if I were bi-coastal."

Vee's smile blossomed all over her face and genuine laughter escaped from her lips. Lots of laughter. She couldn't talk or breathe. Finally, she held up a finger and coughed. "Oh, my God, the woman thought you were confessing your bisexuality. She thought bi-coastal meant bisexual."

He grinned, feeling glad he could make her laugh so hard. "Yes, that's exactly what she thought. It took me a few minutes to convince her they were not the same thing. Bi-coastal simply meant I was working on two coasts: east and west. Her embarrassment was visibly instantaneous. I'm sure that's why she couldn't admit her ignorance of the word. I assured her I wouldn't have expected, much less, *wanted* to discuss another person's sexual history on a first date."

Gasping, Vee hiccupped between laughs. "How stupid could she be? And even if you did tell her that, why would she launch into the details of her own sexual history? I mean… yeah, it's weird you'd pop being bisexual in the context that she took it, yeah, but nothing about it suggested you wanted to hear a long, detailed history of her own. Quid pro quo, I guess?"

He chuckled too. "I tried not to let on how… yeah, how stupid I found her. I tried to reassure her that it was fine, just a misunderstanding and all that… but holy shit. Did she go into detail. TMI. So much I was uncomfortable and I decided I never wanted to see her again for fear of all the strangers she'd tell about our date in gory detail."

"No, that's just plain stupid. There is no confusing those two words. And what adult doesn't know the difference? I love that story. It would have been worth the stupid date just to have that experience, I'll give you that."

She laughed again. It was a husky, spontaneous giggle. "Got any more that good?"

"Not that good… but some that are amusing and harmless…" The other stories were cute, innocuous anecdotes that neither mocked him nor the person he was describing. While Gage talked at length, Vee poured the boiling water into the foil packages and let it sit for the requisite eight minutes. She also massaged the packages to spread the moisture and cook the meal in the bag. All the while, Gage's stomach nearly cramped with desire for the hot, mouth-watering meal. So much better than the cold jerky and power bars he filled up on all day. He ate a warm breakfast but that was more than twelve hours ago, at six o'clock this morning.

She divided the package into two bowls for each of them

and handed him the tin bowl with a fork. He grabbed it eagerly, ending his story nearly mid-sentence, forgetting the amusing anecdote of a woman who wanted him to meet her cat before they went on their first date. When he said "meet her cat," he was deadly serious. The woman formally introduced them and assumed the cat understood.

Gage almost sounded a bit orgasmic in his reaction to the first bite. The warm rice and perfectly seasoned chicken melted on his tongue. Startled, he glanced at her sheepishly. She let out a soft chuckle. "Is it good, Gage?"

"Divine. Best meal anyone's ever served me."

She snorted. "Never been accused of that before."

She grinned and he took that as a sign he was gaining her trust. He genuinely hoped so because he enjoyed her company. She was unlike anyone he ever met before. The weeks she'd stayed up here, lacking any kind of plan or timeline, literally made his brain hurt. Perhaps it was because he'd been a single dad since barely reaching adulthood. He'd always lived his life around plans and schedules and routine. He was always accountable. The stretch he took this summer was perhaps the longest he went without needing to account for himself. He was in the mountains because Andy was attending her horse and track camps and spending time with her grandparents. He often imagined camping just like this.

He got quiet while devouring his meal. And so did she. Vee stared into the cheerful flames as she too ate her meal vigorously. Chewing big bites, she was careful to keep her cheeks and mouth closed before she took huge swallows of the cool water from the stream to wash it down. He did too. It was a whole different world up there that affected one's body and appetite in ways that even the best gym workout couldn't. The physicality of mere existence exhausted one far more than anything in regular life. The chores alone were difficult: lifting, traveling, twisting, and always on uneven ground. The uneven terrain tore up their feet and burned their calves. Food tasted better though, and was probably more nourishing than at home. At home, Gage often ate just to eat.

It was truly exquisite here, eating a meal from tin bowls with the fresh stream water falling right off the mountain. The companionable silence was more than he'd ever enjoyed sharing with anyone. They were mutely staring at the pretty flames that virtually hypnotized them. The exhaustion they suffered was evident in their exchanged glances. When they shared eye contact for a moment, they both had little, soft smiles. He was energized. He felt sure he wasn't the only one experiencing that.

Gage wished he could crawl onto her spare cot and simply fall asleep. His empty stomach now filled, he grew incredibly sleepy. The twilight was imbued with the soft, delicate colors of sunset, falling out of the sky and seeming to sink behind the rocky mountain peaks that surrounded the spot on three sides. Down the trail, closer to his camp were the lower peaks.

But he still had a two-mile hike. At least it was downhill. After amusing her with his funny dating stories, the hours passed quickly and darkness would soon envelop the wilderness.

"Do you have a headlamp?" Violet asked as she took his plate and chucked it into the small camp-side stream.

"Yep." He patted his pocket on the side of his shorts. Though it was a warm summer, he would be very chilled by the time he reached his tent. It grew cold at these higher elevations after the sun sank from sight. He drew up to his full height. "Well, I so enjoyed telling my embarrassing dating stories that I didn't realize how late it had gotten. I'd best get back to my camp so I can go to sleep and handle a full day's work tomorrow."

She rose too. "You're okay to hike in the dark? You don't have a gun on you, or do you?"

"Nah. But I'll be fine. I'm okay."

"Are you sure?" She bit her lip. He liked seeing her concern compared to yesterday, when she regarded him with distrust and possibly fear.

"Sure." He headed towards the top of the trail that led down to the creek. Monty ran up to say goodbye. Gage bent at the waist and gave him a full scratch and a pat and some kind words.

"Will I see you again? Or is that too much visiting in a place you'd prefer to get away from neighbors?"

"You'll see me again," she said simply and without clarification. "You can come back here anytime too. I can always spare you a cup of coffee and a few more meals."

His heart swelled and she made him elated. He was so glad she'd invited him to return. He nodded, trying to keep his grin subtle without eating up his whole face. The last thing he wanted to do was scare her off again. "I think that would be great."

"Me too. If you can handle all the walking and work." Cheeky smile. How old was she? Younger than he for sure. Not quite in her thirties. But not early twenties either. There was a maturity about her. A calmness in her gaze and gait and how she carried and expressed herself. Somehow, he suspected Vee probably lived a different kind of life so far. Perhaps struggle and hardship were the roots of her wariness but he was glad it hadn't totally jaded her.

"I can handle it. Bye, Vee… mountain girl."

"Not a girl."

"Mountain girl is cuter than mountain woman… Can't I call you it for that reason? After all, you won't tell me your name… so please?"

She rolled her eyes. "Fine. Yes. Okay. Mountain girl, but only because you'll never really know who I am."

"Strange. But okay... Mountain girl."

She gave him a cocky side smile. "Goodbye, Gage Sullivan."

He waved and left, his feet walking fast, but his heart wanted to remain with her.

By the time Gage fell onto his half-deflated air pad on the ground and crawled into his sleeping bag, damn! It could have been a luxurious bed in a posh hotel, he was so grateful to be out of the dark, off the trail and most importantly, off his feet. In seconds, he fell into a deep, pleasant sleep.

To his surprise, he dreamt of a girl on a horse. She was riding up the mountain to the very highest peak and calling down to him. He couldn't hear what she said but she looked so magnificent up there, silhouetted against the bright blue sky on top of the world, like the divine ruler of a kingdom, and her brunette hair freely streaming and her eyes bright and... what was her name? She was yelling, but the wind caught it and he couldn't hear or get to her, no matter how fast he climbed...

And of course, the queen perched on top of the kingdom was Vee. The mountain girl he wished he knew the name of although he truly believed he'd never find out.

So, what would you do when returning to your camp, you find a big, strapping, strong man down on one knee, at eye level with a timid, anxiety-ridden dog, who barely lets his own family come near him? Now he was lying on his back, exposing his belly, butt wiggling, stubby tail thumping and licking the big man's hand. His other hand rubbed him with a gentle stroke reserved for a baby. He spoke softly, using kind words and well, hell! Violet finally had to trust him. That sealed it. This man had to be who and what he said he was or she'd have to eat her freaking hat. He was Gage Sullivan of the US Forest Service and he was there to rebuild the trail when he happened upon her.

Then he formally revealed his identity to her at the campfire to make sure she knew exactly whom he was. Just remembering to bring it with him said a lot about him. Hell yeah. How easily she was finding it to trust him.

She enjoyed her evening talk with Gage, and also being quiet, staring at the fire. They were laughing and simply sipping their coffees made from stream water after a hot meal. It was better than any fancy restaurant anywhere in the world in Violet's opinion.

Yes. One thousand percent better.

They were friends. *Friends.*

She felt bad watching him vanish into the deep twilight that night. His physical exhaustion was so apparent in his eyes but he never asked to stay over. And she would never have invited him.

Monty slipped his head under her hand as she contemplated the fire, breaking up the still darkness of the mountain forest. The stream sang a melody to her. The stars were distant dots in the sky, hanging above the constant treetops, now relegated to no more than dark shadows. The triangular mountains became shadows too against the night. It was so glorious to observe. Quiet. Never spooky or scary to her, despite her isolation. She preferred to be all alone there. But she wasn't alone now. She felt her gun and eyed Monty, grateful that Gage Sullivan was the only other person in her forest. He was solid and she liked the way he treated Monty. He was that way with the dog naturally, even when he was unaware of her presence. That was the clincher.

Finally, she put out the fire and did her nightly routine

chores and horse care. She changed into her pajamas and slipped inside her sleeping bag. Monty jumped down to the end of her bed. He looked up towards her and touched her hand with his nose at her hip. She rubbed his head. His big, liquid brown eyes stared at her with unconditional love and adoration before he finally sighed as he shut his eyes. She rubbed his ears and he let out a blissful groan. She blinked her eyes shut, squeezing them tightly as she rubbed her best friend and companion harder. He groaned like a cat purrs to show its love. "How could I get through the day without you?"

Monty answered by thumping his little half tail. Violet blinked and her tears streamed down her cheeks. She used to scold herself to stop them and tried to rub them away. Now? All alone like this? She let them flow at will. Tears would often stream down her face without any thoughts about Preston or the slightest warning she was going to cry.

She cried for Preston still. Very often. As much as the day he died. The trauma never left her. It filled her. It consumed her. It drove her to camp in the mountains, making herself too busy and physically exhausted to do anything else but sleep and relax. Letting her thoughts go. But that never truly worked. Nothing did. She still loved Preston. Grief had simply become her new normal, since it was her emotional state all the time now. And nothing could ever change that. The burden of sadness so often overwhelmed her that she could only wonder how she could continue to live with these feelings? How? How much longer?

Fuck. Rolling over, she permitted the loud hiccupping sobs to escape her. Audible. Plaintive. Mournful. She could do that up here. Just let loose with her emotions. There was no one to hide from or worry about upsetting. Here, no one could judge her or scold her with shocking concern. No one could criticize her or advise her how to fix it. She simply was. Grief still controlled her emotions, despite freeing her this day. Grief was her constant companion most of the time.

Even after a nice evening with a new man.

She snorted. As if that man meant anything to her.

No. He was just a temporary diversion.

Solid and firm on that subject, she shook her head and tried to ignore her thoughts.

The way he'd treated Monty was kind of priceless to her. Golden. Platinum, actually. Amazing too. Something that could change her entire opinion of him.

CHAPTER 5

*G*AGE WORKED HARD OVER the next several days, making noticeable progress on the trail repair. Each evening, he hiked up the trail to his mountain girl where the hot coffee was ready or percolating, and a toasty fire roared beside the chair she set there for him. Best of all? Vee gave him a big smile whenever he climbed up the trail to reach the opening of her camp.

Monty didn't bark at Gage after the second time he saw him. He simply flopped down at Gage's feet in ecstasy while Gage leaned down and patted the dog all over. He would usually greet Vee before asking how her day in the mountains went. Very little ever changed in her answer. She went to the pastures to graze the horses and she would recount the little misadventures they occasionally had. One happened when her horse shied at a boggy spot on the trail. The horse tried to jump uphill to avoid it, and unexpectedly to Vee, the horse veered sharply downwards as soon as it got around the wet spot. In the process, Vee fell off.

She laughed about it when she told Gage as she poked the fire with a stick. "I can't remember the last time I fell off. It seemed almost like slow-motion. One moment, I was on the horse and the next, I was rolling down the grassy mountain. It took a few feet before I stopped and I lay there, shocked for a moment, but feeling just fine. So crazy."

Vee was pretty easygoing and talkative as long as the subjects pertained to the mountain, forest, horses, hiking, trails and his work up there. Nothing personal. Nothing to do with real life... at least, nothing about hers. They discussed him sometimes, but only in the most abstract way.

"I won't be coming by tomorrow. I'm hiking out."

Vee's head jerked upright. "Hiking out? You mean, you're done?"

"No. No. Making my weekly check-in. I need to check in with my family and office once every week. I'll be back."

"Oh." Her *oh...* was it regret? Surprise? Disappointment? He thought perhaps it could be, but with Vee, it was hard to tell. She let small smiles slip past when he amused her or she caught him interacting with her dog. But he never saw any expansive or huge smiles. Just small, quiet ones. Little curves of her lips tilting up with an amused half-roll of her eyes. She seemed rather circumspect, a quiet person, who was as fierce in her abilities as anyone he ever met.

"Well, walk carefully," she warned him with a cheeky smile.

And he took her advice. Taking the quick hike out, and carrying only a small daypack, he immediately called Andy.

"Baby girl! How are you?" He almost wilted with joy when her sweet, youthful voice came over the line.

"Hey, Dad." He could all but see her eye-roll in her tone of voice. Like she expected him to be a dork, but she still loved and tolerated him anyway. "I'm not a baby."

"I know that." He lifted his gaze up to the blue sky and replied, "I missed you so much! Tell me everything. How was the camp? Nana and Papa's? How is Georgia?"

"It's so awesome here. I'm having so much fun. Nana and Papa are the same, and that's the best part of them. And camp was amazing… Dad… oh! The horses! Why have I never ridden before?"

"You liked it?"

"I loved it. *Loved.* I think it's my calling. Horses. Dad… can we get one? Please?"

He chuckled at her exuberance. It made her lose her cool and the blasé tone of being a new-teen in her voice. In that moment, Andy sounded like his little girl again, begging him for a pony. She did that a lot when she was five. Now, at age thirteen, she was doing it again!?

"A horse? We don't even have a fenced yard."

"We can put one up. Feed it hay. Please? Please? I swear, I'll feed it and do everything it takes to keep it…"

He rolled his eyes and let his gaze wander about. Sure, as if he believed such diligence could last. Talk about a passing fancy. "How about taking a few more lessons first?" Seemed like a reasonable compromise.

He heard a huff… yeah, literally a puff of air into the phone that told him she wasn't happy. "Fine. Okay, I guess." Oh, to be thirteen years old and so entitled and all that.

"Well… tell me all about it."

And she did. She described learning how to groom and care for, as well as lead the horses. There were other girls her age that she enjoyed, who were "totally the greatest." On and on she rambled. And holy damn. Did Gage love it. Listening to her voice climb a crescendo, going from high to low, with all the intermediate inflections, she dramatized everything she'd done and heard and the things people said. She was always one for details.

Gage dreaded a time when that might stop, and she'd answer him with a terse, dull, understated "fine" or "okay" before ignoring him. Maybe she could become the exception to the rule, and that terrible phase of needing to withdraw after finding their parents too stupid to understand them might never exist. At least, that's according to what he heard. He hoped and later decided to believe that no way could he and Andy ever become so alienated or estranged.

"So, Dad... how's the godawful forest?"

"Dirty. Hard on the old back." He grinned at her disdain. "Speaking of horses, you won't believe what I found up in the mountains right above where I'm working."

"What? A bank robber? Someone on the lam?"

"Oh... I only wish it were something that cool. No, a woman, camping with only her dog and her two horses. She's got an entire camp all set up. When I stumbled onto it, she came up from behind the trees and she was lugging these huge rounds of tree trunk that she sawed off an old log. She proceeded to chop them as we were introduced."

"Do you think she lives up there?"

"No. I think she's staying there for awhile though. I don't really know for sure. She won't say much. Just that her name is Vee."

"Sounds so mysterious. Maybe it's an alias."

"Nickname at a minimum. That's what I was thinking too. She's pretty private."

"Doesn't she get scared at night?"

"Well, no, I don't anyway. Besides, she always keeps a loaded gun on her."

"Gun? Horses? She sounds pretty cool."

"Seems like a pretty cool customer."

"Is she old?"

"No."

Pause. "Dad? Is she pretty?"

Gage held the phone tighter and smiled. Of course, Andy would ask him that. "Yeah. She is. In an unusual way like I've never seen in a woman before. She's pretty strong and

LEANNE DAVIS

capable and I guess her confidence is pretty attractive."
There. Appropriate explanation for a young daughter. He
wanted her to believe that her inner self contained the key to
her confidence and being "pretty," not her looks… Sigh. Yeah,
he found Vee pretty and yeah, it affected his judgment of her
in a different way than if she'd been sixty years old. He
sounded hypocritical even to himself. He knew that. Raising
a daughter often revealed that to him more often than not. It
changed many of his perspectives, which he might've missed
if he hadn't raised a daughter.

"She's pretty," Andy decided with a giggle.

"Why do you say that?"

"Because when you break into some version of, 'oh she's
strong and confident' when you're trying to sound deeper
than most dudes and not just thinking how pretty a woman
is, it's a dead giveaway. Especially after I ask."

"Well… not always. I mean, she really is strong and
capable and confident."

"Sure. But you get this stressed tone to your voice whenever you talk about the subject with me. So I'm sure she's
pretty and you've noticed. Do you like her?"

"I do. It's nice to talk to another human out here, I'll
admit. There's a lot of alone time up here."

She snorted. "Duh. Which you wanted somehow. But
yeah, totally true. That's cool you found yourself a mountain
girl."

"Ha. That's what I call her. She wouldn't tell me her real
name…"

Andy laughed. "You said she had horses. Is she good with
them?"

"The best, as far as I can tell. I haven't seen her ride, of
course, but she managed to get around the trail I'm fixing
and I'm not sure I could have hiked up around it. She rode

92

around it and pulled another horse behind her, the one that she packs her gear on. So she must be good."

"Do you think she could teach me how to ride?"

"Andy…" he groaned. From zero to sixty went his teenage daughter. "I barely know her, not even her real name. I know nothing about her. I can't just ask her."

"Well, if you like her and she likes you and she knows all about horses, at least well enough to be up there all alone with them… Think about it, Dad… it could be the key to solving our fence issues," she cheekily responded. He groaned and chuckled. It was hard for Gage to deny her quick brain whatever she wanted to argue a problem she thought she already solved.

"I doubt she'll even give me a way to contact her after she rides out of there."

"Lay on the charm, Dad. You can do it."

He could not believe his daughter. She so easily turned his casual encounter with someone into something that benefited her. It seemed so farfetched, he threw his head back with a chuckle. "Andy Sullivan, you have to realize you are not getting a horse. Never. Period."

"Well, we'll see, Dad, won't we?" Andy chirped before doing a one-eighty with the conversation by asking a new question. She was a master at doing that. They were next discussing her impression of Georgia and the upcoming week, and when she would be going back to school. As usual, it was a hasty call. But nonetheless wonderful, and one he loved.

"Okay, Dad… I'm getting hungry and you need to rest and shop."

He shut his eyes as the end of the call hit him. He hated the separation. "Yes. Okay. I love you, baby girl."

Andy sighed but didn't chastise him. "I love you too, Dad.

Go visit the mountain girl. Convince her to give me horse-back-riding lessons."

Gage laughed as he hung up and smiled with satisfaction that he talked to her and she seemed so happy. Then he felt disappointment that it was over. He had to last another week. That was the drawback to the work. He sighed and glanced at Vee's rig. He could take down the license plate and find out her personal information but it didn't seem right. He sighed before heading to the store. He was eager for a hot shower and a good night's rest.

Then he had to get back to camp and go at it again.

THE MOUNTAIN almost felt emptier the next day. That was so silly, Violet kept slapping her own cheek. She didn't see Gage all day. She'd spent her weeks all alone up there before he'd made his presence known. To miss him felt very strange. And annoyingly stupid. She carefully rode up to the small lake that wasn't named. Her family members showed her the way to get to it during their years up there. She never saw anyone else go there. It was very far up the valley, hidden on the far right by a high ridge. The long stretches of forest and rocks were foreboding enough, but climbing a dangerous lip to get there made it kind of a magical spot.

It was shallow and small. More like a pond than a lake. Green with algae now, it was usually gold in the fall when the western larches turned from green to gold in their needles. She believed her aunt and uncle first hooked up there. They never told her that, but there was some anniversary date that they always insisted on spending here. Violet was sure they never missed a year. She grinned, picturing her no-nonsense Aunt Kailynn and Uncle Ian. They were actually quite a bit like Violet, but that was a surprising fact of their long history.

The enduring ride and being in such a pretty spot swiftly ate up the day. Violet was tired by the time she headed back into camp. She buttoned up the camp and checked on the horses before preparing a meal for herself and dropping into bed. Glad not to think or dream or lie awake or contemplate. No regretting. No crying.

No. She slept hard. Morning came and she felt strangely renewed and excited. For what? After she lived up there for several weeks, she got a sense of déjà vu over and over again. It was a familiarity she loved, treasured and counted on. That was why she was up there. But it was not a usual feeling for her to get giddy. She jumped out of bed, jamming her boots on and rushing out... to what?

Even if he came back... it wouldn't be until tonight.

Late.

But what a long hike. No way he'd come up there after returning from the other hike.

So... what if she went down there?

It was an easy enough hike for her. She could visit him for once and be neighborly. Maybe even bring dinner.

Yeah... that would be fun and nice. And... whatever. She almost stomped her foot on her other foot. It truly was *whatever*. It meant nothing. *Nothing*.

Sure.

Violet did her chores with more relish and excitement. Standing under her makeshift shower, she washed her hair and body. The water came from a five-gallon plastic, solar-heated camp shower that hung from a tree. She kept it filled with creek water, hoping a few days of baking in the sun would warm it substantially. It wasn't freezing, but not even close to warm. So her bathing was quick, but effective. She towel-dried herself and put on clean clothes. The day before was spent washing a few underthings and t-shirts. She wore her jeans for several days. No matter what she did all day: cutting wood, making fires, tending the horses, and simply walking around, her pants were usually dirty. But she didn't smell bad. She fingered her hair until it was dry and brushed the straight strands out. She didn't wear a hat on it. She felt almost grand in her fresh appearance up there.

When five o'clock arrived, she all but ran down the hill, past Gage's pile of tools and the latest stretch of new work. She headed back into the woods and down she went, all but galloping. She was happy and why not? It was nice to see someone else. Someone new. Someone who didn't know her history. Especially, someone who didn't know her grief. He knew nothing about it. Not even what her real name was.

He seemed content with that. He hadn't pressed for more than her lame nickname and if she suddenly ceased talking about a subject, because it was too personal, he never pressed for more. Gage made it easy to be with him.

Finally, Violet heard the rushing water from the north fork of Hunter's Creek. She spotted it down the hill through the tree trunks. Rotten logs, rocks, roots and a faint, twisting trail led to the gushing water which connected to the south fork, which flowed below Gage's camp.

She spotted the flicker of orange flames. Her heart skipped. Yeah, so? It sped up a few beats. Didn't mean anything. Easy enough to be glad for company if only to split up the ordinariness of the tedious days out there. Violet loved the horses, and the quiet, and the chores. She even loved the survival skills she practiced to stay alive and comfortable out there… but there wasn't a whole lot to break it up.

Except Gage.

She cautiously took her steps down. No use in spraining an ankle at this steep section of the mountain. When she finally hit the bottom, she could see the tent beyond the creek. It was hidden off the main trail by trees and branches. She quickly hopped across the creek using the flat stones and almost slipped on the wet green moss of the last one. Leaping to the edge and scrambling up the dirt bank, Violet eagerly darted around the trees until she stopped right before his camp. The tent was as she expected: small and narrow, not high enough to stand up in, like most hikers used. There was a small firepit with a fire in it and a few items placed all about. A single burner stove and fuel. A large backpack resting against a log. Not much to his camp. Nothing like hers. She glanced around and didn't spot him, but he had to be there, considering the fire was snapping with fresh wood and twigs.

Then… there he was, coming back from the creek and weaving through the brush. He held a pan which he'd filled with creek water. She sucked in a breath when his eyes naturally lifted to scan the trail. He instantly spotted her, her blue shirt standing out and showing through the otherwise natural setting.

"Vee?" He said her name as if she were an African elephant standing in the middle of his camp, so out of her element that he had to blink to be sure she was real.

"Hey." Swallowing her nerves, she felt sharp pangs of discomfort and was instantly awkward and out of place. She should have never shown up like this.

Then again… Since when did she feel so damn unsure of herself? She knew her place in the world. Since when did she care if others accepted her? She had withdrawn from everyone so epically since Preston died that she seemed to have lost her former personality. The defining features of Violet Rydell. The attitude. The sparkle. God, she hardly remembered all the bling she used to wear on her jeans and shirts. She always bought the loudest women's riding clothes with big white stitching and pockets outlined with rhinestones and outlandish colors.

Remember the fake smiles and snarky comments? All that confidence? Riding the horses so cockily in the arena while daring others to join her tricks and fun. She used to be fun. Once. Now? She rarely smiled. Or talked. Or engaged.

Sigh. She came down the hill to see Gage, someone she didn't know. She didn't have to come there. Someone she barely knew, yes, but whom she strangely missed in the short time he was gone. It had to be the solitude of their campsites. The isolation literally made them seem like the only two human beings in the world for a short period of time. Sheltered in this bubble, they could pretend they were.

"Hey. I didn't expect to see you." He walked forward, his green eyes scanning her with visible pleasure and a welcoming, warm smile. God, it was so warm. She couldn't remember the last person who seemed glad to see her.

No one. No one from River's End, anyway. She was the sad near-widow whose tragic circumstances stopped conversations while others looked on with big, sympathetic eyes, tilting their heads and pursing up their mouths. Never a welcoming, joyful smile.

There was also nothing threatening or predatory about Gage. He didn't look at her like she was a meaty parcel he couldn't wait to devour. No. No creepy vibe from Gage. He was just glad to see her. Pure pleasure. She was sure of it. Which she found so beyond laughable, she almost did laugh out loud.

"Yeah… I thought you might be back by now and I doubted you'd want to walk up further so…"

He carefully set the pan of water on his small burner and lit it. Turning towards her, his smile widened. Her heart clenched when he leaned over and put his hand out towards Monty before giving the dog a huge smile and a vigorous rub on his head. "That's awesome. I wouldn't have wanted to walk any further, but I would have, since I love having company for dinner."

An odd warmth spread through her at his enthusiasm and carefree manner. It was nice to feel wanted and put so quickly at ease. Gage had a genuine friendliness about him, one that was both warm and nice. He also had a good sense of humor and some interesting stories. Not a nice guy in a boring way—like he was so quiet or uninteresting, you couldn't stand it—no, he wasn't boring at all. He was full of laughter and smiles and funny stories. He could be edgy and shocking at times with his jokes or his sarcastic takes on whatever story he was telling. But he was so open at the same time, both with himself and with her.

Violet so obviously wasn't. But Gage didn't press her to be any different.

"Yeah… I brought dinner." She showed off her bag of dehydrated beef stroganoff, her favorite.

Head shake. "Nope. I replenished the supplies, so this is my treat."

"Yes, but it's so much harder for you to restock, so we should use mine. Please? Consider it a welcome back gesture."

She pushed the bag towards him. He nodded and with a sweet smile said, "Okay, when you put it that way… Thank you for welcoming me back."

She found it impossible to resist a smile and almost reflected his in the way it instantly brightened her face. For a moment they stood there, his hand on the bag of freeze-dried food and her hand holding the other edge. Their gazes were fastened on each other. She stared into the green-gold depths that reminded her of the Rydell River when the summer sunlight hit it… She almost shook her head to dislodge the image, it was so romantic and fanciful. Who cared? He had green eyes. *Green.* Just plain green. Nothing special. Just like her. But hers weren't as golden and warm and beautiful.

But while standing there as their grins began to fade, something intensified and... damn it. Violet felt a hard lump of nerves swelling in her throat and she tried to swallow but it was stubbornly lodged there. An objective observer might think they were playing tug-o-war with the damn bag. No, they weren't doing that at all. They were letting the bag act as a link between them.

She let go first, breaking the strange spell that seemed to freeze them. "So did you get all checked in with your loved ones and showered? Maybe a little pampered?" His beard was trimmed up. She turned her face away to hide her rapidly warming cheeks. Why was she blushing? she wondered. Certainly not from embarrassment... but the heat was flushing her entire body now. Damn it. Why? From a single look? From releasing a bag?

He turned away and set the bag down. "All of the above. I slept in a padded, cool bed that felt heavenly and lounged too long in a decadently hot shower, which was absolutely amazing. Checked in the with fam and found out nothing big is going on and the people at work are happy with my progress. So all is good."

He flopped his butt down on a log a few feet away from his fire. His long legs, currently clad in nylon army-green hiking pants with numerous utility pockets down the sides, looked kind of attractive on his athletic, commanding frame. She'd give him that much from an initial observation. He waved toward the small, light-weight aluminum tripod stool by the fire. She sat down on it, giving him a small smile of thanks since it was the only seat. "Family? I thought you had no wife, right? Were you married once?" Why didn't she ever ask him before? She had no legitimate reason to delve into his personal life. Just because they were out in the middle of nowhere together and he appeared to be single. Just a fit, prime guy working on the trail. As if his life were that simple and existed of only what she saw here. How stupid. Of course, he had much more beyond what she saw or wished he had. She liked how simple he seemed... and the way their interactions unfolded. She craved simplicity. It was easy. She was staying in the now. Without complications or messy emotions. She hated sloppy emotions most of all. But there was no avoiding them sometimes. With Gage, at least they were all pleasant and enjoyable.

"Disappointed? What if I was? But I already told you I wasn't," he replied, arching an inquiring eyebrow with a smile.

"It was how you said you had to 'check in'... Not many grown men would hike out just to check in with their parents."

"Well... it was definitely not a spouse of any kind. No. Not me."

She snorted. "Makes no difference either way to me."

He pretended to grab his chest. "You can shoot arrows of indifference better than anyone I know."

She rolled her eyes and couldn't resist another smile, which dug into her cheeks. "Gage... be serious."

"Seriously, I don't have a wife. Never been married. What about you? Since you keep asking me, maybe you really came up here just to escape a deadbeat husband."

Gage meant to sound casually curious and obviously didn't think it was possible she could be married. But all Violet heard was *husband* and it caused her to lower her chin and clench her fist. Fiancé. Husband... she *should* have been married by now. She should totally have had a husband. And should have been a happy newlywed... Perhaps they could have been performing as a couple now... Instead, she was alone on a mountain with a stranger, staring at his small, slowly dying fire and freaking glad for the company.

"No. I'm not escaping anyone." Just things. Her feelings, to be specific. And boredom. Chaos. Hurt. Grief. Okay… she was running away fast and hard from a lot of things.

Gage got up and grabbed a few branches from the small pile he'd gathered behind him. He fed the flames until they danced steadily up. "Well? Tell me, what did I miss on the mountain? How did the neighbors behave?"

Violet's irrepressible, small smile once again tugged at her lips. Lifting her gaze, she met his stare with an eye-roll. "Oh, yeah. You missed a lot. A neighborhood block party. Let's see, some of the guests were the horses, Monty, me and an assortment of resident bugs. A few bees dropped by the camp and I saw a small mosquito. Thankfully, those aren't in abundance around here. One of the few blessings, I suppose."

Gage chuckled when he saw the boiling water behind her. Walking over, he grabbed the pot and opened the bag of food, measuring out two cups of water and dumping it inside before closing the zip-lock and setting it aside.

"Really? I missed the summer block party? Damn, that sucks. What did you wear?"

"Oh… something very shocking…" Crap. Did she really just giggle before adding something semi-suggestive? She couldn't remember the last time she did that. "You know… my freshly cleaned cowboy boots."

He wiped his brow. "You cleaned them? As in for real? You actually cleaned them? That must have been some party. Getting kinda racy around here. I never knew… and I forgot to bring my cowboy boots."

Yeah… she laughed. She finally relaxed as he poured out some of the hot water into a cup with some instant coffee in it. Clinking his tin cup to hers, he said, "I brought in that second cup, and the utensils and another plate, hoping…

maybe not for a block party but to convince you to come and see me. Because... admit it... you missed me."

She raised her glass with a nod before quickly sipping it and holding it in front of her face. She tried once more to conceal the odd, wussy blush on her face. "I admit, Gage, you're a welcome distraction from all the quiet solitude of the mountain and forest."

He sipped his instant coffee as he flopped back down on the stump. He moved with such grace and ease when he was working and walking; but now, he kind of flopped and slouched while relaxing at camp. "Admit it, Vee... you missed my company. And this? How could you not?" He waved a hand down his front with exaggerated bravado.

She clicked her tongue against her teeth and tried hard not to react with a smile. "Oh, yeah... *That!* All that kept me up at night and I was so restless with desire..." No. Crap. No, she never meant to say those words. No way did she sexually want him but that's just how it sounded. Burning fire consumed her cheeks.

Gage laughed and said, "Ahh, Vee, if only you weren't kidding and having fun with me. Fine. Maybe you missed another human voice and any one would do." He sighed and leaned forward, sticking out his lower lip and pretending to look glum.

Like magic, his reaction melted her heart. She smiled and relaxed as she stretched out her booted toe and nudged his leather shoe. "Well... not just anyone. I don't like a whole lot of people, but you? You're not so bad."

His foot responded by pushing into hers. There wasn't a millimeter of flesh touching, just their shoes and their riveted gazes.

"I'll proudly take that as a compliment. I imagine you meant it."

"Why do you say that?"

"You seem like you have pretty high standards. I feel honored that you tolerate my presence sometimes."

She peeked up at him and quickly dropped her gaze. "What about me tells you that?"

"Well, you were living on a mountain alone… all alone… and you didn't seem too excited when I stumbled upon you. Any fear you felt dissipated quickly when you realized I was no more harmful than a fly and you had more bite than me… But I digress, in short, you would rather be all alone than wasting your time with anyone you find intolerable. And I doubt you'd care if you never found anyone tolerable. Getting past your invisible defenses and into your tolerance level? Well, I call it a huge compliment to be included with those few people."

Her lips pressed into a flat line as she withdrew her foot, pressing her elbows on her knees and leaning forward. She was cradling her cup as if it were chalice of liquid gold, not to be spilled. But that was only a prop, something for her to concentrate on. She snorted. "Yeah, I'm a real gem." It was impossible for her not to glance at him across the small space. "I know myself and I'm not."

"You're circumspect." He blew on his drink, smiling at her before dropping his gaze on the flames. "But I like to make you smile. So, the mystery builds: people want to get to know you while hoping you will tolerate them."

Her head was shaking. "Absolutely not. People don't seek me out for companionship. Who'd want that from me? I'm simply more comfortable up here, more than anywhere else." She swung her arm around to include the forest and wilderness around them.

He nodded. "Yes, that's the draw. Again… the mystery."

She bit her lip. "You can't know how wrong you are."

"Then tell me. Tell me something that's real about you." His tone dropped lower, losing the levity and casually flirty tone of normal. That was Gage Sullivan's normal demeanor.

She licked her lips, still shaking her head. "I've told you real things."

"Not much. Not your name. That's usually where one starts with the truth."

Finally, he challenged her.

"I don't want to tell you my name."

"Would I know it?"

"Doubtful. But maybe."

"Huh. So you won't tell me?"

She hesitated, gripping her cup and drinking liberally from it. She finally shook her head to confirm her conviction.

Silence descended heavily. She rocked forward to her feet. "Think that dinner's cooked yet?"

Gage rose and grabbed it, saying, "How am I ever going to cook normally again? After only heating water out here?"

His tone, thankfully, returned to normal. Casual and easy. Thank God the awkward moment passed. "Don't. Just keep eating these premade meals. No doubt they taste amazing. Except the vegetable primavera; that one is flavorless."

"Meat woman, huh? I like them too. But have you checked out the price? I'll be broke after just a few days up here."

She nodded. Yeah, they were definitely expensive. He split the meal in half and handed one bowl to her. She took a warm bite and sighed at the wonderful taste, asking, "You cook at home?"

"Oh yeah... pretty well. Yeah. I do. Couldn't survive on frozen foods forever, you know? Single guys have to eat too. Besides, my mother wasn't willing to cook for me when I entered my early twenties. She made me learn how to cook. She's like that."

"Are you close to your parents?"

"Too close. So annoyingly close… like a five-minute car ride from me. And my sisters. Two sisters…" He winced as if he were in pain.

She laughed and perked up. "I get that."

"You have them too?"

She snickered. He made it sound like a bad disease or rash. "Yep. Three."

He sighed. "Two for me. Younger though. Which makes it seem like I have four."

"Oh. I'm the younger of two and I have one younger than me."

"Third in line, huh? Almost a middle child."

"Best child of them all…" She smirked.

"What are their names?"

She bit her lip and shook her head. "I can't tell you."

"Really? Why?"

"You'd guess my name if I told you theirs. It's a pattern. My parents were pretty lame in their choices of baby names." That made her smile.

"Damn… I thought I saw my inroad. My sleuthing skills aren't so great."

"No. They really suck." A smile was exchanged between them.

It was so easy to fall into an easy banter with Gage. That surprised Violet because she hadn't felt any desire to carry on banter or engage in much conversation over the last couple of years. Having withdrawn from society so completely, she nearly reverted to a life of solitude, emotionally speaking. None of her former friends recognized her now. She used to be boisterous, always the life of the party. She used to be fun and funny. Now? She resembled Iris, her older sister. Iris was always the quiet, solemn one, and very hard to read. But it worked for her. With Violet, sadness was the dominating factor. Everyone knew about it too, which made the entire situation even sadder.

Gage allowed her the space to be quiet and sad. But he also inspired a little smidgeon of her former self to emerge. She found it easy to release a few smiles. Maybe not knowing him allowed her to take an interest in someone else.

Violet wasn't a monster. She interacted with her parents, Allison and Shane, along with her three sisters, Rose, Iris and Daisy, the youngest. "The most beautiful flowers in the world" as her dad used to call them. She and her sisters could only cringe and pelt him with shrieks and feigned swats. They'd wrestle with him and beg him never to repeat his comment outside the confines of their home. Never. Thinking of it now made Violet's mouth twitch. Another saying her dad often reiterated was, "don't wilt with stress over it. It'll be okay…" or some such version of that. He loved his daughters' names and sought little word twists to say about them. Things like, "what does my little flower garden think?" or "how is my favorite bouquet?" or "what do my little wildflowers want to do?" And so forth.

Talking to Gage about his sisters and hearing how much they annoyed him with their constant mothering, even though he was the oldest child, reminded Violet of her own family. She recalled her dad's quirky humor and her mom's warm arms and calming support; they were always was there for her. Her sisters' constant presence in her life was something she took for granted during the last two years and maybe even forgot what a rare gift it was. She lived with Iris and her husband, Quinn, in a huge house on the golf course Quinn owned. There was so much room, and they'd welcomed her after Preston died.

They also worried incessantly about her, especially when she was out here in the woods alone. They worried about her mental health when she was at home in their presence.

"You should be going."

Jolted from her thoughts at his words, she frowned and reacted by jumping up instantly. "Oh. Yeah, right."

He rose too but his gaze wasn't dismissive or annoyed. "Not because I want you to. Only because it's going to be dark before you reach camp and you can't stay here since I don't have any other sleeping accommodations obviously. I worry about you alone in the dark out there."

She snorted and patted her gun and locator. "I'm safer walking on this trail at night alone than on any city street or dark parking lot I can think of. Most of the time, I'm not armed in the city; and second, out here? There's no one to fear but you."

"Along with bear, cougar, wolf and a variety of falling hazards or other accidents we can't foresee. So never mind the attacks. I feel like I should walk you back."

"No. That would be stupid. It's a four-mile hike for you for nothing."

"Knowing you're safe isn't nothing to me."

A surprising zing jolted her spine. Huh. She kind of liked hearing about his concern. But it was also kind of insulting. "It's because I'm a woman, right? You think I'm fragile. You walk back to your camp in the same light each night. And without a gun. You're no less prone to tripping or unforeseen accidents than I am."

"You got me there. Maybe it's because I'm just a natural worrier and it has nothing to do with you being a woman."

She tilted her head. "Nuh-uh. It's because I'm a woman."

He sighed. "Okay, fine. Then it kind of is. It's just something ingrained in me; I have to watch women to ensure their safety in the dark. You know? Two younger sisters and all of that. Mom always had me meet them at the bus stop if she were late getting home from work. I also had to go with them to the store or whatever... My mom always emphasized the need to look out for their safety for reasons of gender and what can occur. It's not because I think you're weaker."

"But out here?" Hand on her hip, she raised her eyebrow.

He tilted his head in defeat. "You're right. No attackers out here. Less likely to happen out here than anywhere else. Okay. Just be careful."

"Same as you should be."

"Same as I should be."

She stepped towards the trail and then looked over her shoulder. "But it is kind of sweet all the same."

Gage finally released his shoulders, which were hunched around his ears. "Well... I didn't mean to be a dick. It was really just out of concern for you. For safety's sake. Whatever. I didn't mean it in any way to make you feel less capable or inept."

"I know. It's just so easy to get you going..."

He jerked his face up and saw her smirk before she released a full-on smile. He blinked a few times but finally smiled back. "You don't smile like that too damn often."

She slowly let it fade and stared at him for a prolonged moment. Then she said honestly, "I don't often feel like smiling like this."

"Well, it suits you. And I'm glad you came down. It was just what I was hoping for."

She didn't smile at that. Or react. She quickly turned and retreated as if she suddenly remembered they were merely mountain neighbors... At most, they could be called *friends*, but nothing beyond that... absolutely nothing more.

As she started up the trail, she whistled for Monty who quickly followed her. Finally, at home in her own camp, it was well after dark. She was honest when she told Gage she had no fear. But the silence seemed louder than usual. And her camp seemed more remote. And it felt kind of lonely.

Her horses, Princess and Peaches, were thrilled to see her and their ears pricked forward as they emitted small whinnies and neighs for her attention. They spun circles in their highlines, no doubt, upset at being left alone for so long, and ready for their evening meal. Twice a day they were fed, per Uncle Jack's express instructions. Violet also had to make sure the horses received salt and sulfur as part of their regular care. It was a trick he learned from his farrier years ago. Decades actually. In the daytime, they grazed on the wild grasses of the upper fields; if they were at home, they'd receive a flake of hay. Here, they also got alfalfa pellets and salt and sulfur mixed with hot water to avoid getting colic.

She quickly fed them, scratching their ears and mumbling lots of kind words before she readied herself for bed. She fell onto her cot. This time, sleep didn't come as fast as before. But neither did the familiar feelings of sadness, loneliness, isolation, and grief. In fact, Preston never even entered her thoughts. The image in Violet's mind was Gage and the hours—four, to be exact—they spent chatting it up with genuine smiles, furtive glances and... undeniable interest. It was the first time Violet felt like interacting with someone in too long to remember. It seemed like a heavy burden was finally lifted off her throat. Her vocal cords felt free again and she could finally talk to another person.

She flipped over onto her side, and Monty groaned at her sudden movement as he rested between her legs. She smiled. At some point, she must have fallen asleep. She was thinking about the things Gage said. Not like there was anything profound about his words... Although they did make Violet feel very nice.

CHAPTER 6

*V*EE CAME TO HIM. Gage stared up at low ceiling of his tent. The shadows from the bright moonlight filled the empty earth. He didn't dare hope that she'd come to see him. Yet from the moment he stepped back on the trail after leaving the parking lot, he wanted to see her. He wanted to be hiking towards her, instead of doing his job. And odder still? It was exciting and almost normal to be going back to her.

But she resisted his ministrations. She allowed him to come and sit in her camp. To eat her dinner and drink her coffee. But she didn't seem to return his interest. Not that he sought her because of it.

In contrast to what he readily admitted to Andy, Vee was gorgeous. Gage crushed on her hard. It was impossible not to. Silky, straight brunette hair that bobbed over her shoulders. Tonight, she'd washed it and left her hat off. Might have been the first time he'd seen her without her hat on. He liked the hat though. It was just her thing. A Vee thing. His mountain girl.

If he were totally honest, he did worry about her. Especially trudging up a damn mountain alone in the dark. Yeah, she had the gun and the GPS locator and she was probably better equipped, skilled and in possession of a richer knowledge base than he had to defend herself out here, but still, she wasn't as strong as him. Nor as big.

Yeah, his dad taught Gage to be conscientious of the women around him and to look out for their safety. The two baby sisters he liked to complain about were always calling him up with women for him to meet or fussing about this or that, but he adored them. He always made sure they were safe and healthy and okay. That included making sure their husbands kept them safe and treated them decently. Fuck privacy. If a single hair was ever harmed on their heads, he'd be there without a thought or care about privacy. He considered it his business. Their safety would always be his business, first and foremost.

And that mission was on steroids with Andy. His daughter. Maybe it was the daughter factor that made him so aware of all the dangers that could happen to women. Of course, way out here, most of those concerns became null and void. But his worry resided at gut level and he couldn't stop it by conscious will or effort. The thought of Vee alone in the dark became one that he couldn't stop thinking.

Why? Because he really liked Vee whatever her last name was. He liked her a whole lot. And her family should have been shot for letting her stay out here all alone. So strange. So anti-social. So isolated.

Vee didn't seem lacking in social skills. She wasn't strange at all to talk to. But the way she lived right now? That was strange.

There was obviously a story there. That fact was evident and all but screamed a huge story loomed there. Something kept Vee back from sharing anything real about herself. He noticed the distrust that lurked in her eyes. And a sadness behind her hesitant smiles. So muted and subtle. All of her body seemed purposely toned down. Like all the factors that combined to create her personality were turned down. Not turned off, but definitely reduced. Whatever made her hide out there was her secret. Hibernating in the summer wasn't a typical activity Gage witnessed in anyone before. He should have found her odd and off limits for that reason. But there was something so compelling in Vee that he could not stay away from her.

And the pleasure that had coursed throughout him when he'd spotted her standing there, looking at him, thrilled him. He'd nearly dropped the pan of water, stomped forward and swept her up against him. He'd wanted to hold her, care for her, and kiss her. She would seem so small in his arms. She was maybe five-foot-four or five. She'd fit perfectly in his warm embrace.

But she was very strange. There was no escaping that.

Perhaps her secrecy pissed him off a bit too. Asking if he were married? Again? She obviously doubted he told her the truth before. She probably just wondered if he had a life at all. For some reason, it made him choose to keep his daughter, the top priority in his life, to himself. She wouldn't share her name so he wouldn't share his daughter with her. His daughter was reserved for those people who were important to him and Vee hadn't earned the right to know about Andy... yet.

Would that change?

Sighing, Gage finally dropped off to sleep. Tomorrow promised another hard day of labor.

And it was tough going the next day. About eleven a.m., he glanced up and saw Vee standing there. She wore the same outfit. Cowboy hat on, hair pulled back in a low pony-tail. She swung her daypack down. "Thought I could help you. I mean, if that's allowed. The exercise would do me good."

She told him a lie. All she did until now was move horses, lift logs, chop wood, and walk on the uneven trails everywhere. It was exhausting and hard on anyone's body and joints. But when she looked at him and her gaze suddenly skittered away, all he could think was, *damn! He was glad to see her.*

He smiled and it was way too big. There was no denying his pleased reaction to her. He wasn't used to that. He was always open and honest so it didn't occur to him to ignore that urge or desire, even with someone as secretive as Vee. Vee no-name. Whoever.

Still, for some reason, he trusted her more than he would many people he encountered in his daily routine. There was something so real and genuine about her that if she told him something new or revealed a secret, he would one hundred percent believe her.

"Yeah, you could be a huge help." Shrugging, he let out a small smile. "Besides, if it were a problem, who would ever know? You're kind of like a ghost to me so…"

"What shall I do first?"

"Well, I have to rebuild the foundation here to withstand the pressure of another heavy rainfall and possible mudslide. It tends to hit this spot harder, as past years have told us. So we need more support here and over here." He pointed as he spoke and demonstrated his plan to secure the bottom section of the trail before addressing the part hikers would actually walk over.

Nodding, she finally smiled. "Well, at least you're not an idiot. What you've done so far seems like it could keep the trail intact and prevent it from washing out next year. They've been doing the same fix over and over and achieved the same results. Imagine that."

"Ahh… and you might be the hardest critic of them all?"

"Well, me and my horses might be the most frequent users of this trail. I always stress over it, expecting that they'll cut funding and the whole trail will wash out. If it fails to get fixed, this end of the trail will be swallowed up by the mountain and the woods. Left to the animals. Like the Hanson Trail to Bear Claw basin. I would be very sad to lose it."

Wow. That was far more than she usually said about herself or her feelings. He cleared his throat. "The Hanson Trail spurred off this one, right? It goes north over Hubbard Crescent and drops into the small basin?"

She smiled, obviously pleased with him. He puffed up his chest like his teacher just commended him for being the only one in class to know the answer. "You know it? That seems like a myth to me. I've heard… well, in the seventies it used to be accessible, but it's been decades now and I can't even find where the trail spurs off. They quit grooming it so long ago that it's virtually lost. I've had some pretty good descriptions of where it's located but I can't find it."

"You actually looked for it?"

"Oh, yeah. Every year I do. Imagine the fun of finding it and seeing a place most people haven't seen in half a century or more."

Gage swung his mallet, going up and back down. He smiled as he worked, knowing she was watching him and the smile was evidence of his amusement. "Vee, you have the oddest interests for someone in their twenties, straight out of any box I've ever heard of."

She nodded, scattering her gaze as she lifted up a spike and braced it near where he was working. She started to bury it into the ground. "Yes. I've been told that. But it would be fascinating to discover."

Gage finished pounding in the spike and tested the reinforcement of his work. "Yeah, I imagine you have heard it before. But by people who probably know your name and have a good idea to whom they are speaking." He stopped long enough to lift an eyebrow to emphasize his dig. She nodded and gave a cheeky smile back in return. Oh yeah, she knew he was getting grumpy about her incessant hedging and hiding. So what if she refused to tell him her damn name? Her voluntary assistance was unlike anyone else Gage ever observed. She worked just as hard and long as he did. She was every bit as strong too. No complaints from her. They worked side-by-side until they finished the bottom renovations. Tomorrow, they were ready to start filling the trough-like base Gage built with Violet's help.

They flopped down on a large boulder, each gulping down water and glancing at each other with tired smiles. The wonderful sensation of being completely united in a singular experience with each other was evident on their faces. He held out his water bottle and she responded by touching hers to his. "Here's to getting that bitch done."

Vee laughed out loud and Gage blinked in surprised. The tinkling sound of her unguarded laugh was both feminine and husky. So unexpected from how she looked and acted and presented herself. She wasn't seductive. She didn't even seem to realize she was a woman and he a man. As with her smiles, outright laughter from Vee was rare. But damn. Was it hot.

His entire body tensed and something new and over-whelming bolted through him. Damn it. He was becoming so interested in her. It had gone far beyond friendly. Far beyond any resemblance to his relationship with his little sisters too.

He averted his eyes. "Well. You sure made quick work of this. Thank you. If you ever seek a career with the Forest Service, you got a job."

Drinking the last of her water, she rubbed her mouth

with the back of her hand. "With you as my boss? No, thank you."

"Ha. You could do a lot worse than having me as a boss. I'm awesome."

"You work straight through lunch without any breaks."

Lightheartedly, that turned into a five-minute back and forth and if they weren't freaking flirting, then his name wasn't Gage. "So… dinner here or up there?"

She gave him a cheeky, arched eyebrow. "What? Who says I'm having dinner with you? You don't know about all the offers I've gotten since my arrival…"

"From the flies or the horses? We should start up the trail. I'll make you walk up now, while you're still tired."

"And keep little ol' me safe from the dark."

He hopped to his feet. "Yep. That's exactly right."

"I can't believe you're serious."

"I am. Now… shall we? I need to eat something more than a glorified candy bar." Gage had several power bars left and some nuts but he was ravenous now. Enough to kill and gut a small animal before cooking it over an open fire. He needed food now.

"Okay… okay, He-man. We'll get you a hearty meal. But you're being a little ridiculous about the dark."

He shrugged. "Okay. You got me there. Your camp is fancier and nicer than mine and the thought of those damn easy chairs… I can feel my ass sinking into one right now."

She took that as a good enough reason and it seemed to soothe her ego. She rolled her eyes. "God, men are always attracted to my finer-ass things…" She puckered her lips, rolled her eyes, and swung her hip out in an exaggerated manner.

Gage burst out laughing at her. "Men? With so many men after you, maybe they can tell me your name if I ask them?"

She smiled. "No. The secret is the key to my allure."

117

"Right… having a name is so strange. You're definitely not a serial killer whose name is posted everywhere and if I knew it, you'd have to kill me too?" Falling in step, he trailed behind her and left his bag. He planned to grab it again on the long hike down. "Wait. There's nothing to that, huh? I was just kidding?"

She turned around, her eyes wide. "Are you serious? You're wondering if I'm a… a femme fatale hiding up here in the mountains?"

"Well… it's weird. Really weird. I nearly went with it at first, maybe just a little bit. The fear that I could be psychotic and seeking to bother you and all. But I think we're way past that now. Those bad first impressions of me… right?" He lifted his eyebrows in visible curiosity.

She nodded. "Yes. We are."

"Then, knowing our real names would be normal about now."

She sighed. "I was hoping you wouldn't press that. Let's discuss it more after we eat."

They had such a fun day. So much comradery and kidding around. He felt sure they were past whatever arbitrary test she'd insisted on putting him through. He'd earned a solid A. He was sure of it. Sweating through the hard, hot, grunt work, they'd stayed in perfect sync and easily exchanged jokes and observations. Everything in total synchronicity. So… what was the big fucking deal? Now it made him crabby. He fell silent while following her the rest of the way. His muscles were screaming and his stomach grumbling.

Entering camp, the dog ahead of them, the horses nickered and snorted their greetings. Vee immediately attended to their care. She untied them and led them down to the small stream. They followed her like eager lap dogs. She petted and talked to them as she stroked their giant heads and scratched their ears.

"Mind if I start a fire and get some water boiling?"

She glanced at where Gage stood inside the camp and a small smile of relief flashed on her face. "Not at all; that would be great."

By the time she finished her horse care and feeding, Gage had a fire blazing and the hot water was already cooking a bag of freeze-dried food. She took the tin cup he handed her of hot coffee and all but sighed in ecstasy as she flopped down on the chair beside the fire. "That's so decadent, having a camp boy cook dinner for me."

He stood in her favorite spot before the firepit. The flames rose mid-calf to his legs. A metal bracket in an upside-down "L" shape was pounded into the rocks beside it. It held a cast iron pot over the fire. She often heated food and water in there. Gage propped one leg on the rocks of the fire. It made the perfect spot to rest his forearms and casually watch her as he sipped his coffee. He smiled at her exaggerated flop into the chair and her loud release of air. Feeling as fatigued as her, he got it, but when she called him *camp boy*, he responded with a harsh scowl.

"There is not one thing boyish about me Vee-who-ever-the-fuck-you-are."

Her head shot up and her eyes widened. "Oh, my God, I've never heard you swear before. Are you... I mean, did I offend you?" Tilting her head back, she erupted into full-on laughing. Again, it was dark and husky, not at all girlish. Or shy. Nothing like the rest of her interactions.

"I'm not a *boy*. I'm a guy. A dude. Just saying, in case you missed that," he muttered. Yeah, he was kind of offended when she laughed *so* hard, she had to set her coffee down. Then she leaned forward and started choking and coughing from her uninterrupted laughter. The coughing ruined her sexy, husky laugh.

"Wow. Sensitive much? Some reason you're so defensive about your manhood? Perhaps you protest too much?"

Oh, yeah, he didn't miss the mirth he saw on her pretty face and a new levity in her usually solemn eyes. Always lovely, the greenness with gold flecks shone in the sunlight like little constellations he could not look away from. This woman beside him with her scuffed-up jeans, dusty shirt, and dirty forearms and hands was just like him. She'd swiped her face at some point and etched the dirt in a line. Her hair was ratty and frizzing out from the elastic band she tried to contain it in. But sweat and running her hands over it too often had taken their toll. Makeup and hairstyling weren't in this woman's vocabulary, at least not since he met her.

Damn. His heart skipped beats and his gaze ate up every detail about her. Most of all, he wished she would stop thinking of him as a camping buddy. He was too harmless to her emotional and mental wellbeing. That was because he was such a good friend. Like a big brother. Was he also asexual? What did she think?

Seeing her smile and then truly laugh at him was a treat. She finally dropped a chunk of the invisible wall she guarded so fiercely. The need to protect herself was epic with her. That paranoia was so intense, she refused to say her name or even her sisters' names.

Smiling, he remembered she was not on the market. She considered him decent company and a camp-buddy so he had to be careful not to cross those boundaries. Being so finicky and hard to pin down as this woman was, as long as she was living alone in the mountains, he could not press his luck... not *yet*.

Lacking any definite timeline for not pushing her, Gage hoped a little more time and interaction would successfully build the trust and comradery he desired. He would broach the limits later. But right now? Finesse and tact would get him much farther than anything else. And with that realization, he instantly began to chuckle too.

"Maybe I was. But damn, Vee, you're pretty hard on a guy's ego."

She nodded, letting her feet fall forward, and tipping her torso to grab her coffee. She sipped on it and stared into the fire. "Because I'm not a helpless female in need of your help or protection? Because I could manage to keep up with you today? Minute for minute. Is that perhaps the reason why?"

He sighed as he hauled his butt to the other chair and dropped down in it. "Yes. Fine. I didn't realize how unused to that I was, but yeah. Maybe."

She gave him an approving glance. "Well, admitting it is half the battle. Now you can quit being a sexist idiot. Once you realize having an equal partner is far superior to being the big man and the hero of every encounter."

"An equal partner?" He tipped his head to show his concentration on her comment. "I'll remember that the next time you threaten to shoot me."

"Well, how could I know what you were like?" As she answered, he quickly divided the bag of cooked food in half on two plates. Her camp was like staying in the Presidential Suite of a five-star resort. His camp was more like the sleazy motel that rents by the hour.

Vee leaned forward to take her plate and they both groaned as the hot food hit their tongues and palates. Grinning at each other, they swallowed and laughed like mirror reflections of the other before taking huge swigs of coffee. She lifted her cup. He liked to see her relaxed, and at ease. She also got all of his jokes.

They ate in silence and synchronicity. Chewing, swallowing and drinking in what appeared to be a choreographed pattern, their smiles acknowledged the obvious link. Finally, he said softly, "I'm not going to press you anymore about your name... but I leave here in a week. Think about telling it to me by then. I hope you can trust me before I go."

She didn't look up as she rose to her feet and collected all the dinner utensils and plates. She dumped them in the small creek near them. Without looking up, she scrubbed everything with soap and a brush. Then she said, "I do trust you, Gage. You're not the reason that keeps me quiet. I just don't want to be that person... with that name. Not right now. Not up here. Not with you. Can you just accept that?"

It wasn't okay with him at all. Naturally, he didn't want to accept her explanation and yeah, he had his doubts about the underlying reason. "For real, level with me, Vee... Is it something illegal that keeps you from saying it?"

"No. Nothing like that."

"Were you in some kind of danger at home? Are you hiding from someone or something there?"

"No. Nothing like that either. My family knows exactly where I am. I stay in regular contact with them through the text on the locator."

"And I should believe all that?"

She shrugged and walked forward with the wet, clean dishes, setting them on the dish towel Gage laid out for her. He spread it on the small table she had near the front of her canvas tent. "You should believe me, but I can't make you. It won't change what I say either."

He stared hard at her and she stared right back. Finally, he nodded and decided to take the plunge in trusting her. Out there, all alone, his normal life was already stripped away. The normal social cues and constraints were missing or at least, they were very different out there. Everything came down to basics. How they lived and managed to survive. The goals they sought to achieve each day. Living in the present moment instead of referring to their to-do lists, and routine chores with endless distractions. There was nothing here to distract them from each other. And it encouraged a fast, tight bond, which Gage felt towards her. Maybe, just maybe, she felt a smidgeon of it towards him too. "I believe you."

She even smiled as if his faith in her mattered. With a head nod and her lips pressed, she said softly, "Good. I'm glad."

She eased back into her chair and so did Gage. The sun began to set and the light started to change. Pearl-white sky glowed over the crests of the mountains and spiky tree tops that he gazed at. "It's weird, you know."

"What? Not sharing my life and history with you?"

"Or your name. Mostly it's your name. But I don't think you're weird. I think you have… your own reasons."

"I do. But they're probably weird since they're specific to me."

"Care to share something? No names or specifics, just generalities?"

She sighed, poking the fire with a stick she held. "I loved someone who died. I haven't felt like being around other people since then."

Must have been a boyfriend or lover. Gage felt it in his guts. He nodded. "Seems reasonable. Now, I can believe you're not a jaded criminal on the run." He spoke gently, letting his gaze fall heavily on hers. Her shoulders flinched and her mouth tightened and relaxed, but her eyes remained fastened on the flames.

"I don't want to talk about it anymore. I gave you the answer."

"Agreed, and thank you for that." His voice was mild as he asked, "So what do you think about tomorrow's game plan?

Bring some fill dirt in and bury the trench? Or do you think we need to shore it up some more?"

Her gaze rose to his, and her eyebrows quirked in challenge, as he hoped they would. In reply, she asked, "Who says I'm coming to help you tomorrow? I don't work for the Forest Service, remember?"

"You're one of those people that can't start something unless they finish it. It'll drive you nuts if you leave it. Plus, it's something good to do. And…" He smiled fully and spread his hands over his torso. "And because you want to be around all this. Why wouldn't you? Don't beat yourself up over it. No one can fight the urge. Who could blame you?"

And like that, all the sadness and distrust she felt left. She rolled her eyes and began mocking him pretty quickly, and it lasted from then until dark. Yeah… they decided they should start backfilling the dirt into the channel they finished today. Yeah. Vee was all in. And Gage was counting on it.

CHAPTER 7

*T*HEY FINISHED SEVEN DAYS work in half that time. Duh. It was expected since there were two of them and Vee worked just as hard and efficiently as Gage did. Without pay or any fringe benefits. She shrugged him off when he asked if that bothered her.

"Not at all. It's something to do. Passes the time. I can barely tolerate you so it works for me on a few levels."

Gage preferred to believe that her desire to be around him was her true motivation. Whatever kept Vee's life tightly bound inside her, and motivated her to hide up here in the mountains under the guise of a retreat from ordinary, civilized life, it also gave Gage the advantage of being the only distraction for Vee. Grief was obviously the root cause. Whatever she suffered was trapped deep inside her. How recent was her tragedy? He wondered because she refused to discuss her life. But she was so easygoing when it came to other things like making fun of him. She liked nothing better than listening to his frequent quips about his masculinity and his annoying penchant for chivalry towards her. Of course, she managed to survive rather well before she met him.

"There... done. Can you believe it?" he asked as he smoothed out the last few feet of trail with the rake. That was the easy part.

She leaned on the handle of the shovel she'd used to loosen the dirt and rocks. Gage used it to fill in the trough he and Vee designed. After making it smooth and level, it became a relatively solid trail surface.

"Sure. I was here. You'd have been stuck up here for another few weeks."

He set the rake aside and gave her a narrow-eyed look. "You think you're so necessary to my success? Well, you managed to let me finish the job earlier than planned. The joke's on you."

Vee kept shoveling, despite being essentially done. "Well... you could just stay here as planned. Who the crap would ever know you finished the job early? I'll never tell. Besides, you wouldn't have done it without the free labor, so you owe me."

"And your payment would be spending some leisure time with me? See, Vee? You do care."

She smirked at him. "I like correcting all your mistakes. I find it more amusing than swatting the flies. Anyway... stay?"

No head lift. No furtive glance his way. He was getting to her. And now, she didn't want him to go. Normally, friends would agree to meet up, you know, in town. There was a small town too, just fifteen miles from the trailhead, so it wasn't like they couldn't do that. Go out for a few drinks. Get some coffee. Go to dinner. But that was not up for debate with this woman. This ghost. This stranger. Yet he oddly felt more comfortable and real and raw and in sync with Vee than anyone else, besides Andy, of course. Maybe it was from the coffee they shared as they stared into their campfires, watching the wispy spires of smoke vanish into the sky, or the fading light of sunset, bathing the sky in rich pastels and quiet beauty. How do you follow something like that? By meeting at a coffee shop tucked at the end of a strip mall with paved parking and late-model cars to stare at? Maybe destiny brought them here. Right here. Gage feared everything would change once they got away from their oasis, their private spot in the mountains. Let them remain lost in the forests and the clear, beautiful streams.

"I could stay. Up until Sunday. Then I really have to go." He scheduled a call with Andy then. He was aching to hear her voice as she began to chatter about whatever she'd done this week. But for now, and maybe for once, he could actually take some time off, some selfish time for himself. Andy was safe and happy. She was being entertained and well cared for, and besides, she wasn't expecting him for another week.

And damn. Gage was having the time of his life. Hard work, hard camping, hard forest floor to sleep on and all.

"Good. Then we'll plan on it."

"Only…"

"What?"

"I'd rather stay at your camp. If we don't *have* to come back down here, it would be nice to relax without hiking up and down the mountain. I fear I'll waste away from all the weight I've lost after so much walking. And you have so many extra comforts in your camp I can only dream of."

Vee stiffened her spine and turned slowly towards him. "You want to stay at my camp?" It seemed as shocking to her as if he just told her the dog was on fire. She could not believe he'd actually uttered those words.

"Don't worry… I'll set up my own tent. You just have better cooking stuff and shelter and fire and easier access to water… and lounge chairs. Mostly, Vee, it's those damn chairs. I'd do anything for a chance to relax in them. Hopeless chair-whore. That's me."

She broke into a smile. Relieved, glad and genuine. "Chair-whore. Sure. Okay, yeah, that works."

Gage secretly hoped she'd allow him to sleep on her second cot. To him, it was a memory-foam, king-sized bed with twenty throw pillows in the way of comfort when he compared it to sleeping on the ground atop his inadequately small air mattress.

"Want me to come down and help you pack up?"

"That would be awesome." He beamed a huge grin back at her. They collected all the tools and carried them down to his camp. After setting them off to the side, where they were relatively hidden, they left them there. The younger summer crew would hike in soon to haul everything back out. Gage almost groaned with relief. He was glad it wasn't left up to him to lug the supplies out.

After quickly dissembling his tent and camp, he stowed everything in his hiking pack. Vee stared at the monstrosity with disdain. "Yuck, that looks heavy."

"Well, Princess, not all of us have two horses to lighten our work for us." He started to heave it onto his back. Fatigued in a matter of seconds, he emitted a slight groan as he wobbled onto his feet.

She gave him a once-over. "You're too tired to carry that. Look… all you need is your clothes, a sleeping bag and your food. You know, you can stay in my tent. I have an extra cot."

Gage fought the urge to dance an Irish jig with unbridled joy. "That would be most appreciated. Thank you, Vee. I accept your kind hospitality." He wasn't too ashamed to almost shout his appreciation with glee. It was all about the bed. Even better than the chair. He grabbed his stuff and divided it between them before stashing it in their daypacks. Then up they climbed. Both grew quiet on the steep terrain. Too tired in their muscles and their brains. Maybe tomorrow, after enduring less hardship, they could get to know each other without extreme exhaustion being the constant link between them.

Repeating the last four evenings, Gage was in charge of setting up their dinner and creature comforts while Vee tended to her horses. She worried they felt neglected and fed them extra treats while promising tomorrow they could spend hours in the pasture to graze. An easy rapport developed between Vee and Gage as they continued to bicker and flirt. It started at dinner and lasted while they did the dishes and gazed at the dying fire and finally, the stars. Gage leaned back, hooking his hands behind his head and staring up at the now dark sky as he propped his feet above the fire. He felt like he might look like a beached starfish to Vee. "Damn... this is real living. Look at me. For once, I'm not walking down the mountain. I can be lazy now and recline in a chair."

"You are so dramatic. And way too easily pleased."

"That I am, Vee-whoever. That I am. A man of simple tastes and needs. Must be why I appreciate your company so much," he added with a smug smile. Without needing to look at her, he could feel her evil-eye staring at him. He liked calling her *Vee-whoever* and did it a lot. Each time, she rolled her eyes and huffed but eventually gave up her protests.

"You're lucky I grace you with my company."

"It must be your charm; yes, I'm sure that's it." His smile grew smugger as his eyebrows wagged.

She rose to her feet. "I'm going to brush my teeth and go up camp. You can go below the horses." She smiled sweetly before she disappeared. Nothing sweet there. He'd have to avoid horse poop as he climbed past their fencing. His exhausted legs shook as he too ambled off to attend to his private business.

He lingered in the dark. Now it was just the two of them in a tent. Vee, who hid everything, even the most trivial facts about herself, like her last name, would surely find the close quarters uncomfortable. Gage hoped she didn't regret her invite. He never expected to be up here without his own tent, so she couldn't be mad at him.

For seeming like the toughest woman in the forest, and possessing a mastery with nature he'd never witnessed, Vee was emotionally as fragile as a hatchling.

Making his way back to the tent, the outer lantern that hung under the tarp was already off. A battery-powered lamp hanging from the top of the tent offered a faint light. She'd shut the flaps. Gage went out to wash his hands, fore-arms and face in the shockingly cold water. He warmed and dried his skin by the fire until Vee finally opened the tent flaps. Was that a sign she was ready for him?

"Can I come in?"

"Yes," she answered and for the first time in their interac-tions, her voice sounded strained. He dowsed the fire, entered and closed the flap behind him, turning to zip it up. Monty was already stretched out on the end of Vee's cot. She was standing beside a table, setting down a hairbrush. She wore pants and a sweatshirt, not lingerie. He'd seen her dressed in less clothes outside, wearing only her t-shirt and shorts. But this was much more intimate. Her silky hair was brushed smooth and free from her face. Her clothes looked slouchy and casual. Comfortable in a way that almost made him grab her and cuddle up beside her. It was a stupid impulse, he chided himself.

Gage collected his stuff, laid out his sleeping bag and added air to his ground mat. He hung his clothes off the end of the cot and changed into his sweats and a clean shirt outside the tent. That way, he could swiftly tuck himself into his sleeping bag. Hers was a large tent compared to his. He could stand up straight for once, which in itself was heav-enly. There was a small black stove, but it was unlit. The night wasn't as cold as it had been. Vee ignored Gage as she started tugging her own sleeping bag open. He waited politely to give her more space. Only after she sat on her cot did he quickly jump into his and slip down inside the bag. An intimacy was shared that went far beyond the time they spent together. The confined space. The white tent walls replaced the trees and night. It was simply the two of them together.

And oh… the luxury of sleeping in a bed off the ground. That surpassed the damn awkwardness of being together. The raw novelty of it. He kicked his legs inside the bag and flopped backwards, unzipping it to his waist. "Oh, damn. I feel like I slipped and fell onto an angel's feathers from heaven." He kept his gaze fastened on the peak of the tent. "Thank you so much for sharing your cozy abode with me."

She reached up and shut off the lamp.

"Yeah… I can see where it would feel pretty good."

"You can't imagine." His gaze was still facing up. Vee moved around on her cot until she finally quit and let the darkness and the quiet prevail. The soft rushing of the creek. Oh, dang, this was nice. Gage released a sigh and let the inner peace he cherished fill him up. He let it comfort and soothe his tired muscles. His eyelids already felt too heavy to open.

The quiet reigned for a long time. Gage wondered if she were asleep. When he finally felt more comfortable under the cover the darkness, he asked Vee something private. "Do you live around here? Or are you visiting from somewhere else? Far away?"

A sigh. Yep, she was awake. "I don't want to answer that."

"So, you're a local. You'd say if it were otherwise, or invent a place I wasn't likely to know."

"Do you live downtown or out further?" Clever change of topic, he noted.

"Outside of Winthrop. I own an acre lot not far from the Chewuck River."

Vee didn't reply for a few seconds. "That's a pretty area." His suspicions were confirmed… she knew the area, which meant she was from somewhere in the Rydell River Valley. It was a long valley. Maybe two thousand residents lived between Winthrop and the inhabitants at the north end and down toward Pattison, which was a good forty miles. There was a lot of space and a lot of land. He couldn't guess what part she was from since he had no idea if he might have seen her.

"Your family lives there too?"

"Yeah. Mostly. My parents and Mom's sister and husband. Two cousins still live in town. My younger sister and her husband and three kids and Grandma Lou are still living on her own and kicking ass. So, yeah."

Gage didn't mention the most important person of all. Why should he? Until Vee offered something real about herself, he could wait. Hell. Why divulge the most important part of his life? His daughter, Andy, of course.

"That's a lot of family."

"Yes. It feels that way at times. But they keep me company. I have a hard time getting lonely."

"Yeah. Family is good for that." Did that mean she had some family? She wasn't a total loner, trying to mend her broken heart out here because she had nowhere else to go? Or escaping her horrible, neglectful family that didn't care or look after her? But she was no more willing to share anymore even here, in this intimate space, than in the broad daylight. Well, at least he learned one thing. She was a local. There was no doubt in his mind that was true.

Luckily, exhaustion overtook him and Gage passed out like a fainting goat. When he awoke, she was already up and out of the tent. He stumbled outside to take a leak and found a fire roaring, the horses eating, and a pot of coffee percolating. He blinked and rubbed his eyes. "Ugh. You're a morning person, aren't you?" Saying it out loud, he had no idea where she could be. He slipped away to take care of his personal business, stopping briefly to wash his hands and splash the ice-cold water on his face. He scrubbed the sleep from his eyes with his fingers.

"The chirpiest in the land of morning people, yes." Her voice made him shiver although he was already shuddering from the low temperature.

"Uh-huh. Of course, you are," he muttered. Blinking while finding his way back to the warm cot before he simply face-planted onto it, he sensed her watching him.

"Are you serious? It's eight-thirty."

He rolled onto his side. "Vee-whoever, there is not one blessed plan on the agenda for today. There is nowhere to be and nothing that must be done. I worked myself ragged on that blasted trail and now I fully intend to relax on your heavenly bed, and gasp! I might lounge here doing nothing until nine or maybe even ten o'clock. So goodnight." He rolled over and let the arms of sleep overtake him again.

When he finally got up, he had the best day with Vee. He kept poking and prodding her as she shuffled around her camp, finding endless chores for him to do. Girl couldn't relax and just be. He gave her shit over it, but asked her a litany of questions like, "Are these your own horses? Did you ride as a little girl? Where did you learn? Who taught you? Did you ever show them professionally? Where did you go to school? Any college? Ever go away to college? Whom did you buy the tent from? The stove…" She was ready to say the name when she snapped her mouth shut.

On and on he questioned Vee all day long, trying to get something personal to slip out of her mouth. She took awhile to catch on to what he was doing. She reacted by storming out of the camp only to come back a half hour later with her head bowed.

"You almost got me. Kudos for your valiant attempt."

She forgave him when he pulled out a chocolate bar he'd been saving and gave it to her as a peace offering. He also helped her with some chores like repairing part of the fencing that broke loose. He stopped himself from pointing out the obvious, namely, that her fence was in no way temporary, nor in an area it was allowed to be.

Night descended again and the fire slowly flickered away. They both found comfort and peace in their quiet time together. Neither suffered from being so damn tired. All the banter they engaged in was irrelevant. It meant nothing important. But there was an undeniable warmth and connection. It had to be real. Didn't it? And as much on her end as it was on his?

With the flames flickering shadows on her face, illuminating it, Gage leaned forward, digging the stick he held deeper into the glowing coals of the fire. He didn't look at her as he asked, "You said you lost someone. Was it your boyfriend?"

He could literally feel the air change between them. An arctic blast swiftly engulfed them and stiffened her entire skeleton. He didn't bother to lift his head to witness it. "Vee? It's obvious something significant happened to you. You don't trust people and you don't want me to know the story. Specifics. But I'm right here. I have been long enough to feel like I know you. What lies at the core of you. Your sense of humor. How to make you smile or laugh or chuckle. How hard you resist my ministrations. I still don't even know your first name. It's an odd juxtaposition that you have put me in. But I want to know more. All about it."

She kept her neck ramrod straight. "Why? Why do you want to know more?"

"Why not? Identifying yourself honestly is usually expected between friends."

"I meant… why do you have to know anymore about the loss?"

"Because it matters a lot. I'm assuming it's why you won't tell me your name."

"Why would you assume that's the reason?"

"Because I'm a man. You try to act like you don't want another one. Well… perhaps that's an indication about what kind of person you could love. But that's how you first reacted to my presence out here and then you kept hanging around me."

She leaned back in her chair. His gaze was glued on the fire. For the first time in over thirty years, he felt nervous to give eye contact to another person. He was pressing her. Hard. And he wasn't ready to stop.

"Yes, I'm still into men. And no, I won't fuck you, Gage."

He didn't even look up. Poke. Poke. Poke went his stick as he stabbed it hard into the coals. "That is not at all what I was asking. I simply asked your name. Not to fuck you. Do you know that your thought process is not quite rational?" His voice sounded as tight as his muscles felt.

The chemistry was undeniable between them. So far, they managed to avoid the sexuality that continued to manifest between them. It was unquestionably there. It existed. Whether or not she told him her name, it would continue to exist. He seriously doubted she would ever give that small flicker of flame any gas or encouragement.

"I'm not rational in your opinion?"

"No. You're not. You equate my request for your name as a request to have sex with you. And for your information, as long as it's already out there, I wouldn't fuck any woman whose name I didn't know."

She snorted. "Bullshit. You would in a heartbeat if I offered myself to you."

"Damn it." He stood up and flung the stick he held. "Why would you say that? Because there's an uncanny chemistry between us? Because you flirt with me twenty times a day and then come back for more while pretending to be completely asexual? When I know you aren't? Or because I'm out of line by asking your name? *Your first name*, for God's sake. Give me that at least. It's so fucking weird you won't even do that."

"Do not yell at me." Her words were tight as she pressed her lips together.

"Why? Why not? We aren't anything. Right? According to you. So what do you care if I'm annoyed at you? Shit. I'll walk out of here and never see you again. That's what you want… right?"

She jumped to her feet, clenching her fists. "Yes. Absolutely. That's what I want. I don't want to see you ever again."

"Then why do you want to see me now? Why? Why keep seeing me? Sharing dinners? How many, Vee? Helping me with physical labor is kind of above and beyond the call of duty if you don't like someone."

"We're friends."

"No. No… Don't you dare use that cop-out. Friends? Sure. I have lots of those. They tell me the most basic things about themselves, like their names, for instance. I even know their last names. Gee. I know where they come from and live and their sisters' names… something about them. No, Vee, we are not friends. Because you won't let us be friends. So tell me why that is. What ghost controls you that he won't even let you tell me your name?"

She glared at him, her eyes almost slits in their narrowness. Her puckered mouth and sunken cheeks looked like she was sucking on a slice of lemon. "It's not funny to say that."

"Did it happen this year?"

Her jaw wrenched back and forth. "No."

"Was it a man?"

"Yes. Fine. He died."

"And you loved him?"

She shut her eyes. "Yes. I did."

"And you think telling me your name will somehow keep you from... what? From falling in love with me?"

Her entire body jerked as if he zapped her with the end of a hot poker. "Oh, my God, no. That's not it at all. I just don't want you to know who I am. No. No, and there's no worry of that happening."

He crossed his arms over his chest and nailed her with his gaze, tightening his jaw. Standing almost toe to toe, glare to glare, locked-jaw to locked-jaw, when Gage spoke, however, his voice was soft. Calm. Almost a whisper. "But I do know who you are."

Her jaw slackened and her mouth dropped open. She swallowed and he knew he'd stunned her... and for once, maybe he'd affected her. He sucked in his guts, along with all his confidence. Every move he ever made for a woman fell away. This was Gage, raw and in the moment, confronting the first woman who could ever have caused his heart to thump so hard and fast. Whose smile made his chest lift with a physical joy that was almost overwhelming. He already felt different about her than any other woman... and still, she shared nothing of herself with him. But he knew her essence and he wasn't wrong about that. He knew he wasn't.

Slowly lifting his hand with infinite care and tenderness, he placed it on the side of her frozen face and palmed her cheek in his hand. "You know it's true. You feel it too. I know you do."

She didn't answer. She only swallowed and slammed her lips tightly shut. Her head shook to deny it.

"I don't know that. I don't feel that."

"I think you're just scared. You might not want to feel it. But I call bullshit that you don't."

Her huge eyes were almost transfixed on him. "No… just no."

"You're so brave… but so fucking scared. Aren't you? Of anything real. Of anything you might actually feel."

She didn't flinch from his touch. There was the smallest, infinitesimal dip of her head toward the warmth of his hand. Her eyeballs spun in her eye sockets as if she were half panicking, but she didn't step back. Or to the side. Or slap his hand away. Or try to speak. She didn't speak a word but she acted so awkward, it verged on being painful. He wasn't sure what to do with that. He expected a hot, fiery reaction of denial or even the opposite. Instead, Vee seemed confused, like she didn't know what to do.

He stepped closer, using the brief respite of sparks in her temper as a signal to push her. He had to try and make her own what she felt. What existed here. And if she didn't want it, then she simply had to admit that. He'd know then. He'd dealt with rejection before. He could now. Even up here, with no escape and a tent to share. But if she felt what he did, it was well worth exploring further. It was the most important thing they could do for themselves and each other.

His hiking boots were touching the tip of her cowboy boots. He lifted his hands and cupped her face as he stared down into her unusually bright green eyes. Same color as his. Their skin tone also matched. They complemented each other. His eyes followed the shadows and features of her narrow face. She had a small forehead and her hair was pulled back. He stared at her closely set eyes, small nose, thin lips and wide smile. The softest spray of freckles over her cheeks was so faint, you had to be close to her to appreciate them. He thought they gave her the most arresting face that ever existed.

Her huge eyeballs were wider than ever as she stared up at him. She didn't deny his accusations. She might have blamed her grief for not allowing this. Gage believed her grief kept her in a state of fear, even if her heart knew what his did. Something real and important had developed between them. Something hot and flirty, fun and exciting, sweet and tender, but mostly comfortable, as if their souls had always known each other in other lifetimes and finally recognized each other in this one. It was a first for him. The very first. Ever.

He lowered his face forward slowly and kept her gaze locked onto his. He finally reached her mouth and he closed his eyes and sank his lips on hers. She was frozen, and her torso became rigid and unyielding. But when their lips touched, her back swayed as easily as a tree branch in the wind and she wilted towards his chest. Her mouth cushioned his and she responded to his lips from the instant he made contact. He leaned towards her and she fell against him until the space between their bodies vanished. He held her face, tipping her chin towards his hungry mouth. She let out a soft sigh that drove his blood wild, surging into his extremities. For several long moments, he kissed and touched her lips with his in a soft, gentle, coaxing exploration.

Coaxing was unnecessary. Her mouth welcomed his. From the simplest touch, he experienced the most explosive response, which he felt inside his entire body. Blood rushed through his veins, spreading intense warmth. Desire for her tightened his muscles. He could feel his heart softening for her. He adored the way her mouth relaxed and seemed to melt under his. The feel of her lips and the soft, sweet sounds she made. He lapped up the heat of her body against his. Yeah, he kissed plenty of girls and women over the years. For at least twenty years. But it never felt like this, not even the first time… So right. He knew exactly what a kiss was supposed to evoke. Natural ease. As if they'd kissed a thousand times already; and even if they kissed a million times, each one would be as perfect as the first.

He held her face like it was a bowl to lick sustenance from. Letting his tongue touch the seam of her lips, he tested and tasted and pressed. Her lips opened at once and he groaned with unbridled desire as he dipped his hot tongue inside her mouth. Savoring the heat and honey taste, she became a lovely combination of smooth silk and irresistible sin. He dropped his hands around her waist and pulled her tighter against him. She had to lean back when their bodies collided and their mouths became fully fused. They opened their lips and clacked their teeth together, tongues sliding all over as they tasted each other. Sighing, her hands gripped his back and the folds of his shirt in restless abandonment. Their tummies bumped together and their hands clung to each other's backs. Both of their shirts were gathered in their fists as the kiss grew deeper and more aggressive. They kissed on and on and Gage could have stayed there forever, basking in her radiant warmth and sweet taste. Her soft lips were just wet enough to be perfectly sexy and sweet. The image made his brain spin with thoughts and melted his heart.

God. Damn. This was the kiss he'd been waiting for longer than three decades.

But she suddenly wrenched her mouth off his with a garbled explanation. It almost seemed as if she were cursing herself, not him.

Gage blinked in shock. First, he was kissing like he never had before and then, all at once, not. Staring up at him with her mouth half open, she blinked several times as if she were clearing her brain of the foggy cloud she drifted under. He was that intoxicated and confused after kissing her that he couldn't register what was happening. The first kiss they shared was everything he'd ever imagined a simple kiss could be.

Her eyes were rapidly growing wider with panic and something more... fear? Yeah, it looked a lot like fear. What the hell? Did she fear him? He had some doubts, but causing fear in the woman he saw before him? There was no way he threatened her and she could have easily said no to him. Of course, she knew that... right? "I—I can't do this."

Turning away, she suddenly bolted, vanishing into the dark night. His shoulders fell forward and he deflated. His body was still riding high with the notion of finding... what? Another kiss from a woman who wouldn't utter her real name? How could he assume she'd even accept a kiss from him, let alone, anything more?

But he'd pushed her. It almost worked... until it didn't.

Now it was pitch dark in the forest. On a mountain top. There was no way she could just avoid him and pretend nothing happened. Or stay separated until her feelings calmed down. Gage grabbed the lantern and started up the mountain after her.

"Vee?" he called out, swinging the lantern back and forth. He called several more times. Stopping dead, he listened for her but heard nothing except the swooshing creek water as it rushed over the jagged rocks to deeper pools. Then he caught the curve of a shoulder and human outline. She was sitting on a high spot above the creek, staring down at a small waterfall and pool.

He wasn't quiet when he came up behind her, setting the lantern beside her. He hunkered down and touched his hand to her shoulder. "Vee?"

She jerked away from him, shaking her head and said, "Go away."

Sighing, he pointed out, "We're in middle of the forest at

night. I can't go very far and neither should you. We're sharing a tent. We'll have to talk about it. Or not. But you still have to come back... right?" His voice wavered. Maybe she'd decide they didn't have to do anything.

"I didn't want to kiss you."

"Okay, I kissed you and I'm sorry. If I overstepped my boundary, I won't do it again. I promise you." Gage was sure she'd allowed him to kiss her and in fact, even liked it. But he would never touch her again. At least, not without explicit permission. "Fine. It was a mistake. A miscalculation. Let's forget it. Go back to being friends with no names. That's fine. Just come back to camp."

Her face turned so he could see just her profile as she peeked over her shoulder at him. "You pressed me too much."

He nodded. "I see that now."

She faced forward again. "I love him."

"The boyfriend who died?"

"Yes. I still love him." *Therefore, I won't love you.* That was loudly obvious even if it remained unspoken.

"I can accept that."

"I don't want to move on and I don't want to kiss you."

"Accepted. All of it. I read you all wrong."

There were long moments of silence until she folded forward, hooking her arms around her knees and all but hugging herself. Did she regret what she'd done with him? "You didn't read me wrong. I'll admit we have chemistry. But I'm not looking for that. I don't want it. I won't act on it."

He almost begged her to reconsider. But judging by the sudden straightening of her spine, she was not budging a millimeter on this. She was done. With love? With sex? With kissing? Everything? It was certainly her decision. He was just relieved she realized that. Maybe she understood why he thought it was okay to kiss her.

"Okay. Duly noted. I won't press you again. Nothing ever

again. Nothing but friends. I must ask you something now that I know you love someone else and there's no chance of anything more happening between us. That's totally acceptable. I can deal with that. But would you consider telling me your true identity sometime before I leave? Or giving me a way to contact you after we aren't here? That's what I'd like most to happen. But don't answer me now. Just think about it."

Her head jerked back. "That's not the reaction I expected."

He gave her a lopsided grin. "What did you expect? That I'd throw you over my shoulder, drag you back into camp and insist that you want me?" He spread his hands open, palms up. "I hope you realize by now that I am in complete control of myself. I will never pose any danger to you."

She nodded with her own crooked smile. "You'd never have made it into my tent if I weren't sure of that."

He nodded. "Well, good… now… come back?"

She slowly rose to her feet and Gage followed her cue. He grabbed the lantern and swept his hands, indicating that she go first. A true gentleman he was, even if she didn't ask for such quaint gestures. But she nodded with a grateful smile and started back to the tent. Did she fear he'd refuse to believe her when she said no? Did she have regrets? Did her feelings for another outweigh anything Gage might have offered her? She decided he wasn't worth those feelings.

Gage accepted it. He would not press her.

But it still felt like she sucker-punched him as hard as she could in the chest. Like his lungs were too tight and contracting until he could not breathe properly. A numbing sensation deadened his body. Damn. Oh, damn… never again. He'd never get a kiss like that with another woman. And he'd never know another connection like the one he shared with Vee. And it also looked like he'd never see her again after they left the mountain. Or if he did, it would have to be without her permission, which would therefore be unwanted. Pushing her? Yeah… and look where that didn't get him. He'd never do it again. Boundaries were engrained in her. And she had issues that were entirely hers. The death of someone she loved, a boyfriend, apparently had lasting consequences on her. It managed to prevent her from taking any risk herself.

But God damn. Didn't she feel the same thing flowing between them? The current of energy? The magnetic pull of their bodies towards the other? How easily they could respond to each other. How quickly their smiles and laughs seemed to synchronize. The natural grace they shared. The beautiful, luxurious comfort they found in each other and both enjoyed.

No, he didn't know her real name, so it was odd. But he still sensed something big between them that was undeniable; he felt it one hundred percent.

But Vee was still nursing her wounds and didn't want it. He should have gotten some comfort that she acknowledged it. But the only thing on his mind was what she so easily gave up. Yeah, best kiss of his life but it would never happen again. Fine. No, he never announced that it was the best kiss he ever had. He guessed her best kiss was with her dead boyfriend. That made sense. But for him? Kissing Vee was the best one in his lifetime.

She walked towards the tent and Gage hung the lantern on its hook. They quietly proceeded with their nightly ritual. The damn day was ruined. Night was almost over. Time to go to bed and let it die in peace. His heart still ached and his extremities felt numb whenever Gage thought about her, which was so dumb. He never really had her. Only a kiss that seared into his mouth, his heart, and his soul.

He dropped onto his bed, leaving the sleeping bag half open. Placing a hand over his forehead, he could only stare up in despair at the white canvas. Vee moved about a bit longer. She went outside, then came back in. Eventually, she slipped quietly into her cot and that was that. What more was there to say? Nothing. It was all over. They'd get up tomorrow and chat as they shared the chores with the graceful fluidity of a couple married fifty years. At some point, one of them would make a joke or rib the other and they would resume their amicable bicker. That would lift his heart and make him laugh.

Yep. They would do that tomorrow. But what about tonight? His chest contracted with the loss of something he never had. He never knew he wanted it. The feelings he couldn't comprehend turned out to be his own.

He lay awake for hours and hours. His brain short-circuited whenever he thought about what he wanted most and could not have. How shocking it was. To feel something that strong and connected while the person he hoped would feel the same did not. Vee never knew the pressing, over-whelming and almost panicky need to be with him. She never debated whether or not to act on those urges.

The creek's loud crashing and swooshing over the rocks slowly lulled his heartbroken psyche into exhaustion and sleep finally allowed him a successful escape.

SOMETHING WAS ATTACKING HIM. One moment, he was in rapturous oblivion; and the next, he woke up to body weight and the feeling of being pressed upon.

He blinked as he tried to figure out where he was and what was going on. Confusion muddled his brain. Darkness inside a tent. That filled his eyesight. A soft light, the glow of moonlight. But the weight wasn't overbearing… it was femi-nine. It had to be Vee. Obviously, there was no one else. Her

LEANNE DAVIS

legs were straddling him and her knees rested beside his hips. Her hands were on either side of his ears and she held her torso just inches off him.

"What the fuck?" he muttered as he awoke and his consciousness became fully aware.

"Violet. My name is Violet," she whispered into his ear. Her breath was warm and moist and he felt it on his ear and neck. Shivers broke out all over him. He gulped in total shock and shuddered with his ragged nerves. If he moved, he feared she'd retreat and flee. He'd lose her again. He never dreamed of this. He held his breath.

"Gage?"

"Violet? That's... really a pretty name." It was such a lame reply. His voice was low and gravelly from sleep and utter confusion. Was he dreaming? She just told him her name? After all the times he'd asked and all of her vehement denials. Now, she simply whispers it to him?

"This is purely sex. We're out here. There is no relationship. No cuddling or affection. I felt something with you and the things you did. But I don't want anything else. Okay?"

His heart hurt when it pounded against his ribcage very hard. He nodded and had to restrain himself from appearing too eager to comply with her conditions. "Yes. Okay. I understand... *Violet.*"

Violet. Vee. She finally told him something about herself. He thought she made the name up and it had nothing to do with her. *Violet.* It was pretty. But he couldn't yet think of Vee, his mountain girl, as *Violet.* It didn't feel right. He couldn't call her Violet yet. But...

Damn.

She was on top of him and talking about sex.

She lowered her head and her mouth covered his. It was hard and fast and aggressive. As fierce and capable as a woman who knows what she wants. The woman he found her to be thus far. So he should not have been surprised when she easily captured his mouth with hers and devoured him.

In no time, Gage realized it was so much more than sex. No matter what she said about it or would later attempt to say.

CHAPTER 8

*V*IOLET LAY ON THE cot, staring up. Moonlight imbued the tent with an other-worldly glow as it illuminated the space. Soft, interesting ambience. Romantic almost.

Turning over, she looked at the canvas wall beside her, glaring hard at it. She tried to forget everything she was thinking and feeling. *Go to sleep. Now. Please*, she desperately pleaded to her overly busy brain and racing heart.

But no. No such mercy. She could not stop thinking about kissing Gage Sullivan. Someone new. Someone so different from her. Someone who wasn't Preston. And the most horrifying part was how much she'd loved it. The feel of his lips on hers, his hands exploring her body, the pressure and warmth... the entire experience spun her mind into a dizzy but wonderful escapade.

She didn't know how to handle it. Gage pushed and prodded her, using valid points, of course, when he'd asked for her name. Her damn name. There was no good reason why he needed to know it if they would indeed remain two people who shared a camp on the mountain briefly. That period of time they spent together as friends was fleeting. But how often can true chemistry exist only to be denied? The energy that flowed between them was too obvious. They both knew it at once. That fact sunk into Violet's brain early on, which was why she'd tried to avoid anything that could lead to a future attachment. She never wanted to fall in love again. She couldn't survive that kind of vulnerability more than once.

She loved generously. She really did. Her friends, sisters, parents, cousins, aunts, and uncles, along with many others who surrounded her received unconditional love from Violet. She didn't go to the mountains because she lost the capacity to love anyone or anything again. She didn't freak out or try to permanently isolate herself from everyone she knew before. No. She wasn't insane. If the close-lipped secrets she told Gage made her seem damaged, he was wrong.

No. She was not quite *damaged.* Her one true love in life was Preston. That lasted forever. Done deal. She had no desire to find another. To open herself up to that kind of pain— chest-ripping, heart-pounding, exhausting grief. There was no way she'd allow herself to feel that again. Not for anything or anyone.

So the simplest way to avoid the issue was to simply not do it. No worries if you refuse to engage in it.

Even when the heat was all but smoking between her and Gage, every time their gazes met, or they exchanged smiles, or their laughs coincided, she'd denied the special vibe existed between them that even blew her away sometimes with its power. But no matter how hard she'd insisted it was nothing and tried her best to keep it neutral and pleasant, staying at arm's length, it seemed to take on a life of its own. It refused to be ignored. It existed.

But Gage wanted more. He'd started questioning her and

probing her about things. Things she didn't want to discuss. They could co-exist without the need to give them voice or breath or life. They could simply be.

Other times, Gage backed off temporarily. Not this time. He'd pushed and she'd responded. The conversation became intimate and personal in ways she never wanted to have with another man again.

Despite the inner conflict, she expected she would want to have sex again. She hadn't felt like it since Preston died, and even the thought of it turned her stomach. But she had to admit that a time might occur when it flared to life. She might eventually have to seek out a man for companionship. Strictly as a partner for sex. That was it. She vowed to always strive to keep any emotions or feelings out of it. Idle distractions. If she got physical with anyone, he would have no other part of her. She'd seek out an attractive man and simply have sex. That was it. A foolproof plan to keep her unattached and always beyond the realm of falling in love.

Until Gage entered her life. *Gage.* Damn it. He was right there. So close, he loomed over everything else in her life. Her fears and resolutions. Her convictions and goals. Everything vaporized in one eye-lock when he'd touched her face. He'd put his hand on her stupid cheek and all she could see and feel after that was him. Everything that came before or what could have come after ceased to exist. Her brain refused to allow her to think about or care about anything else anymore.

All she could do is be. Exist. In that moment. And for the first time in almost two years, it stopped. All of it. Her thoughts and feelings, her anxieties and images of horror that filled her brain and nightmares. She'd swiftly forgot her vow not to be with anyone she had feelings for. She also forgot the feeling she'd refused to have ever again. She forgot where she was. She found herself unable to get away from the person who most upset her. She was stuck with him.

None of it mattered though. All her anxious thoughts and feelings soon faded. They vanished entirely. Gone. She was a collection of cells and tissue and blood, simply existing. There. Right then. That was all that mattered. And Gage's big, calloused fingertips and warm palm cupping her cheek had felt like home. Everything that made her lonely and sad for so long had simply stopped.

Pretty powerful stuff.

His lips on hers made so much sense. More sense than anything else in her entire life. Sure. Those lips should taste hers. Yes. One thousand percent. Why not?

She'd opened up like a morning glory on the first warm spring morning. There was sunshine, passion and a general feeling of goodness. So much goodness.

Anything dark or doubtful had already evaporated like rubbing alcohol. It didn't matter. It wasn't part of this. Even if it should have been.

The kiss was so good that it connected her to the man who already held her spirit through friendship and trust. She wasn't exactly happy about it, but it was the honest truth. Since Preston's death, Violet was always truthful. Even when the truth was hard to accept or something she didn't want to believe. She now believed in it. How can you solve any problems or pursue a life of integrity if you don't start with the most basic thing? Truth. Facts. A common reality. From there, one's feelings about right and wrong and morality emerge. Along with human desires. Later, she could make the necessary decisions and choices.

But now? She had to deny her feelings and emotions and the truth. All things were frozen in suspended animation. Just as she wanted.

Until Gage came. Until that single moment.

She was inundated and overwhelmed by a wave of emotion that completely shocked her. It rendered her mute and immobilized. Only her lips moved as his mouth had surrounded hers. For a moment, her entire being was aware of only him. Them.

Then she remembered. Gage's lips were so different from Preston's. She hadn't kissed anyone like that in two years. Her body was reacting although her heart and brain didn't engage. Her traitorous body liked these feelings. It flooded her with zings and zaps of electricity and radiant warmth. She recognized the urgent feeling of belonging and anticipating and wanting more. So much more.

The sharp, irresistible, unmistakable desire for more overcame her. She'd wanted him to move closer and place his hands around her back, her torso, and up her shirt. She'd wanted to suction cup herself to him and lessen the ache that was so intense, it took her breath away.

She'd forgot.

She really did. She'd forgot how wonderful sexual arousal was. How wild and glorious and new and exciting it felt. How urgent and immediate. The longing inside her so needy, demanding satisfaction right there. Right now. She'd forgot how often she displayed those feelings when she was younger and happier with Preston. She was rarely denied them because she had Preston.

But Gage wasn't Preston. She was cheating. With someone new.

All the grand feelings were funneled into a cold, harsh shower of regret and fear.

No.

She was with Gage. It wasn't love. It was new and strange. She couldn't do it.

So she'd pulled away from Gage and ran.

He was supposed to be a jerk. He should have huffed off

to bed so she could slink in later, cold, hurting, embarrassed and uncomfortable with him. She could silently slip into bed. And tomorrow, they could ignore each other and let it die a natural death.

But no. He came after her. He was not annoyed or angry, but gentle and caring. He approached her with common courtesy and that thing that managed to penetrate her carefully fortified defenses: his genuine warmth. His caring. His understanding... None of which she comprehended. The gentle touch on her shoulder before an immediate apology and letting her off the hook. It was impossible not to like the man. And to forgive him for not being Preston. She wanted to be irrationally angry at him for being there, alive and warm, being able to touch her and receive her touch.

She was angry at Gage just for being alive. And for not being Preston. For making her feel all the things she had only felt for Preston, but now felt for him. She was betraying her heart. Her very soul. Preston owned both of those things. Still.

Even now, the tears streamed down her face. Her nose was almost instantly filled with snot and her heart ached so much, she thought she was having a heart attack.

Gage's breathing sounded more regular. In the few nights they spent together, Gage started out on his back and his breathing was quiet. Then, at some point, he rolled onto his side and started breathing through his mouth. It wasn't quite snoring, just heavier breathing. Violet heard it all. She'd become an insomniac most nights ever since Preston died. Sure, it was related. But she wasn't ready to address it. She was aware of the fact and she didn't sugar coat it. She knew there were things she should deal with, but they were frozen inside her. She found it much easier to escape to the mountain or even her room at home than to chronicle her racing thoughts, streaming tears, sleepless nights and worse, nightmares.

After Gage dropped off to sleep, the even breathing started. He stirred faintly.

Violet finally dried her tears and sniffed. She wondered what he really thought of her craziness. The refusal to provide basic information was something she guarded like a drug dog that was trained to keep the cops away. His questions and confusion were justified. Why he continued to tolerate her empty answers was surprising. Why did he believe her? He accepted her yes and no answers as gospel and never doubted her. He even took her flimsy excuses as the truth.

She closed her eyes and all the images of the evening flooded her, overwhelming her senses. His questions. His words. His soothing voice. It was deep, yet brimming with humor. There was something so glorious and normal about Gage. Where Violet felt strange and odd nowadays, Gage seemed solidly sure of himself, grounded in his confidence, values and openness of the man he was.

His mouth was on her mind as she rolled over. Nearly sighing, she recalled how it felt and all the weird, new things that began percolating in her tummy. Warmth and interest and fire. Throbbing heartbeat from the memory. For so long, she'd avoided a single sip, one taste of desire, and now she wanted to guzzle the whole frothy, wonderful concoction of mutual attraction and sex.

For so long she waited.

She sighed as she squeezed her thighs and the feelings remained. They existed. No matter how much she didn't want to feel turned on, she was. She wanted him. She wanted sex. She wanted to be touched. She wanted Gage.

Squeezing her eyes shut, she reminded herself Gage was not what she wanted. She wanted to *end* her desire for Gage.

She wanted to stay dead inside and never need sex again. She intended to stay in that numbed state. But how? Thinking about his lips, tongue and the pressure of his hands on her cheek and waist were enough to undo her. Squirming. Wanting. Desiring.

She hated every moment she felt it. Asexuality was the goal. She needed it. Forever.

But that wasn't the reality. The truth was a feeling, despite how unresolved and unsolicited it was.

Her desire to have sex again, since she wasn't dead yet, was probably normal and healthy. Her avoidance of sex wasn't, nor her desire to never love again. Not healthy.

But sex? She could have sex.

And why not with Gage? He was handsome, so freaking handsome. Funny. That smile. She adored his laugh and humor and what was sexier than those two factors combined? There was also kindness inside him. He gently addressed her dog, using baby-talk with him when he didn't think she could see or hear him. Their conversation reflected the ease of being together. There was also a distinctly intense and real connection. That kiss. It told her, yeah, they could be hot together.

So if sex were now a part of her life again, her body could say, *hey, Violet I'm still here*. And why not Gage? Why not here? There were no witnesses. No real consequences. No one to observe them. They could be adults about it. With a mutual understanding of what it was. Then they could simply be done with each other. He'd walk out and return to his former life and that would be that. She'd go home and move past it. She'd never run into him before at home, so why would she now? No reason to believe they would have even a chance encounter.

She sucked on that idea for a good half hour before finally nodding in the dark night air. She wriggled her sleeping bag off and slid out from under Monty. He moaned as he turned his head the opposite way and went back to sleep. She sat up, sliding her feet on the ground, which was covered by a tarp. She stared at the faint lump of man and cot.

Man.

Her heart thumped against her ribs. Oh, God, he was big, beautiful, strong and athletic. He really was. All this time, she'd tried to ignore his handsome and intriguing features. Now she could enjoy simply staring at him for several minutes at a time without tiring. His company was fun too. There was nothing that annoyed or frustrated her about him. She felt peaceful. It was so nice to be around him and she could appreciate his good looks. There was nothing she didn't like about him.

Especially, how great she felt.

So why not?

Her nerves nearly made her blood sing and she had to take in a deep breath, lifting herself up before going towards him. She stared down at his sleeping form. Lying on his back, she could just climb on him. That was weird, right? Or should she tap his shoulder and ask him for sex? That seemed even stranger.

No. Go for it. Taking the upper hand ensured she wouldn't chicken out. Breathing slowly, she simply crawled on top of him, placing her legs on either side of his, her hands and arms supporting her torso above his and yes, managing to scare the living crap out of him.

Duh. His entire body jerked when he woke up, and she was sure he feared an animal was about to bite his neck. But then he realized just as fast she was lying on him.

And she told him her true name. He'd warned her he wouldn't fuck anyone without knowing her name, so she whispered it to him. She hoped the uniqueness of her name wouldn't make it too evident.

But he had no reaction to it except to say that *Violet* was a pretty name. She also sensed how odd he felt saying it to her. He didn't yet associate the name with her. She understood. It would be disconcerting to her if he changed his name from Gage to Gavin or the like.

But now she was over his body and he reached around her and tucked his hands firmly on her back. One big hand landed between her shoulder blades and the other went below it. His hands nearly spanned the entire surface of her back. She shuddered at their warmth. It had been so long since those feelings were aroused. She leaned forward and put her head down until finally, their lips touched. It was gentle. Exploratory. New. Tentative. Her lips feeling his. Touching and pressing, pulling back and pushing in. She finally pressed her mouth heavily on his and his hands scrunched up the shirt on her back. He was restless now. She gently licked the seam of his lips. Touching. Tasting. Playing. He opened his mouth and her tongue dipped inside. It was soft and warm and inviting when it glided into his. It was like their first kiss. But this time, it was hot instead of clumsy.

His fingertips traced her spine and she moaned at the intense pleasure of his delicate fingertips. He stopped at the base of her neck, under her hair, and rubbed the bottom of her hairline. It was so sensuous as anywhere a man dared to touch her. That was insane, being so benign.

His fingers moved up along the center of her scalp, and the moan that escaped her wasn't from his tongue thrusting and meshing with hers, which was hot as hell in itself, but the way he touched her head. Specifically, her scalp.

They kissed longer, their mouths twisting and turning in the most perfectly synchronized movements left to right, as if they'd rehearsed it before. No. Instead, it was all spontaneous. Exhilarating. Eventually, Violet sat up, straddling him, and lifting the hem of her shirt before pulling it over head. Her hair fell free for the night, cascading over her bare shoulders and looking soft and sensuous. Her body hadn't felt that good in years. Her heated, sensitive skin felt like it was too tight for her body. Any soft, feather-light touch would cause the nerve endings to explode with ecstasy. Even the sensitivity was arousing.

She was naked now. Her bra was tossed when she'd slipped into bed. Her breasts were mid-sized round orbs with pointy, red nipples that twisted to pebbles as the cool air brushed across them.

She doubted he could see more than a faint outline when his hands slipped to her waist as she sat up. He immediately cupped a warm palm of soft, cushy breast. She sighed at the sensation as he used his thumb to rub the nipple up and down. Sucking in a deep breath, her hips responded to his hard, straining penis that was directly below her bottom.

He suddenly sat up too, gripping her under the armpits and lifting her up to slide his hips back before setting her back down in front of him. He pushed the sleeping bag out of the way until they were face-to-face on the cot, both sitting, their legs crossing over each other's. He let her go briefly as he struggled and pulled until he finally divested his shirt and tossed it away. He pulled her closer, placing her bottom on his thighs before pressing on her lower back to move her as close to him as she could get. She moaned when she felt his hard length straining beneath the cotton sweats. The bulge aimed towards the center of her, which was wet and swollen with desire for all that hardness.

Her hands slipped to his wide shoulders and she held on, using him for leverage. She pressed her body so close to him, a sheet of paper could not fit between them. She ran her hands along his shoulders, loving it. She adored his hard muscles and the slope of his shoulders. His neck was square and strong as it emerged from the base of his wide shoulders. She sighed as his chest rubbed her bare breasts, which squished against him.

He nuzzled the side of her face, her ear and hairline, kissing beneath her neck and chin until she tilted her head and let her hair fall down her back. His other hand grabbed a fistful of her hair, which he used to position her head in a new angle. When his lips came down over hers, she surrendered and allowed him to take complete control of her.

He licked her neck and her chin and her lips. He sucked her lower lip and gently nipped her with his teeth before moving into her mouth. It was soft and easy at first, but when he tugged her head back by her hair, using enough pressure to wield control, he was also gentle. It set off a rush of warm feelings from her stomach and down lower.

Then his mouth was over hers and he quit exploring and teasing her. Now he was prepared to fully plunder her. His tongue dominated her mouth. She leaned closer toward more of his heat and touch and flavor.

He kissed her again and she moaned when his hand released her hair and he held her chin. He squeezed her gently before pressing his mouth onto hers harder. So much pressure. But oh. The delicious things his persistent kissing, licking, sucking managed to do to the rest of her.

She was blazing on fire.

She ran her hands over his shoulders, reaching the short strands of his hair and moving back down the long column of his neck. She was memorizing the texture of his skin. She loved the way it stretched over the straight muscles of his neck. And how it merged into his back and shoulder blades. She found it irresistibly sexy since he was so much larger and stronger than her.

Releasing her chin, he began to lick her lips. He kissed the corner of her mouth before dropping down to the curve of her neck and further down her body. He rained soft kisses as he rearranged his hands. He held her above her waist and below her breasts tightly before he tilted her torso back. He arched her back until the high points on her chest were accessible to his mouth. Violet felt like a mouthwatering appetizer on a platter.

His nose touched her sternum and he planted a kiss on her right breast. Violet held her breath in ragged anticipation. She pressed her shoulder towards him as her unspoken, needy encouragement. He kissed her again. He licked her softness until his lips reached the rippled edge of her nipple. She whimpered her desire, moving her hips with more freedom to let him know... oh, yes. Do that. Now.

But Gage was in no hurry. He kissed her nipple again before flattening his tongue on the end of it and licking it like an ice cream cone. It wasn't long before her head fell back, and she nearly did a back-bend in her effort to encourage him to suck on her nipples. Kiss. Lick. Touch. Fondle. He was literally setting her on fire. She briefly feared she might be dying.

Then he slowed down even more into a measured and controlled touch. He continued to lick and suck her nipples, taking them alternately into the hot depths of his mouth until she was writhing with libido.

Her entire core was reduced to a hot puddle of swollen wetness.

He sucked and bit her nipples, pulling and prodding the swollen flesh before letting it go to do the same to the opposite one. She fell to the mercy of her needs. She sighed and oohed and ahhed while her body begged for more. It kept pushing closer to his wonderful heat and pressure.

When he released her, she scrambled to her feet. She must have surprised him, judging by the jerk of his head as he appeared to look at her. The darkness kept them from seeing clearly, and only intensified her eagerness. The muscles and broadness of his shoulders and chest really turned her on. The hardness of his pecs and his trim waist. He didn't have a six-pack in his abs, but the skin was taut and tight. She used her hands to memorize the way he felt.

Swishing her hips back and forth, she longed to relieve the growing agony that was both sweet and hot, aching and wonderful. She forgot how strong the urge inside her could be. She felt like a rainbow of colors was infiltrating her blood stream.

Gage rose off the cot and stood just inches from her, his height more towering and commanding than before in the daylight. There it was more about friendship. Right now? The goose bumps, power, seduction and urgent desire were magical. Everything about him was turning her on: from his stroking to being quiet, to controlling and commanding her. He decided how he wanted her to be and it was hot. So damn hot. Her needs and wants were being met without her even knowing what they were.

He leaned forward, sloughing off his pants and boxers or whatever he wore for underwear. She could not see him until he straightened up. The energy was radiating off him. His unconcealed sexual desire for her was obvious now. And holy shit. It didn't take much for her body to bend towards him. His jutting penis touched her belly before he encircled her with his arms around her waist.

She surprised herself when she simply wrapped her thin arms around his waist and held on for the ride. They were standing in the center of the tent, clinging to each other. Naked. Blinded. But fully aware of every feeling.

Her heart suddenly dropped like an anvil. Shit. She wasn't at her home or even in town. There were no condoms in the tent. She never had any reason to bring them.

"Do you have a condom?"

"Two. In my wallet." He released her and stepped back. Groping around, he began knocking several items off the table as he patted it down. Reluctantly, Violet reached up for the light and clicked it on. She was a little hesitant to see what was happening. Scared of her own reaction to being naked with another man. A man who wasn't Preston. But her body was so turned on that she felt like a traitor to Preston. There she was. Naked with another man.

She blinked when the small light brightened the space. He twisted his torso backward, blinking as well when he realized the light was on. His bare butt faced her and it was smooth and sleek, with muscular definition from all the hiking, no doubt. Her mouth went dry and she fought the urge to slide her hand over it. Her fingers twitched eagerly and she longed to feel the hollows and swells of it. His gaze sought hers as he turned, easily spotting his wallet. He grabbed it and removed the two foil squares that were tucked inside there.

"Tell me those aren't years and years old."

Gage straightened up, holding the squares, and tossing his wallet on the table. His gaze nearly leveled her. Her breath caught when he didn't answer or smile as he usually responded to their banter. No, his gaze was fastened on her breasts. He didn't blink or breathe although his nostrils flared. His eyes were on her chest. Her tits, to be specific.

Then, he scanned her stomach and the apex of her thighs, taking in the curve of her hips and finally, her legs. He raised his gaze back to her tits, not her eyes.

Surprised, she almost snapped her fingers in front of his face.

The kindness, coaxing and caring she expected from him wasn't there. No. Just hot, turned on, sexy appraisal. Raw desire. His eyes seemed to spark with attraction as he stared at her nipples. They tightened even harder than the cool air already made them. She never remembered feeling so much desire from a hot look.

"Never seen a pair of boobs before?" she finally asked when he didn't speak or give her eye contact. He also didn't answer her.

He smiled. His lips stretched wide and his teeth flashed. But his eyes didn't rise to hers and he still didn't answer her.

She started to grow annoyed… but holy damn. When did anyone stare at her with that kind of appreciation? Want? Lust? Desire? As if she were the hottest turn ever? Honestly? Not too often. Her boobs were small and perky. Not exactly pin-up material.

"Gage?" she said as she crossed her arms over her front. He blinked and his smile faded into a scowl. Only then did he raise his eyes to hers.

"What?"

"You're ogling me. Staring. Like… like I'm the first naked woman you've ever seen."

He shrugged his big shoulders. Her stupid heart reacted by speeding up. He was naked. She let her eyes study his face and chest before dipping down towards his jutting hardness. It strained and bobbed like a compass needle seeking true north: her vagina.

"No. Not the first. Just the best." His smile grew huge then. Lopsided. Sweet. Appreciative. And fun.

God, he was enjoying just staring at her. She switched her weight from one foot to the other. He stepped forward to close the gap and grabbed her left wrist. He tugged on it to prevent her from covering her chest. "Please?"

"I asked you if your condoms were past the expiration date?"

"I heard you. And they aren't. Although I do get laid more than once a decade or once a year even." He gave her a cheeky smile. "We only have two so we really have to make them count."

He took both her wrists in his hands, and moved her arms out again so his eyes had full access to her lovely breasts. "You're impossible. They're just a pair of boobs!" She finally laughed when he could not stop staring. His eyes were sparking.

"No." He finally lifted his gaze up to hers. "Not to me. They're you. All of you. I didn't think I'd ever see you like this or be like this with you. So I fully intend to memorize every single freckle and dimple and angle and curve of your body. You might think I'm crazy. Maybe you don't know that you're the most beautiful woman I've ever been with, inside and out. So I will allow you to watch me devour your looks if you'll try to understand how I feel."

Her breath stopped in her throat. She pressed her lips tightly. Holy shit. She didn't expect that response. He kept staring at her as his words registered in her mind and she met his green-eyed gaze with her own. "You did that on purpose. You turned this into something light and funny and sexy so I wouldn't…"

"Freak out? Leave? Decide I wasn't the right guy and run out into the dark? Yes."

She stared up at this man and her heart fluttered. It hurt. Why did he have to be so perfect? Who did that? She was walking a tightrope emotionally, and only a tiny slip away from falling off it. She refused to allow her mournful memories into her heart.

But did the light cause this? Is that what distracted her? His ogling? Old-fashioned, stupid guy staring at her boobs. But he made it seem funny and not humiliating.

She swallowed the lump that lodged in her throat.

Surprising herself more than him, she launched herself at him. She raised her arms and leapt toward his big, naked, welcoming body. He was full of compassion for her grief, which he didn't understand, but he still cared about its effect on her.

Gage reacted by catching her before her hands clasped his neck and she pressed her face into his chest. She rested her head inches below his sternum. He embraced her, settling his hands on her lower back and pressing her closer. Yeah, she felt his hot, heavy penis digging into her stomach. Her own body was swollen and wet with longing. But it was definitely paused.

The body heat. The mutual warmth. The contrast in their sizes, his being so big and her being so small. His desire to fulfill all of her needs. He dug his fingertips into the skin and muscles along her spine, trying to massage and relieve her by using his own magic: kindness and tenderness.

The light imbued a golden, soft glow. It was kind by making everything pretty and blurred. Her heart hurt. She lifted her head and tilted it back. "I'm not sure…"

His hands simultaneously dropped to her butt and he gripped each butt cheek. He lifted her up on her tiptoes. She cradled his steel-heated length in the V she made with her legs. "I know. But everything feels so right. Just lose yourself in that."

So simple and easy. Stay rooted in the physical, present moment. Of course, he was right, and it felt *so right*. Completely and utterly perfect. But what about the damned hug they were now sharing? It felt comforting. Safe. Necessary.

Fuck. She was in trouble.

He lowered his head to kiss her lips before she could move too far away or get lost in her doubts again. He smiled as he gave her butt a hefty squeeze. "You really have a hot, tight, amazing, little body. So I was staring for me too."

Suddenly finding herself smiling after their sloppy,

connected, fun kiss, Violet thought, *God, he was funny and hot and fun. He's what made this... amazing.*

Then he gripped her under her arms and lifted her up. He was holding her right above his erection and her entire body was being supported by him. Stepping forward, he gently set her down on the cot. He tucked the condom packets on the side of the cot before turning his undivided attention to her.

Her knees poked up and he squatted beside her, stroking her thighs and running his hand down one, making her shudder as he traced the line where her butt joined the sensitive skin of her inner thigh. Her hips strained towards his touch eagerly, urgently, and her eyes fluttered shut as she willed her shameful thoughts to shut down. Be gone for good.

He leaned over her and with an expert and confident touch, stroked her pubic hair, curling it around his fingers as she moaned through her lips. When he sunk his fingers inside her with shallow, explorative strokes, she began biting her lip and squinting her eyes shut. He gently stroked her back and forth. No hurry. He was in complete control of her pleasure and taking his sweet time with her.

She was already gone. Her knees parted and she dug her feet into the soft material of the cot, lifting her pelvis up towards him. But still, he made no haste. He petted and stroked and explored her wetness as it filled her up. He finally dared to dip a finger inside her and her breath hitched before it got stuck in her throat. So good. A mumbled litany of gibberish escaped her mouth but no words. She swung her hips and torso, trying to drive him deeper and harder inside her. She wanted more. She was so hungry. Almost feral.

Dipping two fingers inside her, he stretched her vaginal walls and her aching, needy body nearly exploded. She thrashed about, her eyes slammed shut, and her mouth dropped open in a silent scream.

He moved his fingers further into her body and leaned forward to gently place his mouth on the bundle of nerves that her whole being was focused on exclusively. It was all that mattered to her now. All she wanted. And needed. On and on, Gage sucked and licked her as his fingers dipped inside her until she was lost in the moment. She had no sense of time or space, never mind, what was happening. She even forgot who she was and where this might be going.

Colors started to stream as a series of weird jolts emanated from her core and bolted up and down her body. She left herself. This place. This life. This space. She was no longer Violet Rydell. She was no longer flesh and bone, but waves of light and energy, fire and water. She floated and soared with nothing to weigh her down. No body. No brain. No soul. No grief.

She became pure beauty and heart and soul. She was literally flying. Gone… Lost to an orgasm that was years in the making.

She slowly fluttered her eyelids, only then realizing his mouth stayed on her clit throughout the whole mindblowing orgasm. He slowly withdrew his fingers and finally lifted his mouth off her. He began to kiss the inside of her thighs, heading up towards her belly button. His beard tickled her skin. He kissed her stomach and between her breasts before he finally stopped at her mouth.

It was a gentle, reverent kiss that was so unlike the heated sex glands of moments before. This kiss was soft and caring. It started with a tender touching of their lips. The steam started building as their mouths opened and found each other. Both of them used their hands to cradle the other one's face. That kiss went far beyond what they'd shared until then. Even when his mouth was exploring her most private parts. This kiss was more intimate. It dipped into secrets and emotions, demands and rewards. Expectation and satisfaction. She shut her eyes and allowed herself to be lost. Their tongues and lips and hands kept moving and touching anywhere and everywhere. He slid over her, pinning her down and she loved it. She instantly opened her legs and let him rest on top of her as her body welcomed him.

He barely stopped long enough to grab the condom and slide it on. He was back over her in a matter of seconds and with their mouths reunited, they picked up where they left off. He pushed inside her as naturally as grabbing her hand. He fit snugly. Perfectly.

She took him inside her entirely. Her muscles stretched to accommodate his excessive girth. Her breath stalled. It had been so long since she felt so wonderful and new. And yet, it was also old. Something she perfected with lots of practice and experience. He shuddered when he pushed fully inside her. His head dropped and he held her torso closer, resting his forehead on her sternum. Was he memorizing how she felt?

He moved his hips in and out in one long, slow stroke. She gasped when he did it. He did it again. And again. When she finally caught her breath, he was caressing her body as she happily accepted his.

Then, all the patience and propriety evaporated like a lawn sprinkler on a hot day. They were no more than bodies. Writhing together. Pounding each other. Gasping for air and calling out with glee. Grunting, moaning and laughing?

His hips hammered into her and her body relished every second of it. His mouth sought hers as he jammed his tongue inside hers as hard as he thrust his body. The feelings were soon out of control and she gloried in the moment. She loved losing all sense of time and space and feelings. It was primal.

He needed her.

Her! Now.

It was hot and furious and loud.

Finally, oh, God! Violet couldn't hold herself together long enough to kiss him. Her mouth let his go, and her head bobbed as her eyes rolled back in her head. Gage hammered inside her, pulling her knees wider to get even deeper inside while she screamed with pleasure. *Screamed.*

And they were both lost to the indescribable sensations of their bodies. It felt so new and yet, so old. Exciting and comforting. Wild and tender.

And best of all, Violet adored every single moment of it.

CHAPTER 9

*G*AGE CAME SO HARD he was afraid he hurt her. He lay on top of her for a moment, stunned. He felt like an adolescent again. But this was far better; they both knew exactly what they were doing and so did their bodies. They connected in every sense of the word. From the physical pleasure to the whole gamut of emotions. From greedily taking to eagerly giving. From hot to tender. There were even some moments when his stupid heart actually ached.

The exploration. The adventure. The sense of discovery. It was amazing. But they also had a meeting of the minds and wills. It reflected the time they spent together. Sure, it was hot, incredible sex, but so much more. It was deepening the connection he felt towards her. How he foresaw himself with *Violet.*

It was not an experience he could forget anytime soon. In the first place, they did it on a cot in a tent, something he never tried before. The thrill of knowing her real name almost surpassed everything else they shared in their time together. But no. Together, they were dynamite. Explosive sparks. Rockets in the sky. Like detonating an M-80. But this was real.

Now what? He slid to the side of her. Somehow, they managed to fit on the single camp cot and he liked the way Violet cuddled up against him. They would soon be chilled when all their hormones receded and their overheated skin rapidly cooled in the early morning air. Would she stay in bed with him? Theirs wasn't a relationship. Hell, she seemed to shun affection. Why couldn't he have met this woman with whom he had so much chemistry, who refused to have any strings or other attachments, including her real name, when he was nineteen or in his early twenties? Oh, no. It happens now, when he was so much older and more or less settled. His views about sex, including his preferences as to when and how he did it, were very different now. With few, if any one-night stands to feather his cap, Gage had zero interest in them now. Would he have turned Violet down if she hadn't volunteered her name? Maybe. He needed to know her name. A name he could say to himself and think about later.

He wanted to hug her tightly against him to celebrate the occasion. It was an experience to remember. It wasn't just sex. Not with Violet. Her face. Her body. Her heart. Her soul. This person he'd barely come to know, and still had no clue about. He never felt stranger than he did after their intimate experience.

She was like a wild tiger that he so dearly wanted to hold and pet. Grabbing her by the tail, he struggled to keep her close to him, fearing if he let her go, she would claw his body to ribbons and run away, never to be seen again.

All he wanted was to see her… a lot more.

When he leaned down, he grabbed the sleeping bag and pulled it up to cover them. It was half open so he draped it over them enough to stay warm. She didn't get up and leave.

She nestled on her side closer to him. They embraced and Gage wrapped his arm around her back to keep her from falling off. She did not resist but tucked her legs between his, which he almost called a near miracle. He rested his chin on top of her head and let her get more comfortable next to his body.

Happiness. Peace. Contentment. Joy.

How long had it been since another adult made him feel like he was finally home?

Sure, he got that from his daughter and his close-knit family. But not with a woman. Not with one whom he shared sex and a budding friendship. Not with one whom he worked and cooked and camped and slept beside. No. Never.

Her heart was broken over someone else she loved and lost. She was too young to shut the door on her future. Gage had every opportunity to fall in love with another woman after Dierdre died but he never experienced it. But now? He was feeling something. Something new and big.

And he chose a woman who willingly avoided love. Their friendship and mutual interests aside… she cuddled closer to him. As natural as working together, of course, they could cuddle.

What now?

How could he just go to sleep after that? This thing between them had officially started and yet, if Violet had any control over it, it also ended. *Violet.* Violet… *who?* Hers wasn't the most common name he'd ever heard for a girl. Was there a chance he could find her again in the valley? And if so, would she want him? All he needed was her name and phone number. But no. Nothing. She barely admitted her first name. She really didn't want this to go beyond the confines and safety of the mountain.

Gage lay there without moving the rest of the night, glad she was cuddled against him, especially for the softness and warmth. The chilly air crept in where his sleeping bag didn't cover his legs on one side, but it was worth it to be next to her.

Daylight eventually woke Gage up, and he was glad the tent canopy subdued most of the blaring rays. He lay there until his right arm got numb and his legs grew antsy from lack of movement. He had to get up even if he really didn't want to. His fear of never holding Vee again kept him locked in that position. One which, he had no doubt, would haunt him later today.

He gently rolled over and extricated his hands out from under her. Sitting up, he carefully rearranged the sleeping bag around her. He touched her face and hair. Slipping away, he found his sweats and sweatshirt, which he quickly pulled on before exiting the tent to take a piss. On his way back, he filled the coffee pot with coffee and water and started heating it. The morning sun had just crested over the rim of the eastern mountains and the light shone in soft sprays over the land. Such a lovely way to wake up. Even if he were overly tired from staying up most of the night, he felt alive and invigorated. He was also ravenous.

He found a skillet and cooked up an egg mix, adding enough for Violet. Glancing at his phone, he saw it was nearly nine-thirty, way past her usual wake-up hour. He carefully poured a cup of coffee and carried it to her. She was curled up in his bag with the pillow tucked under her head. Her hair was snarled in the plaid fabric of the travel pillow. Her face was also on the pillow. He looked at her eyelashes, which reminded him of a soft fan.

Leaning down, he squatted beside her, gently placing a strand of her hair behind her ear and rubbing her cheek. He set her coffee beside the cot on the makeshift table.

Her eyelids fluttered. She slowly turned her head and her eyes grew wider. Her gaze skittered to the left and then the right until she saw him. She put her hand beneath her and started to sit up. Gage moved back so her legs could swing forward. "Wake up, Sleeping Beauty, it's nine-forty-five. Thought you'd like to rise before lunchtime. And your horses are getting hungry too."

She nodded as he handed her the coffee cup. She stared up at him for a long moment as if his words made no sense to her, but finally took a long gulp of the coffee.

"I can't believe I slept this long."

He rose to his feet, sensing her cool tones were a clue of how things would go between them now. "Yeah. I'll step out and give you some space."

He turned and went outside to tend the morning camp-fire until she came out. No smiles. She actually looked grim. He all but rolled his eyes at seeing how predictable she was. Sex had been her idea and all that, but she was too worried now to act normal. Or happy. Or friendly.

He gave her plenty of space for awhile. He was more than willing to tolerate the discomfort and awkwardness. He should have predicted it. She started to prepare the horses' food. After they were fed, she returned to eat the meal Gage made for her. She ate without words and the quiet became a physical wall between them. When she finished, she set her dishes off to the side. Gage came up behind her and wrapped his arms around her. "Relax. Nothing has changed."

She jerked forward and shoved his hand off her. "We're not doing this. I told you. No relationship. No acts of affection. No morning coffee in bed… No."

"I was merely making a friendly gesture to the woman I spent the night with."

She ripped herself away from him as if she were a prisoner. "Fuck. We *fucked*. We didn't spend the night together or make love. I thought I made myself very clear about that. I can't—"

"Yep. I know. You can't do this. Or that." He kept his tone calm and personable, as innocuous as the weather report. He infuriated her even more when he dared to place two of his fingers on her lips as if he were shushing her. "Violet, why don't I take a walk? I think I'll go above camp. I enjoy the panoramic view across the valley after spending so much time down below the trees. You relax and have a normal morning until you get your bearings. Take your horses up to the pasture to graze. I'll see you later. Then we can talk."

He turned to go and her expression was one of surprise. She started to stutter with indignation that he dared to shush her, but stopped. His calm, rational words were something only a true friend might say. That started to resonate with her and he doubted she could argue with his sensible suggestion.

She needed lots of space, if only to calm down so she could act normal and remember how normal felt. She obviously, much to his disappointment, couldn't do that with him being there. To avoid having rude and crude verbal bombs lobbed at him—and for his own protection—he thought a walk was the best answer.

He simply sauntered out of camp, heading up the hillside across the creek. He went up and up, huffing and puffing within moments because that stretch of trail inside the cropping of trees was extremely steep. He walked pretty much directly above her camp, scaling the side of the mountain in some spots. Luckily, the long grasses and deep roots kept him steady. After about twenty minutes, he found himself high above the camp and treeline. He sat down on a rocky outcrop and turned to enjoy the view. He saw the valley nestled below the endless spikes of fir trees spearing the sky. The creek's roar shattered the otherwise unworldly silence. The mountain rose up a thousand feet from the base to the top, framed by the heavenly blue sky. The sight was awe-inspiring and breathtaking. Gage scanned the mountainside for animal activity and interesting rocks and brush.

Meanwhile, his heart tried to ignore her harsh words. They would not be allowed to fester. His entire body rejected them. How could he convince Violet not to reject him? Why would she rebuff something so natural that physically and emotionally arose between them? Even their friendship seemed in jeopardy now.

She was like an injured animal, baring her teeth at the kindest hand that only wanted to touch, soothe, comfort, help and fix anything that was wrong. He was unwanted simply because he was the next person to arrive after her worst heartache. But she wasn't ready or willing to allow any person to affect her psyche. Even if she really wanted it. He doubted she could overcome her mental repulsion at the idea, never mind what her body seemed willing to do.

He picked up a handful of gravel and started pitching the small pebbles down the mountain face. He hated knowing the facts. He clearly understood them now. He'd sensed it almost from the beginning with her. Yet he let himself fall in love all the same. He let himself care for her and desire her and have sex with her, knowing she would eventually dismiss him. She would spurn anything more from him. Even decent civility.

Gage clearly understood all of that going in and yet he chose to pursue it and allow it to unfold. He was setting himself up for the same heartache she seemed irretrievably mired in. Damn it.

He threw the pebbles harder, wrenching his shoulder in his effort to release his anger. He was trying not to feel or think about it, preventing it from being real. He had to fight it.

Sex. It was merely a physical release. Something necessary and wonderful... but damn! He was too old for games and drama. The only place he could take out his unreleased aggression was with the damn gravel. Over and over, he threw the tiny pebbles down the hill until his arm grew too fatigued.

After awhile, he heard the snorts and neighing of her horses. He caught a glimpse of them prancing out of the forest before heading up the trail towards the grazing pasture. Good. She would calm herself by doing her normal routine. He finally rose to his feet before tromping back to camp for lunch and a rest. He had to do some decompressing of his own.

Starting a fire, eating, staring at the embers and thinking about every sigh and gasp from the woman he'd watched naked and writhing underneath him wasn't the most healthy or productive pastime. It made him uncomfortable and he suddenly got an uncontrollable hard-on, which was completely unnecessary. It thoroughly annoyed him.

When the sun finally sank in the sky towards evening, he heard the clomping of her horses' hooves and their heavy breathing. Moments later, they flashed across the creek through the tree trunks, appearing above the trail. It seemed like the horses ran a gauntlet, only to be met with more trees. Kind of anticlimactic. But her gaze found him still lounging before the fire. He didn't rise or give her a warm, welcoming smile. He was not typical in his reaction. He wasn't mad but very annoyed. The emotional snub he got from her was still very much on his mind.

She dismounted and patted Peaches' flank. Taking Princess's lead rope, she pulled her into the corral before she let her loose. She unsaddled her mount and stashed all the tack in her usual spot. She was always thoroughly meticulous when it came to her horses and their tack. Always. He watched and waited. She obviously felt his eyes fastened on her because she kept slipping furtive glances his way.

He tried his best to ignore her small, tight ass in her jeans. An ass he remembered very well when he flexed his fingers and recalled how soft and warm it was.

When she cast a tight-lipped face at him, damn. His resolve started to crack. She looked so unsure and nervous. She released Peaches in the corral and paused to take a deep breath before she faced him.

Oh, for the love of all that was green. He really didn't expect her to be scared of him. He rose to his feet and crossed his arms over his chest, feeling as unsure as she looked.

Wondering what to do or say, Gage resorted to his habit of a lifetime: common courtesy. Normalcy. Light conversation.

"Have a nice ride, Violet?" He tested her name, which still felt odd to say. It didn't really match the face he knew.

She glanced at him and then turned away. "I… yes." She all but dragged her feet to walk closer to him. He sighed and jammed his hands into his jeans pockets. Monty came up with his tail wagging. It thumped against Gage's leg as he sat down. He took a moment to pet him before he was back to standing and staring at the only woman who could manage to tie him up in anxious knots.

She looked confused and almost scared. He turned toward the dying flames of the fire. With a deep sigh and a voice heavy of regret, he said, "Don't worry; I'll hike out tomorrow."

Her body stiffened and her gaze whipped up to his. "What?"

He rested his foot on the firepit rocks. "If you're going to say rude things to me and continue to act like this, I have no interest in staying any longer. It was fantastic sex. It happened. You asked for it. Now you're acting like it was wrong or dirty. Like it changed who we are. I don't need that.

I've never had a bad relationship with any woman and I don't need to start now."

Shocked into silence, she suddenly launched herself at him. Just like last night, but this time, they were fully clothed. She wrapped her arms around his waist and hugged him tightly. He reacted without a thought, dropping his leg and turning towards her. Luckily, he'd braced himself to receive her when she flew at him like a brick hitting his stomach. She clung to him and his hands finally held her, although he frowned at her brown-haired head now tucked so tightly against him. *What in the living fuck?* He waited a long moment, but she didn't release him. She clung to him harder. Finally, he dropped his hands to her shoulders, sliding them down her back and embracing her.

He felt her back muscles relaxing. He knew she was relieved he didn't fling her off him the way she'd reacted when he'd hugged her. "I'm sorry," she whispered. Her face and mouth were muffled by his sweatshirt. "Don't leave. Not... yet."

He didn't get her but that was nothing new. However, the two extremes of hot and cold perplexed his weary brain. So... yeah. Great. How could he resist her, when she was exactly the woman that he wanted? In so many ways. Too many to articulate. "Can we just be normal?"

"Not talk about it, you mean?"

"Yes."

"And never touch?"

"No. We can."

He sighed and nodded, gripping her tightly to him. "Violet, you're a goddamned handful."

She finally laughed. "I know. I'm sorry. But please don't leave."

"*Yet.* Right? Because you still won't tell me anything real about you. So this is all it is and ever will be. So you're only telling me not to leave *yet*."

"Yes. Please understand how hard this is for me, and yes, it's all I can offer you right now."

"But you still want to offer it to me? Now? Here?"

"Yes. Desperately. Even with my awkward behavior." He felt her body shuddering. "It's been so long since I felt these things. It's so good... but also overwhelming. I probably overreacted..."

"Yes, you did."

"Thanks for being the adult and walking away before I said terrible things I would have regretted and never meant to say. Thank you for letting me just be me."

He nudged her so she had to look up at him. "I'm actually pretty reasonable as an adult most of the time. So sure. You're welcome. I was just being my normal awesome self."

She finally smiled. "You are annoyingly mature, nice, funny and yeah... pretty awesome."

He squeezed her and lifted her off her feet. "You're not supposed to feel negative with a guy you're fucking."

He set her feet back on the earth and she winced. "Sorry, about that too. No. You made me feel the best way there is to feel and I know I'm spoiled but I should have realized it."

"You should have." Their gazes met and she smiled up at him. He returned it. The smile that was way overdue and which they should have exchanged this morning. Lowering his head, he planted a soft, compelling kiss on her mouth. She leaned toward him, tilting her head, and lifting up to her tiptoes. Yeah, she was right there and wanting him. She was even straining towards him. He lifted his head and caught her with her eyes shut and her mouth eagerly moving towards his. She blinked in surprise as a soft blush flushed her cheeks.

She was sweet and confusing. So hard to know. So easy

to care about. It was a strange juxtaposition he never encountered with a woman before. Not that he had a lot of women in his life that he cared for. He never fell in love before. He liked so many women. His three longest relationships fizzled out eventually but that was because he wasn't in love with them. He was careful to keep Andy away from his female companions for a long while. He feared if she got involved and it fizzled, it could be hard on her. Now that Andy was older, and much more cognizant of his private life, Gage didn't date much. Not until he felt an irresistible interest in another woman, would another one come to his home.

But the way he felt now was exactly what he'd been searching for.

He let her go. "I'm starving. How about dinner?"

She sighed behind him with a laugh. It lifted his heart. He liked her when she wasn't upset or worried. "Yes. I'll make it now."

He snorted. "That loses its impressive impact when all you gotta do is heat up water." If she weren't so goddamned strange and remote, he might have liked to tease and goad her into coming to his house for a gourmet dinner that he would personally cook for her. But he let it go. Unwilling to scare her off again today, his sole intention was to see if this could move forward.

They ate dinner and their mutual contentment filled him with renewed hope. When the night fell, Gage simply flopped on his cot and turned the light on as he asked, "Well... how do we do this? Stay separate like we are? Or push them together? What do you prefer?"

She didn't glance his way but she responded, "Push them together."

He nodded and got up to move the table and his cot. The edges created a godawful ridge for them to navigate over.

LEANNE DAVIS

But hell. Gage was happy for the human contact and didn't care if he had a freaking ledge jutting into his back.

Although they only had one more condom, there were plenty of things he wanted to do to her tonight. He hoped he could encourage her to do some innovative things to him too, things for which they didn't need anything more than their bodies.

DESPITE HOW GLORIOUS the three days were, finally, he had to go.

"Stay one more day?" she begged him hopefully.

"Give me your name and then we could just meet up again at home."

Her head shook. He sighed. "I can't. I have other obligations. But maybe I could come back here on Labor Day weekend. I have three days off. And if you're still around here…"

"I'll definitely be here that long."

"So…?" She smiled. "So meet me then."

He returned her smile with a tight-lipped one of his own. "I hate leaving you."

"I'll be okay. Remember? Loaded gun. GPS locator. I'm awesome too."

He slipped an arm around her waist and kissed her mouth and then her forehead. "You are. You're really awesome. This was so beyond anything I ever experienced or expected."

She patted his stomach. "No one could have predicted this happening. Especially out here. So that's the truest statement I know."

He started to let her go. They held hands until the very last moment when he finally let their fingers slide free. Leaning over, he picked up his daypack, into which he'd jammed all of his stuff, and gave Monty a long rub goodbye with kind words of love. With a glance back, he observed the woman whom he least wanted to leave. But damn it. She refused to let him in.

"Goodbye, Violet."

"See ya, Gage." Her smile was big and her voice was normal. But her eyes? In her eyes he saw a sense of longing.

GAGE MISSED VIOLET. But damn. Hearing Andy's sweet voice again was glorious to his ears and very much needed. Andy was as vital to him as air and food. She was his source of survival. His love for his daughter inspired, motivated and sustained him. He called her as soon as he drove out of the trailhead and had cell reception.

"Did you find her? The mountain girl?"

"I did. She helped me build the trail."

"Does she like you?"

Oh, hell yeah. In so many ways he could never tell his daughter. "She does. I think we're friends. But she lets this sadness inside her about something limit her interactions. She refuses to talk about it and she won't even tell me her last name so there's no way I can find her."

"That's so... cool."

Gage frowned into the phone. "What the heck is cool about it?"

"She sounds really fierce. Like no one else. Living on the mountain alone?! And refusing to tell you her name. What a wild story."

If only Andy knew. It was certainly the wildest story of his life. One that could probably break his heart. Why the fuck did he volunteer for more suffering? How could he know if she'd even be there on Labor Day weekend? She could easily disappear and he'd never find her. God, what a kick in the guts and his heart to imagine that possibility.

"I can't wait to see you. Tell me everything." He redirected his thoughts to the real love of his life and dropped back into reality. To the life that he truly cherished. And within moments, Andy had him fully connected to that life again.

IT GOT SO QUIET. The camp felt like an empty stadium, lacking all the cheers and yelling. Freaked out by the quiet solitude, Violet listened to her horses stomping, the splashes of the creek and the song of an occasional bird. She felt so lonely. So damn lonely.

She didn't cry. She vowed she would not tear up and cry about something that never existed. After Gage left, she took her horses to graze in another pasture that was much further away. She walked until her legs were burning, going up and down the mountain in her effort to work off her excess energy. A new sadness. Fine. So what if she missed him? Being up there just wasn't the same anymore. Not without him.

But he said he would come back. So what? What if he did?

She needed to get out for a shower and to restock her supplies. She decided to leave tomorrow because she couldn't stand it there without him another day. The night only made it worse. Cold. Dark. Tears. Preston. Gage. Guilt ripped her apart. Choking on her sobs and missing Preston much more than before, she awoke from a nightmare. She saw Preston's neck being broken by his fall. She found herself in a cold sweat, feeling miserable.

CHAPTER 10

"OH, MY GOD, I missed you so much, baby girl." Gage swung Andy around in a full circle, uncaring if she were too old or too cool now for it. He tossed her around like he did when she was a little girl and squealed with joy.

She did not squeal with joy now, just annoyance. "Daaaadddd." She hissed his name. "Put me down!" she ordered as she swatted his shoulder.

He did, grinning goofily at her. She rolled her eyes. "You like me entirely too much."

He laughed as he grabbed her rollaway suitcase and carryon. "I do. And maybe next year I'll go with you."

"No!" Falling into step beside him, she was smiling also. She liked him too. He knew that. They chatted and she giggled with the stories he told her. She described all her activities over the last few weeks. It felt more like forever to Gage. Never again would she be away for so long, he decided. Well, maybe after she grew up and went to college, but only then.

"So are we going out or am I making your favorite dinner?"

185

"Let's go out."

He shut the back door on her luggage and jumped into the front seat. "Good. Tomorrow the whole family is coming over to welcome you home. So I'll make your favorite chicken and pesto pizza."

"I can't wait."

At dinner, she asked, "Dad... have you thought seriously about getting a horse? Did you find out anything about it?"

He did not. It completely slipped his mind. He spent a few weeks with two horses and the woman who brought them, but he never even considered getting one. Not even for Andy. "Andy..."

"Can I take riding lessons, then? What about just doing that? I love it, Dad. I swear I could become a... a famous horse woman."

"Maybe it seemed like so much fun because it was so new and rare."

"Dad, really. I mean it. I love everything about it. Please? Can't I just take a few lessons to prove how much I love it to you?"

He sighed as her big-eyed stare melted his heart. "Okay. I promise to consider it..."

"Look what I found." She shoved a piece of paper at him. He sighed as he scanned the flyer she proffered.

"They teach horseback riding right here. Down in the valley... What? Only a half hour away? Come on, Dad... Please? Please... they're well-known and reputable..."

He tried to listen as he read the information and finally shushed her. The flyer advertised a horse camp being offered by the Rydell River Ranch, across from River's End. He knew the small town, although he'd never been there in person. No one could miss the giant spread of pastures, rail fences, and outbuildings across the river from the main highway.

"I've heard of it. But this camp is already over for the summer."

"Right. The charity camp for the kids in foster care around the state is over. Cool, huh? But read the bottom. There is a number there for private horseback riding lessons. Dad, please? I swear, I'll do it forever. I'll quit track. I'll—"

He sighed as he leaned over and ruffled her hair. "You don't have to quit anything. Let's give them a call. We'll see what they offer and then we'll see if we can squeeze it into our busy schedule and how much it costs and all that. So I can't give you a yes, not yet… just a maybe…"

Gage knew Andy only heard "yes" in her excited brain because she gave him a bear hug and got out of her chair to do so.

His acquiescence instantly turned her into a willing, happy and excited dinner companion. That wasn't why he did it. Horseback riding was a healthy pastime, and he couldn't foresee anything bad from her learning more about it. It was safer for Andy to know how to handle the huge animals properly anyway. Better to start early than later on, and he intended to provide her with the proper instruction.

He called the number on the flyer two days later after a big family dinner. Several long talks with Andy about kayaking on the river while lounging in front of the TV detailed her wonderful vacation. Oh, the luxuries he missed. Yeah, he mostly just missed his couch and bed and TV. A lot.

Being back, however, he missed Violet.

Seeking a form of distraction, Gage finally called the Rydell River Ranch. He was transferred to Erin Rydell with whom he scheduled a private lesson for beginners and *voila!* They had an appointment the following Saturday at nine o'clock. Andy was so excited, she didn't complain about the early morning hour. She was bouncing with eagerness and all but shrieking with joy. And oh. The unconcealed displays of affection Gage got for making the arrangements.

That Saturday, they dressed for the occasion and left early. Driving under a sign that spanned the entrance of the dusty driveway with the words, *Rydell River Ranch Est. 1802* overhead, the gate they saw before them was locked with razor wire all around it. They weren't kidding about privacy and security. Erin Rydell, one of the owners, told Gage to press the red button on the display. She promised to leave his name with the security guard so he could get in. Sure enough, he held up his ID to prove who he was before the security detail allowed him entrance. Overkill? Erin claimed that some criminal activity occurred on the ranch in the past so they responded by installing extra security. He followed the gently weaving dusty road. Andy already had her nose pressed to the passenger window as she stared at the dozen or so horses when they came into view. Some stood right at the white rail fence. Others gathered in groups to graze, their huge heads down, a tranquil sight against the open fields, white rail fencing, and brown rolling mountains beyond.

They came to a fork in the road, at which Erin told Gage to bear right. The horse stables were located next to a large indoor arena and guest resort. Erin said she would meet them out front at nine a.m.

Gage drove past more fields. The ones without horses had green carpets of alfalfa growing as far as he could see. On the left, the river shone as brightly as a newly minted coin in the rising sun. A series of small, quaint, adorable cabins hugged the river. He saw lovely landscaped and well-manicured lawns, walkways, fountains, benches and swings. They had a main playground, a swimming pool and other facilities. What he assumed was the check-in office and gift shop occupied a smaller building on the dusty road. Once inside the resort, Gage noticed it was paved in some spots and had gravel in others. A cloud of thick dust followed him as he pulled up a small incline towards a gigantic building: the covered horse arena.

He saw a short, dark-haired woman, whose hair was woven into a braid. She waved as he pulled in. Gage waved back and Andy bounded out like a wild ferret, she was so excited to be there. He chuckled and shrugged at Erin when Andy kept literally bouncing from one foot to the other.

"You must be Andy," Erin said and Gage nodded as Erin gave Andy a huge smile. "I'm Erin. I heard you were recently bitten by the horse bug and want to learn how to ride."

"I was and I do. I went to the most awesome camp where we spent the week learning how to do the basics, so I know a few things. And I love it. Every single moment... and I'd love to get as good as those people that can jump onto their horse bare back and start galloping around."

Erin's broad smile was generous as she watched the thrilled teen. She wasn't the least bit annoyed. Gage wondered how often she must witness that much eagerness and excitement. At least it didn't jade her. "Well, eventually we'll get into the galloping, but you'll definitely get on a horse's back today. And you'll be all the more amazing for it. Follow me."

They entered the arena amidst a series of oohs and ahhs from Andy as her gaze whipped right and left. So did Gage's, to be honest. The elaborate operation impressed him at once by its sheer size and volume. A small group was gathered in the center arena. They were members of the Morgan Horse Riding Association, Erin explained. Pausing for a moment to watch them prance their magnificent horses proudly, Andy's mouth dropped open as she passionately exclaimed, "I want to do that!"

Gage groaned. He could only imagine all the time and money it would take to get her to that stage; not to mention his fear if she did manage to get that far. Erin led them through the stables, past the individual stalls. Some were empty. Others not. She said that many locals boarded their horses during the year, and some of the others were for the horses when they were temporarily using the arena. "We have to employ an entire schedule and management team just for the arena. I don't get too involved with that. My husband and I run the horse rescue at the other end of the ranch. I still give private riding lessons because I love doing it so much. But I'm giving you this little tour just to show you all the opportunities and services we offer. If you're still interested in lessons, either private or group, we give them in here when the weather turns ugly. For now, though, we prefer to use the outside arenas. That's why I asked you to come so early, mainly to avoid the heat." She had such a great smile. Both warm and shy at once.

As they were walking, Erin pointed to the restaurant above them. The walls were made of glass to allow the diners to watch the arena while they ate. "If you're interested, I'll get you a coupon for a discount; you get half off your dinners if you come for the show."

"We're very interested." Andy decided for both of them. "What kind of show is it?"

Erin gave her the most indulgent smile and all of her attention. "We have trained the horses to do tricks with both riders and objects. It's pretty incredible stuff. My husband trains them... with my help, of course," she said as she winked and smiled. "But we attract lots of professional trainers as well as performers. Every weekend night, we try to offer the audience a completely different experience, and judging by their reactions, most of the people are pretty amazed by it."

"Can the horses get hurt? Or be humiliated? You know,

like when the circus exploits animals with no regard for their best interest?"

Startled at her indignation, Gage warned her with his tone, "*Andy.*"

Erin shook her head. "I love answering questions and your curiosity should be encouraged and rewarded. Always ask questions if it's about an animal's wellbeing, I'm for it a hundred percent. Since we run a horse rescue, we're especially sensitive to animal welfare. We only show the horses that are well adjusted mentally and in good health otherwise. Those are the ones we choose to train for the shows. And they have to be comfortable with it too. During their training and perfor- mances, they are also monitored and evaluated. We've had to retire more than a few because Jack or Ian or I realize they don't like the attention or the crowds or whatever the reason may be. We're as careful as we can possibly be. We insist our staff communicate anything they might happen to notice as well."

"Wow. I want to do that too!" Andy shouted as she whipped around. "Dad. Can we come tonight? Wait... Is there a show tonight?" Andy's head swiveled between Erin and Gage.

Erin smiled at Gage and shrugged. He shrugged back with the same resignation, and Erin replied, "Yes. Actually, there is a show tonight."

"Then yes, perhaps we'll come for the dinner and show."

"This is the greatest place ever." Andy purred, bouncing for joy again.

Erin nodded. "I fully agree, Andy. From the very first time I set foot on the ranch. Thirty odd years ago."

"You weren't raised here?"

"Nope. I married Jack Rydell and he and his brothers owned it. Never touched a horse until I was twenty-six and I was totally terrified of them. So it's never too late, and you're so much younger than I was." Giving Gage a contrite look, she added, "If that's okay with your dad…"

"It is. I've never seen her so excited and interested in something."

Erin's grin stretched wider. "I felt like that from the very start too. I was really scared, but also intrigued. I've always credited horses for saving my life. They gave me a direction and confidence and skills… so I really love them for that and I love doing this. Especially teaching. Showing someone who already loves horses how to connect with them safely and inspire their passion even further, to a career or who knows? It's very gratifying."

They walked all around the entire, centrally located, oval, dirt-and-sand arena. The waist-high walls were open so they could hear the riders and horses. A set of bleachers occupied the other side, and a handful of people were seated in them now.

They were just about to turn and head out the doors when Erin mentioned the different types of horses. Gage eyed the wall beside the main door. It featured framed pictures from halfway up to the top. There were dozens of horses and riders. He swiftly scanned through most of them. Some were sitting on horses, performing jumps or barrel-racing and others were just standing beside their mounts. There were some trick horses on the wall also. One showed a horse lifting its front hoof onto a huge, blue ball with the proud rider grinning at the camera. He looked at the next photo where the horse was bowing. The next held a leg out as though it were tapping a rhythm or something. Gage glimpsed the rider… and instantly froze.

Violet?!

The rider was Violet. He was sure of it. He blinked and stepped closer to the wall. Above his head, he spotted the framed photo of Princess, which he could have recognized anywhere. Standing beside her and wearing a helmet and a professional riding outfit while grinning at the camera, was a brown-haired, green-eyed, beautiful girl. With a spray of freckles. And a smile like the sun shining.

Violet.

He never witnessed that big of a smile on her face, but he had no doubt she was Violet.

The horses. He remembered how well she handled them. He'd witnessed it. She was the reason he came there. Violet exhibited unrestrained confidence. If riding horses could build that kind of confidence, Gage would certainly encourage his girl to learn how. Fuck. And there she was.

There she was.

The sight of Violet flabbergasted Gage. Speechless and slightly dizzy, he stared in disbelief at the woman he longed to know more about, especially her current location. Inside the Rydell's arena.

He marveled and stared, his brain spinning. He ignored what his daughter was chattering about as a tunnel-like effect overtook his brain. Staring at her picture, Gage willed Violet to appear, from the picture to him.

He couldn't believe he found her. He almost wilted with relief. He had to resist the urge to close his eyes and sigh, thereby demonstrating his utter shock. He found Violet. Here. At the biggest horse ranch in the entire valley. For miles and miles. Of all the towns. He'd never seen another place like it. So of course, his horse lover, Violet, was here.

Did she work here at some point? The picture younger than she was now. Although he never asked her, Gage assumed she was in her mid-twenties. The picture was less than that. There was a wild zaniness to her smile. A cocky, brashness that she lacked now; but let's face it, those things often get lost as people age. Youth belongs to the self-assured. Life is black and white without all the shades of gray that it eventually becomes. Before adult responsibilities and unpaid bills make people compromise their preferences. As dreams recede to the reality of making money and affording rent, food and raising a child. That photo was taken years ago. But it was clearly Violet.

A lead. A start. Maybe he wouldn't totally lose her after all. His heart hammered with joy and his palms sweated at the possibility of finding her. But the chances of actually finding her were pretty slim. He simply stumbled onto her photograph.

What the hell could he do about it? She forbade him from finding her. She insisted her choice was *not* to be with him. So finding her wasn't exactly a win for Gage. She had the toughest shell to crack of anyone he ever met. This couldn't change it or be a welcome discovery for her... but maybe she would someday change her mind... Maybe she would want him. Maybe there was hope. Something to grasp and cling to.

"...Some of our different trainers and performers over the years." Erin's voice could be heard again. He was still transfixed on Violet's image.

"This... this one of Violet... I've never seen it before." Gage hoped to pull something out of Erin Rydell, praying she knew who Violet was.

"Oh? I'm sure you haven't. That was taken four years ago now. It's hard to believe how long it's been since then. A lot has changed in that time. You know her then?"

"Yeah... she's what inspired me to come here actually. And why I encouraged Andy to pursue the horseback riding lessons... Violet's so good at it."

"My niece is one of the best. It's weird that some of the other Rydell kids have no interest in horses. They were all raised here with horses and plenty of access to them but some just don't care about horses. Some even hate them and roll their eyes, avoiding them at all costs. Others, like Violet, just naturally prefer to be around them. The same with Jack and Ian and me."

Violet *Rydell*. So that's why she wouldn't tell him her name. Rydell was instantly recognizable. Violet. She took quite a risk in telling him that. He wondered how many Violets lived within a two hundred-mile radius?

"Violet is… I can't remember who she said her parents were… not Ian, but…"

"She's Shane and Allison's daughter."

"Right. Duh. Hard to forget the parents of her and her sisters."

"Well, when you name them all after your favorite flowers, what do you expect?" she snickered.

Which was exactly why she wouldn't tell him her sisters' names. Fuck. It all made sense now. From a three-minute conversation. He wanted to thank Erin, but that would have been weird and strange given what should have been a casual conversation, at least, to her. It meant just about everything, however, to Gage.

"It's kind of cute," he muttered, grasping for something to say. He didn't know their actual names, but he soon would. Rydell River Resort was the biggest employer in the valley. He'd figure out who Shane and Allison were. And the names of their flower-children. And how Violet fit into it.

"How do you know Violet?"

"I met her hiking, near her camp."

She rolled her eyes. "Yeah, those trips just about drive her parents crazy. But I think it's the only way she can get through the month of August, you know?"

"Yes. Yep. I totally agree. I can understand their worry though."

"I haven't had a chance to go up there in a year or more."

The Rydells built the camp there. It wasn't her camp, but her family's. They'd probably been camping there for a century.

That explained the permanent appearance of it. The old relics up there. Stuff that he had to pretend he knew nothing about.

But now, he knew something important.

August. What was it about August? Obvious conclusion: the death of her loved one. The boyfriend she still claimed she was in love with. How did that relate to camping up on a mountain all alone?

Erin started for the big barn doors that were now open, letting the morning light and warmth inside. Gage followed her and leaned his arms on the top of the fence. He watched and listened when Erin started the lesson with Andy. She first asked Andy how much she knew about horses and her brief riding history. Then they brought out a smaller horse, and Erin said she was named Sheba, a gentle, easygoing mare. She was a favorite for beginners. Erin told Andy about the need for brushing and grooming, teaching her all the proper techniques and defining the new words. She even learned how to tie secure knots.

"You need to always safely secure your horse so they don't hurt themselves, you, others, or even neighboring horses..." Erin carefully explained all the reasons behind the instruction. But she spent more time with Andy using hands-on techniques, advising her of all the intricacies in horse care and husbandry. She showed her how to properly saddle a mount and cinch the girth. "You won't get all of this the first time, but it provides a good basic introduction and with practice..."

And the next thing Gage knew, Andy was sitting on the horse. Her smile grew as wide as her face. He lifted his phone and captured twenty shots in an instant: Andy walking, turning, and following Erin's horse, falling into step behind her. The constant instructions, telling her to stop and go. Erin told her what to do and then allowed Andy to try it.

The hour zipped by and when it ended, Andy was sold. Gage recognized her genuine enthusiasm despite the wide-eyed infatuation; he knew this was far more than a passing stage. She loved everything about it. The ranch. The horses. The people. The setting. The gigantic arena. The barns, and best of all, the huge assortment of horses.

Andy adored Erin. She loved Erin for her skill, knowledge and natural affinity for horses.

Damn. Gage suspected she'd love Violet too, and for all the same reasons.

He jolted upright at the passing thought. No. Oh, hell no. Imagining his teenage daughter meeting his… what? His woman who wouldn't even tell him her last name? Let alone, her address or phone number. No chance to text her. And here he was thinking how Violet and Andy might get along?

Gage and Andy both flopped down hard onto the truck seats, after many thanks to Erin and promises for next week. On the drive home, Andy gushed about the experience. She was so in love. With the place. The people. The horses. The feeling. Coupon in hand, they planned to return that night.

More than anxious to get home now, Gage planned to do some research. He fought the urge to pull his truck next to one of the buildings and just start asking about the names he already had. But that was too odd, not to mention unwanted by *Violet Rydell*.

How old was she? It never entered his brain. His daughter prattled on and Gage thought they were maybe a decade apart. That would be strange. Not what he pictured.

He shook his head. No. He was getting way too far ahead of what might be.

"I'm going to run over to Sienna's for the afternoon. Okay?" After entering their house, Andy came out an hour later. She was showered and wearing makeup, going down the street to see her best friend.

"Sure. Text me when you get there. Shall I pick you up there for the show?"

She kissed his cheek. "Perfect. See you then. Bye."

"Bye, honey." Ashamed at the relief that coursed through him, Gage nearly celebrated. She was gone. He could feel free to search and possibly find out who the heck this woman was whom he'd grown so stupidly close to, but was still so far from knowing.

The moment the front door shut, Gage immediately sat down at his laptop and clicked on the search box, entering *Violet Rydell.*

He found links to so many Rydells. That would keep him busy for awhile. He hoped to get an overview of her life and her family.

But the third hit down showed Violet's name. He clicked on it and read an online newspaper article reported by *The Pattison Gazette*, dated August eighth two years ago. Sitting back, he stared without any reaction at his computer screen.

Oh, God… Damn. Poor Violet. Chilled to the marrow in his bones, Gage stared at the pictures. He first saw the same one of her that he'd spotted in the arena. Then he saw her fiancé.

The story was straightforward. While performing together inside the Rydell River Ranch arena for a crowd of fifty, someone shot off a gun. Turned out to be a drunk celebrating a bachelor party. The accidental gunshot echoed in the metal-sided building and spooked Preston's horse, causing it to throw Preston into the side wall. He slammed into it, head first, snapping his neck before falling dead to the ground.

And Violet, his fiancée, was right there beside him all the while, witnessing all of it.

Gage's Violet.

Sadly, Violet saw her fiancé's neck snap right before her

own eyes. Considering how much of a shock it must have been, Gage gave her kudos for even venturing near another horse. What happened after that? How did she survive? What did she do? Where did she live? Was she at home still?

August. Violet must have hated to spend August here. That was what drove her up to the camp and why she stayed for that length of time there. She probably went there to grieve in solitude until Gage popped up, out of nowhere. No wonder she seemed so skittish. She still was, and in odd ways that Gage never expected. She suffered more than most women her age. Not many lose a loved one at such a young age. Compounded by the fact that she witnessed all of it; it occurred at her family home; inside the performance arena.

Oh, damn.

What could he do with this latest revelation?

He scooted forward, growing terribly interested in her sad history. He had to know more about the Rydells. He read about the types of horses, and the brothers, along with miscellaneous wedding announcements and births. He read all about the huge fire. They managed to save the horses, but lost their family home along with numerous outbuildings. There were more articles describing the plans for a resort. Then the charity work they did with Shield Shelter, a foundation in Everett that helped plan activities for foster children. For decades, they transformed the children's summers by offering them a stay at the Rydell River Ranch. Plenty of feel-good stories and interviews followed.

He read other news stories about the horse rescue and there were lots of quotes and information about one special Rydell. Jack. Erin's husband. Being central to the rescue, Jack was all over the website and Gage had more than enough information about him. He saw photos of faces that matched the names. He knew Jack, Ian and Joey. Then… he saw Shane.

Violet's dad. The biker guy. Not what he expected. Violet

was a tiny horse woman. So no. Shane was huge. He used to run Rydell Rides, which was now under Iris Larkin's ownership. *Iris.* Sister number two. Larkin had plenty of information to browse through. A billionaire family named Larkin added the golf course to the Rydell holdings.

They were impressive as individuals as well as a family.

He found a Lillian… was she a sister? Sounded like a flower, but not quite… maybe.

Allison. Violet's mom was a tutor for dyslexic students. She wrote several articles as an advocate for the subject. That was something. Then the mention of her daughter, Rose. Aha! Rose, the oldest sister. There was so much more. But his brain was overloaded for now.

He shut the laptop with a snap and got up; he needed to move. He had to fix something. Accomplish something. The lawn needed mowing. He dragged out the mower and bag before starting it up. The engine didn't sound right. Was the damn filter clogged up again? Yes. Yep. He'd just take it apart and fix it.

And he did. After two hours and a trip to the hardware store for parts, he managed to mow his yard. That took an hour. He liked the lines parallel and his younger sister, Greta, always teased him about how anal he was over his yard.

One glance from the street filled him with the flush of pride. Yeah. He should have been proud. It was exquisite. The single-story house was cedar-sided and clear-stained, with a red metal roof and door. A three-car garage with a driveway, and a walkway to the double entry front door. The roof sheltered the front with an overhang. A bench and seasonal flowers and decorations made it a welcoming entry. The lawn stayed green from all the care he put into it. The sprinklers were on timers and he lined the walkways with bark beds. A large island was featured in the middle with various bushes and trees that Gage found and planted with pride.

The backyard was the same. Having long outgrown the swing set and toys, Andy didn't care a fig when Gage replaced it with a water feature. He dug a small pond and filled it with a tinkling fountain and goldfish. It was lovely. They enjoyed the summer twilight as they grabbed a final glimpse of the sunset over their flat yard. Watching the sun sink below far-off jagged mountains was always a treat. There were other houses and the view wasn't as rural as it could have been, but it was usually quiet. Now a mower was buzzing. A car lazily drove past. There was nothing unpleasant or uncomfortable about where they lived or the life they shared. It was great. They had enough money to live comfortably and an amazing house and yard. He loved it. And so did Andy. Happy in school and her extracurricular activities, he was glad to see her confidence expanding. She had the usual teenage issues. But they were nothing insurmountable. He had his parents and other family members close by who stayed involved and they all got along.

There was nothing missing in Gage's life.

Except a woman. A companion for him.

He found one who was irreparably traumatized and hurt so what good did that do him? What hope could there be?

He tried to reconnect with all the things that formerly occupied his time, energy and thoughts. Before Violet, he was satisfied and his life interested him. He wasn't looking for anything more. He didn't want anything more. But since Violet Rydell kept taking over his thoughts and worries, he was at her mercy. How was she? Should she be by herself?

Would she ever smile again like she did in that picture hanging in the arena?

That slammed his guts hard. He never saw her smile that big even once when she was with him. And they had some seriously fun times together.

A sharp stab? Jealousy? Of whom? The dead guy? He

shuddered at his own shallowness. But yeah, it was the dead guy. Oh, damn.

Now what?

Finally, it was almost time to get Andy and go to the very location that he no longer wanted to. The last place Violet smiled. It resonated with her presence even if it seemed to have no connection to her now. It still felt like it did.

After showering, Gage threw on slacks and a shirt before he left to get Andy. Her presence helped ease the moment. They ordered huge hamburgers with steak fries that were mouthwatering. Then they sat down in the bleachers and waited. A woman appeared with a headset hooked into a sound system. She proceeded to give a history of the ranch and showed a photo of how it used to be. No more than a little, wooden-topped arena that burned up in the great fire of '14.

Andy was enthralled at the forty-five-minute show. It was spectacular. And Gage felt stupid that he'd been so close and never came before. He promised to bring his parents and his sisters and their husbands and kids. Andy couldn't wait to show off her new favorite place to hang. The food was decent too. Crap nutrition. Yeah. But what about Violet?

No. No reason to tell anyone.

He didn't know what lay ahead in the future, but there was no doubt he'd continue coming to her ranch. There was the ghost of a chance she'd see him.

He had to go back to the mountain.

As the show ended and the applause thundered, it shook the stands. All Gage could think about was going back to the mountains. Back to Violet. He had to see her again if there was any chance for them… here.

What about Andy? He never left her for the company of a woman. He could just tell her the truth, and *she'd die*, that was Andy's wording, to know the girl in the mountains was a

Rydell family member. This wonderful ranch. Her new fascination.

And his.

But what about Violet? Now, everything about her and his time with her was different. New. Intriguing. Deep. Like they'd been together for years, not weeks. It was new, yet old. Such a weird situation.

Gage had to go back to her just to see if he couldn't... what?

He still didn't know, but it was something.

He'd make plans to go. Labor Day was on September eighth this year. School didn't start until the tenth. So he could go. He could leave Andy with his parents.

He'd bribe her with extra horseback riding lessons. His mom wouldn't mind taking her to them. He was sure of that. As long as he notified them in plenty of time.

Nodding to himself, his brain awhirl with so many things to do, and names he needed to contact... What would she be like when he saw her again? What would her reaction be? Should he bother to go?

Yes, and he would go.

CHAPTER 11

IOLET RAPIDLY WENT DOWNHILL in the two weeks she spent without Gage. She felt lonelier than she could remember. Freaked out by it, she packed up the horses and rode down the trail, loading them into the horse trailer at the trailhead and driving into town. She stabled the horses with an old high school buddy who also let her shower and crash for the night. She went to the store the next day and stocked up on fresh supplies. With the horses rested and overfed, she hauled her supplies back into camp. She didn't go home. Not to the ranch. She just didn't want to. Not in August. She needed a break from her family and their overbearing sympathy and concern. Plus, if she checked in, even temporarily, they'd find it harder to let her go off by herself again. Any physical proximity would prevent her from returning to camp. So she merely called them and avoided the entire scenario: her dad's insistence she stay home with them. Her mom's love and hugs and sympathetic eyes. Her sisters' unmasked concern.

Claustrophobic. Violet could not stand so much sympathy. Yes, she'd watched her fiancé snap his neck. She heard it. Witnessed it. Dreamt about it. Her nightmares relived it often. And no one could significantly help her forget it or get past it.

So, naturally, she didn't want to go home yet.

Refreshed for camping after a short break, she fully intended to banish Gage Sullivan from her experience. She recalled how much she liked being alone, isolated, in total solitude. But she was not lonely before. That was the magic key.

She fell back into her routine. She explored more of the area by taking hikes up to other peaks. She climbed many mountains she never did before. They were exhausting and primarily on uneven terrain, which did the trick: leaving her in a state of exhaustion most nights.

She didn't dream. She didn't cry. She didn't smile.

She didn't think about Preston… or Gage.

But she knew exactly when the Friday before Labor Day weekend arrived. And she wondered, no… she *hoped* to see him and hated herself for it. For that irrepressible hope. For another man. For his company, companionship, conversation, care… and sex. Most of all, she hated that.

But she still hoped for it.

She missed it. She longed for him to show up. She doubted he'd return. Not after he got back to his normal life. He wouldn't care about her. She'd soon become a distant memory. A good lay. A wonderful fantasy.

Why couldn't she believe that?

Gage? No, it didn't fit him.

Finally, the sun began to set. She dipped into her newly stocked food supply and prepared a real roast with fresh vegetables over the fire. A complete meal. She let it simmer and the aroma was mouth-watering and homey. She sipped some cold milk from her grocery run. Living the life of luxury. She tipped her glass in a toast to her lonely fire. Yeah, not exactly what most would call luxury.

But what did it matter? No one else she knew was anything like her.

She sighed and turned and then... she froze solid.

How did she not hear him? See him? Sense him?

So thrilled with her simmering stew and cold milk, Violet failed to realize she wasn't alone.

He was standing right there.

Gage.

Right there at the top of the trail where it entered her camp. There he stood. Staring back at her. Colors turned to shadows over the trees as the sun continued to disappear behind the peaks. He looked back at her, but his gaze was different. Deeper. His eyes seemed softer and more caring too. He didn't smile. His mouth was set in a tight line. He tilted his head and slowly reached up to pull the shoulder strap of his pack off, releasing both sides. He let the entire thing flop to the ground, never taking his eyes off hers.

No reaction from Violet. But the change in his look intrigued her. She couldn't interpret what it meant or remember him being so intense and... what? Emotional?

A flood of emotions seemed to flow from him towards her and worse... she felt it too.

Her mouth dropped half open and she forgot to smile. Or say hi. Instead, they stared as if they hadn't seen each other for many years. Not merely days. Weeks. Two, to be exact.

It felt like forever. Way too long.

When she blinked, he seemed to lose the connection. Taking the four steps that separated them, he was on her. He swooped her up against him, his hands wrapping around her and his mouth claiming hers in seconds. She let out a startled but happy exclamation as she rose up to her toes and crashed against him.

He bent her backward as his mouth ate hers. He kissed her long and deep and hard. For minutes. Breathlessly. Their hearts literally pounding in their chests. Oh, damn.

Damn!

He finally let her go and rested his forehead on hers. She stared up at him even though they were close and she touched his cheek. "I didn't think you'd come back."

"I had to," he answered simply. Then his mouth devoured hers again. And again. She finally let a laugh escape that was happy and carefree, almost girlish. When was the last time she felt like laughing? With anyone or anything? Years. Since Preston died, of course.

She held his face in her hands and let her gaze caress his features. She tried to memorize them. He was so dear to her. Too precious. Considering how briefly they knew each other and lacking any future together, Violet suddenly realized that only now matters. Today. The present. That's it. That was the only guarantee anybody had, the present moment.

She studied him and a smile banished her frowns. Her sadness. Her reticence. "I have milk."

He blinked as happy surprise lit up his eyes. "Did something drastically change while I was gone?"

It took her a moment to get his meaning. Then she snickered and slapped his arm as she let him go and grinned. So did he. "I didn't mean inside my breasts, you pervert. I bought some at the store."

He finally released her after committing every angle and feature of her face to memory. She doubted she was that good to look at.

"I see something simmering too. Did you cook, Vee?"

She nodded cheekily. "Up here I do. I made a roast and

vegetables with seasoning and you'll close your eyes when you taste it and think you're the king."

He let her go again and she stepped back to check on it. He began warming his hands on the fire. "You're the queen out here; I'm no more than a lowly peasant."

"Ha. Why did you call me Vee?"

"I missed it. I missed you."

Why was he always so honest? He never hesitated to admit whatever he was thinking or feeling. She didn't doubt him either, no matter what she asked. He always answered with the truth, and if he didn't want to reply, he'd freaking tell her that too. He was transparent at all times, but he also held himself back long enough to be intriguing and interesting. Violet wondered if she'd ever tire of getting to know all about him.

He had such soft, inviting lips. Hot lips. He could melt her panties with his lips. Yeah, she was hot for him, and eager for so much more.

She pressed her lips together before she said, "I'm really glad you came."

He turned back to her, and his gaze was blistering. Scorching. Intense. The opposite of a moment ago when it was mostly friendship. "Are you? Or just glad to have someone to talk to?"

She stepped back. "Yes, Gage, I'm glad it's you. Only you. You know that..." She wrapped her arms around him. "You see where I am. How I live..."

"Right now. Then you go back home at some point and I assume you return to normalcy... right?"

"Yes. Whatever you call normalcy."

He turned and stomped towards her, taking her face in his hands, pressing his body so close she had to lift her neck back to see him. He leaned down and touched her lips with his. Long. Connected. Demanding. "Tell me who you are. Tell me what happened that made you conceal your real name. Tell me... *Violet*. Tell me all about you."

She blinked and gaped up at him. He'd kissed her senseless and then demanded information that left her brain whirling. Stuff she didn't want to share. No, stuff she *couldn't* share. Sharing would make Gage seek her out. She didn't doubt his magnetic draw to her, and her to him. But going from casual friendship to this, whatever it was, would really be something. And something would only lead to more. He'd want more from her. Like feelings and emotional commitments. But she could not, and she absolutely would not... yeah, like Dr. Suess, she would not, could not, should not... ever experience those feelings again.

They'd hurt her. They'd nearly eviscerated her. They didn't kill her, no, but living with them felt like she was dead. She would never choose to endure that kind of vulnerability again.

It was a little dramatic and strange perhaps to refuse to say her name. But her name was so well known, Gage could find her. There was no chance she intended to continue this tryst once they were off the mountain. It was never supposed to happen up there. She never planned it. Holding back her name and general information was never her goal, and she never planned to hide her name from her lover. A man she... no, there were no words to describe how she felt now. She had no intention of having sex with him or wanting to see him again.

She stared up at him vacantly, speechless as her thoughts whirled around her brain. She shook her head. "Don't. Please?"

He sighed and leaned his forehead against hers. Defeat made his shoulders slouch. "Why? Why not, Violet?"

"I already told you..."

"Yes. I know. No relationship. No love. Because you love

another. But the saner, healthier, stabler, and more rational thing to do in this situation would be to talk to me about it. Tell me your name and what happened to you. Don't you trust me with that much?"

She shut her eyes. The hope and pleading she saw in his eyes, and his obvious concern and feelings towards her buckled her knees. She could feel herself weakening... and all the stupid feelings inundated her at once.

"I can't. I just... I just *can't*." She whispered the pathetic words, hating herself for her weakness. Why not simply jump happily into his arms, and express how glad she was that he was back? That she was in the mountains with him again. They could talk and work together and do menial chores... and have sex. She wanted sex more than anything. But saying her name and where she lived would compel him to see her again at home. She didn't doubt that. Look how far Gage pushed her already. In the end, he had her explicit permission. He was that alluring. That amazing. That convincing.

But the mere thought of going home and dating made her heart beat rapidly and her breath seem trapped in her neck. She did not want that. She couldn't picture it. She wasn't ready. She might never be. She just didn't want that.

She finally added, "It's not you I don't trust. It's myself. I can't stand the thought of dating again. I can't be committed to anyone and I just... I don't want any of it."

He stared into her eyes. "But you want this? Right here and now? And that's it?"

"Yes." How to explain how safe she felt tucked away in the forest and mountain? She could pretend to be normal. It was separate from her life, and all the baggage that suffocated her when she was living it usually. Up here, she could be free from it. All of it. Which was crazy. Being emotions, they went everywhere with her. But she felt stronger and healthier here... and better able to deal with Gage. She gripped his hands in her own. "Can you handle that? If not—"

"Just go?" His eyebrows rose. She saw the humor in his warm face as his eyes roamed over her face and he viewed the compassion in her eyes.

"No." She squeezed his hands tighter in hers. "No. We can just be friends and well... we work so nicely together. So maybe we could just hang out—"

"Yes. We do work nicely together. But I didn't come up here to hang out or work with you."

She swallowed, her heart leaping. "What did you come here to do then?"

He grinned. "To learn you name and your story. Maybe get your phone number. But probably the biggest reason I came back is... to have sex with you."

Her entire middle warmed as her face flushed. She could feel the heat on her temples as she replied, "So, you're still up for doing that?" she asked in a flirty tone and her smile tilted her lips up.

"I'm definitely up for doing that."

She gave him a cheeky grin. "Oh, what a hero you are. Having sex with a woman who requires nothing but—"

She was suddenly being lifted up by him. Shocked, she laughed and wrapped her arms around his neck. Everything inside her was lifted up and she felt full of light and laughter as she contemplated how good she felt. How excited she was. He grinned too, carrying her to the cot, where he lay her down before he started kissing her. She ran her fingertips through his hair. Only then, did Gage lift his head, letting his mouth hover over hers.

"The thing is, Violet, I don't want sex with a woman who asks nothing from me. I want to have sex with you, but I don't want it to end here."

Her smile started to fade so he started pulling on her shirt. "But I'm willing to take whatever I can get with you. All the time." She sat up as he tugged his shirt over his head. Then he grinned again. "And all the sex I can get too."

She shut her eyes and fell into his embrace as his mouth found hers again. His hands slid down her bare back and she shivered as she fell against him.

She wished she could give him more. But at least they had two and a half days together. Days that were priceless.

And they didn't wait a single second. They made love three times that night. Gage brought in a whole box of condoms. Finally, she could scratch the itch Gage created in her. She was hungry for him. Over and over again. And he couldn't get enough of her either.

They woke late each morning and dallied around their cots. Their only goals for the day? Taking care of her horses and feeding each other... Then they had more sex and talked and laughed. They got along extremely well.

It was a sheer slice of heaven. Like the world revolved only around them. Gage and Violet. They were all that mattered.

Gage had to leave soon, at two o'clock on Monday. Violet planned to leave tomorrow. It was imperative they weren't at the trailhead at the same time. It would change the dynamic too much for Violet. For some reason, she had to keep it all here. Right here. In this camp.

Gage didn't question her about it.

When it was time to go, he stepped closer to her, his eyes studying her face and body as if he wanted to commit every feature and curve to memory. His gaze was visibly hungry... and sad. His eyes gleamed with passion. "Violet, this was... everything. I hope I see you again someday. You have my number and my address. Call me. Anytime. Tomorrow, next week, next month, next year, or five years from now. And when you're ready to tell me your full name, call me."

Tears filled her eyelids. She blinked hard, trying to keep them from falling, while gulping over the huge knot that seemed permanently lodged in her throat. He gave her his phone number and address. She tucked it into her horn bag, inside her wallet.

Precious as gold. Maybe... God, maybe... If she could manage to get over her hang-ups and anxieties. She nodded her reply, unable to speak. Gage sighed as he stepped even closer, putting his hand around the back of her neck and pulling her against his chest. He squeezed her neck gently.

"I'm so sorry this has to end. I know you're hurting. It kills me to leave you here in tears. And because you can't tell me your name. But despite all of that, I'm so fucking glad I met you. I'm so overjoyed I found you on this damn mountain. I had one of the best times of my life."

She jerked her head up and saw a smile curling his lips. She gasped a little laugh and smiled back. "Me too."

"Then... that was the point. Right?"

"Right." She smiled again but it wavered to a frown and her eyes became watery. He leaned forward and kissed her forehead. She shut her eyes, restraining her hot tears. He softly touched her lips with his in a long, slow, poignant kiss. A goodbye kiss.

Goodbye... God, she hated it.

She never said goodbye to Preston. And doing it now with Gage just felt horrible.

So horrible.

He turned and left as he released her.

He didn't take a glance back or give her a final wave.

Violet fell forward and collapsed, letting her tears stream down her cheeks. Eventually, she crashed on her cot. She did it. She had an amazing weekend, filled with incredible sex and lots of fun with Gage. She did something positive for herself.

Shaking her head, she scrutinized her fingertips while wondering why... Why couldn't she feel like this at home? Be normal? Healthy? Present?

She lay back and let her heart fold up again.

CHAPTER 12

*H*OME. VIOLET SIGHED AS the ranch came into focus. Why did it seem like so much time had passed? She was sure it hadn't. She'd only been gone a total of six weeks. Actually, home was a welcoming thought to her now.

She first stopped at the barns where her uncle ran his horse rescue and her own horses were kept. It was away from the horses they boarded and trained, since many belonged to their clients. Some were used by the resort guests on trail rides; and others were trained to do the tricks and perform. A few horses were exclusively reserved for private lessons.

But her darlings, Princess and Peaches, belonged entirely to Violet. She quickly unloaded them from the trailer and let them roam free in the fenced pasture. Half a dozen of her Uncle Jack's horses raised their heads when her horses neighed excitedly, kicking their heels to be free and allowed to run loose. They spent a long time in the mountains and were, no doubt, ready to return to their cushy life on the ranch. Fresh hay was hand-delivered to their stalls every day and all anyone expected from them was grazing with their favorite herd in a fenced, safe pasture. Horse heaven. She grinned as they frolicked and appeared visibly happier in their new location.

She slowly backed the horse trailer until she parked it beside the others belonging to the ranch. Jack and Ian shared one that could transport six horses. There was an even larger one for the ranch to use in emergencies. The only personal horse trailers were hers and Ben and Jocelyn's. Actually, Violet shared hers with AJ, their foreman.

She unhooked the trailer and drove off without seeing anyone. She headed out to her parents' house first, knocking once and entering. Her mom and dad recently retired and were almost completely removed from their former careers. Rose and Iris took over their businesses although they still provided consultation services on any new or unexpected issues. They also helped to facilitate the complete transfer. But her parents spent most of their time at home now, where they preferred to be. It was awkward and strange initially since neither of them were used to it. Shane still planned to build motorcycles, but on a very limited basis. He needed something to tinker with, but not a demanding career. Her mom had a million books she intended to read and a few classes she wanted to pursue. A lifelong teacher, she loved to learn for the sake of learning. They were also making plans to travel while they were still young and healthy.

So when Violet walked in the Tuesday after Labor day, they were both at home. The physical relief showed in the way their bodies sagged when they hugged her. She gave both of them an extra squeeze. She knew how hard it was for them to allow her to spend her summers on the mountain without demanding that she come home sooner. Or not do it at all. They knew she was too old to listen to their advice, even if she appreciated how much they worried.

Her mom leaned back and scanned Violet from her fore-head to her toes. "You're still in one piece so I guess nothing too dramatic happened to you."

Yeah, actually, it did. Something huge and catastrophic happened. Something that, in many ways challenged her mental wellbeing. And it came in the form of one Gage Sulli-van. Sex. And the feelings she attached to the sex. She blinked hard, trying not to cry. Why? Because she'd been so scared and unsure to embrace what Gage wanted with her. It always made her weepy. Years ago, Vee would have scoffed and disdained this weak girl who called herself Violet. The old Violet was brash, confident and kick-ass, embracing every moment with love and enjoying sex and her desires with a healthy laugh and a wonderful openness. Now? She couldn't even remember how one second of that felt.

Instead of owning up to her adventure, she lied easily, and with a smile. "Nothing at all. Just lots of hiking. My legs got into amazing shape."

"Your whole body is. I worry about you. But damn, are you brave. I get scared when your dad's gone overnight and I'm sleeping alone in our bed with how many family members right here?"

She squeezed her mom before flopping into a kitchen chair as she chatted. "So anything new happen around here?"

"Always. Let's see, Cami thought she lost Ethan, but he was hiding in a horse stall. We had the entire family and staff looking for him in sheer panic and fear for almost half an hour. Turned out he fell asleep in the stinking stall. Oh my God, we were so scared."

Violet chuckled. But only after the fact. Ethan and Isaac were the six-year-old twins of her cousin, Charlie and his wife, Cami. Ethan, however, was a nightmare to keep track of. He was everywhere at once and possibly hyperactive... well, at least he exhausted her. Isaac was the polar opposite:

all sweet and sensitive, very much aware of everyone else's happiness and an uncanny maturity that went far beyond his years.

Violet sat back and listened while her mom offered her dinner, which she gratefully ate. She enjoyed being with the two of them, the familiar cadence of their loving remarks and joking repartee. "How's Daisy? Has she checked in with you guys recently?"

Her younger sister, Daisy, was in college on the east coast. Now she was trying to make a career in New York City as a book editor. Not exactly the easiest or least competitive industry to pursue. Her dad often shuddered while wondering why she wanted to live in such a crowded place where twenty-seven thousand people occupied every square mile. Daisy's response was that it was a lot better than twenty-seven thousand bugs, or twenty-seven hundred horses, which led to a long debate of country versus city living. But Daisy always longed to leave the valley. And unlike some small-town families, she was encouraged to follow her dream while she was young, before any adult decisions could hamper her choices. Youth was the best time for adventure and trying new things.

Daisy grew up listening to Cami and Charlie's numerous stories of their life abroad. They traveled all over Europe when he worked for an international investment company. They lived in Berlin, London, Madrid and finally in Paris, before they settled down in the valley to have their kids.

When Violet left her parents, she felt calmer and comforted. Sometimes, she had to remind herself that being with them mattered to her as much as anything she valued. She lost sight of that during the last two years. And maybe now, it was time to appreciate some of the special gifts she had in her life. So much more than most people had and she was grateful for everything. Being so morose and confining her interest in all that she lost and a future that could never be, she might've easily overlooked the basics. Things she held dear to her heart, like her parents, her sisters and the rest of the family being right there, all healthy and nurturing, with no end to their opportunities.

Home now. Iris smiled when she walked in. Violet gave Iris a huge hug. "Thank you for letting me stay with you. It's helped more than you know over the last two years."

Pleased, her sister squeezed her and replied, "Anything I have is yours. You know that. I love you, Vie. Are you feeling better now?"

"Maybe. Yeah. Maybe not exactly better, but I'm heading there."

"Your time alone on the mountain helped you? I mean, your mental outlook?"

Violet gave her a small, secretive smile. "My time in the mountains was very good for me." Of course, there was no way anyone could understand the real reason why.

She wandered into her bedroom, more than glad to fall onto the soft bed. Monty followed her and jumped on the bed beside her. She was always thankful that Iris and Quinn were so welcoming toward Monty. He became their dog as much as Violet's. They were probably more relieved he was back than Violet. She smiled as she nuzzled his fur. He was the only thing that could make her smile.

But her smile soon disappeared because the peace of mind she found in the mountains stayed there.

Along with Gage.

The next day, she started down the road to feed her horses and glanced at the arena. That fucking arena. It still made her shudder every time her eyes landed on it. She refused to enter it ever since her nearly catatonic body was dragged from it the night Preston died. The night that changed everything. And ruined her. And left her like this. A shell of the girl who was once full of hope and optimism. A girl who proudly told people her name, Violet Rydell.

Now she hid from people and pretended to be fine while trying not to feel alive. But all she managed to do was keep feeling.

She attempted to enter the arena a dozen or more times since the fatal accident. She tried with her father at her side, and her mom, and all her sisters, both separately and together. All her uncles offered to help her too: Jack, Ian and Joey. Sometimes she stopped in her tracks while she was still in the driveway, barely in view of the stupid building. A handful of times she reached the doorway and glimpsed inside before her stomach sank and her brain exploded and she simply stopped dead. Again. No soothing words or daring challenges could force her to go inside that dismal place where Preston died.

Sighing now, she still had no more desire to enter the building than before she left for the mountains. She wandered back towards the section of stalls dedicated to rescue. She wanted to feed her horses and chit-chat with any family members she saw before going back to her sister's house. Luckily, school started tomorrow, so she had to be back at work. It gave her something important to do.

This year, she would be assisting an autistic fifteen-year-old in the special education room. She looked forward to it. Last year, she filled in for the second half of the year when the teacher's assistant had a baby. She worked in STEM: science, technology, engineering and math. She previously assisted the math teacher and learned volumes of things she never knew before, so she eagerly looked forward to a new change in duty this year.

She spent hours unpacking, doing laundry, and resettling in.

The problem was: every single thing she saw and did

reminded her of Gage. Every moment they spent together, every word, every smile, every laugh and every argument. Each sensuous movement, each caress, each goodbye.

All of it seemed to torture her now and she wished she could forget it. Undo it. It was almost worse to have those delicious memories, and experience those feelings while knowing she was the reason it could never advance beyond that.

SHE ENTERED the restaurant owned by Violet's cousin, Jacob Star. He was actually a step cousin, but she didn't discriminate. Violet mentally traced the family tree for distraction. Jacob and Brianna were the children of her Aunt Hailey, and the stepkids of her Uncle Joey. They had been in her life for as long as she could remember. Who cared about age gaps? It didn't matter that they were older than her by almost twenty years.

Jacob shocked everyone years ago when he returned to River's End after kicking his drug addiction. He almost immediately witnessed and partially prevented a mass shooting at this very café. Later, he married the owner, Luna. They redid the entire café after that ordeal and ran it together now. They also had two kids of their own.

Violet followed Iris and Quinn, averting her gaze after saying a remote, casual greeting to the hostess she passed. She saw a large table with a family sprawled all along it. She had to skirt their chairs. She smiled faintly at the antsy, squirming, little kids. One kid was coloring vigorously on the kid's menu, while two spoke loudly with intermittent giggles, and another sobbed beside an adult woman who was comforting her.

It so reminded her of her family. Anymore, when the

Rydells got together for a family dinner, they pretty much had to shut down the restaurant at the arena, since there were so many of them.

Of course, Violet hadn't attended one in two years. She adamantly refused no matter how hard the others begged her to reconsider. She didn't mind going to this café. But never the one in the arena. *That fucking arena.*

Besides her escessively wealthy brother-in-law, Quinn, loved this place. So she often came here with them.

Her gaze drifted over the table… and she stopped dead.

Rooted to the spot.

Her jaw unhinged; her eyes popped and she blinked. No. Oh, fucking hell no.

Gage. Gage Sullivan. Of course. Not even a month passed and she runs into him? She probably saw him at other times over the years but they didn't know it. She sure didn't fail to see him now.

He was wiping his mouth with a napkin when his gaze clashed with hers and made her almost collapse into a fetal ball. His eyes grew round with surprise and he paused before slowly lowering his napkin without releasing his gaze on her. She felt like he physically controlled her as he rose to his feet, sliding his chair back and setting the napkin next to his plate. She gulped. Audibly. Her hand came to her neck and she became almost dizzy with the impact of the moment.

Gage.

She closed her eyes for a moment to let the feelings rush from her chest into her entire body. Adrenaline made her feel warm, but this was so much more. There were no words for how she felt.

Her eyes scanned the table. There they all sat, she was sure it was the family he talked so often about. An older couple in their late sixties, his parents, no doubt. The other end held his two nieces and three nephews? Most likely.

Beside his parents, she saw two more couples. The sisters. Oh, yes, the sisters. All of them were nearer his age. It smacked her in the face when she contemplated how much younger she really was than he.

But now what? They could only know each other on the mountain. Under the canopy and cover of the trees. Beside the rushing water. Beneath an endless sky.

Not in this ordinary building, sharing food and drink with other people.

She felt so different here. He looked so different to her, being surrounded by family and friends.

His gaze zeroed in on her. As it often did when they were alone.

Her heart pumped with fear and confusion. How fast it happened. How could they run into each other? How unexpected to find him here, tonight. Violet couldn't conceal her shock.

"Dad? Who is that?"

The words finally registered. A lovely, dark-haired teenager was beside Gage. *Teenager!* She was looking right up at him with admiration. At him. Gage.

She had the same color hair as Gage and the same green eyes. The same freaking face too, but hers was more delicate.

Dad.

Dad?

Dad.

The word jangled her brain. Her open mouth unhinged even further.

He broke his stare and glanced at the young girl. "That's… ah… that's… I mean, this is Violet Rydell."

Violet *Rydell?*

He knew.

He knew?

He knew.

All along? He knew her name? His gaze caught hers and she still couldn't move or speak. Her hangdog expression made the entire table look up at her. Some cranked their necks around to see her. Or perhaps the long, heated, intense, unsmiling look on Gage's face was what piqued their interest in her. Neither Gage nor Violet acknowledged each other... but it was entirely unnecessary. Everything was broadcast in their silent staring.

Gage didn't flinch. He didn't shrug or avert his eyes from Violet when he looked from *his daughter*, back to her. His daughter!

"Violet?" Iris's voice entered her consciousness from her right side. It startled her and she swung her head toward her sister. Iris was smaller than her, and her face was rumpling up with concern as her gaze darted from Violet to Gage. Her big sister was frowning with visible worry. "You okay?"

Ever since Preston died, her sisters showed her unconditional compassion and empathy. She now appreciated it and them more than ever before. How could she have managed those first days and weeks without them? They took turns holding vigil over her. As she emerged from her catatonic state, they took her out to dinner or lunch or to a movie. They never left her side. And once that habit sets in, they remained supportive and still worried about her. Especially Iris, since she was always there.

"Um... yes. Can you give me a minute?"

Iris nodded and didn't question her. Iris was quiet and reticent, respecting her privacy, as she evil-eyed the table where Gage was. "Okay."

Violet thought everyone at the table was watching and listening to her. All eyes eagerly aware of her and more than curious. That was due, no doubt, to the strange interaction between her and Gage. Lots of staring without talking. The cryptic words he said to his *daughter*.

Her face flushed in confusion. *Daughter.* What the living fuck?

As she spoke to her sister, Gage leaned down and said something to the teenager sitting beside him before straightening up and looking towards Violet. His face appeared stoic when he tipped his head towards the door. The teenager nodded and was just as unsmiling.

Finally, his invisible connection with Violet broke and Gage turned towards the door and so did Violet. Both of them weaved their way through the extra tables and chairs.

They met just before the double doors of the entryway. His mouth in a tight line, he gave her a cursory nod as he pushed the door and held it open for her, allowing her to go first. She sensed that Gage was full of manners and polite courtesy in his day-to-day encounters. That was so him.

She ducked past him. Her entire body immediately zinging with feelings at being so close to him. Lord, why did he physically have that affect on her? Emotionally? Mentally? Why did her soul all but cry out to him? Why was she so happy and relieved and thrilled to see him? How did she survive a month without him?

Did it matter? He knew who she was. Would he have found her on his own? Did she really think they'd never see each other again? Did she really want that?

Violet didn't know the answers, but the feelings flooding her heart were painful and she didn't want to suffer with them anymore. Numbness. That was her nirvana. What she wanted and needed most. What she craved and the reason why she resisted her desire to see and know him beyond their time in the mountains.

Tears brimmed in her eyes as she passed under the outside lights that filled the space beneath the soffit. She kept facing forward so he couldn't see the tumultuous expressions that were playing across her face. She turned around the edge of the building and walked towards the grass. There was a picnic table there that overlooked the river. She flopped onto the bench.

Gage was right behind her and he came to a stop beside her. Still standing, he jammed his hands into his coat pockets and rocked back and forth on his heels.

Where to start? Her brain was spinning with unanswerable questions and thoughts, what-ifs? and what-the-fucks? but she couldn't find the words to speak. And couldn't decide what to say.

She stared at Gage's legs too long. He was dressed in jeans and a pair of sneakers. Violet never saw him in a pair of jeans. He always wore light clothes made of nylon, specially designed hiking pants, or sweatpants and cargo shorts. He always wore hiking boots too. Always. Her gaze crept higher, climbing up his legs and hips to his shirt, which was neatly tucked in and topped off with a black belt. Neat and stylish. Nothing like he dressed in the woods. His hair had recently been trimmed along with his beard, which framed his face nicely.

He was so handsome, so appealing, so eye-catching.

Her gaze caressed his face. A small smile touched her lips. To a stranger, he could have been her brother; they resembled each other so much in their coloring.

His gaze was stony.

"How long did you know?"

"Which part? That your name is Violet Rydell?"

"Yeah. Yes. Did you recognize me right off?"

He dug his hands deeper into his pockets, stepped forward and hunched his shoulders more. Shaking his head, he said, "No. It was purely by chance. I brought my daughter here for private horseback riding lessons with Erin Rydell. I saw your picture hanging in the arena. She told me some details. I read about the rest from the articles published about you and your family."

That word again. That stunning unbelievable reality. Daughter?! Daughter? Lord. What to do with that?

"When you came back? Labor Day weekend? You knew then?"

"Yes."

"Why didn't you tell me then?" That stung. Like he was lying to her. She remembered how he insisted on knowing her name and true identity. It should have been her first clue.

"I hoped you would volunteer to tell me. And ask to see me, and let me see you again. But nothing happened. You clung to your secrets. You did not appear to want me. So what could I do? It seemed like a fruitless endeavor and I couldn't demand it from you. Your secrecy was more valuable to you than anything that could have happened with us. I had to accept that. Forcing you was not an option. I try not to do anything I might end up regretting someday... and it would probably have happened sooner than later."

"But you... you knew we'd see each other again."

He turned his shoulder and head away. "Yeah. I knew. But I had no idea when. Would it be a week, a month or a year? I didn't plan to meet you here, not like this. With my entire family watching us."

"And what about your... your daughter?" Her breath all but whooshed out of her. The words were so foreign to her ears. Shocking and strange. How could she start to think of him as a dad? "What did you do? Leave your daughter alone for a month? What the hell?"

He bristled and whipped around as his stern gaze hit her. "Don't you fucking dare, Violet. My daughter is none of your business. You didn't even tell me your *name.* Your name. The most basic part of any relationship. So don't you dare talk to me about my daughter."

She jumped to her feet, clenching her fists. "You have a daughter, a teenage daughter, and not once did you ever mention her. What kind of father leaves his daughter for a whole month and never mentions her name?"

"Shut the hell up, Violet. You have no right to judge me or my daughter. No, I didn't tell you about my personal life. And I see no reason to start now. You're just a random woman... a random girl I fucked while camping in the mountains. Right? Isn't that all that happened? That's pretty much what transpired between us, isn't it? Leave it at that? Right? You're still messed up with your past. So messed up, that you can't tell me your goddamned name?"

"Because..." Her thoughts spun without making sense and her speech sputtered out. She didn't know what to say. Yes, she was wrong. Yes, she kept it a secret. But only because she didn't know what else to do. Her oddly surprising attraction and feelings for this man were unwanted. And yet they were undeniably there. She had to protect herself. In whatever way she could. How could he understand her desperate need to avoid him? She wanted to avoid this exact moment that was now unfolding. Seeing him in normal life was impossible and her normal life was empty without him in it.

She dropped her head and let the tears fill her eyes. Blinking hard, she said, "Because my life hurts all the time and I just don't want to hurt anymore. I ran to the mountains to ignore my feelings. To stop being Violet Rydell. I never wanted to hurt you... or myself."

Silence followed her pathetic revelation. There were so many more things she could and should have said, but her words were lodged in her swollen throat.

"But you did. You did hurt me." His tone was as soft as a breeze on her skin. She lifted her head. He wasn't looking at her but staring off into the void of darkness.

"Multiply that by a hundred and you can get an idea of

how I feel these days." She blinked hard and added, "I loved someone. Deeply. I relive his death every single night. When I shut my eyes to sleep and as soon as I wake up. I never meant to hurt you. I only wanted to protect myself. I'm not strong enough to handle it. Not anymore."

Violet was fearless once. Invincible. At least, she thought she was. There was no horse she shied away from riding. Using her natural skills, kindness and confidence, she'd managed to get them to do exactly what she'd wanted. Anytime she'd asked them. She once thought she could do anything as long as she believed in herself. Entertaining crowds? So easy for her. So much fun. A born kickass with a wild, flamboyant style and personality. Nowadays? She was a neutral beige. A muted shadow of the woman she formerly was. She used to smile and laugh and be the source of everyone else's fun. She was the loudest, and the most outgoing of all her sisters. She was just like her dad in her demeanor.

Until that horrible day. The day Preston's neck snapped in front of her, teaching her the fragility of life in the most ruthless way. How quickly the day went from ordinary to eerie, and from fun to horrific. *How completely beyond our control,* she suddenly realized.

That day also seemed to suck her soul from her body. She was left with a vacuous, empty shell, doomed to relive the tragedy every single day of her life.

"Everything else I told you was real. What we shared and experienced. That was real. The only thing I denied you was my last name."

She sounded so weak and lame. Nothing better to defend herself. She missed him intensely. It had only been a month since her return from the mountains, although it felt much longer. Longer, lonelier, sadder than she could ever remember before meeting Gage Sullivan.

He turned his body towards her; was he forgiving her? She peeked up at him. His jaw might as well have been set in granite. The lights of the café cast shadows over him.

"There's nothing more for me to do. It was really great, but fuck off now. I never want to see you again? That's pretty much how you left me."

"No, it wasn't. I was upset. You knew that. Apparently, you even knew the reason why."

"But you didn't know I knew. You let me go without a word. It was so easy for you. So why should I believe you're so broken up now? You don't seem cold or broken to me."

"I felt different with you, even if there was also a lot that I couldn't handle."

"What the fuck do you want me to do? Ignore us? You? What? Like we never met? We never—"

"Dad?"

The timid, hesitant voice cut through the darkness between them as effectively as a butcher knife through a pound cake. Violet immediately jumped to her feet and Gage turned back towards the café entrance. Sure enough, there stood his teenage daughter, staring at both of them. Almost within earshot of his angry complaint about sex. Fucking! The teen's eyes were big and worried as she switched her gaze from her dad to Violet.

"Andy? Honey…"

"I'm sorry to interrupt but Grandma was worried and she wanted to know…"

Gage's expression softened as he crossed the space, closing the gap between them. "It's okay, honey. You don't ever have to be sorry for anything. Um… This is Violet…"

Gage was so kind and open with Andy. He touched her face gently and she stared up at him with big, innocent eyes. She glanced at Violet and swallowed hard. "You mean Vee? The mountain girl? You found out her real name?"

Mountain girl? So even his kid knew Gage didn't know her real name? Crap! Shit! Who tells their kid that kind of stuff?

He nodded. Nodded. So he did tell his daughter about her? Them? Holy shit. Why? For fuck's sake! Why would he tell his daughter he slept with a woman in the forest? And why did he stay away from her for so long? What did it mean? How could it mean anything after she ended it between them? Why didn't it feel ended? His daughter was a fucking teenager. She was taller than Violet, for God's sake. She was also slender and small-boned but she had a good three inches on Violet.

He sighed heavily. "Yes. Andy... I'd like you to meet Violet Rydell. Violet, my daughter, Andrea."

Andrea put her hand out politely and Violet stared at it for a prolonged moment. Her initial shock and surprise worked to make her completely uncomfortable. What the hell? She was meeting a lover's *teenage* daughter. How could this be part of her life?

Her face flushed hotter. So hot. Embarrassed by her discomfort, she feared sweat would soon be streaming off her brow. She didn't know what to do.

She reacted sluggishly and slow as her brain struggled to recall what might be normal social reactions. Delaying for only a split second, Violet stretched her hand out and said, "Hello." She sounded stiff, cold and formal. Like a freaking asshole. Which made her face even hotter. Good thing she had the shadows for cover. Maybe Andrea and Gage wouldn't notice.

"Please, call me Andy. Everyone else does." Call her Andy? No. Oh, fuck no, she wasn't calling Gage's teenage daughter anything. At all. Ever.

Teenage daughter. How was this possible? She felt light-headed and the handshake was short. Barely a brushing of their fingertips. His daughter's tone was strong and full of personality. She didn't talk fast or high-pitched like some teenage girls do. She was poised and gracious. Her shoulders were back and her posture was noble, no hunching over like some tall girls her age tended to do. She had long legs, as slender as a filly, and a lovely confidence that was admirable. Truly.

Andy looked over at Violet and then back at her dad. She licked her lips and studied Violet longer. "Do you... work at the school?"

Shit! Shit! Shit! Of course, the girl went there. Had she seen her before?

"Umm, yeah. Yes. I'm one of the teacher aids."

"I knew I recognized you. I've seen you around there."

Yes, of course she would have. Violet tried not to flinch or shut her eyes lest she reveal her terrible discomfort. No. No. No. Another connection to Gage. Through his daughter?

Violet's gaze sharpened on her. "You're in... let me see..."

"Eighth grade."

"Right. Eighth grade." Duh. Small town. Small world. Small school. Small community. She was doomed to run into Gage now. She hated to be suddenly so aware of his existence. How could she hope to hide? Here? Ha! That's why so many of the native residents left. The familiarity of everyone all the time was inescapable.

She fidgeted and her obvious discomfort was nearly intolerable. "Um... so..."

Gage set a hand on Andy's shoulder after shaking out of his reverie. "Give me a minute to finish things up with Violet. Then I'll sit down at the table again, okay?"

Her smile was quick, secure, and relieved. Taking charge, but including and reassuring his daughter seemed very important to Gage.

His teenage daughter. It still would not compute.

She turned to Violet. "It was so nice to meet you. Sorry I interrupted. I just..."

Gage's smile was quick and loving. "You just had to meet the mountain girl?"

She gave a small, shy smile. She obviously knew her father very well. The kidding and special looks showed how well they got each other. Despite his time away from her in the woods, they displayed a solid and loving connection. "Yes. I'm sorry," Andy said to Violet, "but when Dad told me about you and how you handled two horses up there all by yourself? Seems incredible. I could never do that."

"Well, I grew up on a horse ranch. I was riding horses before I was walking. I'm not as safe or competent behind the wheel of a car as I am on top of a horse." What was she doing? Chatting with Gage's daughter?

Andy took Violet's words with unmasked interest as she swung around, her eyes brighter. "You're the reason Dad let me take lessons with Erin. On *your ranch*. Now that I realize that, is Erin Rydell also related to you? Is she your..."

"Aunt. She's my aunt. She's pretty amazing with horses too. And so nice."

"She is. Do you give riding lessons? Could you teach me to do what you do? I mean, if you can be up alone on a mountain...?"

"No." Violet's mouth was compressed and her tone was chilly. Andy caught that instantly and moved back a few inches as if Violet's reply hit her in the face like a cold fish.

Gage rescued his daughter. "Sweetie, give me five minutes, okay?" He was kind and the nudge he gave her was subtle and gentle. A shield against Violet's frostiness. Violet immediately regretted her rude reaction. It was force of habit. She bristled when anyone asked her for riding lessons now. She could barely stand to watch others ride, even if they were professional, let alone, teach a beginner. All she foresaw was someone getting hurt or maimed or dying.

"Oh. Okay, sure, Dad." Despite Violet's abruptness, Andy turned to give Violet another polite, genuine smile. "Nice to meet you, Mrs. Rydell."

"You too," Violet mumbled. She was not half as polite or sweet or poised as his young teenager. Nor as disciplined. Andy was not shy, but warm and eager. There was nothing about Andy not to like.

Violet nearly shut her eyes. *Mrs. Rydell?* Had anyone ever called her that until now? Even the kids at the school called her Violet. Many mistook her for a student until they got to know her. She wasn't much more than a decade older than them. Now her lover's daughter called her Mrs. Rydell?

Eighth grade? Ugh.

They fell silent as Andy went back into the café after going around the corner of the building. Then Gage turned towards Violet, his eyes flashing and his jaw locked. "Did you have to be such a bitch? She's just a kid for God's sake. She's interested in your unusual gift with horses. God, Violet. So a bad thing happened to you, but when did you lose your sense of right and wrong? And common decency towards others?"

She blinked at him in surprise. He snarled his admonishment at her. He'd never growled or snapped at her before. "I'm sorry. It just popped out. I don't give lessons anymore. I..."

"I know that!" he roared at her, getting so agitated, he started pacing. "But *she* doesn't know that. She doesn't know the reason why. She found you fascinating. As rare and as valuable to her as a unicorn. You could have been a little nicer to her. She's just a kid, you know."

"Yes. Right. She's your kid. How old is she? Are you married? Were you married? What the fuck, Gage!? Right back at you."

Pressing a hand to his neck, he tried to massage the tension away. "No. I've never been married. My girlfriend got pregnant in college. We were both young. She died shortly after Andy was born and I've raised her alone ever since."

"Oh."

"Yeah... Oh."

"How old is she?"

"Thirteen."

Thirteen. Duh. Sure. And Violet worked at her school.

"She's lovely."

"She is. That's why you shouldn't have punished her innocent curiosity with your angry tone."

"I'm sorry. I won't do it again."

"Were you actually born in the family barn or did they teach you some basic manners and social norms? Because I have to tell you, Violet, not speaking your name and living in the mountains all alone seems to have turned you into a Neanderthall. You can't even handle an introduction. Jesus, *read* about proper manners and social norms if you don't know any."

She blinked at his unexpected verbal assault. He was obviously disgusted by her. Embarrassment burned her cheeks. "I'm sorry. She was such a shock to me. You are too. From the time you showed up here..."

He sighed as he buried his hands in his pockets. "I know. I'm sorry I bit your head off. The hairs on my neck stiffen when anyone speaks rudely to my daughter. You made her feel stupid and I resented it."

As any good father would feel. Her own father would have defended her just as fiercely. Her own father... *Gage is a father*. He suddenly seemed much older and wiser than her. Clear out of her league. Not part of her generation. Beyond her feasibility realm.

"She takes private riding lessons from Erin?"

"Yes. That's how I found out your true identity. Andy always wanted to try horseback riding but we never got around to it. After attending a week-long horse camp this summer, she begged me to get her a horse. Second to that wish was letting her take riding lessons. After I saw how well you handled your horses and how confident you seemed, my decision to let her have the lessons was made. So you might as well blame yourself indirectly for allowing me to figure out who you were exactly."

Her mind was still reeling from all the pivotal revelations. His daughter took horseback riding lessons at her ranch. From her family. Specifically, her aunt. "Why did you tell her about us? And *mountain girl?*"

"I didn't tell her anything. Except meeting a strange woman who lived alone in the mountains. Mountain girl was *her* nickname for you." He shrugged. "Okay, and mine too."

"Where was she during that time?"

"She sees her grandparents every summer for a month. Not that it's any of your damn business. As a good father, I allow her to visit them regularly. They live in Georgia and their daughter died very young so Andy is all they have left to spoil. It always kills me when she's gone. That's why I took the trail repair assignment… No, I begged for it. I couldn't wait to get out in the woods. The reason I hiked out once-a-week was to call them and check on Andy."

Now it made sense. It was all normal, well-adjusted and typical. Everything except for Violet.

"Then, you didn't tell her you and I were…"

"No. Of course not. It won't take her long to figure it out now, however, so we'll have to talk about it eventually. This meeting between us was too weird for her not to notice it and hell, wonder about the overtones."

"How will you explain?" *How does one address the subject of sex with one's teenage daughter? Especially when the sex is all about you?*

"I'll just say I care about you. She knows I went back there to see you, and I'm sure she must suspect what that meant, but she probably prefers not to think about it."

"What? You talk to her so openly?"

Gage glared at her. "Yes. I never lie to my daughter. I don't keep secrets from her either. I might blunt the truth, and not mention sex, but I'd certainly tell her if I met someone who became much more than a friend to me. Or if the potential for that existed. Everything I do affects her. Everything I think about affects her. I don't have to tell you how much she already knows about you."

Overwhelmed, Violet turned and flopped down on the bench as if the weight of his words and confessions were too heavy a burden for her to bear by herself. He had feelings about her? That freaked her out. She fought the urge to start running but... crap. There was something more that kept tugging at her... heart? Maybe so. Yeah, probably. Relief? Interest? A glad sense of hope? Did he really feel something for her?

No. She didn't want him to feel anything for her. Fondness. Friendship. Transient things that were pleasant and managed to justify the inevitable sex. But that turned out to be incredible and so much more than friendly. If it were only friendship and fondness, why the intensity? Why the stomach churning and heavy heart filled with confusion? Why was her brain spinning in circles? Why the ceaseless urge to cry?

She shook her head. "I can't... I can't do this. You have a daughter. And she's a young lady. She's old enough to be my sister and..."

"She's nowhere near old enough to be your sister. Grow up, Violet. You were hurt and heartbroken, but that doesn't give you a pass for the rest of your life. You're still alive so you have to interact. Be polite. Show some human courtesy, for fuck's sake, Violet."

"I know." She glared up at him. "I know. I just struggle to conform to society's demands. That's why I don't seek out people. I prefer to crawl away from them. You found me. And you came back and fine. I'm all fucked up. And I know it. I am the first to admit it. It's why I tried to keep you from discovering my identity. To keep you from knowing how fucked up I am."

She rose to her feet as her heated words agitated her. Fists clenched, she all but screamed at him. Was he judging her now? Of course, she tried to prevent him from seeing, experiencing, and living with her anomaly. She never wanted to hurt him.

Tears again blurred her eyes. "I know how fucked up I am. I really tried to keep you away from me. I tried my hardest; you know I did. You kept coming back. You kept pushing me. You kept accepting my excuses. What more could I do? I tried—"

Fuck. She wiped her streaming tears and sniffled when his arms came around her. She hated the feel of them. She detested her weakness and how trapped he made her feel when he held her. She didn't want his arms around her now. She didn't want anyone. She sure as hell didn't need Gage. Not at all. He was too old. Too settled. And too normal and ordinary. Too nice. Just too fucking nice. And he had a grown-assed daughter. He seemed to be a good... no, a *great* father so where did that leave her? Nowhere. It was too weird now. She was too broken and difficult and—

She snuggled into his embrace, gripping his shirt with her fist and letting her head fall helplessly to his chest. Tears made her throat swell, causing a strangled sound to come out of her mouth. How badly she wanted his strong arms to stay around her. Holding her up. Soothing her. Comforting her. Caring for her. Everything she tried to banish from her life. A man's arms. A man's caress. A man's comfort.

Damn it.

Worst of all, she did not want this man's arms around her.

He was too good for her. Definitely long term or nothing. He deserved love and an abundance of it. Someone who could be his equal. Someone with a real job and a home. Someone who could step in and take charge of his complicated adult life and belong. Be part of it. Contribute something valuable to his adolescent daughter.

Gage needed someone to really love him as he deserved. To reciprocate. He needed to have all of someone's heart. It had to be pure and real and filled with goodness. Not a broken handful of shards that could cut him. The jagged edges of Violet's heart would rip his flesh and soul, rendering him as ragged and torn and dysfunctional as she was.

But for now, she snuggled into his chest. Into the warm weight of having his arms around her. He seemed to lift up her pain and hold it inside him if only to keep her standing. For so long, Violet kept getting shoved onto her knees by her sheer pain.

She wanted Gage. But she didn't know how to accept him. She truly cared. She wanted to love him. She wanted to be stronger so she could handle her feelings but she didn't trust herself. She could not stand to be responsible for Gage's heart. And now there was someone else. A daughter! Violet simply could not commit to so much so soon.

She didn't wrap her arms around his waist even though she wanted to. She fisted her hands at her sides and tried to remain still. Stoic. Uncaring. Inside, she ached to launch herself against his warm body, wrapping herself up in his solid reliability and unending stamina.

His lips touched her hairline. Soft. Tender. Comforting.

None of which she deserved. She pushed him away and it took all of her strength.

"I can't. I can't be anything to you. I don't know how to be. You'll end up hating me and justifiably."

"That's your plan? You can't stop yourself from hurting me?"

"I just did it without even trying. You resented the way I reacted to your daughter and all she asked was if I could teach her horseback riding. I'm always moody and I can't control it like I should. I know. I should be better, but I can't figure out how to be. So run, Gage. Run away from me now. I wasn't wrong for doing what I did. It was unconventional, but it was honestly in your best interest."

"Really? Not yours? You think..."

"I can't be with you in any kind of normal way? Yes. I know I can't. I'll only hurt and abuse and lash out at whoever crosses me..."

"What if I say that's fine? I can handle it. What if I say I still want to see you?"

She wilted, but her heart swelled. God, this man. This persistent man.

She lifted a hand, and her brain yelled, *No. Don't touch him. Don't.* But to no avail. She wanted to. She needed to. She feared she'd turn into solid ice if she didn't. Maybe permanently. A frozen ice princess without the capacity for love and warmth. Her hand splayed over his heart. She shut her eyes and savored the healthy thumping of his caring, good, wonderful heart. God, he was the best man she ever knew. So much better than her...

"I'd say, you'll end up getting hurt. Too late you'll realize your mistake. You'll remember that I love someone else. A ghost. Someone I can't release. How long before my dysfunction creates bitterness inside your heart? Hatred? I can't... I couldn't stand that. The thought of hurting you. And I can't give you what you and your daughter need. So it would only turn out bad. I can't... I can't..."

She bit her lip, slipping her hand free of him and putting it back at her side. It required steady concentration to make it stay there.

"Gage... I'm so sorry. But I also can't give you more. Or be more. So please be my..."

"What? Your friend?" He scoffed cruelly.

"No. I see... I feel more than that but..."

"Always so many buts with you, huh?"

"Yes. So it's better to be nothing to me. Pass politely if we see each other."

He finally released her. "I don't want that for a minute."

"No. But it isn't your decision to make. It's mine."

He stiffened, and his gaze grew furious. He did *not* like her answer. Tightening his jaw until it seemed ready to shatter, he replied, "No, you're right. Look, I'm leaving now to take my daughter home."

He turned and disappeared that quickly. Her heart pounded so hard, it hurt. It seemed to send out the Morse Code, tapping a message to her chest... Help. Help. Please help me. Help me learn how to stop being cold, frigid, and broken. I do not like being ruined. Help me live. Help me come back to life again.

But she knew how futile it was... It couldn't last. She'd take advantage of him eventually. She'd become selfish and hurt him irreparably. She would take too much and leave nothing for him.

CHAPTER 13

"SO... SHE'S NOT JUST a friend!"

Gage sighed while slipping a side glance at his daughter in the front seat of his truck. She faced forward, but her gaze was fastened on him. She looked so lovely. Her features were maturing and she seemed more womanly than girlish. Gage was sure a switch was flipped during their time apart. And it managed to change Andy from his young daughter, staring with awed wonder and adoration at him, to not quite a woman yet, but definitely a female. Her body had elongated. Her arms, legs, and torso were longer, thinner and more curvy. Her face was thinner, losing its baby roundedness. Her gaze was also sharper, and much more worldly.

But Gage never lied to her or shied away from any of her questions. He fidgeted in his seat but knew he couldn't start now. It could only get harder. "No."

"So what happened? That was pretty intense. I mean, her eyes nearly popped out of her head. She was so surprised like... like if she spotted a unicorn grazing in the yard."

He chuckled. As always, Andy was very descriptive.

"Yeah. She never told me her name, so I never told her I knew who she was."

"Why?"

"I wanted her to tell me. To trust me that much."

"She didn't trust you? Why not?"

"She never planned to see me again."

"But she sure seemed to want to."

"I thought so too," he admitted honestly. He fought the urge to grill his daughter about her observations in his lover's reaction to seeing him. But that was wrong. Something that left an "ick" factor in his mouth. "But she's just scared."

"No, Dad. She was shocked... but very interested. She's interested in seeing you again. It's how I'd look at a crush, you know?"

Lord. Crush. Dating. It seemed so much sooner than he was ready to handle. "Um... no, I don't know. But I suppose so."

"Well..." she flipped her hair over her shoulder and explained, "I like boys, Dad. So whatever. I know when a girl looks interested and she was interested."

"She can't handle it though."

"Why? What's wrong with her?"

"She lost someone she loved and can't get over it. And she's too scared to venture into love again."

"Wow." Andy sat back. "Wow, that's so romantic. You could like heal her. Help her learn to trust life again, or love again or whatever. It's like a sappy, after school special."

He held in the eye-roll at her dramatics. "It's not. At all. And it won't be. She won't even try with me. She refused to tell me her name, Andy. She can't love me, and I'm no movie hero. I won't beg her to see me. I have my own life to live and a daughter to raise. And maybe I prefer not to have to beg someone to hang around me. You know?"

She turned in her seat, her arms flailing as she spoke. "She didn't know about me, did she?"

Gage had secretly hoped Andy wouldn't catch onto that fact. "I don't share the most important part of me with someone who won't even tell me her real name."

She tilted her head, eyes widening and searching his face as if she were silently saying something. "What?" he asked disturbed by her penetrating look.

"But you would..."

He nearly died with embarrassment. His cheeks flushed with heat that expanded into his entire body. He felt like he burst into flames right there in the driver's seat of his truck. Discussing his sex life. Andy knew he and Violet had sex and they did not discuss his daughter. Dear God. How did his life suddenly get to this point?

"Andy..." he warned her with his tone, wondering what to do.

"Dad... I'm not five anymore. I'm thirteen. I know you had sex with her. I'm just saying... she must have cared. She seemed so confused about me and..."

He could never confirm that. Neither could he deny it without lying; so he thought it best to ignore it. Move on. Gloss over. Pray to God they never had a discussion like it again.

"She's confused. Yes. That's a good euphemism for it. But I think she's too confused to figure it out anytime soon. I prefer to avoid being collateral damage. Look at how she snapped when you met her."

"But I kind of liked her. She's so pretty."

"I can't continue this conversation, Andy. I can't discuss her anymore with you."

"Dad... she is pretty."

"So are you. So what? That's no predicate for love and not the reason I adore you."

She folded her arms over her chest. "I don't think it's why you care about her and like her."

At least she softened her words. She knew how much he adored her.

No lie there. He cherished Andy. But yeah. For the very first time in his life, he wondered if he could direct those feelings toward another person. Another person his own age.

"You never felt this way before," Andy announced. He hated how well she knew that. She knew that her conception was an accident and he and her mother were just good friends, not soulmates. They'd dated casually in college. But as soon as they knew they were having Andy, they'd agreed to raise her together. Sometimes, accidental pregnancy can be very dramatic and upsetting. Deidre knew, from the moment of her birth, that they both loved and wanted Andy. Their youthful mistake turned out to be the greatest miracle of both of their lives. That never changed. And it never would.

Gage had to smile. He felt proud of his relationship with his daughter. They were so close and so open with each other that she did know him exceptionally well.

"No. But it's not possible with Violet."

"Maybe it could be." She stirred around again, excited and energized, it seemed, by Violet's emotional shattering. She seemed bent on fixing it. Yeah, it was romantic, like stars in the sky. It wasn't anything to do with actual life. Or reality. He had to work. He also had home chores and a family and daughter. He didn't have time to chase the stars. Or figure out how to fix Violet. He wanted a partner in life, not a lifetime project.

And what if he couldn't help her? Perhaps what it all boiled down to was fear. Fear that she'd never love him like the dead man—whom she so clearly and explicitly told him about—and the potential wasn't there. Who signs up for something like that?

But damn. He felt like he got socked in the gut when he lifted his head and found her staring at him with wide, green-gold eyes. Eyes that were filled with fear. Shocked? No, the word *appalled* better described the look on her face. But he glimpsed a spark of something more. Pleasure? Was she slightly glad to see him? Yes. He did see something close to that in her weary but soulful eye-lock with him.

That and realizing the young lady who sat beside him was, in fact, his daughter. It seemed to throw her more than he ever expected. He glanced at Andy, trying to imagine Violet's shock. If you're in your twenties as Violet was, you might expect to see a toddler or maybe a child of seven or eight. Not thirteen. Not in the eighth grade. Not in the same school where Violet worked. That was strange to the tenth power so no wonder she found it hard to assimilate.

Why didn't his daughter freak out after discovering he had a girlfriend? And why didn't the idea of sex utterly disgust her? Andy seemed like she wanted Violet to be his girlfriend. Warmth and pride filled his heart. She was so much wiser and more mature than he was and so beyond her years. An old soul captured in a young woman's body. Andy was always that way. Her wisdom was so far beyond her years and Gage recognized and valued it dearly. He culti-vated and encouraged her by listening to her advice and opinions. Their closeness stemmed from that. One that made Andy honestly want her father to let another woman into his life, which meant *their life.* Even though he never did before. Andy didn't react by yelling and screaming, or throwing a tantrum in front of him or Violet. On the contrary. Andy virtually embraced Violet; and Gage adored her for doing that.

"I'm sorry for the way it went down in there. I mean, in

front of everyone. Neither Violet nor I expected to bump into each other, obviously. And since she still didn't think I knew her last name, it made it very odd."

"Yes. But she was super-affected by you, Dad. I don't think you realize how much... Lord, a helicopter could have landed right next to her and I swear to God, she wouldn't have noticed it because she couldn't lift her eyes off you. She was shocked, yes, but Dad... I saw serious undertones of interest that were undeniably there."

"Again, honey, she has so much baggage... I doubt she's the right one. Not even someone I'd like to date."

They pulled into the driveway and he shut the headlights off before they both hopped out and went inside the open garage door. As they entered the rec room, Andy said, "Dad, it might not be Violet... but maybe you should consider dating someone. I won't be here forever, you know. And I don't want you to be alone."

Gage dropped his wallet and keys on the entry table. He stared at her intently as she stood beside the kitchen table, her eyes wide and earnest. "Andy, sweetheart, you really don't have to worry about that yet. It'll be years from now. And even if I don't find someone special, I've never been lonely in my life. I love my job and my pastimes and hobbies. I have Grandma and Grandpa, and with all the aunties and uncles, I can borrow a niece or nephew if I need to see a kid... and of course, I have you. I'll always have you, Andy. So don't stress over an ominous date in the future. I'll be sure when the time comes, and I'll be good and ready for it. I don't want you to start worrying about me, sweet girl. I'll do all the worrying for both of us. Not the other way around."

"But it's the first time I've seen you look at a woman that way. Ever. In my entire life. You've never shown anything but your friendly, neighborly side. You don't look at women as if they interest you at all most of the time. You were passionate with Violet, enough to yell at her, because you obviously felt so much. You should not discount that."

He rested his hands on the back of the dining room chair. Awed and floored by how perceptive his daughter was, noticing all the things he missed before initiating a mature discussion about it? Stunning and clever. "I don't discount anything. But I can't beg her to give me a chance. I did once and she was adamant in her refusal. She said no. Not sure what else I can do while still keeping *some* dignity."

She smiled softly. "Maybe dignity can't bring you happiness."

"Andy…" he warned her with a soft, playful smile. "Enough about Violet, tonight. Okay? And I totally appreciate your opinion and how cool you were about it. I doubt most daughters would… well, hell! We both know there is no other daughter like you."

Andy rolled her eyes but her smile was real. Kissing his cheek as she passed him, she said good night and disappeared down the hallway. Gage flopped down on the sectional, trying his best to forget about tonight. As he checked the game scores, he tried to pretend his heart wasn't injured. He felt desperate to sink back into his former life… without hoping for a fantasy that could obviously never be. Much to his chagrin, he feared he was doing that already.

IRIS STOOD up when Violet walked back inside the café. Violet watched Gage and his daughter and family finally pull out. Hiding on the side of the café, she now knew Gage drove a new red Chevy Silverado with an extended cab. She watched him tenderly holding his mother's arm as he eased her into the front seat of their large sedan. He gave his dad a wave over the top of the car. The older couple were very trim and both had white hair. She realized she knew his sisters, and she observed them when they cornered him for a moment, talking intently. He smiled and shook his head, playfully avoiding them, and smirking when one pretended to slug his arm in frustration. He pointed towards the truck with Andy in it, gave each sister a kiss on the cheek and dashed away.

So that was Gage's family. Still amazing to her.

When she finally re-entered the dining establishment, her sister immediately rose and rushed over. Quinn was right behind her. "Are you okay? Who was that man?"

Violet calmly replied, "Someone I met over the summer. I honestly didn't know he lived near here, much less, that I'd ever run into him like that. Really, Iris, it was nothing. Let it go."

Iris's puzzled look studied Violet as if she were inspecting her for an injury.

"Please?" Violet begged.

If Iris were Rose, her oldest sister, she would have insisted on answers and could not let it go until she was thoroughly satisfied. Thankfully, Iris kept her business to herself and well understood it when other people wanted to. She accepted Violet's reply with a shake of her head. They sat down and somehow, Violet managed to eat her meal. The food tasted like sawdust. Her heart wasn't in it. Despite her responses to their chatter, Violet could not remember a single thing they talked about that night.

All she could think about was Gage. He looked so good. Better than she ever remembered, although she often recounted every single detail about him.

She was grateful she could retreat to her room if only to stop pretending she was fine. As she'd done for two years now. She lay there thinking about Gage and remembering all the things they did together and how wonderful she felt. Her regret stabbed her like an ice pick underneath each rib in her chest.

They'd ended Labor Day weekend, all weepy and clingy and sad. Yet, their goodbye was poignant, heartfelt and sweet. No anger then. But now, there was anger. Violet couldn't stand that. It was silly since she was the one who'd decided they could not see each other. She couldn't get the yucky flavor of her bumping into them out of her head.

She finally broke down and took out the phone number he gave her. Surrendering to an unstoppable force, she had to reach out to him. For what? She didn't know. Something.

She texted: *This is Violet. I just wanted to say I'm sorry for what went down last night in front of your daughter.*

In a matter of minutes, he responded: *Hi, Vee...*

Her damn heart pumped faster and her mouth instantly curled up into a smile. That easily, she laughed out loud. She imagined his tone of voice caressing her name. Her nickname. The identity she'd adopted with him. She instantly shut her eyes and felt like she was right back in her tent, beside him, and nothing more mattered to her but what existed between them. Then and there. Safe. Protected. Cherished. New. She felt brand new and cared for. The sexual urges and sense of belonging culminated as easily as the word he wrote: *Vee.*

He continued: *I don't mind. I would have given that to you at some point.*

Again, he made her smile and roll her eyes. She loved his voice, the warm timbre in his deep baritone.

Gage added more: *The other night was hard. Strange. I agree. I'm sorry too. For all the attention. For not telling you the things I knew about you, Violet Rydell. And especially about Andy.*

She shut her eyes. Despite her iciness in the way she'd approached him and their brief time together, he was eager to let her off the hook. He accepted some of the blame when it was really all on her. She knew it. He had to know it too.

Violet: *You are being too kind. It was all my fault. I'm sorry for the secrecy. For pretending. For not giving you a safe space to share your daughter with me.*

Gage: *Well. There was that. But now I know the reasons for it. You never lied about that fact. I should have respected it more and not been so surprised. Maybe I'm a jerk for not believing you. I thought I could earn your trust and change your mind. You told me no and I should have listened.*

She tilted her head at her phone screen. Yes. Yes, those are definitely the facts. She was relieved that he was not willing to make all of it her fault. Perhaps he shouldn't have assumed some things. He thought she was lying when she said how broken she was. And about her anonymity being the only way she could handle what occurred between them.

What occurred. Meaning, it was over and done. It was over a few weeks ago.

But Gage was all Violet thought about. Being with him was the only thing that alleviated her grief. And living with her grief eclipsed all the joy from her life and daily routine. Her time with Gage was golden. She recalled seeing him in the morning sunlight and breathing the crisp, fresh air. The rest of her life seemed moldy and dark. Confined and suffocating. With Gage in the mountains and woods, she could breathe freely.

Yet any effort to bring that home with her would have totally destroyed it and eventually, her. It would crush her slowly. Squeezing her breath out until she expired from lack of oxygen.

Seeing him so unexpectedly made her gasp and she forced herself to exhale slowly lest she hyperventilate.

But it was much more complicated now. She and Gage had other impediments. It wasn't just between each other.

Their families saw them together. Background stories. His daughter.

His daughter.

Violet wondered how to handle that most shocking development. The last thing she'd expected.

She answered: *I hope you don't hate me. But I was never looking for more than that. I am not ready to handle it.*

Instantly, he texted*: Not ready? Or not willing?*

God, he so quickly sensed her self-doubt and wavering theories. He seemed completely tuned in to her. Not willing? She didn't know.

I don't know. It is different since our meeting in town.

We could agree to talk about it. Without the shock and awe factor. Without our families watching?

We could, I suppose. You always suggest the right thing to do.

I didn't know your name, but I got you, Vee. I don't think any of that was wrong or a lie.

Was your daughter upset about me? Violet really wanted to know that answer.

No. She knew about you before. I didn't tell her we had sex, obviously, but I'm sure she knows now. Andy's pretty amazing for her age. Mature. Kind. Funny... well, stop me before I go on until tomorrow...

She smiled. How could she not appreciate how much he admired his teenage daughter? Teenage girls can be monsters for single dads and instead, he had only kind words and respect for her.

But he still was a father to a teenage daughter. It intimidated Violet and made her feel weird. Like crazy weird. Was she too young to date and have sex with a man who was raising a daughter that old?! It seemed wrong. So Violet wasn't sure she could handle it.

Vee? Did I lose you again? He texted a moment later.

No. I was contemplating your teenage daughter.

Surprised by my youthful physique? My boyish charm and sexual prowess?

She was smirking and laughing out loud at her damn phone. *Mostly by your fragile ego. Seeing how I wouldn't tell you my last name... So much for your sexual prowess...*

Or maybe I overwhelmed you. So you weren't sure you could handle seeing me in person...

That's it, Gage. That's totally it. I could not handle it with others around. You saw me...

I did. Big-eyed, lost, confused. That's how much I affected you. Rendering you speechless. Overwhelmed. Nearly comatose from my manliness... right?

He shot a barb through her heart like a sharp arrow, yet she loved his damn teasing. It made her heart swell with happiness just to talk to him, which was new for her.

Comatose from your manliness? OMG, no. Never. I'm overwhelmed because damn it, I have to talk to you again.

Ahh... inflicting pointy barbs and spurs into my heart.

She made the same analogy. They oddly thought alike, worked alike, camped alike and did their chores alike. They even enjoyed sex alike. It was amazing.

Would you see me again? Go out with me? We could have dinner or do anything you want.

I don't want to date you. But seeing you stirred up everything again. What if we continued what we were doing... you know? Not dating but?

In seconds, he answered: *No. I have a daughter who met you. I won't sneak out to sleep with you in clandestine dates. As if you're ashamed of it. No connection. It's not just sex I want and you know that. I won't continue if it is. I don't want it and I won't have Andy suspecting that.*

Holy shit. Okay. Pretty cut and dried. She was just testing the water, possibly seeing each other without dating. No boyfriend/girlfriend crap. She couldn't stand being labeled such a thing. Being someone else's *girlfriend*. Why couldn't he just accept it? Let it continue undefined? Let it be purely physical and wonderful? Let it soothe her loneliness and heartache without all the expectations and connotations? Why not?

Fuck. Him.

Her heart dropped into her shoes.

I can't. I just can't.

I can't do it again the other way.

She lodged her tongue in her cheek, feeling disappointed. She had to blink her tears away.

I'm sorry.

Nah. Don't be. From the start, you never lied or pretended what your intentions were. The chances you would or would not take. I can't fault you for that. I might not agree with it. I might wish things were different. But I'm an adult. I'll live with it. I'll get over it.

God, the stabbing in her heart again. NO! No, she didn't want him to get over her.

But it wouldn't work. It would never work because she wanted him so badly. She had to be stoic. Friends. Sex-buddies at most. He was fair and understanding. So why wasn't she relieved he felt that way and wanted no more from her?

Nah? I'll get over it? That wasn't enough. Not after what they'd experienced together. It was epic. Amazing. Once in a lifetime. And finding each other again?

It was pretty romantic. She wasn't willing to take a risk and now she was annoyed at him for respecting her decision? For being a fucking adult? Why? She gave him no other choice.

Great. Awesome. He was a well-adjusted, emotionally mature man. Fuck. Raising a daughter. Violet was a stupid, immature girl, out of his league. They would never have encountered each other in River's End or the valley. They would have simply moved on with their respective lives. Here, they could so easily avoid each other. In the mountains? They could not.

Gage was a mature, settled, responsible, older man. Violet was a girl, not much older than his daughter. Ugh. But she resented his easy acceptance of her refusal to see more of him.

She preferred what? Him baring his teeth and slapping his chest with his fists while galloping past her on a white steed and sweeping her off her feet? A white knight? Ha. She told him NO in clear terms. So why the sinking heart and sarcasm? Why was she being so stupid?

I won't. Not so easily. None of it. I'm sorry I can't be better, she replied.

One simple, honest sentence.

I said I would get used to it. I didn't say it would be easy, he answered.

Thank God. She sighed and something made her warm inside. She didn't want to make it easy for him. Not when it felt like concrete in her veins whenever she imagined never seeing him again.

But in the end, she wouldn't see him again. Leaning the phone against her forehead, she blinked back her tears. No. Oh, no. She didn't want to be hurt anymore, not by Gage. She didn't want to invest any emotions in him. That was why she'd kept her name to herself and tried so hard to keep herself from loving him.

None of this is easy.

He answered after a long time: *Life isn't easy.*

Oh yeah, she heard the rebuke in his simple, flawless response.

Couldn't deal with it either. A heavy blob of lead settled in her guts and pulled her down.

CHAPTER 14

TWO DAYS LATER, VIOLET was back at work. Halfway through the week, she glanced up to find Andy standing in the doorway of the classroom. It was lunchtime and she was the only one left in the classroom.

Damn it.

She stared back at Gage's daughter. The reality of that still blew her away. She hated knowing Andy was taller and older and more intelligent than she expected, with her own opinions about Violet sleeping with her dad. She instantly got to her feet. "Andy? Um… hey. What can I do for you?"

"Do you mind if I sit with you? I had a fight with one of my friends and she's being a bitch at the table where I sit, and everyone's taking sides and I just don't want to eat my lunch there."

Alarm bells rang loudly in Violet's head. No. Nope. She should not get involved. She should never know anything about Gage's daughter. Or risk him finding out she did. He'd hate her getting involved when she shouldn't. Girl-drama. God, how she remembered and hated it. She understood Andy's need to avoid it.

Or did this leggy teenager want to have words with the woman she'd discovered most recently slept with her father? What if she hated the idea of it? At thirteen, Violet would have detested any woman that wasn't her mom going near her dad. She still cringed whenever she pictured her parents having sex. She never got to a point where it was something she could easily hear and talk about.

Then again, her dad was always with her mom, making it an entirely different situation than Andy was facing. What did she really think about her dad being intimate with someone? What if she worried that a woman might change her relationship with her dad? Having spent their lives together with just the two of them, what teen would even indulge the possibility of a strange woman moving in? Becoming a stepparent to her? No. Andy could not want that and would probably hate anyone who even slightly resembled that role to her.

But now Violet was at school. This was a student, never mind she was Gage's daughter, and Violet had no legitimate reason to deny Andy's request, despite the insecurity that coursed through her. "Yeah. Sure... yes."

Andy smiled gratefully as she sank down in the chair with her sack lunch. Did Gage make it? Violet's silly heart swelled, as she watched Andy take out a Tupperware with a sandwich inside it. So tidy and neat, she doubted any teen could have made it. No, her father did. Gage made the sweet lunch. Sandwich, apple and a granola bar. A few small chocolates. It was perfect. Violet's chest heaved a sigh. Gage was like no other man she knew.

"So... this friend? Anything serious?"

"Not really. I'm sure we'll work it out. I just didn't want to participate in the drama or sit there in silence, you know?"

A small smile crept over Violet's lips. "Oh, I know. I remember a few silent lunches with friends I got pissed at, but we never actually said so or worked it out. Instead, we'd go for a silent stand-off, and make ourselves completely uncomfortable just by being there."

"Yes, exactly. We don't say what we think outright. And if we do, others think we're rude, when really, all we're trying to do is work our issues out."

Andy was more mature than Violet was, she realized. Unsure of how to answer her, and totally self-conscious over how much she should say to Gage's daughter, Violet went with what seemed like the safest response. "Should you tell your dad?"

"Yeah. I will. He knows about the start of it. But not what happened today."

"That's good you let him offer his opinion."

"Yeah. I tell my dad more than my friends tell any of their parents. None of my friends talk to their dads. Just their moms. But since it's always been Dad and me, he deals with it."

Um. Shit. What should she say to that? Her heart went out to the motherless teen. Violet's mom meant everything to her. Every hard conversation, every secret she couldn't wait to spill, every time she needed help and advice, she first filtered it through her mom. Her mom was the one she went to in tears and counted on for hugs. Imagine not having a mother? Violet felt her face heating up. Perhaps she took her mom for granted during the past two years. She always had both of her parents to rely on for their support, both financial and emotional, and they never judged her after Preston's death made her so remote. They still loved her. No, they adored her. And she insisted on keeping them at arm's length.

Violet turned her attention back to the tall teen she saw before her, eating a homemade sandwich of what looked like tuna on rye with extra mayonnaise and lettuce. "I'm sorry about your mom."

Was that the right thing to say? Was it weak or stupid? Violet shifted her butt, and sipped her water bottle, feeling lost. She had no idea how to talk to the teenage daughter of a *former lover*.

Andy was still chewing as she waved her hand around. "I know everyone thinks growing up motherless is such a trial and whatever, but honestly? I never had a mom, so I never got to miss her. I always had my dad. And my grandparents and aunts were often around me too. Whenever Dad worked, I got to see my grandparents and uncles and aunties. Even after a lot of them got married, I am still a huge part of their families. I've been lucky to have such a big, close-knit extended family."

Violet smiled, relieved she could finally relate to something. "Me too. Where I grew up, I was literally surrounded by all my aunts and uncles and cousins. They were all there. No grandparents, but I have one cousin that's old enough to be my uncle. I can't imagine my childhood without every single one of them. So I know what you mean about having a big family that you love to be around. Thankfully, I still have both my parents."

"Are you pretty close to them?"

Violet smiled down to her fingers as she replied, "Yes. And my three sisters too."

"Three sisters. That's awesome. That's the only thing I sometimes wish I had, a sibling who might get it. You know? Another person who is raised exactly the same way as you are."

"Yes, I know."

"Did you and your sisters fight?"

"All the time. We still bicker constantly."

"Is it real?"

"No. It's all in fun. It comes from our mutual confidence that we can totally annoy each other without having any guts to it. You know? Like we trust each other unconditionally so we can pick and prod each other. Out of fun and love." Her smile widened as she thought about Rose, Iris and Daisy and the arguments and faux-fights they engaged in over the years.

Andy leaned forward and her eyes were bright. "That's what I'd want if I could make it happen. But I have my cousins now. Five in all. They're much younger than me and I'm like their awesome, older fun person. So I think it'll only keep getting better with them. You know? And they add so much fun to the holidays."

Andy finished her sandwich and started on her apple as she chatted with ease and humor about her family. There seemed to be no hidden agenda to her coming there to see Violet, or in talking about her family. She was entirely family-oriented and Gage had every reason to be proud of the teenager he was raising. She was confident, comfortable in herself and her skin, and she ate her lunch with a good appetite and healthy vigor. She ate like any other child. So often, way too often, that wasn't the case for teenaged girls.

"So you know how I said I talk to my dad?"

"Yes." Violet shifted and stiffened her back, folding her hands in her lap to keep from fidgeting. She reminded herself this was Gage's daughter and she had to be careful with whatever she said, and how she said it.

"Yeah, he's always been my dad and mom blended into one. He's pretty great. All my friends complain endlessly about their parents not allowing them to do what they want to do. I just stay quiet, because I don't feel that way about my dad. I mean, I'm not allowed to drink alcohol or smoke or vape cigarettes or pot, obviously. I can't skip class or lie to him or any of that, but I wouldn't want to anyway, you know? Dad's always been open to any questions I have, so I just ask him. Anything. All the time. It's hard to hate your dad when he lets it all hang out. He admits when he isn't sure of the answer to something. He apologizes if he's wrong. He can be strict too. He gets angry quickly if he thinks I did something mean on purpose; but he's also the first to comfort me if anything goes wrong. He made it impossible for me to miss having a mother."

Violet's heart swelled with empathy. What more endorsement could a parent need than such a glowing report from his thirteen-year-old daughter? Some daughters were too busy rolling their eyes in embarrassment or disgust at their parents. This one told her father everything? Even bragging about his fairness and kindness?

"Not to say he's my friend though. He always reminds me he can't be my friend, because he's the parent and he has a lot of rules. I don't know if you noticed, but he's kind of anal in his rigidity. He's reasonable, and I know I can always at least talk to him. Since he usually makes sense, I can't get mad at him."

Violet tilted her head. Why was Andy telling her this? Making Gage sound like the all-around angel as a man and a father? In Violet's experience, she agreed, but why would his teenage daughter seek her out as... what? His former lover? Why would she tell her all this stuff?

"He is fair and kind. I agree wholeheartedly."

She crunched the apple slice. Gage sliced her apple. Nodding vigorously, Andy's eyes sparkled with joy. "I'm so glad you see that. He is. Really. I'm sure when he got a little cross the other night, it was only because he was so surprised to see you. He never had something like that happen before. I'm not sure my grandparents ever met someone, heck, *anyone* he ever dated." Her face scrunched up.

Oh sweet baby Jesus, deliver her from this conversation.

What the *hell* could she say to that? Why was Andy talking to her? So personally? How much did Gage say about their relationship? The time they spent together? What did Andy hear on Saturday night?

"Umm… yes, I guess we were both surprised. We were both slightly… heated."

"I think he got cross because he likes you so much. He wants to see you again but he thinks you don't want to see him anymore."

She nearly burst into flames of embarrassment. "Umm, I just lost someone very dear to me and can't really care for anyone else yet."

"But you seemed to care about him."

Oh, the accurate perception of this teenager. She was so much like her father. The fluidity of speaking her thoughts without screening them or hesitation. The way Violet used to be. Before she learned how to be different. To be cautious. To be quiet.

"I did. Yes. It was a shock. I didn't think I'd ever see him again."

"But once you did, you didn't seem very sad about it."

Dear God, she should become a psychologist. How smoothly she analyzed a single interaction between Gage and Violet. Yes. They totally got along. Yes, it felt good. No, it felt wonderful. Heart-stopping thrill to see the man. But also shock and pain and awkwardness.

The daughter.

"I know I must have upset you the most. He mentioned he didn't tell you about me. I think that was a stupid move on his part. I mean, come on, I had to be an obvious issue, right? I'm his kid."

"Umm… uh-huh. I mean, yes, it would have been nice if I had some forewarning of it."

"He's just really protective when it comes to me. If he doubted you two would go anywhere, he wouldn't mention me. I've only met two women he dated over the years. Two. And they were after months of *casual dating*. That's nice for me, since I never had to confront strange women during my childhood who might have been staying in my home. Do you know not one woman ever stayed over? Not one. I've never awoken to find a strange woman in my house. I have plenty of friends whose parents are single or divorced, and they constantly blab about all the dates and sexual crap they get exposed to. Waking up to a strange woman or man they don't know and being asked to eat breakfast with them. Or strangers virtually moving into their homes after a few months of dating. They all hate it. They also hate the people that are involved, including their own family members. Being strangers in their own homes makes them feel like they don't matter. Don't you see? My dad never did that to me."

Violet did see. Gage was the perfect man. Gage Sullivan was the ideal boyfriend who would later become the ultimate husband. Seeing that as a friend and acquaintance and knowing he was also a father? Well, who could top that? Violet's face almost melted into a gooey pile of pleasure when she thought how wonderful Gage truly was.

Which was why he was so wrong for her.

Violet wasn't wonderful or mature or settled. She didn't know what to do with a man as ideal as Gage. Never mind his daughter.

"He's pretty unusual and special."

"Yes. And don't forget awesome. But I think he wants to bring you home. I want you to know something right now: that would be so cool with me if he did. I mean, you love horses and he told me how well you managed to take care of yourself all alone in the woods and whatever... Seems you aren't ordinary and not at all like the girlfriends some of my friend's dad's end up with."

Violet smiled, biting her lip while picturing Andy's standard of measurement. "Well, you aren't like any thirteen-year-old girl I ever met either."

"I'm not. And that's what I'm trying to tell you. Don't let me be the reason that you won't date him."

Oh? Oh, shit. Andy thought it was her fault. Violet's gaze focused on the soft contours of the girl's round face. Youthful and fresh, without the strains of adulthood yet. "Oh, Andy… that's not why. That's not it at all. I was lost before I ever knew you. You see, I have… my own issues."

"I know; you saw your fiancé die."

Oh. Man. She didn't beat around the bush. The innocence of youth. No tact and all honesty? Sheer, brutal honesty. Violet remembered being like that. Oh yes, she was just like Andy before all the shit hit the fan.

"Yes. It broke my heart. I can't go through something like that again."

Andy put her Tupperware in her bag and rolled up her lunch trash into the paper sack before making a mini-ball, which she deftly shot directly into the trash can. Perched on the edge of her seat, she shook her head. "But don't you see? This time it has to be different. I mean, think about it… What are the odds that your next boyfriend would also die right in front of you? I mean, they have to be pretty small? Right? Statistically speaking, being in a relationship with a person who doesn't ride horses might be the safest thing you could do right now." Tilting her head, Andy's entire face brightened. "I mean, he's a hiker, not a rider. I hate hiking; but oh, man! My dad loves it. See? No chance of fate repeating itself, right?!"

Violet simply recoiled with a small huff of shock as she stared at the girl in utter disbelief. She was beyond good reasoning and way the fuck out there, but she was also almost faultless in her assessment too. The simplicity of it was impossible for Violet to argue with.

Naturally, all the emotions gurgled up into Violet's throat. The ones that mere talking about Preston and how he died always seemed to trigger.

"You should go to law school and become an attorney when you're older," Violet said with a sardonic rise of her eyebrows.

Andy's head tilted and her expression was totally serious. "Dad says the same thing to me frequently."

"Your dad is very perceptive."

"You're avoiding our previous conversation."

"Yes," Violet smiled, "I am. And you are so clever."

"I think you're missing the point here."

She tried not to smile but the girl's tone was so indignant, she had to bite her lip to keep her expression neutral. "Okay, what's the point? What am I missing?"

"You must have feelings towards my dad. If dating him and spending time with him scares you so much, you must fear losing him."

Sliced right to the bone, straight through the skin, tendons, tissue and veins. This girl surgically snipped her with a scalpel, using accurate precision and going straight to the bone. The heart and center of the matter. She did it epically well. Violet could not refute anything that she said. It sounded so lame of her if she failed to embrace her feelings. Maybe she was scared of something that could never happen.

But knowing that a smidgeon of a percent of a chance existed was what kept her up at night. It festered like a virus after lying dormant in her body. Ready to suddenly emerge and infect her, making her as sick as the plague until she died.

"You make very good points."

"And you are very skillful too. You manage to avoid answering my questions by creating diversions. I can see how many people don't even realize they haven't gotten an answer."

"I do care about your dad. Maybe too much. And if I do, it's only because I'm trying to spare him from my screwed-up emotional state regarding relationships."

"What if he doesn't want to be spared? Shouldn't he be the one to decide that?" Andy countered. Violet almost applauded her pluck and stamina. Damn. She was a true master with the snappy retorts.

"Yes. But I also have to be ready and right now, I'm not strong enough."

"What? But you lived in the mountains all alone. How can you not be strong enough?"

Violet took Andy's big-eyed wonder to heart. Andy really meant it. Passionately. She viewed Violet and her lifestyle and physical capabilities as superior to anyone. Andy didn't believe Violet had a frozen icicle where her heart should have been that made her unwilling to take chances. Andy was far more mature and wise than her age would suggest, but her assumption that physical strength and prowess were correlated to one's mental and emotional strengths only proved to Violet how young Andy still was.

But what a teen.

Andy tilted her head, tapping a finger on her lower lip before a warm smile brightened her face. "Okay. I guess that's fair. But remember what you decide today doesn't have to last forever."

Violet blinked. Dear Lord. Was she thirteen or a hundred and three? Where the heck does a young teenager learn such things? By being motherless? By receiving the unconditional care and love that Gage gave her? Whatever. It combined to create the most incredible person. A girl who wasn't annoying, snarky, bubbling, irritating, angry, reckless or hateful. It was hard not to be those things as a budding teenager. And Gage received all the credit for it. On any given day of her life, Violet knew she or one of her sisters were terrible teens.

"I'd better get to class. Mind if I stop by and visit you again sometimes?"

Jolted, Violet shook her head. "No, not at all. But do you think it's necessary? Will your friends continue to pose a problem?"

She waved a hand around. "Oh, that. I made that up. I figured you might feel weird about being alone with me. So it's good. I got a bunch of friends. Sorry, I lied. I don't make a habit of doing it."

Well, shit. Violet should have been annoyed or angry at that revelation, but the girl was so damn honest about herself and guileless, that she candidly admitted things she didn't have to. There was no way Violet could feel miffed or slighted.

"Don't do that again though. I hate liars."

"Me too. Next time I see you, I'll just hang out because I want to."

She sighed. "I have to ask… why would you want to?"

"Because I saw the pictures of you performing on the horses. I want to do that too. I want to learn how to do everything you do… I think you're the most awesome person and why not?"

"Andy, please listen to me. I can't teach you how to do it. I can't stand seeing other people riding horses anymore. So, I'm not trying to be mean, but I literally can't do it now. Every single time I try to force myself to give a riding lesson, my stomach turns flips. Are you hearing me?"

She smiled. And it was huge. "Sure. Got it. Dad explained it. So I'll see you around."

She didn't hear a word Violet said! Frustrated, Violet

ground her teeth and the bell rang before the classroom filled again.

After school in an effort to be honest and forthright, she texted Gage. *Violet ate her lunch with me. She wants us to date. Just so you know. I was honest and tried to decline gently but she didn't hear me.*

Immediately, Gage answered: *Ahh, hell. I'm sorry. She gets something in her head and nothing slows her down. I'll talk to her. Thanks for letting me know. Sorry if she made you uncomfortable.*

Not uncomfortable. She's very smart, astute and observant. She also makes good points. I'm pretty sure she won them all. I was so astounded.

Emojis of smiles appeared. *Believe me, I know. Try raising a child more worldly and wise than you are.*

I wanted you to know the reason I said no to dating. It wasn't because of her...

Nothing for a few moments: *She thought it was because of her?*

I think so. It isn't. I want that made clear. She's great.

She is. And it would make this so much easier. But I know why you said no. I'll talk to her.

Violet clutched her phone to her chest. Damn it, why did his daughter and he make her heart beat too fast with anticipation just to hear their reply? Why did her nerve endings feel so goddamned raw? But they did.

HIS TRUCK WAS PARKED INNOCUOUSLY at the entrance to the arena. Obviously, he was there for his daughter's riding lesson with Violet's aunt. Why the hell did his daughter have to choose to take her lessons here? Riding in that fucking arena. The place where Preston was murdered. That's all she saw when she looked at the arena. Murder. Death. Grief.

She turned away just as Gage stepped out of the main door. *Gage*. Her heart thumped hard against her chest. Oh, God. Gage. The fun she had with him in the mountains filtered through her brain. The work. The walking. The chores. The banter. The contentment. There was nothing about Preston to detract from her time in the mountains with Gage.

It was so pure and pleasant. Just the two of them. Nothing to hinder their connection or fun or friendship.

But now, everything was wrong. Seeing his face in front of the arena almost made Violet nauseous. The death trap. She was filled with dread. He didn't see her. She stepped behind a pine tree. Was he planning to wait in his truck? Or do errands? Violet stood and stared. As Gage approached his truck, he noticed her. He stared for a moment, then he released the door handle and walked towards her. Crossing the gravel lot, he headed to where she'd just returned from feeding her horses.

He stopped a few feet shy of her. This time, the chance encounter was not so emotional. Or gut-consuming. "Hey, Violet."

"Hi." She studied his face, drinking it in. She examined the curve of his brown eyebrows, the sweep of his thick, black eyelashes and the soft lines around his eyes. Even a small smile warmed and twinkled in his eyes. His nose was straight and narrow and his jaw square. Every detail was etched into her brain.

"Andy's riding now."

"Yes. I figured." Silence fell. He glanced away, kicking a rock with his foot.

"Do you want to sit over there?" she asked after several long seconds. There were plenty of benches situated up and down the river of the land they owned. And many others were placed in strategic spots of the landscaped resort grounds. They provided endless views to appreciate so the guests often sat on them. On this quiet Saturday morning in October, no one was out and about, at least not at the moment. They sat down and gazed at a grove of cotton-woods before them. The river glinted through the tree trunks, showing bits of brown and cobalt blue.

"How's it going with the riding lessons?"

"Andy's in love." He straightened his jacket, putting his hands in his pockets again. A nervous habit around her, but it seemed to help him keep his posture.

"I was always like that too."

He stared at her profile. She could feel it. "That didn't seem to change."

"No. I still love them."

"Can I ask you something? About Preston? That was his name?"

Startled at Gage's line of questioning, and hearing Preston's name took Violet by surprise and she looked at him and then away before a frown appeared on her face. "Yes. That was his name."

"After you witnessed his tragic death, what kind of effect did it have on your career? How could you still manage to ride horses yourself?"

She licked her lips. Of course, he questioned it. She refused to give horseback riding lessons to his daughter, dashing the young girl's excitement and hope.

Sighing, Violet turned forward and stared at the paved path before her. Gage deserved some information to explain her oddities. He'd been a damn saint compared to what other men might perceive as games.

"I wasn't afraid to ride. Even right after it happened. I wasn't afraid because I know I can ride. If a horse bolts, I use my legs to squeeze the horse's middle instantly. That keeps me centered and on top of the horse. I can pull back on a rein or grab the saddle horn. I have fast reflexes and I've been honing them on horses from the time I was five years old. There isn't anything I haven't done or experienced on horseback. So I trust myself. It's other riders I can't trust. Most respond with fear. Fear can paralyse a rider when danger strikes and fast reflexes are required. Others have too much confidence, making them careless. Pushing their horses and themselves too far can lead to fatal errors. Since Preston's accident, I can't stand to watch other people ride. All I see are visions of them falling or being thrown, like premonitions, and I wonder where they'll land... I know my anxieties are ridiculous, but I can't shake them."

Gage didn't answer at first. Was he confused by her strange triggers? The way the accident affected her made her rather eccentric. She hoped when he remembered how he met her and slept with her, he wouldn't think so.

"So that's why you went ape-shit when Andy asked you to teach her to ride?"

"Yes. It's strange, I know, but I trust myself with horses. What happened to Preston wasn't the horse's fault. It was caused by the fucking asshole who shot a gun in an enclosed building, making the horses react instinctually as they do when threatened. Fight or flight. You know? That's what they do. Most horses react by jumping or rearing or running before they can obey their riders. It was such a freak fucking thing." She stared at her fingernails, rubbing them together but not glancing up. She could not bear to see the sympathy or annoyance or whatever might be in the face of this new man in her life.

"It's not so odd when you explain it. You can control yourself and handle a horse's natural inclinations. They are not machines, after all. They each have their own personalities, strengths and weaknesses. You trust yourself to handle them, but you don't fully trust anyone else."

"I trusted Preston too. He didn't grow up with horses like me. He learned to ride here. From me. I truly believed he was ready to perform in the show. I pushed him to do it. So he did and that's why he died."

Gage's hand covered one of hers and he squeezed her fingers. Instantly, her hand went as limp as a dead fish. It was an automatic response for her. She bit her lip without looking up.

"How many times did he perform?"

She let out a sigh as she calculated the number of times in her head. "I don't know. For barely three months, a couple of times a week so probably a dozen or more."

There was a long, heavy silence. He didn't lift his hand from hers even when she didn't react. She didn't turn her palm over to grip his, although she wanted to. She longed and ached to squeeze his hand and had to mentally command her hand to stay down. Protecting herself.

Gage wanted to undo her defensive responses. If anyone could succeed, it was this man with his huge, brawny shoulders and chest and his warm, green-gold eyes and dark hair. The freaking beard that never attracted Violet before looked right on Gage. He was so hot and he had the air of an older, mature, capable man with a woodsy wisdom. That was a bit of an aphrodisiac to her.

Gage was the antithesis of young, clean-shaven—could Preston even grow a beard?—athletic, young, smiling Preston. Dying at age twenty-three, he never developed his maturity and wisdom. He had hot, intense, quiet, inborn confidence. Not like Gage in his manliness. Preston was hot in a young, cocky, grab-the-world-by-the-fucking-balls way.

So comparing Gage and Preston was a stupid pastime. Like comparing an elephant to a lion. Neither is better or worse, just different. Different views and perspectives on the world and their contributions to it determined how they lived and thrived in it.

"And nothing like that ever happened before to you or anyone you know?"

Oh, she knew where his calm and reasonable questioning was headed. Many others had tried to take it that way before Gage.

"No. I've never heard of it. Neither did Jack or Ian or Ben or any of my family members who have been running this horse ranch forever. They know everyone in the three-state area. No. It just happened here to Preston."

She knew what any reasonable person would say next. That didn't mean it would ever happen again. The likelihood of that was zero. Even his damn teenager pointed that out to her. But Violet could not accept it. She didn't believe it at gut-level and could not convince herself of it. She told him everything he wanted to hear. But that didn't make it true where her heart, her guts, or her core were concerned.

"Have you thought about talking to a professional?"

She jerked her gaze from her bobbing left knee, which she jiggled incessantly. This topic always turned her into a bundle of energy and frenetic nerves. But doing it with Gage? She felt like she might slip right out of her skin. She thought he'd try to persuade her that her fears and phobias had no foundation. He'd try to make her see how obvious it was, as everyone else saw it. So many people tried. She stonewalled every effort and cut off too many well-meaning family members and friends to even count.

"Like a counselor?"

"Yeah. Specifically, a grief counselor. You sound to me like you suffer from PTSD. You witnessed a loved one's violent death. That's no small thing. Perhaps you're shouldering some of the blame because you taught and encouraged him to ride horses and perform in the show. The thoughts and feelings you discuss don't seem crazy or strange, but they are the triggers. Emotions you can't restrain or control."

She pushed his hand away and immediately hopped to her feet. "What? Should I get all better so I can fuck you and be friendly?"

He sighed. His fingers touched the bridge of his nose and he pressed the space between his eyes as if he had a bad headache. "No. Not at all like that. I want to facilitate your healing for you, Violet. It's not about us. I'm not sure if it ever was. Maybe I allowed you to see a flash for a second that improved your life just a bit. But with so much baggage and trauma, you refuse to even see it. It's sad to hear how much pain you have to live in. That's all. If something could improve it, it seems only reasonable that you should try it."

She fisted her hands and all but stomped her feet, hating Gage for sounding so rational about her. The constant pain in her chest was like an iron lung she needed to breathe. She hated knowing he was right. Everything he said sounded right, and yet... she failed to even try to fix what was wrong. She couldn't stand the thought of talking to someone who didn't actually know Preston. Why would talking about his death help her? How could that ever fix it or make her *feel* better? Did she really want to feel better? Wouldn't that mean she had somehow moved on? Or healed? She still loved Preston and didn't want to lose that connection. Those feelings.

He sighed, heaving himself to his feet as if it took a great deal of effort. "Look, you overreact anytime I try to mention ways to make you feel better. Or talk about us. Then you're sorry for it later. I'm really not interested in pushing you anymore and I don't want to fight with you. I've witnessed your grief and where you're stuck with healing—"

"I will never heal. I can't get over him. That's what I'm

trying to make you understand. To see the whole picture and fully comprehend."

He tilted his head in the smallest nod. What? His first capitulation that she was right? Narrowing her gaze on him, she all but huffed like a child annoyed with a parent.

"Okay. Then remain stuck where you are and never heal. I started to really care about you. You push me away, and say you don't want that, but you can't control me, or prevent me from feeling the way I do. And you can't change my belief that you need some professional help to make sense of what happened to you."

"I have family and friends with whom I've talked about it ad nauseum. It doesn't help. Talking doesn't help it at all. The facts remain, hard and cold, no matter how many times you review them."

"Right. But therapy, especially grief therapy could be different than just talking. Maybe they can teach you the necessary skills to help you overcome the anxiety and panic that cripples you… that keeps you from telling someone your name for example."

She couldn't hold his gaze. It was too clear, concise, intelligent, sympathetic and fuck… *loving* and it roved over her face as he spoke. Speaking kindness and truth. Truth. She hated hearing it.

"You've no idea what it's like to lose the love of your life," she threw out at him like a rock. Hard. Biting. Aiming to hit her mark and make sure he understood she did NOT love him. Or want him.

"No. I agree. I've never been in love with anyone before, although I cared very much for Andy's mom. She was my best friend. My baby's mother. She died at the tender age of twenty-one. The cruelty of it is not lost on me and I still grieve. For her. And myself. But mostly for my daughter who lost her mother."

"Why are you so fucking rational? Love isn't like that. You don't just get over it. Or analyze and understand it. It's hard and messy and unpredictable. It's all-consuming and all-healing and when it's gone..." She leaned over, gasping for breath and finally lowering her voice. "When it's gone, you're gone. You're empty. Devoid of all meaning in your life. Like a bottomless, empty, black pit, and yet you must continue to wander the planet, and try to go on. That is how I loved. That is the only way I could love. And nothing but the love you have for Andy compares to it. Imagine losing your daughter and having me tell you to 'get over it.'"

She nearly screamed with annoyance and the grunt she released was filled with unmitigated anger. She wanted to kick the bench. Gage was so smart and analytical. He sounded so logical. Yes. Everything he said was right. Except the feelings. What happens to your emotions? All the things that make a relationship new and special and different? Being in love and feeling loved in return were what made Violet feel the best ever. Gage sounded like the end of it should be rational; something to be organized and discussed and catalogued and dealt with. No. It was hard and messy and it destroyed you, crushing all your dreams and hopes. All the coulda-beens. All the lost years and standard milestones. For an eternity. When she lost Preston that day, he also vanished from their shared future together. All the anniversaries and birthdays that would have been hers to celebrate were instantly gone. Poof.

She suddenly realized what she blurted out after her emotions got the better of her. Pushing her hands up to bury her face in them, she said much more quietly, "I'm sorry. I didn't mean that... you should never even dare to imagine the loss of... I'm so sorry. That wasn't fair. I just got carried away with myself."

Oh. Fuck. Gage immediately came over to her,

surrounding her with his large, warm arms and tucking her against his broad chest beneath his brown canvas coat. The harsh material felt rough and scratchy on her cheek. She kept her hands over her eyes, pressing them harder to hold in the hot tears. His grip on her was loose, merely his hands on her waist. But he embraced her. Generously offering her his warmth and protection and... oh, God, it felt so good.

"You tend to get carried away."

Shoulders wilting, her anger rapidly dissipating, Violet released the smallest laugh. Only Gage could manage to draw that out of her after the mini-meltdown she just displayed. "I do. Why do you put up with it?"

"Because maybe I like it. Especially if you get carried away with me or something else you particularly like."

His calm words, reflecting his stability, freaked her out. She feared he would wear her out with all his intuitive understanding. He pushed her to her limit and then backed off, letting her grow accustomed to the new space and expanding her comfort zone. She knew he was doing that, and she responded as planned. Fucking A if she didn't make that space part of her zone. She learned to swiftly acclimate to whatever situation Gage thrust her in without hating him for doing it to her.

She took in a breath that made her chest shudder. "Whatever you find positive in me can't compensate for the rest of me that's not."

"Why don't you let me be the judge of that?" He toyed with a strand of hair on her shoulder and her stupid heart swelled with desire. She savored the care he demonstrated while sliding his hands through her hair.

"I can't be what you want me to be."

"I think you can. I think you're just scared to try something different."

She dropped her hands to her sides, leaning into his

warmth. She longed to respond by wrapping herself up around him completely, and her heart ached to do that. But she kept her distance, meaning she hadn't fully fallen for Gage's charm and chivalry... not yet.

She tilted her head and said, "Yes, Gage, I am scared of too many things. The old me would have mocked and laughed at me now. But there it is. I still can't walk into a fucking building that I hung around and loved to be in all my life. *Can't.* I physically cannot do it. I could break out in hives at the mere thought. So yes, I'm afraid. Knowing that and pointing it out and wishing for it to change hasn't improved or resolved it."

He sighed and let her pull herself free. Rubbing the hair that bounced off the top of his head absently, he stared out towards the trees. "You know what they say? Admitting there's a problem is the first step..."

"First step of what? Recovering from alcoholism and addiction?" She finally found a smile that raised her eyebrows. "Not exactly the same thing, Gage."

"No. But I wish you'd consider what I said. When your mind is free and you're alone, try to wrap your head around this: I just want something good to happen for you."

Her heart squeezed with joy. He always knew what to say. He was so... so... what?

Right. Always just exactly right. Just managing to say enough. Wonderful. Amazing.

All at once, Andy bounced out of one of the arena's large doors and Violet nodded toward her as she replied, "There's Andy."

Gage glanced back, pressing his lips together. "Well, now I must endure an hour-long discussion of every single horsey detail she learned today. Wish me luck; I'm going in."

His sense of humor instantly banished the overwhelming, dark, hard feelings, and seeing his wide smile of pride and adoration for his daughter shining from his eyes, warmed Violet.

"Mission impossible." She smiled. She made a silly joke. She was all but flirting. Only minutes before, she was on the verge of crying. Or yelling. Or both at once.

His appreciative smile thrilled her stupid heart, which beat faster, but why? Amusement? Satisfaction that Gage got her lame joke? That she liked their interaction?

Feeling puzzled as usual, Violet immediately waved and left.

She could not bear to watch him greeting his daughter without devouring their interaction. The view of his back-side in those jeans against the dramatic backdrop of the arena... where her lover died.

She quickly left the resort to meet her aunt, Hailey. She'd called Violet and asked her to discuss the schedule for the holiday festivities. There was a lot to arrange between the dates, the vendors and the notes from previous years of planning. The most anticipated events at the resort occurred in November and December, created exclusively for the guests. There were exquisite dinners. And unbelievable horse shows. And the decorating? The most elaborate Christmas decorating took place every year. Violet wondered how many lights they had to hang? Thousands? Probably millions. In the past, the resort won awards and brilliant write-ups in the local as well as international travel magazines. It was featured in Christmas competition websites, blogs and magazines.

Violet liked to help Hailey, who managed the resort side of the business.

Violet hoped that once they got into the plans and assigning the various jobs, she'd forget all about Gage and Andy. And all the logical, goddamned advice Gage gave her.

She could only hope.

"Everything okay?"

She was startled when her aunt snapped her fingers in front of her eyes. Embarrassed, she quickly dipped her head to hide her face and nodded. "Yeah, just daydreaming."

Hailey stopped dead. "Really? Since when did you last daydream, Violet? Did something change?"

Violet sighed. God, she really sucked at being stealthy and secretive. She was surprised Gage didn't guess her name the very first day she hid it from him.

"I just thought about a few good but painful points a friend of mine made. I was trying to remember his exact words."

Hailey's eyebrows all but leapt off her face. "His?"

"Men and women can be friends."

"Right. Sorry."

Violet released a small smile. "But this one was a little more than just a friend, and now I can't figure out what I feel. I told him no relationship because of Preston. He refuses to just have sex." She glanced at her aunt who nodded her understanding without getting shocked or uncomfortable. Violet often helped Hailey at the resort. She'd covered the check-in counter at the main lobby all through her years of high school. She'd also coordinated and led the guests on rides. She was in charge of the horse performances during the year when Preston died. Now, Hailey's husband, Uncle Joey, took over that task. They were both the official resort directors.

Violet was always close to Hailey.

"Do you want to talk about it?"

"No. Just having issues."

Hailey leaned over to squeeze her hand. "I know how hard it's been for you. But love can happen more than once in a lifetime and in ways you could never imagine."

Hailey was divorced before she hooked up with Joey who

was twelve years younger than her. Hailey acted as if it were scandalous that she was thirty-eight and Joey was twenty-six when they fell in love. But no one else agreed, and they all but laughed it off for how funny she was about it.

"I want to know that. But my heart is still full of Preston. It gets all twisted up..."

"Honey, the older one gets, the less clear life becomes. I lived an entirely different life with another family before Joey. I was happily married for years. I loved Brett. It ended with an affair and divorce, but that happened ages before. I was a mom so I raised my kids. I loved him. It wasn't a death I suffered from, but losing Brett was a huge blow to me. It took years for me to fully come to terms with it and finally get over it. Brett and I had fairly young kids together that we had to take care of. I met Joey. There were vast differences in our ages and life experiences. There were so many times that I didn't see how we could find a way through any of it. Our relationship overlapped with all kinds of other things and it wasn't nearly as neat and tidy as my first marriage. It was confusing at first. But in the end, I knew I loved Joey and he was worth holding onto... despite any feelings I still had for Brett. And the family we tried to hold together. I saw how hard it was on Brianna and later on, Jacob with his self-medication. I wished their father would hold me because he truly understood my devastation since he was a father. See? It's complicated. But it never lessened my love for Joey. And loving Joey didn't mean I stopped loving Brett."

Violet stared with big eyes at her aunt. She didn't expect to hear such a lecture and personal advice. It was so honest and real. The truth shone like gold in her eyes.

"When Jacob disappeared, I got to be a mom with a baby again. I didn't want it in the beginning. He was supposed to be my grandson. But as time went on, he soon became Joey's and my son... until Jacob came back. I had to figure out how to love them all. It was never clean and neat. The lines blurred between family members in ways I never wanted. But we don't always get to decide who our family members will be. If you believe everyone enjoys the simple family life that your parents display in their love and marriage, take a look at Jack and Erin; or me and Joey. There is more than one way to find love. Different circumstances, stressful ordeals, and yet, you can work out a lot of it if you really want to. So don't give up totally on life. Or love. Or even a good time with whoever he is."

Violet's mouth was agape. Hailey leaned over and squeezed her hand. "Lecture over. I've wanted to tell you that for a long time now. Don't reply. Just know it's my take on it. Have you ever considered talking to someone who lost a spouse at a young age? Perhaps Jack?"

"Jack? Uncle Jack?"

"Yes. You never knew Lily, and Jack was only twenty-nine when she died. He had two young sons at the time and this ranch. And Ian, Shane and Joey were also very young... it was a lot for him to swallow. None of it turned out perfectly. But everything fell into place. Just consider the possibilities."

"Do you think I should be over what happened to Preston by now?"

"No. I don't think you ever get over it. I think you simply learn to live with it. You learn how to cope. Consider it friendly advice. Now, do you think we need to bother with Santa showing up every weekend, or just during the last two weekends of December?"

Violet smiled as Hailey swiftly launched them back into the business arrangements. "Definitely all the weekends of December." They used a big, white board calendar to write in the dates of special events, and the prepping schedule for each event. It required superior coordination with the vendors, volunteers and employees who helped them. It also kept Violet's brain challenged, which meant she was not thinking of Gage… Now, she was wondering what her Uncle Jack might have to say. She'd honestly never asked him about his personal life.

"UNCLE JACK?" she peeked her head into the rescue barn Jack ran. Four horses that had to be kept quiet were separated from the other horses and people. The equipment inside was on a large scale, from heated blankets to an equine water treadmill and a European exerciser. It gently guided a horse in a circle, and was most often used for injured horses. They had to still move or an even worse injury could occur. A broad, vibrating floor was designed to stimulate circulation for horses that were too injured to exercise. It could tilt the horse gently at various angles and thereby stimulate the horse to rebalance itself. Fresh blood supply and circulation are the fastest way to promote healing in soft tissue injuries, so much of the equipment was primarily there to stimulate the circulatory systems of the animals. Only the top of the line care was provided for the horses there. Jack tried anything that was cutting edge and innovative, but only kept the devices that he felt were safely effective. They addressed everything from joint pain to teeth care and even scheduled chiropractic sessions for some horses.

Jack's assistant, Finn, was deaf and married to Brianna who was Hailey's daughter. Finn stood at the far end of the building. He waved after he noticed Violet. Violet signed the word *Jack*. They all knew some basic ASL since Brianna taught them the rudimentary skills to communicate with her husband. Finn pointed to the second corral where he often put the newest horses to the sanctuary.

Jack was found in the inner circle of the corral. He was

trying to get closer to an obviously distressed horse. Violet's heart twisted. No. She could not watch him. Seeing a freaked-out horse over a thousand pounds wreaking havoc while Jack tried to approach it? No, thank you. She turned to head back into the barn and chat with Finn for a few moments.

But harsh words followed her.

"Violet Rydell. Turn your ass around. You better watch me. I'm the fucking expert on this ranch and it's high time you remembered that. This horse won't hurt me and you're going to watch it and see for yourself."

She flinched. Damn. Jack was intuitive. At seventy years young, her uncle was still a strong, wiry man. His formerly red hair was white nowadays and lines weathered his face, but his blue eyes shone with an intelligent vibrancy and humor that made him seem decades younger than he actually was. Strapping, lean and tough. He always wore jeans, cowboy boots and a hat. He was Violet's first hero when she was young because he could handle a horse like no one else. Not even her.

Jack's daughter, Melanie, was twenty-six and a hellion, who also kept him very young.

Violet tried to ignore him, but finally turned back. He didn't spare her a glance to see if she followed his instruction. He knew she would. Most people did. There was something authoritative about Jack that made people listen to him. Violet was no exception.

Maybe Melanie was, however.

He was right. Jack was no newbie and much more at ease and comfortable on a horse's back than walking. That was how she used to be. Jack had almost half a century of experience on her... so fine. It wasn't like watching Preston or a beginner. Jack was as advanced as they get.

She turned and leaned on the rail as Jack approached a

frightened, skittish mare that seemed scared senseless. Violet's heart lodged in her throat and she held her breath so many times, she forgot to breathe.

After fifteen grueling minutes, Jack released the horse into the open pasture. Lesson over for the day. He coiled up the lead rope and came over to her.

"Thought maybe you forgot all the work I do here. I could use some goddamned help. With Lillian off at vet school and Melanie busy with well, whatever keeps her so busy she's not here... you're very much needed. You're the best of the whole bunch, Violet, and—"

"And I'm afraid to watch anyone ride. You know that. I told you."

He sighed, flipping the latch on the gate and sauntering out. He rested a boot on the rail beside her. They stared out at the pastures of his sorry rescues. Broken, hurt, abused, neglected... They were all horses in need of so much love, medication, and physical therapy. Mostly they required what Jack was just doing. Building their trust. They were afraid of people. They were damaged and broken.

So much like Violet.

Maybe this was where she belonged.

Before the accident, she was a show-rider. A performer. A grinning, gleeful mass of energy, confidence and showmanship. Now? She was no more than a sad shadow of that amazing person. She missed the old Violet, that wild, crazy, fun, adventuresome girl of the past, but she didn't know how to be her anymore.

"How did you manage to remarry after your first wife died?"

Jack's gaze dropped down to the top of Violet's head, but she kept her eyes glued on the horses without emotion.

"Ahh... that's a good question. I didn't remarry for several years. You know, I didn't like Erin too well in the beginning.

Not her fault. Mine. I wasn't receptive to my feelings towards her and I punished her for that. Ask her about it, I'm sure she'll be glad to tell you what a horse's arse I was." He gave a small chuckle at his self-deprecating remark.

She was sure her aunt would give her an earful. But right then, she didn't feel like laughing. Silence fell between them for a good five minutes. More horse watching. She always appreciated Jack's silence. He could wait out any conversation.

"I can't... I can't get the thud of his body out of my head. The angle that his torso was twisted into. I think of it every time I close my eyes. It makes my heart hurt all over again. I know I should get over it. And feel better. I met someone that it might be possible to do that with. But I just can't. I still miss Preston..."

"That was harsh, witnessing it. My Lily got sick and then I found her dead. That was traumatizing too. I still remember holding her and crying, begging her not to leave me. I was so young... barely twenty-nine. I think Ian finally pulled me off her. It was a stressful time. Perhaps that's why I stayed single for so long. Or maybe because I was waiting for Erin."

"You loved her? As much as you did Lily?"

"Yes." No hesitation.

"Did you ever feel guilty about it?"

"Yes. I had to make my peace so I could love them both. I loved Lily for what she was, when we were young, the mother of my two boys, the holder of my young heart. Then Erin came and it was different. Not less. Just different. If you're asking me can you love them both? As in equal but separate. The way you love one child and then another. If a parent has six kids, he or she loves them all equally but separately. Or at least, that's how they're supposed to be in a family. Love is infinite, unending. Even in death. But it cannot fully contain you. It doesn't wrap you up in a cocoon and not allow you to feel it ever again. No matter how deep you think it was or is. There can always be another type that's different. I loved Lily. If she'd lived, I would have stayed married to her to this day. If Erin had crossed my path, I would never have looked at her the way I did because Lily would have been alive, even though there was still love out there for me to find. I was still full of life. I know, honey, I didn't want it at the time either. To take that risk again after losing so much and hurting so deeply? I never wanted to do it again. I wasn't planning to. The fear of that awful pain was too great. Few people experience that or the need to get over it. It takes more strength than just about anyone can imagine."

"I suck at it. I make a terrible tragic figure. I'm not strong or noble."

He snorted and nodded. "Lord, I pushed Erin so far... I was a fucking idiot. For a long time too. You don't have to be good at it. Sometimes, love sneaks in and grabs you, despite it all."

She stared straight ahead, and her eyes remained dry, but her voice cracked when she whispered, "Uncle Jack... I'm so scared."

He turned and wrapped her up in a gentle hug. "You've been scared for a long time, sweetie, but you're still here. You still get up each day and go about your business. You're alive. You'll want to love again someday. If not this guy, another guy. Or girl. Whatever you're into." He smiled at her and she reciprocated.

"Unfortunately, it's always guys for me."

"You should talk to Erin. Ask what it was like for her to step into someone else's shoes. It might give you a better perspective for this guy... Wait, is he a good catch?"

"I think so. Yes. He's got a thirteen-year-old daughter."

"Erin could definitely help you deal with that. Have you told your parents yet?"

"No. They have this ceaseless, unbroken love. Sometimes I get jealous of them. They give me advice and love and all that, but they can't know how much my loss affects me and how hard it is for me to go on."

"I can appreciate that. I'm glad to help but you should know, they understand you too."

"Mom's first marriage?"

"Yep. Shane had to cope with that. Your loss is not so uncommon as you might think. Love is not easy, it's hard; whether or not it's your first time or your last time."

"I know. I loved him and I still love him but I can't figure out how to make peace with that."

Jack ran his hand over his white hair. "Damn. I get that. It took me longer than most. Everybody encouraged me to move on and date; but until Erin appeared, dating never interested me. It was always a big, fat no. Maybe the combination of timing, surviving grief and meeting the perfect next person have to coincide."

"I guess I thought that time alone could cure it."

"Maybe time will help you learn to cope with it." He snorted. "I hated all the platitudes and clichés. I can't tell you what path to take or how to navigate through critical crises. No one can. Not your parents, nor your sisters, not even this new person. If you can't move on yet, then you simply can't. I get that too."

"You don't think it makes me weak?"

"I think it only makes you human. You're still hurting. And everyone's threshold for pain is different, just like the duration of it. I know people who didn't even wait a year after their spouse's or companion's death, before embarking on a new long-term relationship. Several of them even worked out. Does that mean they loved their lost spouse any less than I loved Lily? I don't think so. I really don't. Your strength comes from knowing *you*, including what you need. You have to learn to ignore what others say you should do or feel. Avoid judging yourself through the eyes of others. That's all you can do."

"I hate those stupid platitudes too. I thought I knew myself before. And then I met this guy and his daughter and now I am filled with doubt. Nothing is magically fixing it."

"In my experience, relationships don't always go smooth or easy. But I will say this, despite your fear of watching other riders on horses, you should come here and start working again. Finn and I could use your help and there is an endless supply of horses to work with. Neglected, scared, some are terrified even and you have special abilities and natural intuition with horses, something they sense, which is invaluable to me. I need you. You've learned a lot since Preston's death, being frightened, vulnerable and confused, your confidence was cruelly shaken. I believe that happened for a reason and the maturity and growth and understanding you received have made you kinder and gentler, the ideal person to heal damaged horses. I really see that in you, Violet."

"Me? A healer of horses?" she repeated her statement in disbelief. "Is that what you are? What you do?"

"Yes. Nowadays. That's what I prefer to do. It's been quite awhile since I trained a challenging, spirited, young, confident horse. The kind the rodeos can't even handle. It's been the opposite for me. I rehabilitate the horses that are hurt, abused, neglected and some have even lost the will to live. They have no more fight inside them or survival instinct. It reflects the human experience in my way of thinking. Anyway, the work is tedious, and requires infinite patience and understanding. It can be very frustrating, with slow progress and regular reasons to be annoyed. Occasionally, we have a rare but huge, breakthrough moment, but mostly it's just steady, snail-paced progress. The reward for all your work and tenacity, never giving up, will finally result in a trusting horse that was once too afraid for you to touch it. It not only lets you stroke it, but it eagerly approaches you, seeking your companionship. And well, that's better than any show I could put on with a horse. No amount of applause for my showmanship in the ring could begin to compare to the quiet moment in a small corral when a once nearly broken horse decides to live again and trust a human."

"That sounds like the most perfect moment a horse-person could possibly have."

"It is."

She tilted her head, scrunching up her brows in confusion. "You never asked me to work here before."

"No. I'm very selective about it. Finn and I are very discerning when it comes to this enterprise. The equipment we have is state-of-the-art; it's expensive and means much more than just its monetary value. It's life-saving. The horses we rescue aren't the kind you can train and ride. They are—"

"A version of my spirit right now?"

He smiled gently. "Yes, that's a nice way to say it."

"And you're asking me to…?"

"I am. Are you interested?"

Violet swallowed and turned back towards the small paddock. The horse Jack was working with stood on the opposite side, warily staring back at them with obvious suspicion. Clearly on the alert, she seemed poised to run if they dared to approach her.

"I actually think I am." She blinked in surprise at her own reply. It was the first new thing she'd done for two years. She'd quit her job at the resort: horseback riding and training the riders and horses for the shows. It was a full-time job that she quit without any warning. Other than looking after her own two horses, Violet worked at the school district now. A job she got through her mom's former teaching connections. She filled in as a substitute para-educator and remained with them. They moved her around wherever they needed her. She started at the elementary school but was relocated this year to the resource room at the combined middle and high schools. "I work at the school most days, but I could come by after that... Could I maybe start part-time? I could definitely work the weekends too if you're okay with that."

He gave her a lopsided grin. "As I say with all horse work, they don't care what day it is. They don't take Saturdays and Sundays off from feeding. So any work you can do with them is important."

"I didn't come looking for you because I wanted to start working with horses again."

"This is nothing you've ever done with horses before. You are a gifted, natural trainer. And you know that. You could have stayed busy full-time doing that. I would encourage you at some point to get back into it. But failing to do something with all the horse know-how and talent you have, Violet-girl? That's a sheer waste of exceptional talent. You have an inborn compassion towards horses that is so vital in rescue. No offense, but I don't see the school district as your destiny. It fits someone like your mom or Rose... but not you. Iris loves to work in mechanics, and you were born to sit on the back of a horse. Professionally and personally."

"You thought this out before?"

"I thought of it right after Preston died. You needed time before getting to a place where working with horses seemed acceptable again. You were on my horizon. But you came to me on your own... to discuss things entirely unrelated so yeah, it was the perfect opportunity I was waiting for. How about Monday afternoon? Say around four?"

"Yes. I'll be here."

She blinked back the tears in her eyelids and quickly turned and fled. Her tears were different this time. Not from sadness or because something triggered them about Preston or the accident. It wasn't from regret and heartache over who she was failing and what she wasn't accomplishing.

No, this was totally different. Tears of relief. Relief. She wanted to do something with Jack that finally captured her interest. Her goddamned curiosity was piqued. She wanted to know what Jack and Finn did to calm the rescued horses. She wanted to go with them on a rescue mission, anywhere from down in the valley to across state lines. Sometimes, they had to cross several states to pick up the pathetic, desperate, abused, neglected, and often beaten horses.

An inherent sadness accompanied this new venture too. At times, the kindest and most humane thing Jack could do was to put a horse down. But that was Jack's last resort. Always.

She had so much to learn. They rehabilitated horses and sold them to people they screened very carefully. The money they earned funded the River's Rescue operations. There were a few big-name donors from whom they always accepted any donation, no matter how small. It was a not-for-profit endeavor that turned out to be highly profitable. They also used the proceeds for the charity foster children camps in the summer. Violet used to perform for those kids. Maybe she could help them in a different way now.

She used to be all flashy with her flamboyant style and her need to stir up the excitement and be the center of attention. She now preferred the quiet. Only quiet. None of the attention and accolades that used to drive her appealed anymore. Maybe Jack was right. Her new demeanor was better suited to the broken-spirited animals he wanted to save and recuperate.

Maybe by helping them, Violet would find a new way to help herself. Something that might be nicer than hiding up in the mountains every August. She was working a job she had no passion for, which didn't pay well and offered no future.

By accepting the job Jack described, was she finally starting to foresee and believe in a future? Did she actually have one?

More tears dampened her eyelashes and she wiped and dried them before making her way home.

Home was the house her brother-in-law built. She was invited to live there only a few months after Preston died. Grateful for the change of scenery, she eagerly took the spare bedroom. They didn't seem to mind her presence there. Iris was always busy at the shop and Quinn was working on his golf course. The progress of it was slow and time-consuming, but Quinn seemed invigorated by the work. They were together most evenings, taking in the panoramic views of their mini-empire and the other Rydells below them. She could make out her parents' house, a speck of color on the banks of the river, just past Rydell Rock.

No one was home. Sighing, she dug out some pasta and made a quick, easy dinner.

Iris and Quinn weren't the ones she wanted to reveal her mini-breakthrough to. Oddly enough, it was the man she didn't really know that well. The one she ran from and kept running from.

I did something new today. That was all she wanted to text him.

She wanted to see him.

She wanted him to hold her again, sweeping her up against his wide, comforting chest. She wanted to listen to the deep, calming voice with a warm smile poised on his face *for her*.

But of course, she'd only shunned Gage. She'd rejected his

comfort and support and friendship. She'd offered him a chance to feel the physical, but reserved the emotional. The piece he most wanted and which most scared her.

Not true. The physical side scared her equally, for deep in her guts, nothing was simple about anything they did together or felt. She sensed what they had could be real and deep and healing. And she didn't know how to accept it. Honestly? She wondered if she even wanted it. Perhaps that was the hardest part for others to understand. If she *could* feel better, why wouldn't she?

Maybe because she simply wasn't ready yet. Maybe the crushing guilt of moving on from Preston loomed over her, and was much too powerful still. Maybe she just didn't have enough strength to handle so much emotion towards another person. Feeling numb simply was easier.

CHAPTER 15

*C*RAP, IF ANDY DIDN'T come into her classroom at lunch. She sat down, eating her Gage-prepared lunch, chit-chatting about school, but mostly talking about horses. The girl couldn't fake her unquenchable interest in them. Violet hoped she wasn't the type of girl who got crazy excited about something new only to abandon all interest months or even weeks later. Maybe she was a phase-oriented person and horseback riding was her latest phase.

Violet soon learned that Andy got straight As and school for her was a breeze. She ran cross country for track and liked it but didn't love it. She doubted she'd continue to do it in high school because they ran much further. She wasn't ready to commit so much of her time to it. Since most of her friends were on the team, it wasn't a cut-and-dried decision. She was a bit torn.

Violet knew all of this because she was quiet around the girl. Sure, she answered her direct questions but mostly, she listened to Andy. And that seemed to go a long way.

Andy might as well have screamed how much she liked

Violet. There was no earthly reason for it, at least, none that Violet could find. Why did Andy like to hang out with her?

Violet started working at the rescue barn, and was glad she had new things to tell Andy. Andy squealed with unmasked delight when Violet told her what she planned to do after school. The first thing Andy asked was when could she be allowed to come there?

Violet restrained the urge to say there was no "we" about her new job. But she didn't. She wondered how to deal with Andy's ceaseless interest in her ranch activities.

Later that afternoon, walking up to the rescue barns, Violet's heart started to beat too fast. She felt odd wearing her cowboy boots and hat, walking the dirt paths again, with the intention of helping a horse. The rescue barns were located on the southeast edge of Rydell land. It sat up on a bank, overlooking the river. The family's private houses were downriver and visible to each other but not so close they could yell back and forth. The rescue barns faced the river and spanned the Rydell orchards. The land for the resort, the horses, the rescue barn and residences ran along the east side of the Rydell River. There was a section that jogged off towards the west, which was visible from the rescue barn. The orchards of cherry and apple trees were recently harvested. That turned out to be an unexpectedly lucrative branch of the ranch income.

The resort was north of the rescue barn and the arena was above that. Violet could not see the arena once she headed to the barn. The trees blocked the view. The land curved around and away from it too, creating its own little island. It was one of the few spots on her family's vast acreage where Violet felt free. The view and accompanying stomach-wrenching sensation of *the arena* no longer bothered her. That fucking place. It was so impressive with all the facilities and the cleanliness they maintained. The pristine conditions of the stables and inner arena were pretty remarkable. The outside construction was beautiful, matching the ranch buildings and resort façade. Everything fit in as part of the landscape, without dominating it.

Sure. There was so much to be grateful for.

But it was also now the main source of Violet's hurt.

She was glad she could work with the horses without glaring at the arena. It was a true blessing that made Violet release a sigh. Maybe, just maybe, she could do that. Maybe this could work. Imagine that. Her working with horses again. And succeeding? She felt too rusty to consider it. From the age of fifteen, she'd been training horses and working at the resort. She liked being part of it all and a central contributor to her family. After the disaster struck, she retreated into an inner shell. What if this new job marked the start of her emergence from it?

What if that actually happened?

She kicked a nearby pebble. It didn't matter at that second. Right now? Jack was waving at her and she was eager to start her new job.

"Well, you came on the right day. We had a call from a family who bought an old farm…"

She winced. "No… please don't tell me—"

He nodded, and his mouth became a grim line. "Yes. They found an old mare in the barn. She's starving and covered in sores. They aren't horse people so they don't understand the full extent of her deplorable condition. You'll start right off seeing how hard this can be. But when the process works, it's so fulfilling."

They were walking in tandem. "And when it doesn't?"

"It's the saddest fucking thing you ever witnessed. So… there's that too."

Her mouth was also a grim line. "I guess that's life, huh? When it's good, it's great, when it's not, it's horrible."

"Just about." They climbed into the cab of the truck with the words *River's Rescue* and their logo on the doors. It was designed by Brianna years ago. Brianna did most of the marketing and internet advertising. The double horse trailer was already hooked up. "Ready?"

Violet nodded, sitting up straighter for the first time in a long time and something churned inside her. Interest? Curiosity? Ambition? "Yes. I'm ready."

She wasn't really prepared for what they found when they saw the poor mare. No one could be prepared for it. The previous owners deserved old-fashioned, vigilante justice for what they did to her in Violet's opinion. They should be hung, shot and flogged. That was no punishment to equate the suffering they'd inflicted on the horse Violet and Jack found.

When they pulled into the old farm, which was a good hour's drive away, the lady who met them was older. She wore shabby clothes and had frizzy hair and her face was pulled tight as she said, "You can't help the poor creature fast enough." Violet instantly liked her. The lady pitied the poor horse and immediately reached out to the local authorities. The police came to take pictures and gather evidence to investigate further. They needed to know who left the desperate animal in such a terrible state and how to find them. Reaching out to River's Rescue, which was known for its successful rehabilitation cases, was the best solution, no matter how desperate the horse was.

Violet sucked in her exclamation of shock. The animal was the most pathetic thing she'd ever seen.

Jack was brilliant. If she hadn't liked and respected her uncle before this, which she did, afterward? She was in total awe.

The horse was covered in scabs and abscesses. Many were unhealed or badly scarred from not healing properly. Her ribs were all visible. The horse's eyes were filled with fear and when Violet saw her, she needed no more reason than her true desire to help her.

Jack entered the barn. His patience was legendary and his experience was pivotal at making horses trust him. Violet doubted he could be successful with this one. Not many trainers can calm a terrified horse.

"You stay back. Our safety matters first, despite how bad the creature appears. The truth is they are so rattled by fear and distrust, they can strike out and hurt us. So always stay back. Be aware. Never let your compassion replace your need for safety. Right now? Stay back. Far back. This isn't your job. You're just learning it." Jack pulled a pair of gloves on his hands as he scanned the old, decrepit barn and decided what to do.

Violet never considered his job to be high-risk or hazardous. Never. She didn't realize how easily Jack could be kicked, trampled or shoved. Hooves could hit his face, temple, head or chest. Feet could be crushed, broken and bruised. Abused horses were nothing like the healthy ones. Maintaining their peak physical and mental wellbeing were required at the Rydell River Ranch. The horses they boarded and trained were given only the best treatment. From their food to their veterinary care and even the farrier they used. Only the best horse people could work there too. Jack relied on them. He demanded integrity from everyone who worked on the ranch.

Including her.

Violet used to think she understood abused horses. And rescuing them. But no one knows how hard it is until they encounter it. No one can comprehend the sheer strength these poor animals have, even in such dilapidated conditions. Violet never factored in all the hazards and risks involved in any attempt to save them. The mere acts of moving them and feeding them and trying to help them could easily get a caregiver killed.

Jack requested the presence of the local veterinarian in case he needed to sedate the horse. But that involved another slew of problems. Jack backed his trailer right to the gate of the stall. He stood on the high side of the gate, placing the fencing between him and the terrified horse. He had to unlatch the stall and he couldn't with the trailer in the way. He used some old fencing he found to line the stall to the trailer, which he secured. He made it so there was no other place for the animal to retreat but the trailer. He created a makeshift funnel to guide her. Puzzled when the gate didn't open, Jack used a hammer to start busting up the rotten wood until the whole gate was demolished. The hideous noise scared the poor creature even more, of course, but there was no helping it. Violet knew that someday this would be the best day of the horse's life. But right now, the mare saw them as the enemy.

Jack gave Violet a tight-lipped smile. "Be ready for the worst part. I'm going to scare the living daylights out of this poor animal."

Violet nodded, totally on par and understanding. But the feeling of pride that surged through her was new and strange. Not because Jack had to scare the horse, but because she was helping Jack. He trusted her with such an urgent, hard, and delicate process. She totally got what Jack was doing and why. There was no judgment, just total awe and respect.

He climbed up the back wall of the stall, and the horse huddled against the other wall. Jack lifted one of those air-horns that people use in stadiums at games to make loud, blaring noises.

Violet was wide-eyed, instantly understanding there was no other way. No gentle coaxing could get the horse from point A to point B. The horse simply refused to cooperate. She did not trust them. But they had to get her out of the barn or she would die. There was no choice in the matter. Jack grimly nodded as he blew into the air-horn.

Violet knew it was coming and still, she was startled. She jumped and covered her ears.

The mare went insane. In a blind rage, she shot forward, hitting the trailer. Jack was right there, ready to drop the specially designed door on the trailer. It rolled down from the top, using gravity to close it. Finn was up on top of the trailer, poised to release the door at the exact moment the horse's back hooves were inside it. When the horse realized it hit a dead end, it tried to turn around, but too late. The door to the trailer was already shut.

The petrified mare kicked the sides of her new jail cell but to no avail.

Jack moved the fencing and put his hand on the door. Violet literally sensed his empathy and sorrow for the horse. She was going insane and Jack shut his eyes and said, "I hope she doesn't do too much damage."

"That's what all the padding is for?"

"Yes. We've run across this level of fear before. It's never easy when they panic. I hate putting them in so much distress. But we need to move them and we can't just lift them. They have to walk on their own feet. And here we are. Thankfully, the customized additions make it a little easier, and now you know why."

Violet stared at Jack and Finn in unashamed awe.

Eye-opening described Violet's entire evening.

The property owners gushed their thanks and gratitude. Finally, Violet, Finn and Jack were back on the road after a wave and the promise to let the people know of the horse's progress. It was dark so Finn, who was riding in back, could not even see the signs she and Jack made to include him.

"Do you think this horse will recover? I mean, do you think you can cure its trauma? Or…?"

"I do. I always have to think I can. But I also consider the worst-case scenario. I can't be so hopeful and optimistic, or I'm being unsafe and stupid. You saw the worst right now. But tomorrow, I'll start you out better. And then I'll show you how to get from one stage to the other."

She was breathless with anticipation, thinking this was exactly where she belonged.

Miles flew by. Then Jack asked, "I know you struggle watching others ride. We have to deal with lethal, insane, and unpredictable horses. Can I ask you something? How were you able to do that and not the other? The other, which is far safer and saner?"

In the dark cab, she made a face he could not see. "Oh, now you question my sanity? I don't know. I just can't stand watching others ride. But this is so different. You know? I guess the horse's obvious misery makes mine insignificant. I suppose…"

"Oddly, that makes sense to me."

"Does it ever scare you?"

"Oh, hell yeah. If you're not scared, you should never do this. Horses are very dangerous. They aren't cruel, awful, or terrible but the treatment they received was. That doesn't lessen how dangerous their abuse makes them. You need to maintain a healthy respect and fear of that."

"Does Aunt Erin do this?"

"No. She hates to see all their misery and mistreatment. She can't handle it. We also decided years ago we each needed to do our own thing. Working together, at the exact same job and living in the same home on the same ranch…"

She gave a small smile. "Maybe too much time together."

"Yep."

"Thank you, Uncle Jack. That was strangely illuminating

and hard, but I know how important it was. Hard but necessary."

"Yes. I hate the pain and suffering. Even when I sometimes am the cause. The end justifies the means eventually. It doesn't ever make it easy, however. But I do it for the end result. The best outcome I can give to the horse. I figure, even if it turns out to be a painless euthanasia for a sick or injured animal, it's still a better outcome than if I didn't intervene. Finn feels the same way."

"Yeah. I can see that. You two make a well-coordinated team."

"Yeah. Honestly. I always thought I'd work with Ben on this. But he likes working with Ian better... maybe another necessary separation. But you know that."

"I get it."

"So... do you want to join the Rescue staff?"

"I do. Yes."

"Then consider giving the school district notice and committing to us full-time. I can find more than enough work for you, and I think it would do you the most good. More than everything else. You were meant for this as much as I was. I see it in some, but in many, I don't. Erin had it. And Ben does. But Ian and AJ were more interested in working the land on this place. Not the horses. My love for the horses exceeds everything else. No matter if they're ours or not. Horse people are very special to me. Often, I can spot them even before *they* know they're horsey."

She smiled, thinking of Andy. That was the definition of Andy for her. The girl was screaming horses, even if she were green. So new, she squeaked. Violet saw the excitement that was once her sole motivation.

But crap. Damn. What could Violet do for Andy? Besides, Erin was already helping her.

But to Erin, Andy was just another client. Another rider.

To Violet, Andy was Gage. And what? So what if she cared that Andy rode? Or if she helped her cultivate her newfound love?

But what if something happened? She tried to imagine how Gage would react to that. How he would respond. She shuddered.

"Violet? Full-time?" Jack's voice interrupted her. The escalating thoughts were getting away from her.

"Yes. Okay. I'll give two weeks notice. But I already promised Hailey I'd help her with the holiday stuff for the resort…"

"That's fair enough."

Violet gave the school district notice. She told Andy on the second to the last day what she was doing.

"I won't see you anymore?" Andy's despair was real. Her eyes got bigger and her mouth puckered in a look of genuine confusion and sadness.

"Well… not here. You take lessons at the ranch. I'm always there."

So much more now.

"Wait, you said you'll be doing the rescue thing? That's different than the resort or the arena?"

"Yes. You can't see the rescue barn from the resort or arena. It's located in the heart of my family's land, near our private homes. It's a non-profit and has no access for the public, due to the fragile and sometimes dangerous disposition of the horses in residence."

"Can I see it sometime?"

Violet frowned and then shrugged. "Sure. Sometime. Yeah."

Andy nodded. "I'd like that. And I want to see you again."

Violet didn't make any promises. She was wondering if it were better to cut ties since she would be out of the school district now. Working in an area that Andy couldn't randomly visit because of the tight security the ranch now employed. After Iris was raped right there in the center of their land, they completely secured the ranch. Since then, chain link fences with razor wire surrounded all the residences and Rescue areas, separating the resort and the arena, the more public venues, from their private domain. Their personal horses, houses and the rescue barn were located downriver. The new version of Rydell Rides was still near the center of the ranch, with some public access, but much more secure now with twenty-four-hour video, steel gates and twenty-four/seven security personnel observing everything. The resort and arena only had public access on the high side of the resort, the opposite direction. Hence, Violet had no chance or reason to see Andy... or her sexy father.

A stab like a knife in her stomach surprised Violet. She only thought about not seeing Gage again and received a physical reaction from it.

Violet worked full-time with Jack and Finn rescuing horses, however, she spent most of the day with Finn. Jack was the "face" of the organization, so he had to schedule time to meet with investors and other interested parties. He also handled all the calls for pick-ups, evaluated the new horses' most urgent needs, and devised all the programs for rehabilitation. Jack's grand-daughter, Lillian, had aspirations of becoming a large animal veterinarian.

Keeping the healthy horses well required adherence to the recommended care. The special cases of the rescue needed emergency access to a veterinarian all the time. Right now, that was their greatest cost, according to Jack.

With Violet on the payroll, they could handle more rescues, which pleased Jack. It also gave Violet a steep surge of pride. She was finally contributing something of value, her time, and Jack didn't miss a single second of it. Her presence there was prized and appreciated and instead of feeling like she was just taking up space, Violet felt important. She hadn't felt like that since Preston died.

After a few weeks into it, she got a text from Gage. Her heart pinged with instant eagerness and excitement. Admonishing herself, she waited until she finished rubbing down Maximillian after his workout before she clicked on it.

First snow of the year is scheduled to fall this evening. We're celebrating with a backyard fire. If you like s'mores, come join us?

What? After a month since their fateful argument and hug at Andy's horseback riding lesson, he invites her to his house? Like it was the most normal thing in the world? Like they were friends? Or… what? Something? What was it? An olive branch? Something more? Something she repeatedly told him she could not do.

However… it was only s'mores. Not exactly a marriage proposal. It didn't even cost much money or time. So it was… what? A friendly gesture?

She was friendly. At least, she could be.

It was only s'mores.

At his house.

But who didn't love the first snow of the season? It made the air brittle and the land stark, turning it into a different place.

Did it mean anything else? She contemplated the same loop for three hours. Shall I go? Or not go? It meant something. It meant nothing. Could they be friends? Why couldn't they? Did she even want that? What if? All the what ifs had her feeling dizzy.

But it was just s'mores.

The most sane and rational reply was the simplest. She texted: *Sure. What time?*

Heat rose on her skin the second the message left her thoughts and went onto her private phone. It was now lost in the cyber world where she could not retrieve it. She was stuck with her decision. Did she want to see more of the man she kept saying no to? It made no sense. Yet she could no more resist him than a kid could resist a chocolate bar.

Seven work for you?

Sure.

Nothing more. Her nerves immediately fluttered and she hated herself for what happened next. She went home, showered and tried to decide what to wear. Something casual that seemed as if she just slipped it on to go visit her *friend*, Gage?

But damn if she didn't wear her favorite jeans, the ones that made her butt perkier than the others did. And the sweater she wore brushed her hips just the way she liked. It covered the upper body but showed off her slimness and curves. How silly. With the first snow coming, she'd be buried inside her large blue ski coat. With warm gloves, hat and boots. Her thick, wool socks wouldn't fit any of her cute, summer shoes. She'd wear her cowboy boots even though they weren't warm. At least they were stylish and could accommodate the wool socks. And they weren't as bulky and boring as her snow and winter boots.

Sitting on her bed, she pulled her knee up and aligned her blue and brown leather cowboy boots that she never actually wore, neither outside around the ranch or on her horse. They were strictly for fashion.

A knock on her door startled her. She glanced up with a half smile at Iris. "Yeah?"

Iris entered, her hands on her hips. "Are you wearing those?"

Violet jammed her foot into the boot and stood to stomp her toes all the way in with the bulky socks. "Yeah. So?"

Iris's smile was quick and surprising. "You haven't worn them since… well… since Preston died."

Violet was just tugging the right one on when Iris's words stumped and shocked her. "I haven't?"

Iris sat beside her where she flopped down on the edge of her bed. "No. You haven't. You used to wear the sequined jeans and every fashionable boot and cowgirl ensemble out there. You were a walking advertisement for all trends western. Flashy..."

Violet looked down and a small smile filled her face. She used to say that a lot when her sisters teased her fashion sense. "Flashy and fantastic."

Iris sucked in a sharp breath as if the words that came from Violet's mouth affected her. "Yes." The smile was gentle and kind as she set her hand on Violet's head and ran it down her hair like she was a child. "Flashy and *fucking* fantastic was actually what we said."

Violet stared down and Iris stroked her hair as her mom often did. She smiled at Iris. "I guess I forgot what was so fucking fantastic about me."

"Everything. I know what it's like to have your entire foundation and your whole identity shattered."

She grabbed Iris's hand and squeezed. "I know you do. Sometimes my grief makes me so selfish."

Iris waved her other hand around as she returned Violet's squeeze. "Nah. We all get that way. I went through it after I was raped. The ridiculous things I did and tried to do to Quinn and Mateo? I'm grateful that others are so forgiving. I don't think I deserved their forgiveness. But they gave it to me anyway, and that's exactly how I feel about you. One thing I never told you is that when I was raped, I had an orgasm. That nearly devastated me. It ruined everything I thought about myself. It kept me from reporting the incident. I showered. I didn't get a rape-kit or tested. I always believed I was strong and rational enough to go to the fucking hospital. Instead, I cowered alone in horror and disgust at myself. I was too embarrassed to tell anyone. At all. I lost myself for so long. Rebuilding Iris was a steady process and who I am now bears no resemblance to how I started out. You know? I see that happening with you. I hope you realize someday you're just as flashy and fucking fantastic as you ever were, but you look very different now."

"What? You're saying I'm still me? Just different?"

"Exactly." Violet leaned her head on Iris's shoulder. They sat there for a moment, just letting each other feel their own hurts and the support each girl offered the other. She always appreciated that with Iris. Iris didn't say empty platitudes or try to fix things. Their oldest sister, Rose could actually fix just about anything, but found it hard to allow her loved ones to vent and just steep in the pain or emotions they felt. Violet used to be a take-charge-and-get-shit-done kind of girl, very much like Rose. But since her life imploded, she became more introspective, and crawled inside a tiny world she never used to inhabit. Iris was the easiest sister Violet could stand to be around. That was why she found refuge there, in her house.

"I'm sorry about the rape. I never knew the part about the orgasm. My God, Iris... what you had to endure..."

She squeezed Violet's shoulders in an embrace. "It's different but just as bad as what you went through. Don't lose sight of that. Okay? Hurt and grief and sadness are a soupy mixture and almost everyone has to experience them at some time or another."

"I know but you're so strong."

"So are you, little sis."

Violet squeezed her eyes shut and hoped it were true. She needed something to believe in if only for tonight. Friendly and casual and maybe something more were what she aspired for, and yet, she wondered if she really wanted that and would be disappointed if she weren't like that.

She finally leaned back and wiped her teary eyes and runny nose.

"Where are you wearing those fabulous shit-kickers?"

Violet laughed. Iris wrinkled her nose at horse poop and anything else horsey. She was a shameful derelict at ranching and often resented the land she was born and raised on. But she flourished around the nasty odor of oil, lubricants and rusty metal. Iris all but sniffed it for pleasure like perfume. Violet and Iris were the two most similar in their demeanors of the four sisters, but their opposed career interests were like comparing hay to oil.

"Umm… this guy…"

Iris jolted around, twisting her body, tucking her leg up, and widening her eyes with unconcealed curiosity. "The guy from the restaurant that we couldn't mention?"

"Yes. Don't make anymore of it. I'm already a mess. We met while I was up in the mountains. He's great. He has a good job… no, *a career*. He has an entire adult life and a thirteen-year-old daughter."

"Oh? That might not go so well."

"No, I thought the same thing. But she started coming into the classroom with me to eat her lunch and she seemed to like talking to me. Several times, she gave me a thumbs-up to date her dad. Erin's been giving her riding lessons and—"

"Oh, that girl? Yeah, I met her. Andy Sullivan?"

"Yes. Gage is a bit older than me."

"About the same as Quinn is for me," Iris reasonably pointed out.

"Yes, but Quinn started out as an emotional child who missed having a family and had no true values. Gage has everything together already and he's raising another human being and he seems to be doing an amazing job. Why he likes me and wants or at least, did want to go out with me is still a mystery but I want to pursue it and then I get—"

"Scared. Things you can't explain suddenly stop you in your tracks when they overwhelm you."

"Yes."

"So why the fancy shit-kickers?"

"Because he invited me to have some s'mores tonight in his backyard. The first snow is predicted to fall tonight and it sounds like the thing I want to do most. But after I texted back *yes*, I almost had a panic attack. That's when I put these stupid boots on."

"Boots you haven't worn in a very long time."

"It doesn't mean anything since I can't handle it."

Iris rose to her feet. "Then it doesn't mean anything. They are simply boots. It's supposed to snow. Makes sense. Doesn't need to be any deeper than that. Right?"

Violet nodded with a wan smile, relieved at Iris's crisp tone and black and white summation. She found refuge in Iris's no-nonsense way of explaining everything. "Right."

"Then go tonight. Eat the best dessert in the world and try to enjoy yourself. That's it. All you have to do tonight is wear a smile and enjoy a warm fire. That's it. Remember that."

Her heart slowed down and she let a breath out gradually. "Iris… thank you. I was starting to get freaked out."

"You're always starting to. Just take one moment at a time. You don't have to attack the big emotions or analyze the long-term ramifications to absolutely everything you do. Otherwise, you'll continue having panic attacks."

"Do I do that?"

"That's all you do. You spend two months alone in the mountains just to avoid one day: the anniversary of Preston's death. Yes, honey. You've always been known for your overreactions. Especially now. It comes out a little different than before, but it's still big. You're so much like Dad…"

Violet saw it as a blessing sometimes to be so well understood by her sister, when it wasn't a total curse.

"Okay. I can do that. Have a smile. Sit by a fire. Watch some snow fall."

"See? Easy."

Iris started to leave when Violet called her back. "Iris? After the rape, was it hard for you and Quinn...?" How to ask if post-rape sex was still possible to enjoy? She never asked Iris about it, but she wanted to know.

"To have sex? Yes. It's totally possible. It was hard at first, however. I had a lot of guilt about the orgasm, my fault or not, and it was tough for me to accept. I felt like my body betrayed me. I hated it for awhile and I had to learn to forgive myself. Sex after the rape started out very slow, Violet. Kind of like what you're going through now. Just a kiss here. A touch there. It took months and months before I was ready to have sex. Enjoying it again was a whole new process after that. But somehow, together, Quinn and I found a new way of being close. We have a deeper under-standing and we trust each other more because we are more honest with each other now. I'll never be glad it happened, but I'm glad Quinn helped me survive it in all ways. And I am especially glad I can enjoy sex again."

"I enjoyed sex with Gage." Violet rolled her eyes, admit-ting it while blushing. Why the blush? They were both well past adolescence. It was stupid not to talk about it much. "But the commitment part and opening up everything else stopped me... I feel all blocked up."

"Then go enjoy a fire. Together. Start there. That's my advice. Don't think beyond that or what it might be building towards. It could just be a fun night. Right now. Tonight."

She nodded. "Thank you. You don't know how helpful that is."

"I actually think I do. And you can thank Quinn for that. He was really good at keeping me grounded in the present moment. Allowing small things to eventually get big."

"I knew I liked the guy for more than his stupid-fat wallet."

Iris let out a loud laugh. "Exactly what I had to learn as well." They exchanged sisterly smiles and something shifted in Violet.

Small things. Just tonight. A smile. A fire. And staying grounded in the moment.

She could do that. Even in kick-ass shit-kickers that really were flashy and fucking fantastic.

With a deep breath and a stomach full of butterflies, Violet left with the address she had for Gage and Andy Sullivan.

She pulled into the driveway. The street was a quiet side road, that branched off one of the main avenues. There were only a few houses on it, and all were widely spaced, imbuing the area with a pleasant, neighborly feel. She gulped and stared at the beautiful family home. It was a fancy rambler. This was no spec house. It was custom-built, with an ornate, double-door entry and classy, etched glass relites flanking both sides. His lawn was immense and pristine, with perfectly mowed rows that were visible to the naked eye. Professional landscapers could have designed and maintained the grounds but Violet assumed it was most likely Gage.

She sucked in her courage. One night. One fire. One smile. That was all there was to it.

Armed with her strong spirit, she stood at the front door and dared to knock. No answer. She mustered up more courage and rang the doorbell that pealed loudly. The obnoxious noise made her stomach butterflies feel like small birds taking off. Holy shit, she was nervous. As if she were fifteen and preparing for her very first date.

CHAPTER 16

*A*NDY WAS PARTICULARLY SILLY and talkative tonight. She begged for Gage to fix her his gourmet pizza, one of his specialties. Using his own secret tomato sauce, he topped it with chicken slices and pesto. Chatting to her dad about school, gossiping about her friends, and analyzing what they did or didn't do. She kept cracking herself up with her own lame jokes, and Gage laughed but not because they were funny, rather because he found her so amusing.

It was a favorite tradition, the first prediction for fresh snow, and whenever they were at home when it came, they built a bonfire in the backyard and bundled up to watch it. Tonight, he built a blazing fire as the temperatures were rapidly dropping as soon as darkness descended. Despite a few neighbors' lights in their yards, Gage had a mostly unobstructed view from his backyard to the tiny pinpricks of starlight above. How could it snow tonight with such clear skies? Yet three different weather channels forecast the same conclusion. Glancing up at the stars reminded Gage of the pure clarity he experienced on the mountain with Violet. He clearly recalled staring up from a fire on nights like this one. Sighing, he flipped a log into the rising flames. He thought of Violet much too often these days.

Andy came out all bundled up and flopped in one of the chairs. When they built the patio, they'd poured a concrete slab that began at the French doors in a circle and led to a path that meandered into another circle in which the firepit was located. The centrally placed fire radiated lots of heat and the ample seating made Gage's backyard quite inviting. With such a large, close-knit family, Gage's house was often the first choice for picnics and bonfires.

Andy swung her feet over the opposite armrest, and tipped her head back while her feet jiggled. Looking innocent and young despite her height and long hair, Gage couldn't help thinking she was growing old so quickly. There were still a few precious moments he intended to capture with her as a little girl. His little girl.

"Wanna grab the stuff for the s'mores?"

Andy swung her legs forward. "Can't we wait just a little while? My stomach will burst if I eat one right now."

"'Course we can." Gage sat down, putting his hands over the fire.

"Did Violet really cook her food over an open fire?" Andy's voice jolted Gage from the pleasant reverie he was enjoying while staring at the hypnotic fire. Damn. To Violet.

He snorted. "Most of the time, all she did was heat up hot water for a pre-packaged freeze-dried meal. But I remember a few times..." and he proceeded to tell Andy more about her even while his brain screamed, *No. Don't say anything.* He did not wish to encourage anymore interest from Andy for a woman who didn't want him. Why bother? She could never be part of Andy's life. But instead of abolishing the idea of Gage dating a new woman, or acting bitter and scared that a new woman could drive a wedge between them, Andy shocked him with her response. His special teenager seemed mad and disappointed at him for *not dating* Violet. How many times did he try? Too many times. But since Gage still liked her, he found it easy to talk about her.

Eventually, the front doorbell rang. "Ahh. Hell, who do you suppose that could be? You think Grandma and Grandpa smelled our fire?" Gage teased and Andy giggled. Like clock-work, his parents often showed up on the nights he and Andy built a fire in the backyard.

Ambling through the house, he was slightly surprised they didn't just enter. If Mom thought they were outside, she wouldn't walk inside lest she accidentally startle Andy.

He grabbed the door handle and flung it open. A welcome smile and a sarcastic greeting hung on his lips when he stopped dead and his smile faded. His eyebrows furrowed upwards. His jaw stiffened. In a weak voice, he said, "Violet?"

"Umm... yes." She tilted her head, plunging her fisted hands from her sides into her coat pockets. She held her shoulders back as she raised her head and looked at Gage with flashing eyes. "Didn't you say seven o'clock?"

"Seven o'clock?" he repeated absently.

"For s'mores?"

"S'mores?"

"Why are you repeating everything I say?" she snapped.

"Why are you *here*?" he shot back.

Her entire face flushed with embarrassment. She dug her hands deeper into her pockets and took out her phone, waving it in his face too fast to read it. "Didn't you ask me to come? Text me to come for s'mores? To celebrate the first snowfall?"

Her phone wasn't even turned on. He had no idea what she was talking about. "I didn't text you about s'mores or fires... I mean, I would have if I thought for a second that you might come but you were so adamantly sure you didn't even want a friendship with me so—"

She gave him a puzzled look. "So what?"

"So... did you come by to be friendly? Just because?"

"Yes. But you really didn't ask me to come?"

For the first snowfall? No one did that. No one he ever heard about. It was their special thing, just Andy's and his. Other than the family, no one else knew about the private tradition. He sucked in air and closed his eyes, swearing softly. With a quick glance over his shoulder, he saw the inside of the house was empty. His daughter's form was standing in a shadow by the fire. The fire she'd insisted they have tonight. And the ingredients for the s'mores were also bought at her insistence. Her unreasonably heightened excitement over the snow forecast started at six-thirty tonight, and now? Violet appears out of the blue?

He was more than shocked she showed up regardless of who sent her the text. But she came all the same.

He nearly groaned when the full understanding dawned on him. It hurt but also sent a warm current that flowed from his heart to his extremities. Andy was so damn sweet; he was so lucky she was his daughter. She was wrong, of course, and she shouldn't have tried to manipulate anything between him and Violet. Or push them together when they weren't ready. But she wanted to see her father happy. What teenager thinks more about her parent's happiness than her own? She even sought out the woman of her choice. Which made a lot of sense, since technically whomever her father chose would affect Andy's life too.

But then he thought about the strong, uncanny bond Andy forged toward Violet, which was a bit disconcerting.

"Andy must have done it. I'm guessing Andy texted you from my phone."

Violet's eyes rounded wider and the whites got huge as

they framed her tawny eyes. "Oh. So you didn't ask me to come here tonight?"

"I certainly would have if I thought there was any chance you'd do it. You denied me every time so far and shut down all my attempts. Except this one." He tilted his head. "Interesting. Huh? Why is that? Did you miss me?"

She puckered up her lips in a prissy look and gave him the evil-eye. "No. I just love s'mores."

"Well, this is your lucky day then. Andy insisted we buy them, so we got 'em rarin' to go. Come on in."

Violet hesitated as usual. Gage shut his eyes and pinched the bridge of his nose. Fluttering his eyelids, he ground his teeth and said, "Violet, you came here thinking I invited you. You were coming to be with me. So don't act weird now or get cold feet. Come in, and have some s'mores. We'll chat and catch up. It's not a lifelong commitment. I swear." Violet eyed him skeptically. Finally, he shrugged and said, "I double dare you."

Violet nearly hissed as she glared at him before whipping past him and entering his house. She acted as if she just cleared a difficult hurdle or climbed up a high mountain instead of simply walking inside his house. He resisted an eye-roll at her dramatics. She stepped past him, then whirled around. "So you think Andy set us up?"

"I think Andy set us up. Yes. I'll have a long talk with her. But it was only because she took a liking to you. So I apologize, but there are worse things than having a teenage girl like you. Believe me, I always hear the opposite from what she says her friends tell her."

"That's so true. I often heard the girl cliques in the hallways. Lord. Squealing their protests. Lots of *waits* and *likes* and *oh, my gods*. And *you won't believe* this or that. And it spills out to everything else. They get overly dramatic just choosing which table to sit at to eat their lunches and gossip."

Gage escorted Violet through his entry, passing the sunken living room and the kitchen and dining table. It was all one open space, with vaulted ceilings and skylights. The hardwood flooring was everywhere. Violet's gaze couldn't take in every last detail, but she nearly gasped her appreciation. Even as she spoke, she chattered. It was almost meaningless, but at least it helped calm her nerves, he guessed.

He grabbed the back door handle. The entire backyard and far beyond were visible. She stopped dead and stared at the panorama. The wide-open sky and unlimited space. Miles away, the trees and mountains seemed to embrace them. A blanket of tiny stars filled the sky. The embers in the fire glowed, and it wasn't completely dark. "My God, it's beautiful," Violet commented as she glanced around. "Your entire house is amazing. I'm speechless."

"Really? Coming from a ranch-girl. You have seen where you live, right? Aren't you staying on your sister's brand new golf course?"

"Ha. It's my brother-in-law's golf course. Iris wouldn't claim ownership except with an eye-roll. She's unimpressed by material things, only cars and mechanical objects that she can tinker with and fix. I realize we have an awesome spread too. But yours is truly lovely."

"Thank you, Violet." He stared at her upturned face, as she took in his yard and grand view. She didn't realize he was taking her in also, feeling drunk from the sweet line of her cheek where it met her eye and slid up to her brow. Her hair cascaded around her shoulders, but some strands got caught on the hood of her warm, puffy coat.

She glanced up when his deep, serious tone registered in her mind. She knew he was marveling at her, not the gorgeous view or his house. With a small smile, she slipped under his arm, which was holding the door still. He followed her with a sigh and shut the door behind him.

"Andy? Can you imagine who showed up here at seven o'clock for s'mores?" he teased as they walked up on his daughter.

Andy had the grace to duck her head down, but her little grin wouldn't cooperate or stay hidden. "You are both so stubborn. It was the only way."

He put his hands on his hips. Wearing a coat as puffy as hers, Gage hoped he didn't resemble a snowman, which would have diffused his perceived toughness. "Daughter, you are not supposed to schedule my dates. It's weird and it's wrong."

Violet stepped towards the fire, keeping her head down so he couldn't see her face. She put her hands towards the heat and his entire being shifted at the memory of her doing the same thing at their camp. Suddenly, she seemed so familiar. So reachable. So much what he wanted.

But he zoned back in on his daughter.

"I really like her. She likes us and everybody likes s'mores. What's the harm in it? Unless you two can't handle seeing each other? But that would mean your relationship is more than just friends!"

Thankful for the darkness and its rapid descent, Gage endured his burning cheeks of embarrassment. He was glad neither she nor Violet realized how childish he felt. Like back in the day when a girl discovered you had a crush on her. It was so stupid. He did have a crush on her. She knew it. They had sex. Lots of sex. They held each other and cuddled and kissed... oh, the kisses... and now he wasn't sure how to handle the possibility he might feel something more for her? He had to man up.

"Don't do it again. It's manipulative to Violet. You have to think about the position you put her in. You gave her the wrong assumption and the wrong information, right?"

Andy finally seemed to get it and her gaze immediately

narrowed on Violet. "Oh. I didn't think about that. I'm sorry, Violet. I just thought we'd have fun and we aren't at school and you like my dad..." She got to her feet and stood closer to Violet without touching her. Her head hung forward, looking sad and pathetic. Gage rolled his eyes. She could so easily turn his annoyance into sympathy toward her. But no! He had to stay strong. Andy was wrong. She did wrong and he needed to see this through. But oh, hell... how sad she looked. How sorry she seemed. How desperately she yearned to reach out and hold Violet's hand.

It would have been comical if it weren't so sad. What did she see in Violet that she liked so much? A motherly figure? It didn't jive, not to him. For one, Violet was a few inches shorter. His leggy daughter towered over her, although she looked like she wanted to curl up in childish desire, pleading for forgiveness. Violet was still young. So much younger that she lacked any maternal tone in how she spoke and treated Andy. Was Andy thinking Violet could be her stepmother? She never had one, and never seemed to mind, but maybe she did. Especially now that she was entering her teens. But *Violet?*

It seemed so. Violet.

"It's okay. I was glad for the invitation, so I guess you were right."

Violet peeked at him, then away, growing confused and flushing with heat. Then she leaned over and squeezed Andy's hand in hers swiftly. Andy looked down at their joined hands and then over at Violet with obvious relief. She was glad, beaming a smile of joy at being forgiven. Gage's heart swelled until it hurt at seeing the small interaction. He didn't expect Violet to handle his daughter so correctly. So right. So easily and kind. But she did.

Fuck! His stupid, fanciful heart enjoyed the sight of these

two women standing together in total cohesion and care. Damn it!

No.

It could not be. Violet refused to allow it. He wasn't sure he wanted it anymore. But hell, it was the first time he ever considered it... and the idea of sharing Andy with any woman was new to him. He never cared about any woman before. Not like this. Not to this capacity.

What would he do with it?

He didn't know. His poor heart was about to be crushed, perhaps broken, and he knew not to overstep his boundaries with the one woman he actually wanted.

A sharp, intense, poignant energy flowed between them. Their gazes met and they both hastily looked away. There was no imagining the connection. The same things Violet didn't want and proclaimed she didn't need. Leave it to his go-getting, no-holds-barred daughter to see the solution, even if she erred by finagling the situation. She had honorable intentions.

Then Violet surprised him by slapping her hands together. "Whoever texted me doesn't matter since it doesn't change the invitation for s'mores and I haven't seen one yet! False advertising is much worse than crossed messages..."

With that, Andy let out a gleeful yelp as she ran towards the house, calling out, "I'll grab all the stuff!"

Gage kept staring at Violet. "Thank you for not taking it out on her. I will talk to her again. But you were really good with her. That means a lot to me." He couldn't help himself. He leaned forward, taking her small hand and squeezing it in his. She stared at their linked hands and then up at his face but she didn't pull away. She didn't even glare.

She nodded and smiled. "I really love s'mores."

He let out a laugh that relieved the strain. "Well, I do too.

Another thing we share in common. Hey, we never made these in the mountain camp…"

Violet laughed too and all the tension evaporated. They were the same two people who shared a mountain again, and who connected despite everything that clashed in their lives. At the core, the essence of their connection was real and lasting. Was it the simple addition of the damn fire? Is that what made them drop right back into the zone? That connection existed so often in front of their mountain fires. Just as it was now. But this was even better. His daughter laughed and talked freely. For the next hour, they competed making gooey, melting marshmallows. Many fell victim to the smoldering coals of the fire. Lots of flicking gooey strings of sugar at each other. They finally managed to make the golden-rimmed s'mores with melted marshmallows, chocolate bars and graham crackers which they quickly ate before going right back for *s'more*. Gage was laughing as he reached out and rubbed off the dried, sticky goo on the side of Violet's lip. He smiled when she turned her hot eyes on him. Startled, he was mesmerized for a long moment, caught in her stare. "You… you had a long string of marshmallow stuck there for the last ten minutes. I couldn't take it anymore."

He didn't move his hand afterward. Holding his fingertips on the side of her face, near her mouth, she swallowed and he felt it in his hand. He was lost in her eyes and she was drowning in his. He licked his lips and finally withdrew his hand.

She rubbed the spot, sad for the loss of his touch. It tightened his stomach and released a radiant warmth in his body. She was, as always, raw heat and sex, tenderness and compassion; at least she was for him.

But Andy was there now. She was chatting while flicking bits of marshmallow and it was fun so they did it for hours. Eventually, they were just talking and gossiping. The people they knew in common who lived in the valley. And horse stuff. And Violet's new job. Shit! She took a huge step forward in her healing, and he was so proud of her. It bore no reflection on him, but he wondered if she hadn't met him and experienced a tiny bit of healing, maybe she'd never have even tried the horse rescue business.

Her face glowed now with hope and pride and joy. Keen interest. Seeing what it did for Violet Rydell, Gage was all for it.

When Andy finally got to her feet, she stretched and said, "I'm going inside to watch some TV. I'm getting cold now."

"What about the snow?"

She glanced up. "Well, the clouds rolled in finally. But they obviously missed the forecast." And with that, she was gone, disappearing down the hallway. Moments later, her dark room shone with light, but her shades were shut.

Gage sighed as the quiet fell between them. The fire flickered. The night was getting colder. The air seemed more brittle. The stars vanished under the soft cloud cover and night shadows. The sky was completely different. Insulated almost. Cozy. Then after a few minutes, Gage saw it.

The very first snowflake.

"Hey, they weren't lying. It is beginning to snow. That clear sky nearly convinced me they goofed even if it is cold enough."

Violet tilted her head back. The flakes were small and few. But it was definitely snow. The very first snowfall of the season. She smiled as she bent her head back down and turned to him. "As promised. A fire. S'mores. Way too many, but still s'mores to celebrate the first snow... damn! Andy sure can plan a date!" Her soft smile was kidding and the warmth of her voice thrilled Gage.

It went straight into his gut and lodged there. Her tenderness. Their closeness. The word, *date*. Even if she were teasing. "Is it a date?" he asked, leaning closer to her, breathless. They each had their arms on the armrest, but their coats touched. It was oddly erotic, without a millimeter of skin contact. The electricity from being so near was undeniable.

"It doesn't matter. It just is. How about that?" she challenged him.

He nodded and let his gaze hang on hers. "How about that?" he mimicked her. Uncaring what they said or why. Gage was entranced. No, he was totally captivated by her.

Firelight flickered over her smooth face and he lifted a palm to her cheek. She tilted her head into it, closing her eyes as a soft breath escaped her mouth when her lips slightly parted. It sounded like a sigh of gladness, like when you finally come home after a long trip.

He touched her cheek, holding her closer. Cupping her face, he leaned forward to kiss her. Lips touching, the snow fell cold and wet on them, but the hot fire melted it, creating the perfect moment. The perfect balance of hot and cold, wet and dry, night and fire, joy and fear.

Fuck. It was brilliant. Their lips fused, each holding the other's face since there was no other skin showing. Their puffy coats and cold weather clothing notwithstanding, the skimpy touches they engaged in were that much more profound.

Why couldn't she see how far she'd come in her journey of life after Preston? That happened before he knew the story or her name. It happened in the mountains. Doing new things with the rescue reminded Violet of her love and natural skills with horses. But her heart was too stuck in the past to recognize it.

However, her body realized it. She easily surrendered to the kiss. There was no hesitancy. No confusion. Just tenderness and warmth. The familiar desire, building in anticipation and urgency, couldn't just be his imagination. She leaned her face towards his and twisted her entire torso. Half her butt was lifted off the seat in her attempt to get closer to him. Their lips were pressed together, sliding off as their tongues danced, licked, stroked and played together. It was so hot, it bordered on ripping their clothes off if the straining got any hotter.

His daughter's bedroom overlooked the backyard. As if a bucket of snow were suddenly poured on their heads was how fast Gage released Violet. Breathing so hard, like they just ran a marathon and sprinted over the finish line together, her eyes were eager with desire and he imagined his own were the same. He leaned forward and kissed her lips. "Stay here tonight. Come inside with me, Vee."

Seamy breaths mingled as Violet blinked through the fog in her mind that always seemed to epically surround her in his presence. She barely had the wherewithal to close her gaping mouth. Leaning back for more space and to calm herself, she replied, "I thought you never allowed women to spend the night. No awkward mornings for Andy."

His eyebrows furrowed. "How did you know that?"

"She told me. You never made her aware of any women you were dating. Except for those two times when it was kind of serious; but even then, she doubted you were ready."

Gage's tightening, turned-on body began to relax. "My daughter told you all that?"

Violet smiled with genuine warmth, tenderness and amusement regarding her memories of Andy. "Yes. The very first time she ate her lunch in the classroom and talked to me. I think she hoped I would be different."

He released Violet as he rose to his feet. The temperature noticeably cooler now, he stepped closer to the fire. Staring down at the embers and low flame, Gage said, "I hope you're different. But she's right. I never subjected her to a strange woman being here in the morning. She'd stay with my

326

parents if I wanted anyone here or went to their place. Which wasn't very often."

"But you want me to stay?"

He could have sworn she could reason that out for herself. "Yes. I didn't even think it through. I just said it."

She rose to her feet and stood beside him. Mimicking him, she reached out her hands and said, "See these boots?"

Startled by her swift change in topic, he nodded and looked at her. "Yeah. They're much girlier than I've ever seen you wear."

"They are. They are flashy and fucking fantastic. This is how I used to dress. Even the outfits I performed in. Geez. I was my own flaming Vegas show."

Now, truly interested, Gage fully turned towards her and asked in disbelief, "You?"

She nodded. "Me. I was flashy and loud and outrageous. I had unlimited confidence and a firm belief in my own immortality. People would often shake their heads at me while claiming how much they loved watching me perform."

"And after Preston died?" Gage finished the story for her.

"After he died, I turned quiet, sullen, and never smiled. I started wearing dark brown boots and plain but functional jackets. I buy my jeans from the local hardware store now. I'm a muted version of myself now. Beige. Boring—"

"There is not one thing *boring* about you, Vee aka Violet Rydell." Gage loudly interrupted.

She inclined her head his way. "Touché. Perhaps you don't see it. But everyone who used to know me does."

"But you're wearing the flashy and fucking fantastic boots tonight?" He felt unsure about what that meant but it obviously held some significance to her.

"Yes. I am. Although I'm no longer the way I was, tonight was the first time I felt like remembering that, you know, what I used to be. What I once was."

"Violet?" He stared down her but she kept her face downturned.

"I don't know what I mean. But I felt like wearing the boots tonight."

He set a hand to her shoulder. "I'm glad you did. Would you like some…"

Glancing up, her weariness and uncertainty were reflected in Gage's eyes. "Pizza? I made my famous gourmet chicken and pesto pizza at Andy's insistence. Wanna piece? You need something to nourish you after all those sugary s'mores."

Her weariness became a huge smile. "Yes. Actually, I would love to try the pizza."

He nodded. There was nothing more he wanted either. Calmly, chatting comfortably, they walked inside after he doused the dying embers of the fire. Violet took her coat off and sat down at the breakfast bar on the center island. He pulled out the refrigerated leftover pizza and started the oven to reheat it.

"Care for a glass of wine?"

"Hmm… that's a bit more daring than just s'mores."

"Because that's just the kind of sophisticated guy I am." Gage spread his arms boldly as he showed off and she smiled and nodded.

He poured a glass of wine for her and leaned on the counter as they talked. When the timer dinged, Gage arranged the pizza on the two plates and sat down beside her. He touched his glass to hers and she gazed up at him with curiosity. "Here's to being flashy and fantastic."

She said, "Here's to being flashy and *fucking* fantastic."

"Right. *Fucking* fantastic." His heart beat faster as he watched her kidding around and smiling. She looked comfortable and at ease in his home, eating his food and drinking his wine.

She bit off some pizza and closed her eyes. Her facial expression reminded Gage of the one he saw when he gave her an orgasm. He had to look away to avoid the usual effect that image did to him.

She groaned and said, "Oh, my God, no. Nothing is so fantastic as this pizza. It's fucking fantastic. I had no idea you could cook like this."

"Oh, that's just the tip of the iceberg. My talents are unlimited," he bragged with an eyebrow wag. She laughed and his heart lifted. He kept thinking this would all turn out well.

She stayed for two more hours and they finished their wine in the living room. They talked about movies and TV shows they binged on and books they loved to reread. They smiled and talked until it got late and Violet began yawning. "I really should go."

He didn't argue with her. Perched on his tongue, he wanted to say, *no, stay here tonight.* But his sleeping daughter's presence kept him quiet. Violet gathered her coat and scarf, putting them on. Gage startled her when he said, "Let me have your keys."

She looked at him inquisitively. "Don't worry about me. I'm fine to drive. I waited long enough since my last glass of wine."

"No. Let me warm your truck up."

She dug her keys out of her pocket and tossed them to him with an appreciative smile. "Thank you." Her terse answer was brimming with gratitude. Too much. It wasn't more than a kind gesture. He started the truck and let the heat blast until the cab was warm.

They lingered another few minutes to give her frigid truck enough time to heat up. When they were standing at his front door, he reached out and grabbed her puffy coat in his fist, gently drawing her towards him. He dropped down so he could kiss her lips with a long, lingering kiss. She sighed when he reluctantly pulled back. He kissed her forehead and squeezed her against him in a long hug. She didn't resist but actually burrowed deeper into him.

"I'm glad my daughter was so inappropriate. At least she lured you over here."

Violet had a gleam in her eyes. "I wasn't quite lured. But yeah, I'm glad too."

He released her without anymore promises. Holding the door as she brushed past him, he restrained the urge to say, *please stay over here.* You can be flashy and fucking fantastic, or quiet and muted. He didn't care. Just stay here and be Violet. She was the only woman he ever wanted to spend the night with. Or for his daughter to get to know.

And thankfully, his daughter wanted that too.

She smiled as she passed him, waving goodbye, and he watched until her taillights turned the corner. Missing her again, Gage grinned wider than he had in years.

HE SLEPT in later than usual, and took a shower and put on sweatpants, a t-shirt and slippers. Grinding the coffee beans when Andy shuffled out, he looked up to say good morning. Her hair was ratty and her pajama pants did not match her shirt. He loved seeing her like that. Grumpy. Half child-half young woman. "Good morning, Princess." He always teased her about her morning surliness. For a usually even-tempered teen, Andy was notorious for being moody at least a good half hour after waking up. She glared at him as she glanced around. "She... Violet didn't stay?"

Gage turned to pour the coffee that barely covered the bottom of his large cup. He had to have something to do. "No. Of course, not."

Hearing a heavy sigh behind him, he turned when Andy said, "Dad, you must realize I know you've engaged in sex without benefit of marriage or I wouldn't be here, right?"

He winced. Lord. Duh. Why was she saying it? Discussing it? He hated such moments. He replied, "Yes, but that doesn't mean it's a proper subject for us to discuss..." Yeah, not saying that out loud.

She nodded, staring down at her hands. Then, in a mature, calm voice that didn't match her messy hair and funny outfit, she sounded more like his equal not his daughter. "You know, I wouldn't mind waking up to find Violet here. No, I wouldn't mind that at all."

Wow. That can't be common for teenage girls to tell their single dads. Especially after a lifetime of not sharing him with anyone else.

"That's not going to happen."

"Fine. Send me to Grandma's like you usually do. But listen to this: I don't mind. I like her. A lot. I could easily care deeply about her."

Irresistibly lulled into her conversation, Gage sat down beside her. They seemed to be doing this whether or not he was willing. "Can I ask you why? I mean, she's not much older than you. She's not particularly maternal either, which is my guess what you want. So why her?"

Andy's smile revealed a surprising amount of wisdom. "Because I think she's the first woman I've ever seen you in love with. You seem happy around her. I like her. I think as I got older, we'd become good friends. I don't need a mom... I've always had you. There's nothing I need from her. She's a nice, decent person to me. And she has a sense of humor. She has all the things I value in a person. And she isn't overbearing, rude or annoying. She doesn't walk in and act like she owns this place or you. She's respectful to both of us. I think she'll always be that way. That's probably what I like the best about her. Second is how happy you get around her and with her. From the first time you mentioned her, the mountain girl, on the phone, you sounded different. Because it was all about her. The excitement in your voice had never been there before. I was fully prepared to hate her, for all the dumb, generic reasons: not wanting her to come between us or flaunting her authority over me… you know, all that adult power-trip crap. But she isn't like that. I do like her. So I don't mind. Plus… she has that huge-ass horse ranch. That part's pretty cool."

Gage smiled and almost cried with a rush of gratitude. How did he get so lucky to have this child? She was amazing. Every inch of her. Her selflessness could be the most precious part of her.

"Andy, I'm happy. With you. With us. Our life. You know that."

"I'm happy too. But I won't be here forever. And I think you could be a little bit happier. In Violet's case, I doubt she could infringe on you and me. So maybe I could be happier too."

He fondly hugged her and kissed the side of her face. "Whatever happens, have I told you how proud I am of you?"

She patted his face and nodded, rolling her eyes as she got up. She sauntered to the cupboard and pulled out a Pop Tart. Opening it, she started munching, casually. "Duh. Like everyday."

"Well, I have reason to everyday. I don't know if Violet can ever get over her issues."

"Then let's help her figure out the best way to overcome them."

"That's so much easier said than done."

"Well, who said it was easy? I think she's worth figuring out. You could try different approaches… like asking her to do something without calling it a date. She came over for s'mores and a bonfire when she thought you invited her. So why don't you try being more direct?"

Andy was too smart. He got up and hugged his incredible daughter. "You are freaking brilliant, Andy. Why didn't I realize that?"

She patted his shoulder. "Because she hurt your feelings when she said no to dating you. But if you come up with some specific plans? She'll respond."

That's exactly what he decided to do. It only took his intuitive thirteen-year-old daughter to point out the obvious. He was tired of how Violet was reacting, and now he knew what to do in order to change it. Yeah, he conceived a brilliant kid who was well on her way to becoming a brilliant adult.

CHAPTER 17

*T*HE WORK WITH RIVER'S Rescue was invigorating. Exciting. Varied. Plenty of nuances to learn and all of her prior competence and skills were put to good use. Each day she answered directly to Finn, and her duties were increased as she proved her proficiency. Jack was in less and out more, tending to the big picture as well as teaching. But each day, Violet's confidence and spirit grew. To be honest, she felt lighter, finding contentment more often and in places she never expected. Once, she could only be happy alone in the mountains. Occasionally, she passed the arena and wondered if she could stand to go into it now? Was she strong enough yet? Had the memories faded? Had the triggers been deactivated? Could she take the risk? Could she finally enter the arena again?

Maybe.

"Why does my brother have to be the one to tell me what my daughter is doing?" Violet winced but smiled when her dad's voice interrupted her as she shut the barn up for the night.

She turned slowly and replied, "Hello, Dad." He stomped forward and swept her up in his big, burly hug.

"Hi, Daughter-I-Never-See."

She rolled her eyes. "You do too. Rose lives in freaking Rhode Island; she's the one you never see," Violet pointed out correctly.

He dismissed her comment with a wave. "Well, why didn't you tell me you were working here? When did you quit the school district?"

She leaned over, shutting the containers of food and medicines she used today. She was trying to avoid eye contact but her dad grabbed her arm and made her stop and face him. "Please tell me what's going on."

"I met someone."

"You... you met someone? As in... a man?" Something flared in her dad's eyes. Possibly hope and anticipation.

She yanked her arm back. "That's why I didn't say anything. I didn't tell Mom either because she'd tell you."

"I don't understand..." His woebegone expression matched his stunned and hurt tone. He let her go.

She started pacing and shook her head. "Oh, Dad, I didn't mean to hurt you. I've been going through some difficult things over the last few months, and I still need to go through them. You know? Like... listening to my own voice speak from inside my head, all the thoughts that come from my own heart and soul. I have to figure it all out. I don't know what I want. Deep down, I want to see what I can do and handle. You always reach out to help and try to fix me. But this? It isn't anything like Iris's ordeal. When she was raped, she became a victim of unwarranted violence. She thought she needed validation just to exist, which we all gave her, but she also needed to work things out *for herself*. You demolished your old shop so she could start to heal. But we can't demolish the space that hurts me. It's very different. I don't need anyone's answers or guidance. I just need time. I was hurt and sad, for good reason. I could never have gotten through that initial nightmare without you guys. You remember…"

Shane clenched and unclenched his fists. "Yes, I do. Of course, I do."

"I know how much you always want to help me. But I think I've been really stuck for a long time. That's my fault. And now I'm trying to figure it out. It seems easy for everyone else to see, but not me. I need to do this on my own or I might stay stuck for a longer time."

"Are you saying I tried to fix too much? Or expected you to fix too much?"

"Yes. Kind of. But it's not your fault. I needed you and Mom, God, I don't know what I'd have done without your unconditional emotional support and love. I was such a mess. I also relied on your financial support, falling into a depression, and not being able to work at first. I have an endless amount of gratitude—"

"Don't even thank me. Us. Jesus, Violet, you're our daughter. It's what families do."

She smiled. "Not every parent is like you and Mom." Maybe Gage was. Perhaps that's why she contemplated something more could happen with him.

"Every parent that's worth a damn would. If not, they're not a parent at all in my estimation. But do you think it became harder for you to figure it out because we smothered you?"

"No. But I saw the glimpses of hope flaring in your eyes; you both wanted me to get better and over it; to a place where I might be ready for someone else. I met someone, but I don't know if there is any reason to hope, not just yet. I don't know how far to take this… or not. I'm not sure what'll happen but it's the first time I wanted something different and new since Preston died. I'm trying to fan it and give it some oxygen. But I don't know if the flame will grow. So I just need a little more time… and space… without any expectations. That way, if I'm really not ready yet, I can live with it."

"So you prefer I should try to be less sheltering and overprotective?"

She stopped and stared at him. His big shoulders were hunched. At sixty, gray strands streaked his once all black hair. But he still wore it long and tattoos still covered his arms. Just like Iris. He looked like a big, grumpy, old biker. But he wasn't. Shane was a sensitive, sorrowful, sympathetic dad, who desperately wished he could stop her pain simply because he loved her so much.

Violet launched herself right at him. Into his chest she flew, knowing she was more than welcome. She had no doubt he'd catch her in his arms, which were always open to her. And Rose, Iris and Daisy too.

She felt him gasp as his big paw of a hand patted her back. "Ahh, Vie, we just love you so much. We worry all the time about you after what you suffered."

She looked up at him. "I know. But maybe there's a small sliver of light in this dark tunnel I crawled inside. I just don't know yet… I don't even know all the questions I want answered."

He squeezed her. "So, I'll do less poking around. You don't need to hide from us. You can tell us when you're good and ready."

"Yes, thanks and I will. And since I've been working here, it's going great so far. Rescuing horses is still very new. But I don't freak out every time someone goes near a horse, anymore, so there's that."

"Ahh… darlin'. That's huge progress." Her dad's voice was as proud and cheerful as when Violet took her first step as a baby. He was always her best fan. He couldn't restrain his exuberance. She sighed as she smiled. He didn't even know how he came across. He wasn't trying to guide or pressure her. He was just proud and wanted her to know he was totally behind her.

"Well… it's baby steps, I guess, but it's some progress."

"And this fella? Is he a good one?"

"Yeah. He is. Better first impression than you got with Quinn, I'm sure. But give me a little more time before I introduce him. He… he has a teenage daughter."

"Oh." That tone. She leaned back. She understood his hesitancy when he said, "oh." He worried about that small fact.

"She's a great kid. And she likes me. Honestly? I don't think she'll become an issue if we do end up… you know, whatever."

"How did you meet?"

She told him the story of running into a hiker in the mountains. Her dad nodded, listened and didn't say anything. He just listened, which turned out to be one of the best conversations she'd had in a long while. They sat down together on an old bench near the barn door. It was cold, but both of them were dressed for it. Shane simply listened without judgment or trying to read between the lines. He asked a few questions and encouraged her to open up more when she said Gage suggested she might have PTSD triggers.

"That's not so far from what your mom and I believe. But you always resisted any kind of help."

"I know. I still don't think it's what I want. But I'm feeling stronger. And his daughter tricked me into coming over to their house for s'mores, pretending she was her dad when she texted me, and I should have been furious, but in the end, I was glad. Why? Because I had a great time."

"The daughter texted you to come over to their house?

For a date with her dad? That is a positive sign." And Shane listened again. Violet used only good, positive words to describe Gage… and Andy. How easily she became excited when she spoke about them. How much more real they became in her life and she liked that.

Perhaps there was more healing taking place.

Shane pulled her up when she'd finally talked herself out. He hugged her and took her home. "You think you could repeat all of that to your mom?"

She laughed. God, it felt so nice to laugh with her dad And, she told her mom everything that she'd told her dad. She said it all over again, and it sounded even better the second time.

So often Violet tried to enter the arena and never managed to make it this far: the damn threshold. She stared at the door. Putting a hand out, she pushed but nothing happened. She pushed it a little harder and it opened a few inches before her heart started pounding against her ribcage. Daylight revealed the inner sanctum and she saw that particular area as she peeked inside it. The wood boards around the lower walls… the sand oval… the bleachers…

No.

Turning on her heel, she all but ran away from there. She crossed the parking lot and headed down the gentle slope towards the resort. Hurrying past it, she went through the locked gate that was installed after Iris was raped. It required a code or a key to enter now. She bypassed it and headed for the rescue barn and private homes as her heart hammered in her chest.

She raced past her aunts' and uncles' houses and the one that her cousins, Ben and Charlie, lived in. Following a short trail on the rocky section of the beach towards the river rapids, she only stopped when she got there, watching the streaming water. The sand felt soft under her boots. She tried to breathe slowly to stop her racing heart and thoughts. They spun in circles. She paced. It wasn't helping. Being here made her stomach churn. Sometimes, the familiarity of the beach and river was almost zen-like, and never failed to calm her. She always found comfort in nature. But not now. Not after seeing that.

Another failure. Another panic attack. More tears. More heartache. When could she stop hurting? It still freaking squeezed her heart in two, and left her longing to see her damn Preston alive again. Alive. Like he never hit that fucking wall and dropped to the ground. Crack. Thunk. The screaming crowd and her own bloodcurdling screams all congealed into sickening images and sounds, like a hideous soup inside her brain.

She wanted to stop hurting. Why couldn't it get easier? When would she feel better? Healing or some kind of progress toward normality should eventually occur. She felt so sure, this time; so sure, that she dared to peek inside the damn building. It was only a building. Not a murder scene. Yet, she saw it that way. People assured her that two years was the magic number; now her grief would start to ease but it was as sharp and fresh as ever. Tears filled her eyes. She gripped her sore stomach and choked on her tears and sobs as she held herself. Flopping to the ground, she rocked and cried. She remembered everything in detail and ached over it.

Preston had wild, red hair and bright, blue eyes that twinkled with mischief and joy. He fell in love with the horses and couldn't wait to perform on them. He loved performing with Violet and thought what they did together was awesome. Inspirational. He'd have done it with or without

Violet. She realized that. But she couldn't make her peace with it yet.

She cried her tears out, leaving a dull ache and recurring emptiness that always returned. It was intolerable. Sometimes she'd seek out her parents, or her sisters, or she'd take a ride on a horse alone, far into the hills above the ranch.

None of that appealed to her now. She wanted something more. So much more. She wanted to feel better.

The best she ever felt since Preston died was the time she spent with Gage.

Gage. Fuck! She wanted to see him.

But why? So she could grieve for the boyfriend she loved? That didn't make any sense. It wasn't fair. But that's all she could think about. And damn. There was no fairness in any of this.

She finally rose when the sun began setting and the air instantly cooled. Snow already covered the entire area. A white, pristine blanket that crunched under her boots and required her to wear a thick coat, hat and gloves. The sun's angle in the sky was much lower. The pastel colors above the shocking white landscape was breathtaking. Temperatures dropped into the twenties now at night. Winter was rapidly approaching.

Minutes later, she was in her truck, driving up the valley towards Winthrop and... Gage's house. Lord, what was she doing? Why? Tears dripping from her eyes, she wasn't okay. She wasn't calm. This time, she didn't want space. She didn't want everyone to stay at arm's length. All she could think of was Gage, hoping he could make her feel better. Right or wrong, that was her sole intent at that exact moment.

His house was lovely. Fuck. He was grown up and successful, raising a teenager and he lived in this fantastic place. Violet lived at her sister's house in a bedroom. In contrast to Gage, she was a mess. Sad. Confused. Fighting phobias and trying to resist triggers. But here she was... Eager to see him, just to hear his calm, even voice. He was so manly and his smile was kind, watchful, and always concerned.

But right then... Gage was the only one she wanted. So... she went to him.

As soon as she parked in his driveway, she jumped out of the vehicle before she chickened out. She stood at his front door and rang the doorbell.

Tapping a foot, her nerves overtook her entire body. Butterflies fluttered in her gut and her heart hammered in her chest. She heard him undoing the deadbolt and then... the door was opening a crack before... there he stood.

He wore sweats and a sweatshirt. Was he lounging on this weekend night? What did he do for fun in his leisure? She wanted to know. She should have known. This was the real world. Not their mountain. But God, how she missed it.

Suddenly, Violet wanted to know everything about Gage. She was hungry for all of it.

When she saw him, her emotions flooded her like a tsunami, coming out of nowhere. Her tears streamed harder. Gage was all she wanted.

"Violet? What happened?"

She shook her head. "I tried to go into the arena. I got to the door. I pushed it and looked inside the fucking center. I saw the spot where it happened and I couldn't go in. I turned and ran. Like always. I wanted to go in so badly. I wanted to face it and be strong. I wanted to get over it and start to feel better. But I can't. I think about Preston all the time. I cry too much. I hurt too much. Nothing ever helps. Even when I try to get better, I seem to take a step back. I miss him so much."

Gage leaned his shoulder on the door jamb, and his gaze was hot and heavy on her. She stared at their feet, still crying.

"But... but the most confusing part is this: the only thing

that makes it even tolerable is seeing you. I don't get it. Or understand it. I cry for Preston. I miss him. I do. I know I'm not over him but the only damn time I can stand to live with it... the only time when I start to feel better, is when I'm with you. You, Gage."

Her choking tears made her voice waver and she stepped forward, nearly throwing herself at him. She needed his mass around her. His wide shoulders bore her burden, and his broad chest shielded her from her grief. But he didn't fully embrace her.

He set her back a bit and said, "Violet... this... there're... some people here."

He stepped back and she saw all the witnesses to her confession. An entire freaking roomful. Andy was entertaining three of her friends, two girls and a guy that all looked her age. She also recognized his parents, and his sisters and their husbands from the night she ran into Gage at the café. A football game was on the TV. There were bowls of snacks and pop and beer on a buffet table and strewn about. Violet got bug-eyed and her tears were instantly forgotten. She flushed and simultaneously overheated. She wanted to sink into the floor and vanish. Her face exploded with flaming, burning heat. It had to be the worst embarrassment on the highest level of humiliation.

They heard it all. She was in the spotlight. She couldn't see them behind Gage's huge, stupid chest and shoulders. Her words tumbled out in a fast diatribe without giving him the chance to even reply. She started to step back. Licking her lips, she shook her head and said, "I'm so sorry... I'll..." *Go!* Disappear and maybe never reappear. Slinking away, she turned to leave the front porch when she heard a call after her.

"Wait!" Andy jumped up and ran over to the door.

"Dad... go outside!" Andy hissed at Gage. Turning to

Violet, Andy grabbed the front door and said, "My dad will take you to get a coffee."

"No. I disturbed your family time. I'm so sorry. It was thoughtless… and careless of me." Andy had the good sense to close the door behind them, ending the show for the entire room for now.

"It's okay." She gave her dad a physical nudge on the arm. "We'll be fine. She needs you right now. Go." Andy gave Violet a kind smile.

Gage glanced at her and then at Violet. "Dad, really…" Andy tilted her head and popped out her eyes. Somehow, Gage got the message.

He stepped forward and kissed the top of Andy's head. "I'll be back in an hour. Thanks, kiddo." He smiled at her, then turned back towards Violet, taking her arm and pulling her forcibly down the path. Andy grinned and disappeared through the front door.

"Give me your keys," Gage said, not unkindly, but lacking his usual warmth.

Tears gone, Violet was silent now. She quickly dug the keys out of her pocket and tossed them to him. He nodded and took them. She sat in the passenger side. He was quiet. His jaw was locked and he spoke not another word. She choked on her swollen throat, congested from so many tears, but remained silent in her embarrassment and confusion.

He pulled into a small coffee shop in Winthrop. Only a few couples were walking around on this Sunday evening. A known tourist town with a western theme, all the storefronts of the Main Street looked like the set of a western movie. But now none of the gimmick and artifice appealed to her.

Gage didn't say anything when he got out but pointed at the coffee shop. They both ordered from the counter, taking their drinks and sitting down.

Violet stared at the hot coffee. She spoiled everything.

She wanted to go home. She wished she could cry quietly in the privacy of her dark room. Like she usually did when she couldn't stop thinking about Preston. Why did she assume this would be better? It wasn't. She only managed to embarrass herself and interrupt Gage's house party.

But she thought she could count on him. She wanted to. So badly. But then again… no, she didn't.

The silence was stiffly unnatural between them. Finally, Gage took a large gulp of his coffee and set his cup down. He spoke softly. "I'm sorry you tried to enter the arena by yourself. I don't think you should do that alone."

"I thought I could," she muttered. "I thought I was better and stronger and had made more progress but it was like reliving the whole ordeal in that moment."

"Maybe you have progressed, but not quite as far as you believed. You know? Taking baby steps means you have to take a lot of them. Maybe you tried to take a giant leap, which skipped a hundred little baby steps, that you should have taken before the giant leap."

"I shouldn't have come tonight. To your house." She stated the obvious finally. Staring hard at the dark swirling coffee in her cup, she asked, "God, what does your family think of me?"

"Well, they know you're someone special to me, that's for sure."

Embarrassment made her physically hot. She tried to hide her gaze by staring into the coffee cup. She finally sipped from it but it didn't taste half as good as the percolated coffee she made on the mountain, over their own fire, with a gorgeous sunset streaking through the tips of tree foliage— thousands of trees that spiraled higher than anything manmade… She missed their glorious mountain. "This coffee is not as good as what we drank on our mountain," she finally mumbled.

His small smile had the warmth and familiarity she craved and needed. It was finally there. "No. Not half as good. Not even close. The open fire made it taste perfect. The heat from the flames… and you."

"I'm right here," she whispered.

"No. You haven't been with me since we came out of the mountains."

"It's different here. In real life."

"Yeah. Duh. Of course."

"You don't want to see me?"

"I do. So badly I want to see you. But I can't see you the way you've been doing it. Don't forget, I'm setting an example for a teenager and I'm also her primary caregiver. She has some friends over tonight. I can't drop everything, at least not as a rule, just because you show up crying at my door. Once in a while, yes, but not often. You're not seeing me, or dating me. What do you want, Vee? Friendship? It can't be like this. I can't dramatically rescue you every time you break down over Preston. I can't be that guy for you. So if you want to date me, we can talk about it… I'm willing. But I can't be your go-to relief package when you need a shot of feeling better. Not only don't I want to be that, I can't be. I have a daughter. She comes first. Always. So for me, there will be boundaries for whomever I date. No huge proclamations can be announced in front of her either. It's weird and awkward. It's not the kind of stuff she needs to see or be a part of, frankly. And between you and me? I'm confused by it, so she doesn't need to know."

Violet's head spun. Burning up with new embarrassment over her assumption he could be there for her, when no, duh! They never agreed to be anything. He had a teenager. But Violet wanted to see him and only him. She acted it out. Now she dreaded going home alone. Without him. But staying wasn't any option. Now what?

"I get that. I wasn't always the dramatic one. Ever. I used to be calm and fun. I wasn't clingy or needy and I rarely cried. Now... now I don't even recognize myself."

"You talk of how you used to be. The thing is, Violet, I like the woman you are now. Today... even crying. Even when you're upset. I just need to set some boundaries to clarify what we are. I can be your friend. I can. Or your boyfriend. But I can't be nothing to you and then have you show up. I can't do that. I need a straight answer. Do you want to date me? Be my friend? What the hell is this? What was tonight? I wouldn't call that what happens between us friendship."

What did she want? He deserved to know. He was right, he had a complete life and extra responsibilities. She could either join him or leave. It wasn't unreasonable. And he had a daughter.

She didn't want to leave him. Not for a second. But God, what if she couldn't handle it? And Andy? What about her? She wasn't planning to ever become a stepmother, especially to a teenager? She was far too young for that. That was Gage's life and his responsibility. She wished... no, that wasn't fair. She would not wish he were childless. That wasn't reality. She needed to be rooted in reality.

Andy would and should always come first. There were obvious parameters Violet had to follow. They'd be set by Gage, and nonnegotiable. Could she deal with that? Did she want to?

And the alternative? Not having Gage? That felt so much worse at this point. And would she want him so much if he were any less with his daughter? No. He was amazing with Andy. Always. It wasn't a question, but a fact. Andy came first. Andy was the number one priority and she trumped everything. And always would. Violet knew it because that was how her own dad felt toward her.

But Andy seemed so old. Violet wondered what their

347

relationship would be like. What she wanted it to be like. And the girl was so nice to her, even when it wasn't necessary. There was no reason Andy had to like Violet, but she did.

"What would it be like if I said we could date? What would we do next?"

Gage stilled. He went completely stock-still. His eyebrows rose. "First? I'd kiss you. Hard and long. Then… I guess, I'd go home because I promised Andy I'd be back in an hour and it's football night and I have a houseful of people. Then I'd ask you to join us—"

She gave an emphatic head shake no. He grinned. "No?"

"Not after what I said earlier tonight."

"Okay. Then I guess you'd drop me at home. Then… tomorrow I'd ask you to go on a date with me."

"A… a date? Like dinner and movie? Like we never met on a mountain and shared a bunch of meals…and… and….?"

"Yes. On a date. Dinner and something. And we'll see."

She nibbled on her lower lip. That sounded pretty reasonable. Doable. Not so dramatic. Not as scary as the dating that her brain kept going off on. "What about Andy?"

"Well, I'd prefer to leave her at home… but if you need her there…" His smile was small and his teasing made her relax.

"I guess I meant… will Andy be okay with that?"

"She's fine. It's me who's not."

"And no more drama?"

"You get a few passes for drama. But no. Not all the time. I don't have the patience or the inclination and I won't allow it in our household since it's never been that way for Andy or me."

"And Andy comes first?"

"Always." His tone was final. But his expression was open

and hopeful. She did not doubt how much he meant that. "Consider if you can live with that."

She didn't have to. She nodded. "I can. And I'd like to go on a date with you."

His eyes gleamed and he smiled. She glanced at him and then away. Finally, she said, "I thought you were going to kiss me first. Before everything else."

He smiled, looking a bit shy for once. Then he scooted over in his chair, leaning on the table so he was close to her. "So I did." His gaze started on her forehead, and his eyes caressed her face until she smiled at him. He leaned forward and his lips touched her in a soft, sweet kiss that promised much more... but he held back. He did it just enough that she reached for more when he released her mouth. She blinked.

"I forgot how good we are together."

"We are so good." He grinned too.

They finished their coffee, and the conversation was lighter until she drove him home. "I'm not going to kiss you goodbye; Andy's head just ducked below the living room window. So she's waiting up and spying on me. But..." He gave Violet the sexiest, hottest smile and her stomach fluttered in excitement. "I would like to do so much more right now. But honestly? I can't wait for our date."

She grinned at him. "Me neither."

WANT TO GO SLEDDING? *Taking Andy and two of her friends. Not a date so much as a rescue mission; saving my ears from a lot of squealing and gossip.* Said the text a few days later. Violet was anticipating the next time she would see Gage and almost held her breath waiting to hear what their "date" might be. But sledding? With teenagers? After reconsidering it, she decided it could turn out to be the best way to start this whole dating thing.

Couldn't be that threatening, right? Teens. Snow. Sleds. Yeah… and lots of squeals. Sounded pretty non-threatening so she agreed.

Violet drove to his house. Gage, Andy and her two girl-friends were waiting and ready so they simply rushed out when they saw her. Violet walked into his three-bay garage and saw his large, four-door truck. Only a year or two old, it was very high end. Violet sighed. So beyond her budget.

But Andy gave her a huge smile and eagerly introduced her two friends.

The girls piled into the back seat and Violet sat in the passenger seat. She was fully prepared for the cold, wearing her snow coat, snow pants, hat and gloves, as did everyone. She glanced back and saw the sleds already loaded in the bed. Then Gage came out. He was still tugging his coat on. He smiled at her when he saw her face through the windshield… and damn! Violet's heart leapt into her throat before plunging into her stomach all at once.

He got in. "Hey, Vee… did you meet all the drama queens?"

"Ha ha, Dad. Yes, she did."

"I did." Violet laughed.

Gage backed out and started down the street, heading off towards the Chewuck River. He took some turns until the empty highway turned into country lanes, and they passed old farms and pastures, slowly climbing the low-lying mountains and pine forests. Finally, the road narrowed down to one lane and became gravel. And soon after that, fresh snow appeared. The drifts on the roadsides grew higher the farther they drove. They were following a mostly frozen stream. The trees were covered in white, brilliant snow that stood out in the brittle, afternoon blue sky. After a few turns on old logging roads, they finally reached the pine forests, in the middle of nowhere and snow was everywhere they looked. Fluffy and white, it looked as soft as duck feathers.

The drive up there was a fairly fun ride. Thankfully, there were no intimate discussions. Or furtive glances. No way. How could there be with all the loud banter from the three girls? Violet found it impossible not to relax and enjoy it. After Gage parked, they got out and Gage lowered the tailgate before pulling out sleds and saucers in differing shapes, sizes and materials. The squealing teens ran off, leaving only their backs to Violet and him. Violet grabbed a sled, but Gage didn't let go; he used it to pull her toward him, giving her a cocky grin before bending down and brushing his lips over hers.

"I thought we weren't calling this a first date. You know, all the squealing teens? And how I couldn't let you face it alone?"

He released her, turning away to grab his own sled and shutting the tailgate. He pocketed the truck keys, and slipped his gloves on. "Gotta cop a quick one when I can." He wagged his eyebrows before sauntering away from her. She was staring after him, her heart beating fast and hard and her freaking stomach bubbling with feelings. Violet was delighted that he did that. Her entire body was pleased by it from a single damn smooch. No more than that. Gage kept walking and Violet watched him, framed against the snowy hill and the dark line of pine trees, she was enthralled. She readily admitted it for a guy, a man, who was funny, cute and interesting to her. Who took his teenage daughter and her friends sledding and handled it all with familiar ease and charisma.

Gage wore black snow pants with a black and red parka. The matching black hat and gloves made him look like an advertisement for a popular skiing or snowboarding magazine. But Violet knew his hiking skills were top of the line, so he was no model in an advertisement but the real deal. Fully knowledgeable and well-acquainted with outdoor equipment. Violet really loved that.

Her dad preferred anything related to cars, motorcycles or mechanics. Violet was always more nature-oriented. She liked camping, horseback riding, hiking and swimming. As well as all the winter sports.

She shook her head at her musing. The man snow-skied? She had also spied a snowmobile in one of his garage bays, which made her contemplate taking up a new snow sport. The ranch and resort owned a few snowmobiles. Violet had access to them her entire life but never once asked to use them. Her dad would have liked her to ride them. But she never had any interest.

Until now?

Ugh. She had to quit thinking so much and so hard. She grabbed the sled and quickly followed everyone else. They were already at the top of the steepest hill. Obviously, it was once an old logging road, which kept it skinny with a large berm on one side.

Andy wasted no time before she flew by screaming and laughing. Then her friends took their turns. Then Gage, who caught Andy before she reached the end of the long hill. When they landed and fell off, Gage jumped on his feet and threw snow at her. Then at her friends. In seconds, they were all screaming, running and squealing shrilly. They sounded as if they were drowning in the river, not having an innocent snowball fight. But oh. Were they having fun.

Violet waited until their frolicking was over before launching her own sled down the hill. The wind felt cold on her bare cheeks. The snow was slick and icy and it seemed much closer to her face than she remembered. How long since she'd last sledded? Middle school maybe? She slid down the hill at the ranch, but it wasn't nearly as fast or as long. Violet was cheered on by the girls who were now trudging back up. When Violet reached the bottom, oh! She knew Gage was still there. She rolled off and ducked her head at the same time he threw a snowball, of course. Duh. Scrambling to her feet, she threw three in a row at him. They were snowballs she'd made *before* she started her descent down the hill, which she hid in her pockets.

Her first snowball smacked Gage on the bare cheek and he was stunned. Utterly and completely shocked that Violet threw it. She laughed and turned to run but Gage didn't wait long before hurling one at her. Sliding on the snow and unable to get her footing, she wasn't as fast as she usually was. She barely reached the trees when two hands grabbed her around the waist. Gage had a hard time hanging onto her under all the cottony layers she wore, but he finally found something to grasp. She was suddenly in the air, with her legs out from under her and being plowed into the ground with Gage on top of her, holding her down. Grinning wildly with a gleam in his eye, it wasn't sexual at all, more like "gotcha!".

Turned out Gage was more than competitive as he triumphed and she lost. He used his knees to hold down her lower half, laughing maniacally as he shoved the handful of snow into her face and ground it in with his hand.

Violet squealed like one of the girls. She even ate the snow when it filled her mouth and nostrils and eyelids. Sliding down the rim of her collar and onto her neck, it instantly chilled her whole body.

"I give up. You win!" She laughed but it was muffled by all the snow pack in her mouth.

Gage finally relented, sitting back and using his glove to wipe the snow off her neck, chin and face. "You should have known better than to even try."

"Oh, Gage Sullivan, I will always try. Even if I can't win, I'll always freaking try."

He gave her searching look, then nodded at her as if he were satisfied. "Competitive?"

"All my life. You only win with practice and muscle strength. Speed? I could have ditched you if I could have only run in the snow. You'd have never caught me."

He leaned over her, placing his face right above hers. The sparks in his gaze went from joy over winning to a deep staring and he looked serious. His nose touched her cold nose as his lips landed on hers. "When I first met you, I doubted you ever tried. Not even to win for fun. But now? You do. So you might think on that. You say you were always competing? I think that's the part of you that's been missing for awhile." He leaned back on his haunches, giving her a little wink before he rose to his feet.

Violet lay there a moment longer, staring at the tops of the pine trees, their needles a stark emerald green against the pristine white snow, which silhouetted them. The sky, an intensely bright blue, played peek-a-boo through the tree tops. She closed her eyes. It was so pretty here. The cold air was so crisp and refreshing. The girls' voices blended, rising high and low as they laughed. Then they yelled. Then they squealed. Lord. They did that a lot. There were more shrieks and lots of laughter.

Life. Violet felt very alive in this frozen, white world. The gleeful sounds of joy and fun included her; she was right there. She liked being competitive again. She liked winning. She used to be the most competitive of her sisters. She loved to make bets in poker or thirty-one. She loved to race horses and she usually won. Pouting sometimes when she didn't, which was not her most attractive quality. But how she missed this. The urge to win, outsmart, outperform and be the best. To be... Violet freaking Rydell.

Since Preston died, she stopped caring about competing. It seemed stupid and unimportant. But it wasn't. It was a huge part of her personality. And feeling that wonderful urge again made her heart swell with joy.

She had renewed hope.

She rose and wiped away the snow on her clothes. Some melted on her skin and even inside her bra, making her shiver. She opened her coat and rubbed the wet spots dry before bundling herself back up.

Right back in the thick of it, Violet was racing, sliding, and spinning before trudging back up the hill to do it all over again. And again. So many times, she lost count. Then they had races, organized by Andy. She was bossy and liked to be the leader. Violet loved that. So they had races and winners and contests right up until the end. She and Gage were the last ones standing.

"No fair. His weight takes him farther."

"Yes, but you have a faster sled." Gage argued.

They discussed it for a good five minutes before Andy made the decision. "Violet gets a ten-foot head start. That'll even it up. End of discussion."

They glared at her and then at each other in tandem. Violet muttered, "Stupid rule."

"Unfair and unnecessary handicap," Gage muttered back.

Violet stuck her tongue out at him. He showed her his middle finger. Andy finally snapped. "Enough. You two are worse than any teenagers I ever met. Now get ready, set, go."

Down they went.

And damn if Violet didn't win. Barely, by a hair, but she won. She jumped off her sled, rising excitedly to her feet, and began exclaiming, "I beat your ass. So hard!" Then she realized what she said and smacked a gloved hand to her mouth. Her eyes got huge as the girls came running toward her, but Gage was laughing so hard at her that he seemed pleased by the smackdown she gave him. He ignored her choice of words about it.

The girls circled Violet, all but dancing and singing how amazing girls were in general. Girls rule, and all that, and Violet felt like one of them. She was laughing and carrying on and so freaking happy. In that moment. In the snow. The cold air was exhilarating. With Gage. And Andy. And her friends.

Violet laughed and yelled and talked smack and best of all, she felt alive again.

And it didn't hurt. It just felt amazing.

When they were all too exhausted to climb up the hill again, they piled into the cab of the truck. The sun was setting, and they took off their gloves, hats and boots. Violet tucked her feet under the seat and set her frigid hands in front of the car heater. Everyone groaned for more heat. Gage rolled his eyes. "You guys are such a bunch of girls."

Violet and the girls responded with an earful of arguments that detailed how stupid and sexist that was…

He lost.

Halfway home, Andy said. "I need tampons."

Startled by her comment, Violet glanced back, but Andy was staring out the window. Gage didn't answer. A minute later, he pulled into the parking lot of the grocery store. He glanced at the back seat. Andy had already taken off her coat and shoes. He parked the truck and casually asked, "Anyone need anything else?"

Violet shook her head no. Andy's friends each asked for some candy bars, but Andy overruled and told Gage to get them a brownie from the bakery that they all could share.

Violet flipped around as soon as the truck door shut.

"He buys your tampons? Without a single word of protest or a grumble?"

Andy lifted her head, raising her eyebrows in mild surprise. "Well, sure. What's the big deal?"

"Most guys I know, including my own father, wouldn't say the word, let alone, touch the things. How does he know what type to buy?"

"Because he buys them every month. Always has. Duh. Sometimes I ask him to try a new brand. But I always let him know first."

She kept her father apprised of her preferred brand of tampons? He always bought them for her?

Violet faced forward and her thoughts were spinning.

If that weren't a reason to adore the guy, well, hell what could be?

Andy leaned forward, resting her hands on the console and peeking at Violet. "He's really awesome. I know he's my dad, but he was always like that."

"Yeah, my mom makes him an example for my dad when she wants him to do more crap around the house or be a better father. My dad doesn't do any of the things Andy's does," Andy's girlfriend chimed in.

"Well, most fathers don't," Violet replied. She was raised around a lot of men.

But Gage was a manly man. And now he was in the store, buying his daughter's preferred tampons simply because her boots weren't on. He never even questioned it. Not a groan or harsh word. He just went inside and bought them.

Gage was walking across the parking lot, a brown bag in his hands and Violet's freaking heart felt strange. She saw the hat on his head, the brown bag and the casual way he carried it before everything seemed to go all warm and gooey and squishy inside her. He was so damn hot. And very kind. He got into the truck, setting the bag between them and smiled when he noticed her gawking at him. Turning back to Andy,

357

he said, "They don't carry your favorite brand here. So I got the off brand. Sorry."

"That's all right."

Sorry? Violet stared at him. A lot. He looked over only to find her open-mouthed as she watched him. He gave her a little smile before facing forward and shifting his truck into gear. The heaters were blaring while he was in the store because he wanted everyone to be warm… What chance did she have with this man?

When they got back to Gage's house, he parked the truck in the garage, and the girls jumped out, with Andy taking the bag. He and Violet were still in the truck when Violet turned and her hand grazed his. She glanced at him.

"You okay?" Gage asked. "You got quiet all of a sudden after I went to the store."

"You… bought her tampons."

His raised eyebrow showed Violet what a small deal it was to him. "Who? Andy? She needed them. She started yesterday and the first few days are hell on her—"

"Yes… I know that," Violet interrupted. "I get it. I always use the off brands. Would you buy mine? I mean, if I needed them?"

"Crap. Do you? I asked you before I went in the store."

"No, I don't need them right now. Not today. But you'd buy them for me? If I needed them?"

His eyebrows scrunched up again, and she knew he was thinking, *what the hell?* But he humored her. "Sure. If you let me know. Of course, I would. I'm sorry; what's happening here?"

She stared at him and a soft smile formed on her lips. Leaning over the truck console, her lips found his and she kissed him hard and long. He responded in kind but after she removed her lips, she looked at him with big eyes when he asked, "Do tampons turn you on or something?"

"No. Knowing you would buy them without freaking out. And even say the word *tampon* without cringing or softening your voice. You're fully aware of when your daughter gets her periods, without flinching and even when I, the woman you slept with asks—"

"No cringing or flinching. Does that make me special?"

She smirked as she looped her arms around his neck. "Very special. Yes. You are... yes. In general. All the time. In the way you treat others. And Andy." She kissed his mouth again and added softly, "And me."

He pulled his head back, and let his gaze drink her up, starting with her forehead and scanning her entire face. "Violet?"

"Your daughter is right when she said what an awesome man you are."

"Really? She said that?"

"Yes. She did. I agreed."

"Are you okay?"

Violet gulped and closed her eyes, resting her forehead on his. He wondered about this sudden emotional but strange response from her right now, sitting there in the cab of his truck, parked in the garage. But it was a breakthrough for Violet. Her heart was lighter and surer and free. She no longer doubted him. Or why she was there with him.

There was no other place she wanted to be except right there. Finally.

She gently kissed his lips and leaned back and said, "I'm fine. I'm really, really okay, Gage. With you. And with Andy. And everything that's happening to me right now."

His back straightened. "We're talking about something besides tampons here, aren't we?"

Her soft laugh seemed to release years and years of grief. "Yes. *Yes...* We are. I'm talking about everything. About us dating and being together. About making a commitment and

359

thinking about a future… and imagining that it all could work."

"You and me? Like, for real?"

"Do you think I could stay?"

"Always."

"I meant overnight, Gage."

"Yes. Yes!" he said with a long sigh of audible relief. "I never thought you'd ask. Or that you'd want to."

"I do… more than anything else in my life." Then she suddenly eased away from him, leaning back to her side of the truck. "But what about Andy and her friends? I mean…"

"She said she was all for it. She insisted that you stay. To her, it's perfectly normal. So… come inside?"

Violet nodded, grabbing the door handle. Gage waited at the front of the truck, holding his hand out to her. When she slipped her hand into his, it felt as snug as a key sliding into a lock. Perfect. Right. Home.

They shared a long, searching smile until he blinked. "Someday, you'll have to explain why buying tampons is so meaningful for you."

Of course, that made her giggle before he tugged her inside his house.

The garage entrance opened into a large, airy mudroom. The washing machine and dryer were on one side, and hooks holding countless coats covered the other. All the shoes were lined up neatly and pairs of boots stood at attention, waiting to be worn. A large sink and counter allowed for any projects. The girls' snow gear was hastily discarded every-where. Gage had no remark about it but released Violet's hand before he grabbed a jacket from the floor to hang up onto the hook. That way, it could dry. He did the same routine with all the snow pants and coats. Then he tossed the gloves and hats in the dryer and turned it on. Violet slipped hers off and hung them up. Wearing long johns and leggings, a turtleneck, a bulky sweater and warm wool socks, she seemed anything but sexy. She liked to be wrapped in her most comfortable-fitting clothes.

Gage glanced at her as if she was a goddess. Even as she simply stood there in his laundry room.

Yeah, Violet tucked that look away too. She added it to his list of attributes: buying tampons, hanging out with his kid, being kind, teasing her, getting grumpy when Andy tricked her into coming there, caring and understanding why she did, gourmet cooking, smiles and the patience he always showed with his daughter. His daughter who told Violet only an hour earlier that he was an awesome man.

And he was.

His gentle smile prodded her forward. The laundry room opened into the kitchen and the great room. The girls were in the kitchen, collecting food. Hot water sputtered in a coffee pot and cups with hot chocolate were waiting for it to brew.

"Want some hot chocolate?" Andy asked as she entered the kitchen behind her dad.

"I would love some," Violet replied with a smile.

The friends chatted as they carried bags of chips and pretzels, loudly disappearing down the hallway as Andy finished pouring the hot chocolate. All five cups. She dropped little marshmallows in each cup.

"Marshmallows are a favorite around here?" Violet inquired with a smile.

Andy grinned as she replied, "Totally."

"We're getting ready to watch the new horror movie. So if you hear any screaming, don't bother to come running." She gave Violet a cheeky smile.

Violet had a dirty thought that swiftly passed through her brain: if they heard any screaming from Gage's room, don't bother to come running either. Her eyes met Gage's gaze,

361

and the heat flickered like flames in his eyes. Instantly, both of them burst into huge grins; of course, they were thinking the exact same thing.

Gage's mouth turned into a flat line and his eyes followed Andy's retreating figure. Then he looked at Violet but she wasn't sure what it was about. He acted like a man headed for the gallows.

Then Gage said gently, "Hey, Andy?"

"Yeah, Dad?" She was busily stirring the hot chocolate.

Gage visibly swallowed. "Um… Violet was… that is, I wondered if…"

Andy lifted her head when her dad's loss of words and stuttering caught her attention. She looked at her dad and then at Violet before a huge grin split her face. "Yes, Dad. It's fine with me if she spends the night here. Well, goodnight, then. I have to prepare for our sugar coma." She winked and gave them each another cheeky smile.

Gage all but wilted against the counter with Violet right beside him.

"Did she just give you permission for…"

He rubbed a hand to his forehead. "This'll get me the blue ribbon for Worst Father of the Year."

Violet put a hand on his forearm. "Really? Why should it? Asking your teenage daughter *for the first time ever*, from what she told me, if a woman can spend the night at her house? Because you didn't want to upset her? Or blindside her? Or shock her? No, Gage. It makes you…" She could not find words to describe him. Or why she was there. Why she failed to resist him despite her most intense efforts. Despite her grief for someone else. He prevailed with his kindness, caring, warmth, tenderness, toughness, humor—(good God, his humor!)—strength, hotness, stability, love for his family and most especially, his love for his teenage daughter. He broke down all of her defenses and helped her heal some of her wounds.

His gaze was sharply studying her face. "It makes me what?"

"Awesome. The care and concern and warmth you show by parenting her. The way you love her. Everything you do magnifies…"

She shook her head, getting choked up. Overwhelmed, she turned away. But wonderful, caring, sensitive Gage came up behind her, slipping his arms around her, crossing his hands over her stomach. He gently brought her back against him. His breath was warm on the shell of her ear. "Magnifies what? Your fears? Your worries? Your grief?"

Her head shook vigorously in denial. "No. It magnifies the reasons I fell in love with you. And no matter how hard I fight it, it's undeniable. There is no way for me not to love you."

His entire body strained and straightened. Her words seemed to physically assault him like buckshot. His arms tightened before he flipped her around. His gaze scoured her face from her forehead down to her chin and back up. His eyes finally rested on hers. Searching. Reading. Trying to understand.

"Do you mean…?"

She gave a hopeless, little shrug with a small smile and her eyes shone with the feelings she kept trying to smother and ignore. Love. New love. Scary love. She felt timid and unsure but she was ready to love all the same.

"I mean I'm falling in love with you. Yes."

Gage didn't answer but simply swept her off her feet and carried her, like a freaking, caveman turned he-man, down the hallway into a dark room. He used his foot to shut the door and gently lay her on the bed before he disappeared.

Locking the door, he came right back to her, tugging off his shirt.

She grinned and elevated herself onto her elbows. "Does this mean you're not going to worry about teens and…"

He crawled over her, placing his knees on the outside of hers; then he popped his head up and stared at her. Leaning forward, his answer was a long, deep kiss that stole her breath, her heart and her words.

Kissing her lips, and peppering more kisses all over her face, forehead and hairline, Gage whispered, "I wish this were candlelight and wine. That we were alone tonight. I wish you could scream out the pleasure I intend to give you… but this is my life. I'm surrounded by girls. Lots of girls. Andy's popular and spends a lot of time with her friends. And cousins. So many cousins. We… we'll have to muffle our pleasure. But if you're willing, Violet… *Vee.*" His tone changed when he spoke her nickname, and it sounded deeper, huskier and more tender. "I love you. I think I always will love you. Sharing all that is mine with you is what I'm offering. If you want it."

Well, what could she say after a declaration like that? Tears, happy, gleeful tears sprang from her eyes. How right this felt. She blinked to be sure she wasn't dreaming then she smiled. "Oh, my God, I don't want candlelight and wine. I want you… a man who puts his daughter's happiness and wellbeing above everything. And raises her alone without allowing her to miss out on anything. Because she has you. A man whose love goes beyond the moon and stars and who doesn't ask for anything in return. That is the man I want. I want raging campfires and gooey s'mores. Morning coffee together as we hurry out the door and decide who has the time to grab the groceries. I want to live again, Gage. This life you have here… if this could be my life someday, it would be the greatest honor. I can't imagine anything nicer than being included in the family you two have created."

He lowered his head to her chest, placing his face right between her boobs. She stared at the top of his head. He could be so... reverent. He kissed her before simply wrapping her up in his arms and holding her so tight, her breathing was almost compromised. But she let him do it. She hated to remember all the hurt and anxiety *she* caused him. Telling him she'd never give herself to him... Yet seeing all that he did for her proved he was willing to totally give himself over to her.

Humbled, grateful, overwhelmed with love and joy and wallowing in the depths of it... Violet relished him holding her. She kissed his head and rubbed his hair.

Then she pushed him until he turned and fell on his back. Rising off the bed, she slid off her shirts and bra and Gage gasped, suggesting he could see her. Moonlight fell through the open curtains. It was a shadowy, soft, beautiful, white light. She hoped to see his bedroom at some point. Someday, maybe this could be her bedroom too.

She couldn't live worrying that someone she loved with all her heart was going to die. She couldn't do that now. Not anymore. And she didn't want to.

She grabbed the waistband to her pants and shucked them down her legs, pushing off her socks too. Naked, she got up. Gage sat up too, as if he were suddenly prodded by a crowbar. He got off the bed and discarded everything he was wearing as quickly as Violet did. They stood staring at their naked bodies in the moonlight leisurely with a warmth and comfort they didn't experience before.

She set her knee on the side of the bed and he did the same. With their eyes fastened on each other, they crawled over the bed and met halfway. They were both kneeling. He wrapped his hand around the back of her head, tilting it back as he whispered, "Hi."

She inhaled his word, savoring the soft, tender tone and the hot, sparking gleam in his eyes. Oh, God, his eyes. His smile. His voice. Wow.

"Hi." She nearly gasped. His thumb stroked her jawline.

He leaned forward and pressed his lips on hers, knowing he already stole her heart. She no longer refused to admit defeat. She was finally ready to embrace the foregone conclusion. She was already his. And he was hers.

She was eager to commit to everything now.

They kissed and groaned softly into each other's mouths. His tongue explored hers and her hands found his shoulders, which she used for better leverage. His strong, deep, wide, manly, protective, caring shoulders. God, how she wanted to share her burdens and joy with him. Now she was ready and willing and happy to. No longer so needy and sad.

She stroked his muscles and moved down his shoulders to his back. He all but purred at her firm but gentle touch. Looping her hands, she touched his clavicle before sliding down to his pecs. Trying to memorize each contour of his muscles, the more she touched him, the deeper his kiss became. He tilted her head back and his tongue fully plundered her. His straining penis was hitting her stomach as her inner core pooled with its own wonderful, wet desire.

She dropped her hands to feel his hot, thick, pulsing erection. How badly he wanted her. The engorged shaft strained and swung as the tip wept with need. She grabbed the thick rod in her hand and he groaned as he kissed her mouth. She smiled around his lips, saying, "Shhh." Then she wickedly stroked and pulled his length. His heart beat faster as he lost track of their kiss.

He rubbed the tip of her straining nipple with his tongue before putting it inside his mouth. His hand dropped down her body and found her wet, warm, eager entrance. Swollen now with her own need, she gasped at his touch. His wonderfully hot, bold touch. Using his fingers to separate her lips, he simply plunged two of them inside. She bucked and arched her back as her eyes grew huge. She pulled on his hard length in response. Perhaps a little too hard but he responded. They were both tugging and pushing and pleasuring each other with each stroke of their hands. Mirroring the intense pleasure as they watched the other, it was the most erotic, intense sexual experience Violet ever had or imagined.

He gently grabbed her under each armpit and lifted her up before setting her down on the bed. He left her for a brief moment, shuffling around the drawer of his nightstand for a condom. When he returned, he kissed her long and deep as his body entered hers. Her mouth gaped open, and her eyes must have all but popped out of her head when her legs opened wide to accommodate his hips. With the first thrust, he pushed in deep and high. She seemed to inhale him with her vaginal walls. He began leading her in an ancient dance of love and sex and primal fusion. She moaned her appreciation and joy. He used a bunch of pillows to support her, until his chest was even with hers and they discovered the most perfectly synchronized rocking together. It was slow and languid like a slow burning wick.

Filled with blissful pleasure, her eyes slid half shut and she allowed his constant sliding and grinding to propel her into an extended, intense orgasm that seemed to last forever when it consumed her whole body, from her toes to her head. She gathered handfuls of his bedspread to stop her sighs and moans, trying to remain silent. But Gage used his mouth to cover hers and virtually swallowed her ecstatic sounds. Seeking his own release, his hips began thrusting harder before he exquisitely buried himself deep inside her.

His entire body jolted before he collapsed and his body heat radiated and enveloped her.

She gripped him closer. She held and cuddled him as he nuzzled at her neck. Eventually, he lifted his head and asked, "Do you want some pizza? I'm starving."

Violet burst out laughing. Dinner was the last thing she expected him to suggest at that moment. But it was the best ending she could think of and they pulled on their sweatpants and socks and sweatshirts before quietly exiting his bedroom. Stealing down the hallway like naughty kids, the only noise they made was when they got to the kitchen. Gage took out his wonderful homemade pizza from the fridge and they ate the leftovers while gazing at each other. It was magical: eating cold pizza and swigging cold beer at his breakfast bar. Talking softly and drinking up each other with their loving gazes. It was home. Family. And real. Violet was the most healed she had ever felt before.

And when they tiptoed back to bed, it started all over. Except this time, they prolonged the foreplay and delayed their lovemaking. Violet felt the budding of love as she engaged in the sex, laughing and belonging to a family she never imagined or wanted, but needed.

When they emerged from the bedroom in the morning, both were showered, dressed and proper. They were careful to get up early since teenaged girls liked to sleep until noon. When they saw Andy standing in the kitchen at eight a.m., they both froze as it was not what they expected.

"Andy?" Gage blinked several times and seemed lost for words.

Andy, however, didn't freeze or hesitate, but gently asked, "Coffee, Dad? Violet?"

Gage couldn't even look at her but nodded as he quickly skirted the island to pour some. "What are you doing up so early?"

She yawned and smiled. "Better to ask me why I'm up so late. I haven't gone to bed yet."

"Oh? Right. You know how I hate it when you stay up all night."

She nodded. "Uh-huh. I'll go to bed now and sleep half the day. We watched like, three movies. I got a stomachache."

"Are you okay? Do you need some antacid?" See? Gage was the ideal father.

"No, I'm okay now. Just had to eat something halfway decent." Lifting the bowl of oatmeal, she finished her explanation for her early presence.

"Yeah? That… that looks *good*. Oatmeal. Uh… Violet?"

Violet sat down feeling very awkward as she replied, "Sure." She nearly spat the word out and her cheeks were red.

Andy stared at her and then at her dad. She munched on a spoonful of oatmeal. Then she swung around on the stool and asked idly, "So, Dad, how was your night?"

Gage stiffened. He appeared stricken and almost scared to reply as he gaped at his daughter and mumbled, "Uh… um…"

Then Andy burst out laughing. "God, Dad, relax. I'm not interested in any details. Calm down." She walked around and kissed his cheek while patting his arm. "I intend to fall into a coma now for a few hours. 'Night. Love you." Then she gave Violet a wink. "I'm really glad to see you this morning, Violet. You should stay the whole weekend. We can make s'mores again tonight."

God bless this girl. Violet blinked back her tears when they filled her eyes. She glanced at Gage and replied, "I think I might. Thank you, Andy. You seem to be the only adult in the room."

She shrugged. "Yep. That's me. Now, Dad, serve the woman some oatmeal and coffee… remember your manners, dude. Manners."

Andy wandered down the hall and that was it. No trauma,

369

LEANNE DAVIS

no drama. She spent the night in Gage's bedroom, and Andy knew but the world didn't end because of it.

"I really have the best child that ever walked the earth."

Violet got up and approached him like a cougar stalking its prey. He stared at her warily, unable to see her clearly in the dim light of morning. She wrapped her arms around his waist in a hug and replied, "That's because she has the best dad. Andy really wants you to be happy. So yeah, she's selfless and kind and mature about something other girls her age usually hate and mock and are awful about. Andy isn't and that's strictly owing to you, Gage Sullivan."

He let out a deep sigh and stared at her with a small smile. Brushing a stray strand of hair off her forehead, he said, "No one ever told me that. Besides my mother. I never had anyone close to reassure me or bounce my ideas off... You really think you can handle the parent side of me? It'll have to dominate our lives, Violet. At least, for another few years."

She tipped her head back. "Gage, don't you know that's what I love about you? Yes. If you can handle it, I can. I'm younger than you and not really maternally-inclined, but of course, I'll be here. Andy has to take priority and I'll fit in somewhere. But I want to be here with you however that looks."

Releasing a sigh, Gage hugged her and smiled. "Right now, it looks like oatmeal and coffee and what do you think about shopping for snowblowers? I need a new one before the snow starts falling. Last year, mine went south and shoveling the driveway is a bitch, especially on my back..."

She smiled as they shuffled around the kitchen and made plans for a trip to the hardware store. Violet could not remember the last time she looked forward to the day so much. Now, she could look forward to her entire life and future as much as she did that moment.

She didn't have to cross an imaginary finish line to heal

370

and be herself again. She just had to start living again and now that Gage and Andy were in her life, she wanted to.

~

AFTER A FULL YEAR and a month and six days from when she first spent the night at Gage's house, Violet entered the arena. It was Andy's very first 4H Club show and there was no way Violet could miss that.

Andy was about to become her stepdaughter. A year and two weeks after that pivotal night, while sledding on a snowy hill, Gage asked Violet to marry him. Naturally, Violet said yes, and now she was with her fiancé and his daughter in her family's arena. She felt okay. She could breathe again.

Gage gripped her hand tightly as he leaned down to whisper in her ear. "You okay?"

She glanced up with gratitude and love shining from her eyes. "I'm okay. You just concentrate on your amazing daughter. Wait until you see what I taught her to do."

On horseback.

The pride bubbled up in Violet's chest as she watched Andy perform on the gentle mare. It was a demonstration of Violet's expert training and teaching skills. Her future step-daughter began as her friend and student, but she turned out to be the best treasure that Violet and Gage could share. When she perfectly executed a round figure eight, the audi-ence clapped and cheered but no one applauded louder than Violet Rydell.

Even as she was sitting in that fucking arena.

She still hated it. She could never truly enjoy being in that space again, but she did overcome her phobia and managed to use it regularly for horseback riding lessons and perfor-mances like this.

And to Violet, that felt like a win.

In fact... nowadays all of her life felt like one giant win.

But after the performance they needed to get back to Gage's and get some rest. They had a full day tomorrow... they were fencing his backyard, in preparation for Monty and her two horses, to have a safe spot to live. She simply could not leave them on her family's ranch. They were as much her family as Gage and Andy were now. So Gage had given up his perfectly coifed and landscaped back yard to fence in the large portion of it where her horses could graze and a modest barn would soon sit. All in prep for her impending full-time move into his—*their*—house. Home.

Forever. She didn't qualify that. She simply chose to believe it was fact.

ABOUT THE AUTHOR

Leanne Davis has earned a business degree from Western Washington University. She worked for several years in the construction management field before turning full time to writing. She lives in the Seattle area with her husband and two children. When she isn't writing, she and her family enjoy camping trips to destinations all across Washington State, many of which become the settings for her novels.

Made in the USA
Columbia, SC
05 August 2020

15497052R00207